Three: A Tale of Brave Women and the Eyam Plague

by

Jennifer Jenkins

This is a work of creative historical fiction. Whilst the author has made every effort to ensure character names, dates and locations have been drawn from historical records, some events in the plot have been fictionalised.

First edition May 2021

Book cover design by David Jenkins

For more information about the researching and writing of this book, you may like to visit the author's website: https://jenjenkinsthree.wordpress.com

This book is dedicated to my boys, David, Jack and Finn, to all my girlfriends-turned-proof readers and literary cheerleaders, to all who encouraged me to write a story that just wanted to be written, and to Emmott, Catherine and Elizabeth.

Prologue

The laughter drifted upwards with the smoke, an archetypal incense for a future salvation they didn't yet know they needed. The Wakes- Eyam's annual festival of St Helen- united the village and brought in visitors from far and wide; a veritable procession of people all entering Eyam to dance gaily and sing ale-soaked songs until well past dusk. The village was brimming with the excesses of a feast day amongst the endless days of labour and struggle, and it was with genuine happiness that many laid their merry heads down on straw-filled pillows that night, grateful for a sun-steeped summer and quietly contemplating the season of change and all that it would bring...

1

Emmott

26th August 1665

Emmott gathered her skirts in about her slim waist, folding the fabric into a concertina and tucking the wadded material in behind the band of the old leather belt, once her father's and now twice-wrapped around her middle. This dress had been her older sister's, and whilst she cherished the pattern of delicate flowers on the simple slip and Ellen's gentle generosity, she lamented her willowy figure and quietly wished for real hips and a frame that seemed to promise babies and plenty of them.

The Wakes offered a chance to subtly show Rowland how much she looked forward to their life together and in her simple preparations for this evening she let her mind drift towards this same time next year when they would be married. She imagined the house that the village men would build for them, all clay and many hands' work, with its small hearth and modest rooms. The love she imagined they might make there, it made her cheeks burn to think of it, and yet these days she thought of little else but him and their future wedded bliss.

Waiting was agony and yet somehow, they bore it, keeping that modest distance expected of courting couples, but The Wakes would be the chance to be up close and next to him, pressed together as they danced and he spun her round and round, laughing as the compact village whirled with the rainbow colours of an uncircumscribed life. The breath in her lungs billowed out from her parted lips in anticipation of the evening's revelry and she released it slowly, letting her cheeks puff out.

As she skipped over the threshold and down onto the dusty path that led out onto the main village road, Emmott could already hear the sounds of mirth that carried on the late summer air. The evening was balmy and she didn't really need the shawl she had slung around her shoulders and let it fall to her waist as she walked along. The likelihood was he was already there, drinking ale with the Eyam Torres, some of his more distant kin than those of his home village of Stoney Middleton, yet an important focus for him at the annual gathering. He would be listening to their stories of the year half gone and encouraging them with smiles and full-throated laughter. The thought of his handsome face, softened and illuminated by kindness and ale, made her quicken her pace a little.

The day was one for merriment; the jubilant festivities that always accompanied the Feast of St Helen and brought a light and merry air to the village. As a child she had watched wide-eyed as overly-joyous friends and relatives raised unceasing tankards of ale under the stare of the frowning rector, professing love for all to family and strangers alike.

On arriving at the green, she found the crowd much swelled in contrast with her previous recollections of this time, The Wakes at Eyam clearly having become the destination of preference for all in the surrounding Derbyshire vale this summer. They spilled out down the road, a merry procession coming forth from both of the village's two ale houses like a procession of ants intent on carrying away their nectar of hops and grain from The King's Head and back again to The Miner's.

She made her way through the teaming masses of people, nodding at friends and greeting neighbours who she had seen only last night at the vigil in the church and again this morning for rush-bearing. The younger children, including her own younger siblings, had taken advantage of the distracted rector's gaze, whipping each other with the rushes while Reverend Mompesson spoke with his more pious parishioners.

Later some boys drove a cow into the sacristy, upsetting the rector's young wife, Catherine, who believed it to be an act of profanity, defiling the sanctity of the place and ushering in a bad omen. William Mompesson had stopped short of voicing his disapproval during his late-night sermon and Emmott hoped Richard, her sweet-natured but easily led brother, had not been involved in the incident with the heifer.

On the village green huge groups of people were gathered. The laughter and gaiety she had heard on approaching now translated into a mass of men, women and children all brightly coloured with their best garments on and ribbons being festooned as the children ran and leapt about their parents with excitement. Her eyes found Rowland standing with a group of his Eyam Torre kin, his eyes smiling along with his grinning lips as he nodded his head in earnest; a dedicated audience for his gesticulating relatives. She loved this about him, how even listening could be expressed with such kindness.

He seemed to sense her as she approached and turned his head towards her, his reassuring grin somehow just for her even amongst all these crowds.

"Next year," he whispered, so only she could hear.

"Next year," she whispered back.

Next year, at The Wakes, they would be married. She tried to imagine herself in a white dress, flowers picked freshly from the dale woven into her hair like embroidery. She let him keep his arm around her waist just a little longer than was probably wise with her father present, enjoying the ale and company of his friends near the sheep roast. It was this closeness, such that they only really ever got fleetingly, not wanting to attract the judgement of their neighbours, that she was desperate for. A year seemed so far away.

The revelry of the annual festival lasted late into the night, with the villagers and the Wakes' visitors frequenting the Eyam ale houses. The Miner's Arms was full and The Royal Oak, named after the restored King, Charles II, had people spilling out onto the street outside, flagons in hand.

Emmott could still hear their songs and laughter as she lay in her bed that night. Bagshaw House was quiet but she lay awake, thinking about her life a year from now. She tried to imagine a larger bed, Rowland lying next to her, his warm body close to hers and the fever of their love reaching its pitch. Her heart beat faster and she felt an ache down in the pit of her stomach that surprised her.

Taking care to not wake her sisters, Ellen and Elizabeth, she got out of bed and tiptoed to the casement. Across the street she could just see the rectory next to the

Church of St Lawrence. She could just make out a candle still burning in the upper window and imagined the rector, William Mompesson, scribbling his sermon for tomorrow, no doubt addressing the incident of the heifer and reminding Eyam's inhabitants of the merits of temperance.

2

Catherine

27th August 1665

For Catherine, the sight of the heifer inside the sanctuary was entirely unacceptable. Since moving to the village, she had adjusted her sense of propriety to make room for the idiosyncrasies of Eyam's rural inhabitants, but the cow in the church, a prank initiated by some of the village boys, was a step too far. Such sacrilege! She was at great pains to ensure every last trace of it was gone, and there were many traces! She had swept out the muck and straggling bits of straw from the chancel floor herself, though she had half a mind to ensure the boys did it themselves. In the end, her conscience felt more at ease in taking on the task herself. It would be considered service to St Helen and she could ensure the cleanliness of the sanctuary was of the highest order.

It seemed no wonder to Catherine that the village boys had procured a cow so easily for their mischievous scheme. When the feast of St Helen arrived on the 18th August the whole village seemed to down tools, abandoning their jobs and some leaving their livestock to wander in and out of the village untended, whilst they threw themselves wholeheartedly into revelling and amusement. She encountered several bewildered beasts on the road in front of the rectory and she supposed it was one of these that the boys lured into the churchyard and through the doors of the nave.

William was of the opinion that The Wakes was a source of gluttony and debauchery for the villagers and Catherine would not be surprised if next year he attempted to tame the villagers into a less exuberant celebration of the feast; at least one that was more reverent towards St Helen herself and magnified the more spiritual diversions of The Wakes, like the rush-bearing and the midnight vigil. Perhaps next year less people would throng to Eyam to guzzle ale and gorge themselves on roasted mutton and spend more time in prayer and contrition? But for this year, the village played host to an enormous crowd of people, come to sing and dance and make merry into the small hours of the next day. She wondered where they could possibly all have come from. It was as if all the other villages around had emptied out into theirs, such was the attraction, like bees circling pollen-rich flowers.

The Mompessons had first arrived in Eyam during the Spring of last year and she had instantly fallen in love with the beauty of the village. The inhabitants had taken a little longer to warm to. Most of them were sceptical and suspicious, seemingly holding Catherine and William Mompesson to account for the misdemeanours and abuses of the previous incumbent; a Reverend Shoreland Adams, a man by all intents and purposes a rector for gain and ease of lifestyle, and not for any sense of spiritual direction or duty to shepherd a flock. She wouldn't have been surprised if it wasn't the reverend who had amplified the merry-making of the feast, whilst letting the more mystical merits of such an occasion slip by the wayside.

On arrival in April 1664, they had also discovered that in addition to carrying the cross for Reverend Adams they must also live in the shadow of the retired Puritan minister, Reverend Thomas Stanley. Despite losing the parish on St Bartholomew's Day 1662, following the passing of the Act of Uniformity, Reverend Stanley- most unusually for a disposed minister- remained an inhabitant of the village and still preached in private homes. He retained a sizeable following and this, coupled with the hangover of displeasure created by Adams, meant that they had spent their first year trying to make themselves acceptable to the villagers. Catherine was of a patient disposition and she worked hard to overcome her judgement of others and meet them with grace, but even *her* commitment to the task had been tested over the last nineteen months.

William had many ideas for developing the parish and had thrown himself into documenting them with gusto in the confines of his study in the evenings. 'Nothing without trust', he had told Catherine, resisting the urge to pioneer anything without bringing the people of Eyam along with him. Trust-winning was a long endeavour and many still held him at arm's length. She had tried to listen carefully to conversations between villagers at the market, gathering knowledge of the types of trials and challenges their parishioners faced as they carved out their lives in Eyam. Her sincere offerings of much-needed food, or the lending of a required tool to halve the effort needed to complete a job, were at first met with suspicion but in recent months she had seen some softening towards her and a quiet friendship with Elizabeth Frith, the wife of the church warden, was beginning to grow and bring some happiness to Catherine's days.

Catherine was of delicate health, having become consumptive in the years following their marriage and this exacerbated further by the strain of pregnancy and childbirth. Sweeping out the church to rid it of all traces of the bovine intrusion had depleted Catherine of her strength and left her coughing into her lace handkerchief, a gift from her husband put to good use on such occasions. She stood outside in the lychgate to calm her breathing before heading back to the rectory.

Her gaze was fixed upon the old Saxon cross, a beautiful reminder of Christianity having spread out roots here long before a church was built on this land. The sounds of merriment from the village square drifted on the warm August air but she was not inclined to follow it towards any amusement, though it would be a good opportunity for her to enter conversations with villagers she did not yet know. A voice reached her on the breeze, close and deep.

"You alright there Mrs Mompesson?" the voice enquired. Turning towards the street, she saw Marshall Howe, the village sexton, passing in front of her, no doubt on his way to one of Eyam's teeming ale houses. She did not know much about the inhabitants of Eyam but she did know Marshall liked a drink.

"Oh yes, Mr Howe, quite well. I just needed a moment," she assured him. Doffing his cap in her direction, he continued on his way, upright and solitary as he made his way down the road away from the church. Catherine sighed. William was not enamoured with Mr Howe and she had done her best to encourage him to be more open to some possible redeeming qualities in the serious man.

Once she had steadily walked home to the rectory, Catherine found William hard at work in his study. His face was the picture of concentration, his brow furrowed and his lips gathered together like the drawstrings of a purse; his usual look when something had his full attention. It was this ability to be so devoted to something; a task, a project, a person, that had drawn her to him in the first place. How earnestly he had held conversation with her father, never distracted by trifles in the room about him and always asking such earnest questions to know more. Imagine being loved by someone with the capacity to be so devoted? She had discovered the joy of it when they married and he had been a wonderful husband to her ever since, although at times somewhat stubborn.

"William," she said, gaining no response from him on her first attempt. "William!"

His head lifted from the books in front of him and he slid his reading spectacles down his nose so as to see her without the magnification of the lenses. It always surprised him, even now, to look upon her suddenly and find such a beautiful woman standing in front of him. She was of delicate, English complexion, pale and with a slight blush to her cheeks. The consumption had robbed her of the glow that once illuminated her face but she was still a very attractive woman and he enjoyed being confronted by this fact so spontaneously from time to time.

"Yes, my love, what is it?" he said, beginning to stand.

"You had best stay seated," she said, and a wary look crossed his face at her words. "Some boys, from the village, well, I'm sure they meant it for an amusement of some kind, but they took a cow into the church." She could see his eyes widening, even without the lenses of the glasses, which were still on the end of his nose. "I suppose it was one left to wander freely while…while all the villagers are enjoying the diversions of The Wakes. I found it in the sanctuary William and insisted one of the boys come in and take it out, which they did. The Syddall boy I think. But anyway, it was a mess, a real mess in there William. You can imagine. I have swept it all out now, so the altar and all around is clean, but I think perhaps you should…"

"I shall write it into tomorrow's sermon," he finished her sentence. "Yes, yes, I will. I have held back on many things in order for us to better get to know our parishioners without vexing them. But this, this just won't do. The whole Wakes festival, it needs to be re-thought, to have its roots rediscovered as a celebration of the church and of St Helen herself." Catherine was nodding. "Nothing can be done about this year of course; the festivities are well and truly established. But next year, I want to bring some good, old fashioned Christian sacraments to the fore…."

"Well, I know of a planned wedding!" Catherine interjected, happy to be able to contribute something to her husband's plan. "Young Emmott Syddall, the second oldest of John and Elizabeth's daughters, is to marry Rowland Torre at The Wakes next year, or so it is planned. They are betrothed."

"That will work marvellously as a centre focus, and we can have other things to bring the village together and focus on more spiritual pursuits also. Do I know this Rowland? Is he kin to Godfrey and Edytha?" William liked to know as much about the people he was shepherding as he could and knowing where his flock had their connections and interconnections greatly aided him in his role.

"He is of Stoney Middleton, my love. Though I dare say he is of kin to any number of Torre families here in Eyam." William nodded thoughtfully, pushing his glasses back up to the bridge of his nose.

"Tomorrow's sermon?" she enquired.

"Yes," he replied, and once again he was absorbed back into his work and so Catherine retreated from the study and went up to the bedrooms where their children were snoring softly in their beds.

Elizabeth, the oldest, always slept so still in her bed, hardly moving at all from the moment she was kissed goodnight and laying serenely composed as if like Sleeping

Beauty in the fairy tales Catherine was told as a girl and which she now told to her own children. George, on the other hand, was always such an active sleeper. When she approached she saw his arm was trailing out onto the wooden floor and he was lying diagonally across his bed, his hair already wild and ruffled like a baby bird's downy feathers. She smiled to herself as she straightened him out and tucked his arm back in under the covers. The births of her children had weakened her as much as the consumption but she carried no regrets at bringing them into the world. They were such a delight to her days and she could never imagine life without them.

As Catherine pottered about the rectory, setting things straight their maid had left undone and preparing herself a light supper of bread and a small slice of cheese, her thoughts drifted back to the cow in the church. It bothered her. Some would call it a bad omen, a portent of some dreadful thing set to beset them with misery. She was not a subscriber to outright superstition but the old traditions are sometimes hardest to shake off and this night her soul was most definitely more unsettled than she would have liked.

3

Catherine

7th September 1665

William and Catherine had made plans for a quieter morning. Their maid, Jane, had taken the children out into the garden to assist her with some harvesting of vegetables from the kitchen garden. She had set George Mompesson the task of pulling up onions, much to his disgust at having to get his little hands dirty, and his sister Elizabeth had gathered her skirts up into a make-shift basket and was collecting the apples Jane handed down to her from the rectory garden's apple trees. The trees were bowed low with the fruit, each bough heavily blessed this year compared with last Autumn. Catherine enjoyed watching her children with Jane, seeing their personalities played out in George's mischievous compliance and Elizabeth's dutiful forbearance whilst quite taken away from the task by daydreaming.

William and Catherine had left the productive trio and taken a walk up into the fields behind the rectory above Town End, walking up into the woods. They paused to rest by a well up on the hill and looked down over Eyam.

"Do you like it here?" he asked his wife and Catherine was touched by the genuine note of concern in his voice. She reached a hand over to his arm and gave it a gentle squeeze as she answered him.

"Yes, William. Yes, I do." And she nodded her head as she said it, so that her brown curls fell forward from her shoulders and gathered about her face. He reached over to sweep them back and took her cheek in his hand, looking searchingly into her brown eyes, that always reminded him of the colour of the cocoa pods his father's seafaring uncle had shown him as a child.

"You are so good at following me about the land, to and from my different parishes. I never hear you complain, at least not out loud, but I do hope you find this village to be homely. I can't help but notice you appear to be on friendlier terms with Elizabeth of late. Do you find her companionship brings you satisfaction?"

Catherine nodded her confirmation. Elizabeth was not as learned as she was but she was quick-witted and Catherine liked how Elizabeth could make her laugh so readily.

"Yes, I like Elizabeth very much," she said. "It is nice to have a friend."

William put his arm around his wife's shoulders and pulled her close. The church was his great passion but his wife, dear, beautiful Catherine, was the greatest gift God had ever bestowed on him, and then she had given him their beautiful children and sacrificed her lasting strength in the process. He could hear from her breathing, as she exhaled deeply next to his own chest, that the climb up to the woods had worn her out and he encouraged her to rest in the warm September sunshine before they made their descent and rescued Jane from having to entertain the children in the garden. As he looked around him he was quite thrilled by the whisper of autumn in the air, the way the smell of ripened fruit was wafted by the autumn breezes and the leaves began to hint at their future glorious transformation, a rim of gold or red appearing at the edge of them, like an ornate hem on a simple garment.

When they arrived back at the rectory Jane was all of a fluster and pacing in the front garden, the children nowhere to be seen.

"Oh dear," whispered Catherine to William conspiratorially, "Do you think they have been wayward again?" In the first week of their arrival the children had knocked over one of Jane's buckets during a game of chase that had unwisely taken them through the kitchen, resulting in a sopping wet floor and a truly sodden and unimpressed Jane. William chuckled a little but then fixed his stern face, ready to deal with Jane's complaints and the chastisement of the children for disobeying the maid's orders.

But Jane's face looked more serious than he had ever seen it and as they drew nearer she threw up her hands, uttering a heartfelt 'thank goodness you are home' into the air between them.

"The children, have they…?" Catherine enquired concernedly, reaching her hands out towards Jane and resting them on each forearm as she looked into Jane's troubled face.

"No, no, Ma'am, not the children. They were good as gold and better. I sent them inside. It is George." She sobbed, and fell quite unabashedly onto Catherine's shoulder. William and Catherine were aware that George Vicars, Alexander' Hadfield's tailor assistant, had become sick yesterday and was being tended by Mary Cooper, Alexander's new wife. Fearing the worst, Mary had sent word to say George had a fever and requested some holy water from the church stoup so she could make the sign of the cross over him. William had provided the font water himself but had not gone in to see George as Mary was at that moment bathing the man and it had not been convenient. He had planned to return to enquire as to his condition this afternoon as was his custom when villagers were ill, often visiting them for several days for prayer and anointing until they recovered or he was called to perform the holy unction or the prayers for the dying. Had he thought George was in imminent danger he would not have tarried.

"What of George?" Catherine asked gently, managing to smother her impatience at the maid's slowness to convey what ailed him.

"He is dead!" she cried, "and most horribly! Mary is…", her voiced was broken by sobs, "Mary is of the opinion that it might be…it could be…plague!" and with that she covered her eyes with her hands and gave full throat to her sobs.

"Plague?" repeated Catherine, horrified, turning to look at William. She had not seen her husband look so pale, as if the blood had quite drained from his face. He looked aghast, but only for a moment, then she saw him gather himself and his back straightened as he addressed both women.

"I will go to the cottage and speak with Alexander and Mary. You must not worry until I return with the facts. Catherine, I suggest you spend the moments I am gone in prayer. Jane, you can join her." Jane, who would usually have resisted being so corralled into prayer by insisting she had essential housework still to do, nodded her , clearly terrified by the prospect of the pestilence that ravaged London having reached their tiny village. He turned and left them, striding out of the parsonage driveway and into the street beyond. Catherine turned Jane towards the house and as they walked, it was not of George but to the cow in the sanctuary that her thoughts turned.

4

Elizabeth

14th September 1665

"Folk getting right skittish down there," Elizabeth Hancock said, laying both her hands to rest on her husband's shoulders. She could feel the knots beneath her fingers, the hard flesh proof he had spent all day in the smithy, and every bang of hammer to anvil seemed recorded across his taut muscles. She traced the length of each muscle with her fingers as she spoke, applying a little pressure and rotating her thumb to the depth he liked best.

"He had all the symptoms of it. Something in that box from London, John," she said.

"They say it was cloth from the capital yes, but nobody can confirm it came from an infected house. I had some folks up here from the cottages down by the rectory earlier today. They said it was pieces of cloth that arrived and it appeared damp and so Viccars hung it up in the Hadfield workshop to air it. Whatever it was, he sickened a few days after. There's no telling what it was though Elizabeth. No one else sickens, do they?" John asked, turning in his chair to look at his wife. Elizabeth returned his gaze for a moment before she answered. The house was hushed in a rare calm, with all their children outside on the hill, taking advantage of a balmy evening and the lingering light to introduce their youngest siblings to the pleasures of rolling downhill. If she strained her ears she could hear Oner's beautiful giggle, like a brook bubbling just off the path in the woods. It brought a smile to her face, despite the serious nature of their discussion. John so liked to see her smile.

Reaching her hands up behind her neck to wrangle her long blonde hair back into her cap where it had escaped during the searing task of producing a meal for eight hungry mouths on a stove in a house already warmed all day by the overly-generous sun, she proceeded to answer him.

"Nobody else *so far*," she confirmed, running the back of her hand across her forehead and shifting some last straggling tresses from her eyes. "Yet I do not trust we know all the truth, John. There are whispers already that he had those tell-tale swellings. Many down in the village don't want to count their chickens before they hatch, but you should surely know what eggs you be coddling!" she declared.

John laughed at his wife and her suspicions. Elizabeth resisted being told the reports about anything without having to see for herself. He was surprised she had waited so long to go into the village to find out for herself, it having been a full week since George Viccars had died and been hastily despatched into the ground of the churchyard.

"Do not be laughing there John! If it be the plague come from London we had best be on our greatest guard. I shall go down to visit with Mary Cooper in the morning," she decided. This was not the visit John would wish for her to make to find out what was happening, though Mary was the closest in terms of approaching a reliable source, her being the one to have nursed George in his ailment.

"Elizabeth, do you truly think that wise? If what I have heard be true, it was Mary who tended to George, seen as he was under her roof as Alexander's assistant. For all we know, if it is the pestilence come to visit the village, Mary could be the very next person to sicken!" John said, taking her hand in his. "I would have you stay away from those cottages for now. Perhaps ask Humphrey Merrill what he knows if you must go into the village tomorrow."

Elizabeth felt the conviction of his words jostle with her own desire to hear a first-hand account of what had gone on in the house of the tailor last week. She simply could not put the idea of plague to bed in her mind without some further investigation, though she never liked to be down in the village for long. The apparent need for small talk and incessant questioning as to the affairs at Riley always aroused caution in her. Why were people always so keen to know what was going on in the places their eyes could not quite reach? She liked the autonomy that living up here on the hill brought and the gaze of the villagers over her affairs unsettled her.

"Yes, I will go down and speak with Humphrey Merrill," she told John, placing herself gently in his lap so she could take his face in her hands. "Don't you worry John Hancock," she continued, kissing his cheek so that the soft whiskers brushed her face. "I shall be very careful, but we cannot keep our vantage of being safely up here if we do not have the knowledge of what it is we are supposedly safe from."

"My wife is both fair and wise," he declared with a chuckle, and he kissed her hard on her mouth, making her wonder if he might sweep her onto the table while the children still played outside. Despite her tiredness, she found herself wanting him to and a slight disappointment found her when he simply kissed her a second time and then stood up to announce his intention to go back to the smithy to finish the new halberd he had been requested to make for the night watch.

Probably best, she told herself. She was near the middle of her cycle and, though Oner was over two years old and there had been no further signs of pregnancy, she could not be sure any encounter with John would not produce another child. Elizabeth loved her seven children with a patient and intense love, but with the ages of the ones still at home ranging from sixteen down to two years she so often fell into her bed at the end of the day so utterly spent that the thought of another baby growing in her womb and sucking at her breasts brought its own level of exhaustion just in the considering.

Pressing her hands flat against the wood of the table, she pushed herself up and began the process of cleaning the range and sweeping out the living space of their farmhouse. The Riley Farmhouse had several rooms, yet with so many of them living there this rare occasion of being alone in the house with just her thoughts for company was quite a novelty. The jobs done, she sat at the kitchen table again for a moment, the house quiet, unnaturally so. Ordinarily, the very walls of the farmhouse echoed the constant trilling of her family from dawn until dusk and there was very little room for silence.

She heard the faint crying she recognised as Oner's. She had named her after a difficult birth, one in which she had been forced to entertain the very real possibility that she would not live to see her new child. Even now she could recall the moment of dread with such clarity that she felt her heartbeat quicken with the memory it. Yet by some miracle she had shifted from what had appeared to be her hopelessly stuck position and slid out, all bloodied and perfect, looking around the farmhouse with her dark, inquisitive eyes.

She had named her Oner, knowing its meaning to refer to a remarkable person or thing. She had seemed so remarkable in that moment, like a soul who had been here much longer than her few minutes of being born and had merely struggled in her arrival and not her existence. When she cried it pulled at Elizabeth in a way it didn't always with the others. Her cry was a reminder that Oner lived and so did she.

When she pulled the door towards her and stepped out into the gentle evening she could see William, her oldest boy now Joseph was pursuing his apprenticeship in Sheffield, carrying Oner across his arms, and Anne, her second daughter, tickling her gently, so that her cries turned to little peals of laughter as seamlessly as Elizabeth saw the seasons change up here on the edge of the wood. It always amazed her how you could look out just days after a balmy summer's day and realise the leaves had suddenly begun their changes, gathering gold and bronze edges to their green leaves. William put Oner down and she ran to Elizabeth, toddling in her uneven but rapid gait until she reached her skirts and wrapped her little arms around her legs. Elizabeth ruffled Oner's golden curls, before calling the rest of her children in for supper and preparations for bedtime. John, a sweet boy of five, asked her if Oner would be alright. She was moved by the real concern in her son's face.

"Oner is just fine, John. Don't you worry my boy," she said, and at once he was at peace. The power of a mother to ease her children's fears. She had always had it just like her mother had before her; the soothing influence of her calm words that could bring an end to calamity. As a mother she was not easily ruffled.

She watched them all troop into the farmhouse one by one and it was hard to resist a sense of achievement, even if she knew it was just the natural way of it when a womb had nothing to prevent it from filling and emptying again and again. She was tired though and for the first time in a long time she felt an unease. It ruffled her hair and ran its fingers down her back so that she felt a chill. There was little to be afraid of up here, so detached from what was happening in the row of cottages at the centre of the village, and yet she did have a growing, nagging doubt about the security she usually felt at Riley. As she entered their farmhouse she tried to shut it out. She would not want to show fear to her children for all the world.

5

Emmott

24th September 1665

It had only been a couple of weeks since the village had welcomed masses of joyous visitors to the village's annual Wakes, but at the start of the new month a visitor of a different nature had arrived in Eyam. George, the journeyman tailor, and lately assistant to Alexander Hadfield, living in the same household as him and his new wife Mary Cooper across the street, had apparently taken receipt of a box of cloth from London at the start of the week. The box was clearly not just transporting fabric and patterns and, having hung it up to dry in front of the fire, George Viccars had developed a fever and now he was dead.

This was the account Emmott had heard from Mary Cooper, no stranger to death as a widow only newly married to Alexander, and it had caused her great shock. Mary had recounted the symptoms of the unconfirmed illness with great detail, turning Emmott's stomach with the talk of pus-infested lumps in his neck and armpits. Mary's voice had reduced to a near whisper as she speculated with Emmott and her mother about the possibility of this, God Himself forbid, being the pestilence from the capital.

Emmott and her mother were stood at the cottage door with Mary standing on the path and at these words Emmott made some excuse to step away and busy herself in the cottage's small but cosy kitchen. The hearth was warm with the flames she had kindled that morning in order to warm oats in a large pan for Joseph's breakfast. On the table were a few crumbs; she leant forward, her willowy figure bending at the waist and her slender fingers gathering the crumbs into her delicate hands.

A small fear crept into a forgotten place in her heart and appeared to fuss and swell before settling in. *Could this really be the plague from London? Had the Black Death stalked them here and made its silent but deadly presence known in the body of George?*

Nearing the doorway again, she again heard Mary's voice. She was now talking about Marshall Howe, the village's appointed gravedigger, who had been rather rough with the corpse by all accounts. Tying poor Mr Viccars into a shroud, as a precaution he had then slung a rope around his neck and pulled him out, muttering that he would 'take no chances if this were the killer from London'. George was buried in the churchyard by Marshall Howe, with Alexander assisting and a blessing was said by the village rector, William Mompesson. Mary had finished recounting by saying that her son Edward was a bit quiet today. Emmott knew how Edward liked to help George; handing him needles and yarn and watching him work, often taking the scraps of fabric to play with. He was three years old, the same as Joseph, and a happy, energetic boy. Being quiet was not like him.

She felt the fear in her heart flutter a little and took a deep breath, letting it escape from her lips slowly as she turned to go and find Joseph. That boy was overdue a few cuddles and she was sure he would enjoy playing with the wooden soldiers her father had made for him last Christmas.

George had died on the 7th of the month and for a few days everything seemed to be normal, with this part of the village going about daily life as usual. She saw Robert Thorpe on his way to the market and asked him if he would mind fetching her a few eggs, which he did very willingly. When he returned, she handed over the oat cakes she had made for the family as a thank you for Robert's errand. Emmott's affections were worked out through baking and cleaning and doing little kindnesses for the families she had been surrounded by all her life.

The Thorpes were a kind and considerate family. With five children, they lived in the row of cottages adjoining that of the tailor, opposite the house Emmott shared with her parents and siblings. The family was a little younger than the Syddalls, with 16-year-old Robert being the eldest child, but they had been there for as long as Emmott could really remember, her being only five years old when they had first moved in to the cottage as newly-weds.

Over those first weeks in September, a shadow gathered in the minds of those who lived on this row of cottages. They kept up the smiles and nodded and waved to their fellow villagers across the street but not far from their thoughts was the possibility of a dreadful fate imbibed in the bricks and mortar in which they spent their days. Emmott caught herself wondering about it when she should have been completing her daily tasks. Her mind seemed unable to concentrate as it should, with the constant suggestion of an unseen threat waiting just outside her conscious mind. She shook her head in an effort to bid it gone but in the middle of her next task she would find the question was back again; *would George really be the only one to get sick?*

On the 20th of the month Edward Cooper's quietness was accompanied by a fever and chills that wracked his little body. Mary, overcome with worry for her youngest son, had sat on his pallet bed with him for two days and nights, attempting to bring down his body's heat.

On the second day the red marks had bloomed across his chest, like the roses that had their second bloom during September in the cottage gardens outside. She had seen these scarlet markings on George's chest when she had washed him before Marshall Howe's unceremonious arrival and the awful removal of his lifeless body. With trembling fingers, Mary had felt her boy's neck and into the space under his arms, and her worried fingers had pressed against the hard lumps. Her son's body squirmed with the touch and she held him close to her, not caring for the danger and wanting to comfort him and save him with her mother's love.

It had broken Emmott's heart to hear Mary's wail when Marshall Howe emerged with Edward's lifeless body, limp across his arms like one of those woeful bales of cloth that had arrived in the box a fortnight earlier. Emmott was glad to see Marshall taking more care over young Edward. He still had him shrouded and had wrapped him in a heavy rug but had spared Mary the pain of seeing her little boy dragged out of the family house.

Emmott knew Marshall had a little boy of his own; two-year-old William, who was the only child of Marshall and his wife Joan. They lived on the other side of the village, out towards Town Head, but she had seen Joan with Marshall at the market in Bakewell, leading the little boy as he toddled round while she shopped for their necessities. Perhaps it was this gentle unit of mother and son alone that tempered Marshall's practice.

When news of Peter Hawksworth's death the day after Edward's reached Bagshaw House, the Syddalls were forced to acknowledge the danger was creeping ever nearer to them. Peter lived at the end of the same row of cottages as the tailor and his cottage was directly opposite Bagshaw House. Jane Hawksworth was desolate, left suddenly all alone with her one-year-old boy and her fear. The Syddalls couldn't see this phantom, and the mysterious pathway it progressed along could not be traced. But it was clear it had taken a hold of the cottages across the street, spreading out between them, stretching its deadly reach into every home and grasping anyone it reached with the grip of certain death. Now the question that was in all their minds: *would it, could it, cross the main road of the village to reach them?*

Emmott shuddered as she stood at the window looking out at the affected cottages, and pulled her shawl tighter around her. She was no stranger to imagination, harnessing it to tell stories to the neighbours' children when she had opportunity for an audience, and as she stared at the closed door of the Hawksworth cottage she could imagine with unnerving ease, a hooded creature, with a black mantle and a cruel scythe in hand, making its way along the path and marching up to their own door, rapping its deadly knuckles on the wooden door of Bagshaw House. Except it wouldn't announce itself like that would it? It would creep in, silent and deadly, and the first she would know of it would be the look of sickness in the eyes of one of the people that she best loved. She realised she had been holding her breath, as if somehow the stopping of her breath could stop the horrible threat from being released upon them. But how could they stop it?

Her mother had just ordered Sarah -her twelve-year-old sister- back from the Thorpe cottage, where she frequently whiled away the days when she wasn't doing chores or trying to learn simple letters, in the company of the Thorpe's twelve-year-old daughter, Alice. Sarah had come away reluctantly, complaining that nobody was sick and why should she not play with her friend? She now sat in the window seat looking across at the row of cottages with a grumpy frown on her face. Despite the apprehension Emmott felt, that nestled-down, unwanted fear growing in its nest in her heart every day like a cuckoo, Sarah's face made her laugh. A chuckle escaped from Emmott's mouth, reaching her eyes and making them crinkle with laughter, and finally making Sarah give up on her frowning too.

"I'm sure you can play with Alice again soon," she said kindly, tucking her sister's long plaits behind her ears. "Nobody knows what is happening, so I think ma and father just want you to stay here for a while. I tell you what…" She trailed off as she went upstairs, returning several minutes later with a doll. It had seen better days. The delicate features on the wooden face were barely visible and the cotton of the dress was worn very thin but still soft to the touch. In some ways it reminded Emmott of herself.

"Father made me this when I was about your age. I call her Margaret. Would you like to have her until things seem better again?" She lay the doll in the girl's lap and saw her sister brighten as she picked it up.

"Thank you, Emmott," she whispered. 'You always know the right things to make us feel better." Emmott smiled at her and watched the girl skip off to play with the doll by the hearth where Joseph played contentedly with his soldiers.

Something else swelled in Emmott's bosom. Kindness brought its own rewards. The flush of appreciation made her think of Rowland and his kind-hearted way of approaching the world. She hadn't seen him for several days, instead fixing her attentions on calming her near-hysterical mother and helping her neighbours in the little ways she knew made life easier in troubled days. She'd like to see him.

Perhaps he would visit today? Though if just thinking it could summon him she knew he would be at Eyam all the time.

Though his family were from the neighbouring village of Stoney Middleton, rooted there by generations of Torres spread in homes across the village, Rowland had reassured Emmott he would take up residence in Eyam when they married next year. Cupping her face in his calloused but gentle hands, he had looked her in the eye and told her he knew how much she loved her family, especially her father, and how home would be anywhere with her. She had collapsed onto his shoulder in gratitude and hugged his body close. She suddenly realised it was all she wanted right now, carrying the weight of her mother's fear on her back and her own fear growing quietly but insistently in her heart. Rowland had a way of making her feel that she could do hard things. Without him to remind her she had to draw up her own strength, as if from a deep well, and the effort was exhausting and her strength seemingly finite, challenged daily by the weight of all the questions and uncertainty.

She took a walk out of the cottage and down towards Cucklett Delph, looking over towards Stoney Middleton Dale and hoping he would sense her need and come to meet her. But the Delph remained silent and solitary, with only her footsteps leaving an impression upon the grass as she walked. She sat down in the rock archway and uttered a few words in prayer. None of the highfalutin prayers from the church, just simple utterances that carried her hope and her fear, in equal measures, up to the God she hoped was looking down on their village right now and would spare Eyam the pain of loss that would cripple them.

6

Emmott

30th September 1665

Emmott tried to help her father, taking the bowl and wet rags from his trembling hands. It unmoored her to see his strength so weakened by fear. In the next room, she could hear the wailing of her mother, climbing and peaking like the fever that was reaching its highest pitch in Sarah's convulsing body. The girl had complained of a headache yesterday. Just a headache. It seemed nothing. But when Emmott had put her hand to her younger sister's brow the heat that radiated into her palm was an instant signal that the ghoulish spectre she had so vividly imagined had in fact reached their door, crossed the threshold and come inside whilst none of them were aware.

She had thought then of her father's regular turns as an Eyam night watchman, carrying the lantern into the night and taking with him the large wooden halberd to keep prowlers out and keep the village safe. He was a vigilant and conscientious watcher, always staying awake until dawn and leaving the weapon and watch-bill at the door of the next man in line for the next night's watch at first sign of morning. Yet nobody had been able to leave them a halberd to keep watch and keep *this* threat at bay. Not the Hadfields or the Hawksworths, not little Edward Cooper or Thomas Thorpe, nine years old and now cold in his grave.

It was too much to see Sarah so changed. Only days ago, she had sat in the window looking out at the Thorpe's house across the road, cross that she could no longer play with Alice. Now Emmott would give anything to see that grumpy face. Instead, Sarah's eyes rolled back in their sockets and the large buboes on her neck made her twist and turn on the pallet bed uncomfortably, gripped by her delirium. Emmott's heart thumped in her chest. She didn't want to do this, to live through this, to navigate this with her family. A flash of impious anger burned in her chest to think her prayer, so heartfelt and honest, had not ceased this moment to be. She knew she should feel contrite for her ire but she could not let the feeling go.

They sat for hours, her father and her, applying the cold rags to Sarah's red and shiny face and looking for signs the fever would break or she would be able to do what their neighbours had not and overcome the infection. But as evening quietly fell Sarah also fell still and her breathing became shallow, like those breaths when you first fall asleep, but accompanied by a sinister and deathly rattle that clutched Emmott's heart with an icy grip. The room smelled of vomit and sweat and the utter stench of threatening death. A wave of sorrow and despair rolled over both onlookers at the same time, and she stepped forward from her respite in the shadows, placed a hand on her father's heaving shoulders and gathered Sarah's head into her lap.

As her sister took her last breath she heard the sob escape from her father's throat and he covered his eyes with one hand, and found his dying daughter's lifeless hand in the other as she left this world for the next, ahead of him. Emmott could see on his face the agony of a parent sending their child into the unknown and being unable to go with them. Despite her anger at her prior prayers going unanswered, she could not stop herself from issuing one more; that she would not live to see a child of hers go into the grave without her.

Emmott crossed herself and recited the snatches of prayers she knew from hearing them read from the Book of Common prayer by the minister when older relatives and neighbours had died. She could barely believe she was saying them over her own sister. Death was no stranger to their life and yet even though they knew this, when it came so close and so personally it was still the greatest of shocks. Looking down at Sarah now, a far cry from the desperate tossing and turning of just hours ago, she seemed absurdly at peace. Her lips were slightly parted and her eyes looked towards the window, as if to catch the last rays of daylight before nightfall. Her father recovered himself and leaned forward, tenderly he closed her eyelids, moving delicately with his big fingers.

They both became aware of her mother standing in the doorway at the same time and turned to see Elizabeth frozen in place, her eyes looking out towards the bed yet somehow glazed and un-seeing. John expected his wife to resume her wailing but she remained silent and still, staring and motionless. He got up and went to her, encircling her with his solid arms and leading her out of the fetid room.

"I will lay her out…" Emmott called after them, her voice feeble and weakened by the grief that had already smothered her. She saw her father nod, leading Elizabeth to the staircase. She would have Sarah ready for when Marshall Howe arrived. She shuddered to recall Mary's story of how he had so brutally dragged George from the tailor's cottage and hoped he would pay Sarah the tender respect he had shown to little Edward. *Perhaps they would not need Marshall? Perhaps her father would do it?* She could help him. They could take her to the church yard if Mompesson would allow it. She knew it would be too much for her sisters, Elizabeth and Ellen. They had offered to help nurse

Sarah but the fear in their eyes, reminiscent of that seen in the eyes of rabbits caught unawares on the path during her walks with Rowland, had led her to tell them she would do it and they need only keep a prayer vigil in the kitchen, fill fresh bowls of water when required and take care of Alice, Richard and Joseph as best they could. Her younger siblings were aware something was not right. They had seen their father carry Sarah upstairs and they knew something terrible had happened to Edward Cooper and Thomas Thorpe. Yet they asked no questions and continued their games as normal, though sometimes exchanging glances with each other that betrayed their concern. Emmott would soon have to interrupt their childish ways to tell them of the fate of their sister, though she wished she could avoid such a terrible imposition.

As she had seen done before, Emmott laid Sarah out on the bed. She arranged her hair so that the sweat-soaked strands stretched over the straw pillow were gently gathered around her neck and shoulders and covered the swellings in her neck. The tresses had already begun to dry and curl. Next, she pulled up the bedclothes so they covered Sarah up to her chest, so it looked like she was really only sleeping. A vase on the window ledge held flowers she had picked the day before in the dale so Emmott plucked them out and lay them on top of the bed clothes. She washed her hands in the water that remained in the basin and resisted the urge to kiss her sister's forehead. It was now cool, finally having reached their intended goal but in the way she had most dreaded. She imagined her sister awaking in eternity and hoped she would be contented there. Involuntarily, Emmott's hand came up to cover her mouth and with her eyes closed, she allowed herself a moment of uncontained grief for her sister. Her father would need her to comfort her siblings and so she could not afford to descend into uncontrollable mourning, no matter how much her heart ached with sorrow. She allowed herself this one moment of expressed mourning.

7

Catherine

1st October 1665

After Edward died Catherine could see how much the pain took hold of Mary Cooper. The tailor's wife, who some regarded as a gossip because of her propensity to know everyone's business, actually had a heart of gold and it pained Catherine to see her so bruised. Catherine could not imagine losing one of her children. After Edward was buried in the churchyard, a tiny mound disrupting the flat of the sacred soil, she had crept into their room late at night and held her children tight. George had woken up and given her a quizzical look through drowsy eyelids but she had only hugged him the tighter.

Catherine offered to help Mary with her usual chores, procuring goods from the market and delivering clothes made by Alexander, which was Mary's job to support her husband's trade. With George dead, Mary had more to do helping Alexander and on Catherine's visits to their cottage she could see Mary's actions were slower than usual, her fingers slowed by the effects of grief and her eyes moist with sorrow. Yet there was still compassion in her heart for her fellow villagers, and when she handed Catherine the parcels she would often give her instruction to ask about so-and-so's welfare or offer Mary's sympathies on a particular challenge a customer was facing. Not a gossip, Catherine had decided, just someone who made it their business to know as many people as possible and make their lives a little easier if she could. It was an admirable quality.

"This is from Mary Cooper," she would say and she would see the eyes of the person light up just a little at being remembered and it was with a smile that they often took the package from Catherine, who received the reward of Mary's kindness. Catherine was a quietly pious woman and she turned to the scriptures for guidance through the days and the scenarios they presented, but in this village she found herself tutored in acts of practical kindness by a woman who barely attended church services. Another rector's wife, with more pride than Catherine, might have reacted with irritation, but Catherine's heart was big enough to accommodate the quiet challenge she found in Mary's simple compassion and she spent some time musing over what other kindnesses she could show to the people of the village, their parish. In the meantime, she focused her sympathies on the bereaved mother and did whatever she could see to ease her burden. It wasn't long before Mary was out in the village again and Catherine was humbled by this other mother's worthy resilience.

Catherine was up early and hanging lavender sprigs up to dry when Jane quietly entered the kitchen and informed her that the Thorpes had been afflicted by a second loss. Thomas had died just four days ago, quickly and quietly and to the utter shock of his wife. The signs of the disease were clear upon his body and he had not put up much of a fight as it had overtaken him. William had been called to perform the last rites on the dying man and through what he had heard from Elizabeth Thorpe, his assessment had been that a transmission of 'plague seeds' had somehow occurred during the handover of the watch bill, with Peter Hawksworth passing the pestilence to Thomas as well as the halberd that was used to defend the village from unwanted night time visitors.

Peter had sickened shortly after and died, and Thomas three days after him. There was also talk about the village that whatever had arrived in the box of cloth from London, was also at large in Eyam, silent, unseen and deadly. William had done his best to quell these fears, weaving his sermons through with the encouragement of his parishioners to trust God and keep their eyes fixed firmly upon Him. Fear could disable a village as quickly as a plague and when it infected the hearts of enough individuals it created a growing and thickening shadow that was heavy for all to bear. But the truth was that William was worried and Catherine could do little to resist sharing his concerns.

"It is Mary M'lady. She has died in the night, and not only that, the Syddall girl too." Jane said, her face full of sorrow. Catherine knew the two girls were friends and she had seen them often together playing in the street that ran between the rows of cottages. William had asked to be kept informed of any other bouts of sickness and Emmott Syddall, Sarah's older sister, had knocked at the rectory door just two nights ago to say that her sister was sick with a headache and lethargy and that she and her father were tending to her. They had not heard anything since, although she had found Emmott sitting quietly at the back of the church yesterday morning with her mother.

Catherine had not wanted to disturb the two women as they appeared to be still in silent prayer and when she returned a little while later they were gone. Catherine had hoped the lack of further news had been a positive sign. She sighed heavily at the news, her shoulders slumping down and her hands gripping the window's ledge. She told Jane she would inform William but for a moment she stayed there standing in front of the window, gazing out at the homes that stood all about the rectory and asking God for an end to this most troubling evil that had appeared amongst them.

She went first to the study but found it was empty. After calling his name without reply she made her way out of the cottage's back door and found William in the garden inspecting the vegetable patch.

"There's more to be harvested," he said, turning to face his wife. She saw his countenance fall to match her own, the gravity of her message obviously showing on her face.

"Another?" he said, sweeping the back of his hand across his forehead. She could see he had hoped there would be no more deaths. He stood upright and his eyes seemed to gaze through her and past her for a moment, like a sailor staring out with concern at a choppy sea. He reminded her of Canute, and she hoped he would be strong enough to try to hold back the tide should they be overwhelmed by this. He swallowed before looking at her, waiting for her reply.

"Two. Both children. Sarah Syddall and Mary Thorpe." Catherine told him.

"Such a burden on poor Elizabeth, already in grief over the loss of Thomas." He brought his hand to his breast as he spoke. Catherine was always deeply moved by William's ability to feel the pain of his parishioners. Jesus wept and so did William.

"Yes, it is too much to bear to lose a child. We should pray and then we can make a visit to both families. If you think that wise?" Catherine asked. She would have been most at peace had he said no, that it was not wise. She was not immune to fear, nor to her sense of duty either. He nodded his assent and she took his hand.

"If we can only have an October clear of this plague. Let this be the change we see, even as the leaves die and are shed from the trees." she whispered. Yet in her mind she saw the leaves falling and piling up and she could not help but think about what devastation could befall them.

"I will suggest they bury them on their own land," William said. He had allowed for George, Edward, Peter and Thomas to be buried in the churchyard but with two deaths today he had become convinced that the safer way would be as he had now said. He would visit and do a blessing after Marshall Howe had put them in the ground, if the families wanted it. Catherine knew this new instruction would be received with some pain by the afflicted families but she could see her husband's logic in restricting the gathering of people in the churchyard and she wondered what else he would be forced to put in place should this pestilence really take hold of the village and shake it.

8

Emmott

4th October 1665

Emmott sat at the kitchen table to write a letter to Rowland. Since Sarah died they had met secretly at the village gate after dusk but now they made the decision not to meet in the village at all, instead meeting only in the Delph, calling to each other across the wide, green expanse that this space afforded them. She was grateful for the way the space, a natural amphitheatre, carried his voice on the light breeze to her keening ears. God, how she missed him! To hear him saying 'My Emmott' and asking her how she was, telling her how much he hoped her family would now stay well and how much he longed for her. She longed for him too, so much it brought colour to her pale cheeks. Since they had stopped seeing each other in the village, she found her thoughts were so often consumed with him and her efforts for sleep were frequently thwarted by thoughts of him, running away towards scenarios that caused more than her cheeks to burn.

The house was a dark and solemn place since the death of her sister; her mother having gone from wailing to near silence and walking the house like a spectre, and her father's head bowed most of the time as he went about his daily tasks, as if in constant penitence. She had heard him whispering to her mother one night, asking her why he had not been able to save Sarah, his only duty as a father to bring her safely into adulthood having been denied him. Her mother had remained unresponsive and Emmott had closed the door, giving the scene the privacy it deserved.

Her siblings had learned to do everything more quietly in the wake of their parents' grief, even finding ways to entertain little Joseph that were relatively subdued, though Emmott was revived by the giggles she sometimes heard from him when he was playing with the toy soldiers in the cottage garden. Even amongst the hardest of sorrows and the most crushing anguish, laughter cannot be resisted when it comes to the ears in its purest, truest form.

Putting her thoughts into words was difficult. She had learned to read and write at the insistence of her father but her spelling was poor and she was struggling to find vocabulary for the things she felt and the things she wanted to say. How did you convey this feeling of invisible evil? How could Rowland understand the fear that threatened to strangle her? Frustrated by the inability to capture what she felt in words, she resorted to the things she did know how to say- that she missed him and she thought of him often and imagined near-hourly the next time he would be able to hold her in his arms like he did on the rare occasions when they were alone.

Finishing it quickly, she folded it several times and used her father's wax to seal it. When she saw the boy who carried the mail to Stoney Middleton pass the cottage window she would be sure to go to him, ask him how his mother was and ask him to carry her note to Rowland. She was almost ashamed by the longing she felt to see him. In the note she had asked him to come to the Delph next week where at least she could see him, even if it was from a distance for fear of somehow helping this unseen thief plunder another village of innocent souls.

9

Emmott

14th October 1665

Richard died. It took him suddenly, much quicker than it had Sarah, and Emmott had felt the abruptness of her sister leaving this earth as keenly as a knife slicing through flesh. Like Sarah, Richard had complained of a headache and taken himself up to the bedroom he shared with Joseph. An hour later, Ellen had gone to check on him and found him red and disorientated with delirium. The fever was already well established when they rushed to the boys' bedroom with bowls of water and rags to cool his raging temperature. He had begun trying to pull at his neck, with uncoordinated, twitchy movements and Emmott had already been able to see the swellings beginning to protrude from behind his ears, thickening his neck.

"Check his armpits," she had whispered to Ellen, and lifting his arms slightly, Ellen had felt into the cavity and Emmott could tell from the way her head dropped down towards her chest that her sister's fingers had encountered the hard pustules that most clearly signalled the infection. Just last week, Emmott had listened, horrified, as Mary Cooper had described how Peter Hawksworth's boils had burst, leaking pus and blood onto the sheets and causing his poor wife to vomit even as she tried to help her dying husband. Emmott had prayed, fervently bartering with God, that this would not be the case for Richard, and this prayer had been most mercifully answered.

Just turned seven, Richard was mischievous and often led into trouble by the older boys in the village, but he was funny and she was always overcome by his cheeky manner whenever she thought to scold him for his misdeeds or penchant for trouble. To see him now, unable to crack a joke or make a witty comment was almost more than she could bear. Yet still, he had died, whether she could bear it or not, and Bagshaw House seemed to grow ever quieter.

It had been two days. Marshall Howe had helped her father with Richard's body, deciding to bury him in the earth of their back garden, next to Sarah. Her father had erected two crosses, made from lengths of wood retrieved from the wood pile next to the house. She had watched him work on the crosses for hours; much longer than was necessary really. They would not be forgetting what lay beneath the mounded earth and a simple, crude cross would have sufficed. Still, the lack of sanctified ground had bothered him, especially with the churchyard sitting so close across the road and yet deemed unsuitable for the burial of those with the pestilence.

He had snuck out at night with his trowel and brought two small mounds of dirt back from the churchyard, instead bringing the hallowed ground to them. Now with the crosses erected, John felt as a father he had done everything in his power to bring eternal rest to his children.

John left the garden and returned to the house. It was his turn to do the village watch tonight as he had volunteered to take the place allocated to Thomas Thorpe, who had perished in the interim between the writing of the rota mid-September and the date for which he was assigned. He took up the halberd and the watch bill, scratching out Thomas's name and writing his own. Emmott watched him. His breathing seemed a little laboured and his face was red, though she believed this to be only the natural consequence of the flood of tears he had wept over the crosses as he made them to memorialise his two children, now cradled in the ground.

"I will just rest a while before I leave for the watch," John said, squeezing Emmott's shoulder as he passed her at the kitchen table.

"Your mother is already sleeping. That concoction from Humphrey Merrill seems to have quieted her somewhat and I hope she will sleep now until the morning. Her grief exhausts her because she doesn't express it. It just stays trapped inside her like your linnet in its cage. She needs to let some of it out. Perhaps tomorrow she will?"

"Yes, perhaps she will. Shall I wake you in a couple of hours?" she asked him.

"Aye, that would be good," he replied, his feet finding the first stairs. He turned back to look at them and Emmott, Ellen and Alice all saw the wearied look upon their father's face. They smiled, and as he turned, each sister's face seemed to mirror the concern they all felt. That fluttering fear, well-nested now in Emmott's heart, moved and shifted and made more room for itself; the dread expanding and pressing on her from the inside out. Smoothing out her skirts, she endeavoured to keep her trepidation from her sisters.

"A sleep will do him good. He's tired from those hours spent on the crosses today," she said. Her sisters agreed and they each went back to their evening tasks, preparing the vegetables for tomorrow and mending clothes. There was much to do since their mother had taken to spending each day and night in her room or standing still as a scarecrow in the garden, barely eating and gazing at the wall for hours at a time. Emmott wondered what response the two crosses would bring forth from her mother the next time she ventured to the window to look down over the garden. Part of her hoped it would make her wail and shriek again, anything that would be a sign of life and end this death-like shroud that had fallen over Elizabeth since Sarah's death near a fortnight ago.

On entering her father's room Emmott could tell something was wrong. He was lying across the bed, as if he had fallen there. One arm hung limp and his hand was resting motionless on the wooden floorboards. His shirt was open and she could see what looked like roses blooming in a violent bouquet across his chest. Down his neck Emmott glimpsed red scratch marks where he had clawed at himself in discomfort. He was emitting a deep, low groan and she could see by the way he moved his head from side to side that he was in the sudden grip of a fever. Knowing he would be too heavy for her to lift, she ran back to the stairway and called down to her sisters. They came up the stairs so fast, she knew they had correctly read the urgency in her voice.

Ellen and Elizabeth immediately took their father's weight while Emmott scooped up his legs. There was a heaviness to him that told Emmott the volition he had over his own body was lost. He would never have sought to make it so difficult for his daughters had he been able to help them. Between the three of them they managed to lay him so his head was on the pillow and his tall body was stretched out full. Emmott pleaded again in her mind with the God she hoped was real, asking him to not take her father the way he had her brother and sister. She wondered where her mother was but the task in front of them was urgent and could not be made to wait in order to search of her. It was then that she saw the 'abracadabra' charm hung in the bedroom window, dangling next to a small bouquet of tied herbs. It seemed impossible to her that her mother could have known her husband was ill and done these things instead of alerting Emmott and her sisters so they could tend to him.

Running to the window, Emmott could see her mother below. She was walking the garden, her hands moving constantly as if she was kneading dough. *She knows*, Emmott thought, the idea an uncomfortable mixture of sincere compassion galled with anger.

"Mother is outside. Alice, see if you can fetch her in. Get her to sit down and give her some sweet honey tea. Then please can you go to the Ragge's and tell George that father cannot do the watch tonight. Do not tell him it is…the…this. Just tell him John sends his apologies and will do another night. Hurry." She did not know why she did not want Alice to tell George Ragge what it was that afflicted her father. Perhaps it was the sheer terror that saying it out loud would bring. This was her father. The idea of him, such a strong and ever-present man, being felled by this indiscriminating disease was unthinkable.

Emmott wondered what it was like, when you had the realisation that your body was accommodating an unwelcome guest. Could you feel the swellings growing in your neck and armpits? Did the red bloom that spread across your chest ache or itch? How quickly did the fever render you insensible to your own plight? She chastised herself for using her imagination in such a macabre and terrifying way but she couldn't help but imagine herself the documenter of her own demise. Would she soon be on her own bed sweaty and suffering? The thought brought her heartbeats up to a galloping pace and she had to take some deep breaths to feel calm enough again to be of any use to those in the room.

Emmott saw Ellen smooth down her father's hair and plant a kiss on his feverish forehead. Her mouth opened to admonish her older sister for such a reckless action but she could not find the words and admitted her own strong desire to reach out and hold him. Instead, she silently slipped down stairs and poured water from the pitcher into a bowl and brought it upstairs along with the new rags they had made, having burned the ones used on Sarah and Richard under the guidance of the rector. These repetitive actions were becoming her family's silent, desperate litany as they engaged once more with this unseen foe. Emmott could barely believe how many times this tragic ceremony would be theirs to perform. Would she always be here to go through these heart-rending motions?

People had begun to talk of the cloth George Viccars had brought from London. The little news they received from the capital was that the plague was overrunning the city and thousands were dying each day. It seemed incredible to Emmott that the same disease could be here in their village but speculation about what may have come *with* the cloth, and was unknowingly brought into the Hadfield house by the tailor, was mounting and many now spoke of 'plague seeds'. What Emmott could not understand was how such seeds were travelling from house to house. She had not been inside the Hadfield's house and neither had any of the other Syddalls as far as she knew. How could they have picked up these seeds? How could they have sprouted and borne such evil fruit? The not-knowing was paralysing. Her mind was always flooded with anxious questions, such that at times it had felt like drowning.

Her father died quickly. There were no further conversations with him; 'Aye, that would be good' were the very last words she would hear him speak. There would be no more times spent with him showing her the skills he would also show his sons, no learning how to work wood or build a wall or skin a hare caught unawares in the woods surrounding the village. There would be no more laughter, no more comforting hand on her shoulder. She grasped his hands then, taking one of his strong, sturdy hands between both of hers. The heat was already beginning to leave them. She sobbed, letting her tears fall down onto these hands, the fading emblem of his paradoxical strength and gentleness. He had often told her how much she reminded him of himself and she hoped it was in this, in the unlikely combination of meekness with fierce strength, that she most resembled him.

They worked quickly to wash and shroud her father's body, bringing out a freshly mended white linen sheet to wrap around him. Emmott tucked a bouquet of herbs into the final wrapping and some of the flowers she had picked that morning as she took her daily, solitary walk in the dale. Ellen had already slipped out to fetch Marshall Howe, knowing that they had struggled to even move their father on the bed, let alone bring his lifeless body down the stairs and out into the garden.

When he arrived, the sexton looked genuinely harrowed by the passing of John Syddall. He bowed his head to the sisters as they stood aside and let him pass, Alice sobbing into her sisters' skirts. It struck Emmott that they stood in a line as if for his funeral procession, though she knew there would be no time of gathered mourning for the villagers who had esteemed him and loved him. The only farewell John Syddall would get would be the harrowing chorus of their combined cries and the undertaking duties of Marshall Howe. As a courtesy Marshall tied his rope around John's feet instead of around the neck, having known and respected him in life as one of the village watchmen and an upright and respected citizen of Eyam.

Though he was careful and measured in his heaving down of John's body, every thump of every step drummed a pounding rhythm on Emmott's fragile heart. She wanted to scream at him to stop, though she knew Marshall risked much to enter homes and retrieve the dead. Rumour had it he also required much, so in payment for his services she had laid out a pair of candlesticks which had belonged to her paternal grandmother. She did not think her father's mother would begrudge this payment to ensure her son's body was correctly interred in the soil.

"How many?" she asked him as he came back in from the garden hours later.

He wiped his brow with the back of his hand on the inhale and exhaled loudly before answering Emmott's question.

"I've been to the Bane's, the Thorpe's and the Torre's this fortnight. Infection seems to mainly be in those families. And your own." He lowered his eyes with those last words. They all knew the reality of having lost three of their number but there was still something shocking about saying it out loud, even for an outsider like Marshall. Death was an expected part of life and often families would lose children to sickness or accidents but to lose so many at once was a hardship few saw. Her father had died two weeks to the day they had lost Sarah, with Richard's death between them and Emmott wondered, would death now be satisfied?

Ellen looked exhausted. She gave her thanks to Marshall Howe, who left with the candlesticks, an acceptable reward for seeing three Syddalls safely into the earth behind Bagshaw House. Emmott wished still that it was the hallowed ground of the churchyard, protected by the overseeing of St Helen herself and in the shadow of the Saxon cross that had been such comfort and direction for devout Christians centuries before the church was built. She wondered about the people who had stood before that cross, of prayers they had uttered there; some desperate, some full of gratitude, some whispered in tentative hope. Would anyone ever pause to ponder the prayers said here, in this house, by those desperate to know there was someone in control and that their fates did not rest solely on spells written on parchment and posies hung in windows?

10

Catherine
16th October 1665

What had happened to the Thorpes and the Syddalls tormented Catherine's heart. To have lost so many family members, in a succession of days like a macabre parade, was unthinkably painful. She could see the rawness of it in the eyes of the surviving members of these families and for a moment she had faltered in making visits because she simply did not know what she could say in the face of such loss. She had searched both the Bible and the Book of Common Prayer in her pursuit of a soothing balm but had found that nothing seemed quite right for the magnitude of their suffering. When it comes to times of trial and sorrow, some convey too much that was unintended by saying nothing at all, and others drown the already flailing victims with careless and empty words. Catherine was caught between the twin fears of doing either and it made her restless while she puzzled out what her response should be.

Catherine knew the decision to cease burials in the churchyard had added to the grief of the Syddalls and the Thorpes, though she believed William's decision to be one of genuine protection and not devised to cause further harm. Even so, looking them in the eye after this news had been conveyed was immensely uncomfortable. She had decided to visit with a selection of wild flowers from the dale and those she had carefully selected from the rectory's grounds. She was at pains to include cornflowers in her bundles as for many it was considered to represent heaven and Christ's triumph over the devil. Of the few she found, only a handful of cornflowers were still vibrant and retained their petals due to the lateness of their blooming season, but she carefully placed them into her basket anyway.

Catherine sat at the kitchen table, watched by a curious Jane who did not ask what she was doing but had as much of an eye on her mistress's work as she did on her own. Catherine's long fingers worked nimbly, teasing out the stems of the various flowers and laying them down in bunches, so that each was a flourish of colour, with the blue cornflowers front and centre. She tied these with the rough twine William's manservant had woven for securing packages of goods on the wagon whenever they travelled to and from the village. Eight bundles; four Thorpes and four Syddalls, a perverse symmetry of loss, all buried in their family's respective land by Marshall Howe. Emmott had lost her sister Ellen the day after her father. Catherine knew how terse Marshall Howe's manner was at the best of times and shuddered to imagine the abruptness with which he collected bodies and put them into the earth. The thought of George or Elizabeth in his hands was too much to bear.

Yet this is what her neighbours, their parishioners, had borne. This was the reality of their fate. Two fathers gone into the soil, and a mother too now in the Thorpe's case, leaving a handful of children to find their own way in the world. Elizabeth Syddall had been left as sole parent with the death of John, and from what she had heard from Emmott, she had all but disappeared herself, retreating into herself as a snail that pulls deeply into its shell when winter comes or danger threatens.

She wondered if she would flounder so utterly without William. If it were just she and the children, how would she lead them? But they were only here in this village because of William. They were living in Eyam because of his ministry to this parish. She tidied the thought away as she replaced the bundles into the basket and requested Jane remove the leftover leaves and fallen petals from the table.

"I shall not be long," Catherine told her. "I am to visit the bereaved families. I will be back before it is time for the children to eat." Jane nodded and watched as Catherine swept out of the door. This display of confidence was only for the maid. Catherine did not feel at all assured of the success of her visit and she did not wish to convey more pain on those who already suffered by arriving when what was wanted was solitude and private mourning. Still, to do nothing in a time of adversity was worse, or so she told herself as her hand reached out to knock upon the door of the Thorpe cottage.

They had most recently lost Mary, a girl of eleven, just days after their mother, Elizabeth Thorpe, had succumbed to the same agonising end her husband had. Catherine hoped they had not nursed her alone and she chided herself for not knowing how this dedicated and gentle woman had left this life and who had accompanied her in her passage into death.

She had made the decision to take the flowers despite knowing what the impact might be. These small resolutions, just a tiny series of decisions made to the best of your ability, are what shape who you will be and Catherine desperately wanted to be someone who did not flee from the hardship faced by others but someone who could pull up a chair and cry tears of pain or laugh with peals of joy. She reached out and knocked at the door, not knowing who would answer. The family had no maid or manservant as she did and the principal adults of the house had been so cruelly taken that the only souls left inside who could admit her were Robert, Alice or Thomas, who were all over the age of ten and their little brother William, only four years old and likely dependent on his older siblings for his every need.

Several minutes went by and she heard no noise within to indicate anyone was approaching the door to admit her. She could just go now and tell people she had tried to call, but the desire to know how these bereaved children fared insisted that she stay and knock for a second time. The second knock brought Robert to the door and the sixteen-year-old young man stood on the threshold of the house looking at Catherine. Recognition was slow to reach his face and she was familiar with the numbing effects of grief on even the most basic senses. She smiled at him and it seemed to bring some remembrance to his countenance.

"Mrs Mompesson," he said, bowing his head slightly as he said it, something which might have caused Catherine to giggle if the circumstances for her visit were not so sombre.

'Please, call me Catherine," she told him.

"Catherine," he said, and managed a small smile himself. "Do you want to come in?" he asked. She had thought about what her answer would be to this question and, whilst she desperately wanted to go inside and make sure the remaining children were not living in squalor, she thought it best for the safety of her own children to talk with him at the door. It had been a day over a fortnight since their mother had died and Catherine felt another week should see them safely on the other side of the infection.

"I won't trouble you this morning," she said, silently asking God to forgive her lack of bravery on this occasion. "But I shall come again next week," she added quickly, noticing the way the young man's face fell just a little at her refusal. How grief tipped the scheme of things on its head! Where children who would usually be so disinterested in visits from their parents' peers would now crave for adult visitation once left alone. "I can bring George with me," she added. "He will be a good playmate for William."

She could see the little boy playing where the door at the back of the house opened out to the garden behind, beyond him the three mounds of earth in the garden where Marshall Howe had interred the other members of the Thorpe family. Catherine felt a lump grow in her throat and her eyes began to swim with the tears she needed to hold back. It would do Robert no good to have a weeping woman on his doorstep when he was trying to be so strong for the rest of his family; the man of the house.

"He'll like that Mrs…Catherine…" he said. She looked down with embarrassment at being able to offer so little, and immediately seeing the basket, lifted her head and smiled again.

"I have these…for the…", her glance found the piled-up soil again, "For your family. They say the cornflower represents heaven. You know they are at peace there, with

Christ and the angels?" She saw him look down and shift his weight from one foot to the other and back again. Her words had meant to bring him comfort but she could see perhaps it only agitated his grief to think of them not here but in some other place.

"It doesn't make it less painful though does it? For them to be there and not here?" she added. She saw him straighten and his eyes lift back towards hers. He nodded slowly and the sorrow in his eyes pierced her heart like a briar. His eyes were awash with the emotion he silently and bravely carried. She reached out and touched his arm, placing the three bundles of flowers into his hands.

For a moment they both breathed in and sighed out together, two people united for an instant in the rhythm of death and loss. She saw Alice come in from the garden leading little Thomas by the hand and the sweet girl was gracious enough to offer a wave. It moved Catherine to see these children taking care of each other so affectionately without their parents. She knew the village had been kind and generous in their gifts of food but she could see from her interaction with Robert that these children also needed human touch and genuine affection in their sorrow and as the rector's wife she was the one who should try to provide it.

She said her goodbyes to Robert and returned Alice's wave, reiterating that next week she would return with her own George so the two little boys could play. It would be safe by then wouldn't it? The infection had stuck to households- the Banes, the Torres and the Syddalls, in addition to the Thorpes- and she hoped that in the case of the latter the passing of two weeks without further victims was a good sign. It was to the Syddalls that she would now go.

It was Emmott who answered the door. Catherine knew from Mary Cooper that it was Emmott who had nursed her father and her oldest sister Ellen. Rumour flew about the village that Elizabeth, John Syddall's wife, had become unreachable, retracted deep into her own mind so that were even a hand passed in front of her eyes no reaction would be seen. Catherine saw the sorrow in the young woman's face, sketched there so hastily by grief and a witness to the heavy burden of keeping the family together. Emmott Syddall was a pretty girl, her dark hair framing her brown eyes in wispy, wavy lines. But the girl looked tired and drawn and Catherine saw in her face the strain that facing this deadly visitation had put on her.

"Mrs Mompesson," Emmott said, still offering a smile despite her harrowing circumstances. She did not invite her in, probably on account of the state her mother was in, and Catherine was ashamed of her relief.

"Catherine," she replied. "Call me Catherine," she said and she saw Emmott nod.

"Catherine, then. What can I do for you?" she asked, and the way she asked it seemed to Catherine as if she really meant it, as if this girl who had already suffered so much would be willing to grant her neighbour a request should they have one.

"Really, nothing, my dear girl. I just came to ask after your mother and the health of your household, and to bring these," she said, glancing down at the remaining bundles of flowers in her basket.

"Cornflowers," Emmott said, and Catherine nodded. She had often seen the girl in the dale and walking through the Delph. Clearly, she had an interest in flowers as much as Catherine herself did.

"Do you know what they symbolise?" Catherine enquired.

"Heaven," she said, and her eyes took on a faraway look, as if she were seeing quite past Catherine, even past all that was in front of her, and into another space, another place just out of her reach.

'Yes," Catherine said. "They do. And the triumph of Christ over the devil." Emmott seemed to approve of that. Her sister had died just yesterday and Catherine supposed Emmott had battled for her sister's life, but in vain. She had been the seventeenth soul to perish, the fourth in this household, and the numbers creeping up had set William on edge. The recollection of the danger made Catherine step back slightly, and again she felt a flush of shame and she hoped Emmott had not seen her retract.

"I thought you might like to lay these on the graves…" Catherine almost whispered. Emmott reached out and took them from the basket, thanking Catherine and lightly touching her arm in a gesture of gratitude. *Such a warm and friendly girl despite all she has suffered* thought Catherine and she was of no doubt that Emmott and Rowland's wedding would be exactly the wholesome, community affair to bring the more pious tone to The Wakes next year that William had envisaged. After enquiring after her mother and Emmott's remaining siblings- Elizabeth, Alice and little Joseph- and finding the village rumours to be at least bordering on truth with regards to her mother's state, but her siblings still well, Catherine said her goodbyes. It was with slow steps and pensive mood that she made her way back towards the rectory.

William entered the house just moments after his wife, having come from the same direction. She could see from his face that wherever he had just been had upset him. His eyes glistened where the light found them, showing her that tears were collecting there, though whether some had already traversed his cheeks or he was holding them back she could not tell.

"Oh William, what is it?" she said, rushing to him.

"'tis the Hawksworth boy," he said.

"Oh, not little Humphrey," Catherine cried, the tears springing to her own eyes. Humphrey Hawksworth was a sweet-natured little boy who had only recently learned to walk, to the delight of all who lived in the row of cottages adjoined to the Hawksworth house, the row that had now become a row of death. He liked to toddle up and down the street, holding his mother's hand. Catherine could not bear the idea of his smiling face so touched with death and so still, or his little body assaulted by the horrifying signs of this disease. She sobbed into William's shirt and he stroked her hair.

"I know," he said. "This thing has come upon us, and it is determined to steal from Eyam the things we all hold dear." He led her to the house and she thought about poor Jane Hawksworth, alone without her husband and carrying their second baby that would arrive in the Spring without father or brother.

11

Elizabeth

18th October 1665

It was with reluctance that John had answered the rector's call and gone down into the village. William Thorpe had taken sick and William Mompesson, the rector of Eyam, had called upon John, climbing up to their house at Riley and asking him to witness William Thorpe's will as he had requested. The rector had not been long in the village and the Hancocks were not often in the habit of attending the Sunday liturgy, but John sympathised with this young gentleman who was doing his best to hold back a sense of growing panic in the village. John had discussed it with Elizabeth and she had reluctantly agreed. He would go.

Elizabeth's own trip into the village to speak with Humphrey Merrill had preceded the subsequent deaths that had followed that of the tailor in September. It was not Mary Cooper who sickened next but her young son Edward, who died on the 22nd of that month and the Hadfield's neighbour, Peter Hawksworth on the next day. Since then, what now appeared to almost certainly be a visitation of plague, toyed with two families, crossing back and forth across the street as if by an invisible thread. The Thorpe household's demise had begun with the death of Thomas Thorpe the head of one of the village's Thorpe families who lived on the row of cottages adjacent to that of the deceased tailor. It had since also visited the Syddall's at Bagshaw House, beginning with their girl Sarah and claiming three more of the family after her.

John had recounted the spread of fear in the village when he returned from signing William's will. William Mompesson had informed him of several more dead children in the Thorpe household and a new infection in the Banes household too. John found himself unexpectedly impressed by Reverend Mompesson.

"He commands respect, that new rector," John told Elizabeth later. "Not like that Shoreland Adams was, always making you feel like an inconvenience. He has an impressive air about him, though it seemed that there was some sort of dissention down there. The Reverend Stanley? Some been asking him to help sort their wills it seems. Mompesson seemed not too bothered about that mind. I think it is more his wife who has some concerns."

"Rector's wives are always having *concerns*," Elizabeth said in reply. "Did you know the Bradshaws have left and gone to their other property and rumour is the Sheldons and Furnesses won't be far behind them? There soon won't be anyone left in the village but those two parsons to command any kind of authority! Just like the rich to run away," she said with some bitterness. "The king stays away from London you know. It appears he left in the summer, that's according to what Humphrey Merrill had me believe. With the means to escape calamity there is the chance to outrun death I suppose."

"You are always so very dramatic Elizabeth. You don't think if we had the means we would take off too?" he asked her.

"What need would we have for that John? We are protected up here at Riley so long as they stay down there and we don't go down there either, at least not more than we need to. How many dead at last count?" she had asked him, and John's reply of twelve, including William Thorpe, who had died very soon after John's signature had dried on the parchment, had shocked her. She was not expecting so many already.

This afternoon she planned to go over to the Talbots to find out if they had more news from the village. Leaving Alice in charge of the family supper, something Elizabeth had recently decided she needed to do more of, now the girl was thirteen and should be increasingly educated in the means of keeping house, Elizabeth set out across the stretch of hill that stood between the Hancock and Talbot residences at Riley Farm. Elizabeth enjoyed the feel of the autumn breeze on her face, cooling her skin. She reached up and touched her face, feeling the lines that gathered in creases around her eyes like the feet of crows and the way her skin felt taut and leather-like, no longer the smooth, soft skin of the bride she had once been.

She remembered John bringing her up here to Riley, how she had stood that first evening looking down over Eyam as he worked in the smithy. She had fancied herself a bit of a queen then, overseeing her new kingdom, young and foolish in her daydreaming. How silly it seemed now. Like a different life. How strange that we can look down the tunnel of our own past sometimes and not even recognise ourselves in the spectres of our past selves we find there. There was no time for her fanciful thinking now; six children and a hard-working husband left very little time for it.

When she reached the Talbot farmhouse she knocked on the door firm and hard; with eight children all doing their usual routines with very little attention paid to volume control, often Catharine could not hear her visitors arriving over the din. Catharine was Richard's second wife, though she was the only wife of his Elizabeth had ever known, her being already married to Richard when Elizabeth had married John. Bridget was the only child from that first marriage and she was still living under her father's roof now, despite being almost thirty years old. It was Bridget who opened the door.

"Good evening Bridget, are you quite well?" Elizbeth asked. This had become the standard greeting since the end of September when it was clear George Viccars was the first victim but would not be the only one to be struck down by the deadly disease. Now everyone in the village viewed their fellow villagers with some mild suspicion, enquiring as to health before even the weather could be mentioned. Bridget looked in high colour, which could easily be the start of fever, but her answer allayed Elizabeth's fears.

"Sorry, yes, I'm quite well Elizabeth, just a little flustered from racing round after Anne!" she said, still clearly out of breath. Elizabeth chuckled. There was a certain physicality about toddlers that certainly helped to keep the accompanying adults active. Oner was only two but she was fast and Elizabeth spent a lot of time racing to keep her from mischief or asking her siblings to do the same.

"Ha, yes! If little Annie is half as much trouble as Oner then I am sure you are quite exhausted Bridget!" Elizabeth replied. Bridget gave a smile and then told Elizabeth that Catharine could be found around the back of the house gathering in the linen that had been hung out to dry. Elizabeth thanked her and headed towards the rear of the farmhouse.

She passed John and George, both young men in their twenties now, chopping wood and piling it up under a sturdy cover their father had constructed. They stopped for enough time to raise their hands at her before proceeding with their task. She could see the sweat gathered on their foreheads and the way the muscles in their arms rippled as they lifted the axe or heaved up the chopped logs onto the growing stacks. They reminded her of John when he was in the prime of his youth, how he would emerge from the heat of the smithy all hot and glistening with sweat and a lusty thought passed through her mind at the thought of him, and she quickly moved past the young Talbot men.

Catharine had her back to her and was plucking the family's washing from the lines strung up across the length of the land behind the house. Each piece on the line fluttered in the evening breeze, like the sails Elizabeth had once seen on the painting of a ship when she had taken a job for a while at the start of their marriage in the grand house down in the village. She had found the piece fascinating; *where was the ship going and who or what did it carry in its hold to necessitate leaving where it had been and setting out in search of somewhere new?* Captured by her daydream, Elizabeth forgot to speak for a moment and Catharine stood in front of her bemused.

"Hello there Elizabeth, you were miles away weren't you?" Catharine said with a chuckle. Elizabeth shook her head as if to shake away the distraction and returned Catharine's laugh with a smile.

"I suppose I was!" she said. "I just came to see if you had heard anymore from down in the village? I did go to see Humphrey Merrill a week or so back but John is getting worried about me making any further trips without knowing what's what and Joan mentioned you had been down when she came over to play with Anne yesterday," Elizabeth enquired.

"Aye, yes I did go down yesterday. It is a sorry place down there right now Elizabeth. I had a brief talk with Mary Cooper. Her eyes were red with crying, still in great pain over little Edward. The Syddalls have been badly visited you know. Since Sarah they have buried Richard, John Syddall himself and their oldest daughter Ellen. Mary says Elizabeth Syddall is completely overcome with her grief. She neither cries nor speaks but sits or stands as vacant as those statues you can glimpse through the hedges in the grounds at the manor house. Mary says Emmott has had to take on the duties of the household, especially their youngest boy, Joseph. I believe he is not yet two and may as well be an orphan!" Elizabeth's thoughts again went to Oner. Joseph Syddall was only a little younger. In other times perhaps, she would have invited Elizabeth up the hill to let the two children exercise their infant curiosity together. But not now.

"And the Thorpes?" Elizabeth asked.

"So far five Thorpes in the ground, including both parents and little Mary, although Mary Cooper held out little hope for their son Thomas who is now also sick and unlikely to recover now the red marks have appeared on his chest. It is as a bouquet of doom. As soon as they appear they send for the sexton," Catharine said. "And I've heard he doesn't hang around." She added.

"Does he take them straight to the churchyard? Wrapped or not wrapped?" Elizabeth asked.

"No, not the churchyard now," Catharine said, shaking her head. Elizabeth and John were not regular churchgoers despite the threat of fines for non-compliance and they were not raising their family to be routine little liturgists either, but Elizabeth felt the shock of the closing of the churchyard to those who regarded it as sacred on behalf of her more pious fellow villagers. For her, the ground all about her was her sacred territory, the places she left her footprints and claimed as home. When the time came, she would be happy to be laid down up here on the ragged hillside, with the long grass and wild flowers all about. But for some, the churchyard was the only place they imagined themselves or their loved ones to be laid to eternal rest and closing it was significant, and unsettling.

"Yes, wrapped. Though I hear from Mary that Marshall Howe lacks tenderness on retrieving the corpses," she continued, noticing how Elizabeth's hands were now covering her mouth and pinching her lips between her fingers as she listened intently to what was happening down in the village. She carried on, "He ties a rope to their feet or neck and drags them out and into a pre-dug grave on their own property," Catharine said. "Takes a pretty price for his services too I hear. Joan will be furnished with many a trinket if this goes on." Elizabeth couldn't imagine Joan Howe in trinkets and finery. She had only seen her a few times but she seemed plain and homely, utterly doting on their son and not giving off much of an air for the finer things of the more affluent.

"And the total number of dead now?" Elizabeth asked.

"Twenty," Catherine answered, and Elizabeth did her best to not look shocked. After Catharine had relayed the fatalities in the other stricken houses, the Banes and Torres mostly, Elizabeth bade her farewell and walked back towards her own house. As she walked she cast her eyes down over the village. All looked as it should be from up here. Smoke still billowed from chimney stacks and she could hear the lowing of animals being gathered in at the end of the day. There were no signs from up here that something was stalking the village below, no evil portents hung in the air and no malevolent charms were carried on the breeze. Perhaps it would go away as fast as it had arrived she thought as she closed the door onto the gathering night.

12

Catherine

1st November 1665

November came, cold and crisp. The leaves had finished their majestic show of colour which had made the woods surrounding Eyam seem as if they were burning; a ring of fire that encircled them and dared them to cross. Now all along the streets the leaves had blown in and gathered in the doorways of houses and against walls. They were brown, dead and rotting, sticking to the bottom of the shoes of whoever walked along the roadway and imbibing the air with the sweet rotting smell of decay. Inside the houses of Eyam the smell of death was also settling in, a pervading odour for some families who lost their members one after the other. Such was the tragedy of several families that bordered the rectory and Catherine was extremely sorry that Emmott Syddall suffered further losses; her younger sister Elizabeth taken on the 22nd of the month and her youngest sister Alice dying in her arms just last week.

Catherine knew that Elizabeth Syddall, Emmott's mother, continued to be a shadow of herself, occupying the rooms of Bagshaw House yet to the two children she had left she appeared trapped in some parallel twilight existence. Catherine couldn't bear the thought of Emmott struggling alone in a huge, empty house with only the memories of her family and a dependent little boy for company, and her mother, who she undoubtedly was desperate to receive some comfort from, just staring out with vacant eyes. Elizabeth was unreachable, trapped inside herself and entombed by the heavy weights of her losses. Catherine had resolved to make more visits, overcoming her fear to go inside the Syddall home and sit with Elizabeth. She knew it would give Emmott some relief to have someone else sit with her mother, even if Elizabeth didn't speak or even acknowledge she was there.

Catherine spoke to Elizabeth of scripture and told her of the happenings of the village; all those normal things that just carry on no matter how desperate matters get or how heart-breaking they become for some. Babies were still being born, the fields were still being ploughed, metal was still hammered into tools and washing found itself onto washing lines with unrelenting regularity. All the time Catherine talked Elizabeth merely sat, but there were times she thought she detected her looking her way or a change in her breathing as if she gave the smallest of sighs at hearing good news from outside her own walls.

As Catherine left the Syddall's house she saw Alexander Hadfield airing fleeces in the garden outside the cottage he now shared alone with Mary Cooper. The pain that had been inflicted upon poor Mary two days before was immense, like the double blow of a hammer on her already broken heart. It had been over a month since George Viccars had died, and was tragically followed to the grave by Edward Cooper, Mary's youngest son. Her grief had been as a quiet shattering of the vibrant woman Mary was, yet Catherine had seen how she gathered the pieces and still tried to be the broken version of herself. And for a few weeks she had succeeded. Then two days ago, Jonathan, her kind and thoughtful eleven-year-old, the boy who had first made her a mother, had taken his last breath, never taking his eyes off his mother as he passed, and now she could no longer pretend she was whole.

But Mary Cooper was not simply a broken version of herself, she was a new incarnation of courage sealed with sorrow, like a butterfly crushed inside its cocoon, and though Catherine knew she would emerge again in time, it would be with crumpled wings. Some people are akin to sunshine and Mary Cooper was just such, and the village would bathe in a lesser glow because of her diminishment. Death is greedy; it takes with it some of those it touches as well as the person that they love.

"How is Mary?" Catherine enquired with Alexander as she drew near to the low dry-stone wall that surrounded the tailor's property. He continued to fold the fleeces as he answered her.

"Well, you know Mary. She tries to hold everyone together. Sometimes I wish she would let someone else hold her... Let me hold her..." he added in a whisper. "She needs to fall apart," he said.

The rector's wife in Catherine wanted to rail against this idea, to tell him that the Lord *binds* the hearts of the broken hearted, not lets them scatter and shatter like the fragments of a mosaic. But the mother inside her said yes, yes this was true, she was destined to fall apart. Without her child a mother's world *would* disintegrate, and with the loss of two children who could resist the descent towards a total unravelling? As they always did, Catherine's thoughts went to her own two children. She was fearful for them. Increasingly she asked Jane to keep them indoors and her trips into the village which they would usually accompany her on were now reduced to solitary outings. All around there seemed the possibility of peril and Catherine feared were she to lose her own children all the faith in the world would not save her from simply fading into dust.

"Take care of her Alexander," Catherine said. "She still needs you. Her grief will find its way out in time." He seemed satisfied with her answer and she bade him farewell and continued towards the church. Here she found Elizabeth Frith sitting on the ground outside, leaning up against the

Saxon Cross as she sorted herbs and edible flowers gathered from the churchyard.

"You caught me," she said to Catherine, a grin on her face despite the obvious irreverence of using the ancient symbol as a leaning post. For anyone else, Catherine would have reserved one of her suitably pious speeches, framed with questions meant to get the hearer to reflect upon their actions, but there was just something about Elizabeth's ability to be both mischievous and yet still endearing that turned Catherine's response into a good natured '*Elizabeth*!'". The woman stood up, and dusted down her skirts, gathering the collected flora into a loosely woven basket that stood to her side. She was older than Catherine, past her fiftieth year, and her hair was peppered with grey and the skin around her eyes bore many creases, each one a testimony to how much Elizabeth had laughed during her life, and she had laughed a lot!

"There really isn't the need…" Catherine began to say, though she was actually glad Elizabeth had decided to relocate herself.

"I was starting to get a square rear anyway," Elizabeth declared, and Catherine couldn't help but giggle.

"Elizabeth," she laughed. "You do rather say the things most wouldn't dare to!"

"I do! Because it seems to me that this life requires a certain degree of honesty, wouldn't you say? If you can't be honest about your own backside, you won't be honest about much else!"

Catherine smiled at her improbable new friend. They were an unlikely mix, quite contrary in many ways and yet there was something so refreshing about the way Elizabeth was determined to interact with the world on her own terms. She was unlike anyone else Catherine had ever met, and in truth, she would likely never have dreamed of pursuing a friendship with Elizabeth, on account of their many differences. But Elizabeth's husband, Francis, was the churchwarden of St Lawrence's and so naturally their husbands were together a lot and the wives frequently found themselves in the church or churchyard together for one reason or another.

"What are you doing with these?" Catherine asked, nodding towards the flowers and herbs gathered in the basket.

"I'm delivering them to Humphrey Merrill," was Elizabeth's reply. "He has found himself rather busy of late." The reality of what that meant hung between them for a moment. Humphrey had done what he could to help afflicted families, sharing his known remedies and coming up with new ones. But in the end even his well-nurtured apothecary skills could not put a stop to what disease and death had conspired to do.

"Twenty-nine dead now," Catherine said. "Humphrey Torre died today."

"Humphrey Torre was sixty-five-years old," Elizabeth said. "It's the babes I can't stand to hear about. Just little ones. And to be taken so horribly too. Fourteen below the age of sixteen Francis says. Its unbearable."

Catherine noted the genuine sadness in Elizabeth's eyes, and something that looked like fear. Half of the Frith household were children under sixteen and Catherine guessed Elizabeth was worried about their safety.

"It *is* unbearable," Catherine sighed. "And yet we must bear it, alongside those who already suffer. But we can do our part to help. I'll bring these to Humphrey Merrill with you. Perhaps there is more that can be done. I shall ask him."

The two women left the churchyard and walked up through Orchard Bank, turning right on the road that led them up through Hawkshill to Humphrey Merrill's place. As they walked the silence on the road was eerie in its rarity. This part of town was usually bustling, with those who lived up on the surrounding hills, like the Talbots and Hancocks at Riley, coming down into the village on this route and several of the village roads intersecting like tributaries on a river. Today though, all was quiet, as if all Eyam's inhabitants were behind closed doors holding their breath, waiting for what December would teach them about what it truly meant to be incarnate in a fallen world.

Humphrey Merrill was surprised but grateful for her offer of help.

"Aye, Mrs Mompesson, that would indeed be of great service to me. I am uncommonly busy with this visitation and I find myself quite stretched to both mix my remedies and deliver them," he said, reaching down to rub the side of his knee. "And my legs aren't as young as they used to be. This knee gives me terrible trouble," he said. Catherine was glad to be able to help him, glad to be able to *do* something practical and of consequence.

"Shall I help you now?" she asked him.

"I have no remedies made up," he answered. "I was about to begin making my first batch for today when you arrived."

"Then let me help," Catherine replied, folding up her sleeves and reaching for an apron that lay on the table in front of her. Humphrey Merrill seemed surprised but accepted her offer to assist him. Over the next hour he showed her how to chop and prepare his most simple preparations, those he shared with the villagers for common maladies of head, tooth and ear ache. She was a remarkably quick learner, swiftly retaining the quantities and ratios he described and her hands working expeditiously to sort, chop and stir. The old man marvelled at what women could do when given opportunity.

With Catherine safely working capably on his most basic therapies, he was able to turn his attention to plague cures. He took from the shelves the stoneware canisters in which he kept his herbs. Mustard, mint and vinegar all found their way on to the table, alongside borage, violets and the seeds from several fruits. He was planning to create a new tincture, using the holy thistle and wormwood, the former known for its ability to relieve fever and the latter's capability to induce sweating, which he hoped would draw the infection out and cause the plague seeds to leave the body.

In a conversation with the apothecary from Stoney Middleton across the safe distance afforded by the Delph, Humphrey had been made aware of the properties of quail feathers for drawing out the painful swellings that seemed to be prevalent in the neck, armpits and groins of the victims. His encounters with the symptoms his remedies sought to treat had been thankfully few, but he had seen them on the body of George Ragge days earlier when he was forced to enter the cottage when nobody came to the door to admit him. The stench was unbearable and he surmised that one of George's pustules had burst, as had happened to Peter

Hawksworth. The harrowing appearance of the disease on the body of its victims turned his stomach and he was quick to leave the preparation and exit the condemned cottage and re-join the fresh air of the street outside. He had taken large gulps of it, as if to purify himself and rid his lungs of whatever sickness could be borne in the air, if any. For how it spread, non-one knew.

The unknowns of the spread of the disease caused great anxiety for most in the village. Nobody really understood how it moved from person to person and home to home. In their mistrust they stayed away from each other. It was strangely comforting to him to have this new woman here working alongside him. Catherine worked for a solid hour and her swiftness greatly reduced the amount of effort that would be needed from him this day. He was grateful for the gift of rest, having been wearied by his increased demand.

"Thank you mistress Mompesson," he said to her, hoping his words carried the sincreite he felt. "You have helped me a great deal."

"I've been happy to," she replied, making promises to return the next day to begin the delivery work.

"If you have the time to do some preparing on occasion I would also greatly appreciate that," he said and Catherine assured him that now she knew how to make his basic remedies she would most certainly do this. On the walk home to the rectory she made plans for a herb garden next to the land set aside for growing vegetables. Onions were also being used to treat the horrible swellings and she could set aside some from their Autumn harvesting to offer as treatment to those who were in need. Working with Humphrey had deeply encouraged her and his praise for her efforts was most welcome. William did often lay praise upon her and her efforts but to be commended by a stranger not obliged to approve or love her had its own special merits. To be of use and to be commended for it was itself a tonic in these testing times.

13

Emmott
25th November 1665

It felt oppressive. She looked out of the window but couldn't see anything beyond the dead flowers hanging there and another damned abracadabra spell her mother had scrawled across a ripped piece of parchment and fixed there, as she had in so many of their windows as if this were a working cure. How could Emmott keep herself away from something invisible? Now her interactions with her neighbours were full of suspicion. She looked for the slightest sign they might not be well; a sniffle, a flushed cheek, a sweaty brow. It didn't stop her kindness, compassion just flowed out of her like a natural spring, but she felt that every action was accompanied by a shadowy mantle of fear.

Outside, between two tall, narrow slabs of rock that formed part of the wall that surrounded Bagshaw House, she saw one of her father's gloves laying limp and damp in the November drizzle. The way it lay there, so inert and entombed, it reminded her of the first time she had been brave enough to gaze upon the mound of earth that contained her father's lifeless body. Even now, weeks later, she still could not bear it, and the sight it conjured of the rope around his feet and the shroud pulled tight as the sexton struggled with his weight over the threshold. If she closed her eyes she could almost feel her father's hand on her shoulder, his fingers pressing in in just the right way that felt reassuring, affectionate but with the firm confirmation of being loved. She would do anything to feel that hand on her shoulder one last time.

She closed her eyes. The sound of a crying baby found her ears. It was fractious, likely colicky, as many of her younger brothers and sisters had been. She remembered helping her mother rock them to sleep. She had held Ellen and Elizabeth this way at the end. Her grown up, beautiful sisters taking their last heaving breaths with their heads in her lap. Ellen had followed her father remarkably fast. Fighting it at first, she begged Emmott to make poultices and drank down the tincture Emmott had purchased from Humphrey Merrill. But then she seemed to realise her utter inability to overcome this foe and quietly gave in, releasing her grip on life. Emmott had felt the passing of her only older sister like another parental loss. That last breath from Ellen had made Emmott suddenly the oldest of the Syddall children and somehow it had left her feeling even more responsible for the welfare of the family that remained, with only one grown up sister left and her mother still walking the cottage, a maternal nothingness.

When Elizabeth died it was exactly a week later. Emmott hated the exacting nature of this cruel regularity. It was just enough time for them to believe it had desisted from its killing spree. Her and Elizabeth had even taken a walk together that morning. She had noticed her sister lean a little more on her arm than usual but thought it only fatigue, as Elizabeth had taken on the primary duties of caring for Joseph since her father was gone and her mother was still so withdrawn. By evening time, she complained of a headache and Emmott stayed up with her through the night, watching all the signs of infection spread through her body even as the first rays of the sun reached across the sky and in through the window. Elizabeth died and Emmott began to wonder why she was always left to face the possibility of the next death, like a series of challenges set before a gladiator in ancient Rome. Must she battle again and again with always the same outcome? Would this tyrant never be satisfied?

Alice had been the last, just yesterday. Only nine years old, she had allowed Emmott to carry her upstairs. Her passing was mercifully quiet, her body still as if in surrender to that which had taken most of her family. Perhaps she felt at peace to follow them, knowing she would not reach the shoreline of the next place without those she loved waiting eagerly there for her? Emmott thought she heard her whisper 'Father' as her pulse grew faint and then disappeared. Emmott had sobbed into her hair and reached over to cross her arms over her chest.

It had stolen its way into their home, this vicious, thieving, silent thing, and crossed the street from the tailor's house, finding its way in. They were a bustling household of nine at The Wakes that summer. Now she rattled around in this house with the shell of her mother and her toddler brother who still laughed and jumped and sang little songs, the little boy not grasping quite how much it felt as if the world had ended. How could one heart endure it? Yet she had. She settled her mother into bed, unsure she really understood how many of her children had been claimed and placed into the earth by Marshall Howe. Her letter to Rowland that night was short: *please come*. Tomorrow she would send it and she hoped the day after that he would come to Cucklett Delph and the comfort she craved would be found in seeing his face across the stretch of land.

14

Elizabeth

26th November 1665

The traffic on the Manchester to Sheffield highway above the Hancock's farmhouse and smithy had slowed considerably, as if all about had found out about the coming of plague to the village below and now took more circuitous routes to avoid it. Never had she heard hammer rattle on anvil so little in all the years she had been married to John. Even when they welcomed a new babe into the world, his toiling in the workshop paused only for a few hours, and even less than that once they had older offspring to assist Elizabeth with the demands of new-borns. She looked at John with concern. His smithing was part of who he was, his identity, and she wondered how he would fare with less of it.

To make up for the drop in demand, he busied himself with fixing things about the homestead which she had long since given up nagging him about. All of a sudden, the fence post was fixed so that it met the gate more flush, there were brackets for her cookware above the hearth and everyone had new belt buckles and shoe fastenings. Tending to his family seemed to give him a similar pleasure to that of smithing, at least for now. He was a warm and loving father, sitting down with his children as often as he could, which was considerably more now there were not near-constant calls requesting his skills.

Stepping out of the farmhouse and onto the hill, Elizabeth noted a real chill in the air and drew her shawl around herself a little tighter. Above her the full clouds looked heavy and the village below was beginning to be lost beneath a bank of white. It was comforting to Elizabeth's mind to see it disappear for a while and she stood and watched the clouds draw in like a billowing white curtain. She did not enjoy social interactions in the way that other women seemed to. She was not impatient to race down to the village every five minutes for gate-side gossip and a glimpse of the latest finery the rich families had on show. In these times she felt herself even less inclined to make the journey down, though necessity demanded she must, as the drop in income from John's smithing meant the sale of their eggs and butter in Eyam had become much more important.

Her last visit, just a few days ago, had led to her own chance meeting with Mary Cooper, who was out in the village looking to buy eggs. The news had not filtered up to Riley that Jonathan, Mary's other son, had also sickened and died, so when Mary relayed this to Elizabeth, with the thickness of grief still in her voice, Elizabeth was moved beyond measure for the poor woman.

"You nursed him?" she had asked, her voice dense with compassion.

"Yes, as I did my Edward. Both my boys in the grave! I cannot comprehend it," Mary replied. Elizabeth tried not to imagine it, though, as happens with most things that we try to resist, the image of her own children dying crowded into her mind and she was unconvinced she would survive such a happening in order to buy eggs and walk about as Mary did. "But I have to," Mary had continued. "You never know what you will have to suffer or how you will be required to manage it do you? Lord have mercy," she added, as if by some compulsion.

"Aye," Elizabeth replied and then asked the question that had formed in her mind, her thoughts frequently following pathways of analysis that she didn't often find in other women. "You nursed George Viccars, Edward and Jonathan, yet you have shown no signs of sickening yourself Mary. Do you truly believe it to be the plague that has taken them, as is widely accepted in the village?"

"Yes, I do," was Mary's answer. "I have seen the swellings in the groin, armpits and in the neck that marks it out, and both my boys had the red bloom across the chest and a crippling fever I could not get down no matter what I tried." Elizabeth saw Mary's eyes glisten with the memory of it for a second, before she carried on. "I am not the only one to nurse the sick and not sicken myself, though many do and die themselves soon after. Emmott Syddall has nursed and lost six of her family and remains well and healthy to this day, it being a month now since Alice, the last one to die in their household." Elizabeth nodded. October had been full of deaths, with twenty three souls crossing over into eternity, but November had proved less greedy for the grave, just four deaths.

"Perhaps the cold will be our saviour?" Elizabeth asked Mary.

"Perhaps it will," Mary had answered, before taking her eggs and going on her way. Elizabeth had managed to sell all the eggs and butter that day, but now watching the village disappear from view she was not inclined to venture down again, at least not this day. As she stood watching some thin trails of smoke from Eyam's cottages find their way into the cloudbank, she felt the first snowflakes begin to fall. They fell on her nose and gathered on her eyelashes, so that when she blinked it felt cold. She was in her forties now and the years had traced themselves in the lines on her face and the wrinkles on her hands, but when she stood with the snow falling she felt like a girl still. Her mother would always call her to come inside when the snow arrived but she would resist her calls and stay out in it, letting it fall on her. No, it felt like a cleansing, a return to innocence and simplicity and a welcome break from all the constant thinking that was so very exhausting.

The change in the landscape as it accepted the layer of white reminded her that whatever this time was, it would not be unending, no matter how much it felt as if it would. Within an hour all was lost in an eerie whiteness and the edges of farm and dale, house and smithy, Riley and Eyam, were blurred together into a rolling blanket of snow. Any traveller not knowing their story now would not so easily discover it beneath the shield of white. A wanderer could pass this village wrapped in the beautiful arms of winter and never know that beneath the pure, dazzling brilliance a deadly foe had slipped uninvited into warm cottages and caused such pain and loss. Elizabeth hoped a foolish childish hope that the village would stay buried beneath the snow for the winter, smothering the pestilence and thawing only when the danger had passed, but the next day her adult eyes would see the village emerge once again as the snow thawed, a visitor departing more quickly than the plague had proved to, and December would write its own chapter in these difficult times.

15

Emmott

30th November 1665

Emmott climbed down the hill towards the Delph, the winter sun was low in the sky and sent sunlight streaming through the trees and lighting up her dress in radiant stripes. She hoped he would be there so she wouldn't have to wait. Waiting would let the thoughts in and she was trying so hard to keep them at bay. She knew that burying her grief like her mother had was not going to lead her to any place good but, for the sake of the now small Syddall family, she had to be the one to keep going. Joseph needed feeding and entertaining, the household needed keeping and she was sure her mother would not eat if she did not put the food all prepared and ready in front of her. They sat at the kitchen table at meal times, like a sad trinity bereft of speech.

Typically, at mealtimes, Joseph wriggled in the silence until she let him down to play in the garden, his one and only solace from the desolate adults now his sole minders. She watched him as he incorporated the mounds of his father and siblings' graves into his games, making them hills for his soldiers to climb and the crosses providing shade and shelter for his exhausted troops. She had wrestled four crosses from the wood in the yard, calling to mind all her father had taught her about working with wood. She tried to imagine his hands as she turned and shaped the wood with the chisel. Hours of toiling and several painful blisters later, and with a smooth finish bought with the delicate top layer of her fingers, she had driven four crosses into the ground, again whispering the few prayers that she knew. Again, humbly asking that these be the last graves her hands would tend and wondering who would bury her if it came to that…

At times Emmott wondered why she had not succumbed to the plague herself; how she had tended to all of the sick in her household but plague seeds had not crossed over to her as they had the others. *Was there something about herself she was unaware of? Some sort of unseen magic?* For a moment it had made her feel important, special, and then the shock of her pride had deflated her so utterly she was ashamed to even talk of it, even with Rowland.

Catherine Mompesson, the vicar's wife, had called round during the week following the deaths of her remaining sisters and had been so compassionate. She wasn't much older than Emmott and her eyes showed a kindness of soul that Emmott really warmed to. She had brought bread, still warm and likely just baked by her maid, and enquired as to the health of Elizabeth. Emmott had led her mother to the parlour and had her sit in her father's chair. Emmott was surprised to see Catherine gather Elizabeth's hands in hers as she prayed over her. There was no recognition in Elizabeth's vacant stare that she had received this gift of compassion but Emmott saw her mother's hands squeeze Catherine's almost imperceptibly.

Catherine held Emmott as she left, pulling the other young woman into a short but warm embrace before taking her leave. The solace and reassurance that can only come from human touch had consoled Emmott in a way she had silently craved during the heavy, lonely times of the past months. To have someone else hold her, though even for a fleeting moment, was such a tonic that it was with some reluctance that Emmott released Catherine from their embrace. She thought Catherine valiant to meet them with such warmth despite the novel danger this unseen foe presented.

On leaving, Catherine fussed Joseph's hair, saying how much he reminded her of her own little son, George. Emmott knew she had a little girl too, a year younger than her son. The Mompessons had not been in Eyam long. Before their arrival the incumbent of Eyam Parish had been Shoreland Adams, a rector poorly suited to village life. She shuddered to think how his leadership would have fared in the current circumstances. There was also Reverend Stanley, a decent man of Puritan persuasion relieved of his official duties to the parish when the Non-Conformist Act came into being, but still very much respected within the village.

Though people were wary of the Mompessons at first, many still favouring their allegiance to Reverend Stanley, yet the Mompessons had proved their commitment to their new flock, visiting those who had lost loved ones to offer what little comfort they could and to advise on burial. Catherine had made herself an ally in Humphrey Merrill, who served as the village apothecary, taking his herbal concoctions into afflicted homes and sometimes mixing remedies of her own in the rectory kitchen. After seeing her out, Emmott noticed Catherine had left a small muslin bag of herbs on the table by the door. The nestled, fearful thing inside Emmott again stretched and made itself known. She hoped she would not need to make use of these, other than to season the pot when she next managed to draw upon what she could from her father's hunting abilities and bring back a rabbit for stewing.

As she approached the outcrop of rock that William Mompesson used as a pulpit, their church services being held outside as a precaution to fend off the risk of contamination with plague seeds, she could see Rowland was indeed there already and waiting for her. He was kicking at a loose bit of rock and she could hear his whistling as she drew nearer. It amazed her to hear such a joyous sound. The village was near always still and quiet these past few weeks, as if all inside their homes were holding their breath and praying urgent, silent prayers that they and their loved ones would be spared. When people spoke, it was most often to ask if so and so was well or enquire if you knew what was happening in such and such house. The only residents of the village who made any kind of noise really were the children. They played separately, siblings playing in cottage gardens and looking longingly over into the gardens of their neighbours next door or across the street. Their proximity was reduced but their jubilant play was not. They found cheeky ways to still play together across the divides their parents had established, as children always do find ways around the rules of adults.

The news had filtered through to the children on the row of cottages about the death of their friends, of Robert and Sarah and Alice, and Emmott had it from Mary Cooper, whose son Jonathan had joined his brother in the grave in the tailor's garden, that each child in the row had cried and said extra prayers before they slept whenever they were told of the loss of a play mate from this end of the village.

Emmott knew there had been deaths at Town End and Town Head and the pestilence was starting to spread its deathly fingers through the village, snatching children, men, women, old and young. If she thought about it too much it kept her awake late into the night, though now she felt she was like the widow in the Bible story, with only a mite left to offer should death require more from her. Her most acute fear was for Rowland. Though she was desperate to see him up close, to touch him, to stroke his face and wrap her arms about him, she could not put him in danger. Even her growing notion that somehow she might have something within her that resisted the infection stronger than most, she could not test this idea with Rowland's life. They must continue to only send letters and to meet from afar in the Delph; the theatre of their lovers' tale of loyalty and love.

Rowland's face met Emmott's with a smile that she could tell reached his eyes even with the distance between them. His genuine joy at seeing her settled the fearful thing that was her near-constant companion. When she made Joseph's breakfast it was there, when she took the vegetable parings out to the garden it was there, when she kissed her mother goodnight it was there. She had continued to help her neighbours, even looking after a toddler while a woman at Orchard Bank gave birth to her baby. Emmott could not imagine giving birth during such times. She knew from her mother that childbirth went best when the mother was relaxed and surrounded by loving safety, and bringing a baby into the world at such a time would surely feel the opposite of all that. She had kept the toddler away from Joseph, just to be on the safest side of prudence, though she would have dearly liked her little brother to have had a companion his own age if only for a few hours.

"I wish I could kiss you," Rowland called out. "You look sad, my Emmott."

"I suppose, because I am," she called back, trying to force a smile.

"I can't even imagine what you have been through, these past months. To lose them. So many of them. I wish I could take it all away and I promise you Emmy, I will try to make your life so much better, so much happier, once we are married. How I'll fill up this big hole that has opened up with so much love… And children."

It was odd hearing their private feelings broadcast so loudly, and that he had mentioned children when she had lately been so glad to not be in the position of some of the village women, bringing babies into the world at such an arduous time and constantly worried for their little ones. She looked around and hoped nobody else was in the Delph. She couldn't risk getting closer. The rector was already fearful for those living in the surrounding towns and villages of Derbyshire. If the disease were to break out from here it would spread, all through the county and maybe beyond. Already twenty-nine of the village had perished since the ill-fated box of cloth arrived and took George Viccars as the first victim of many.

"Did they suffer, Emmy?" he asked, his voice dropping slightly and his head bowing towards the floor. Emmott breathed a sigh and gathered herself before replying. Her palms pressed into her belly as she recounted it for him, as if the pain was trapped there and if she touched it she could make it less.

"They all had fever and sickness. All but Alice got the lumps in the neck and their armpits. I didn't check the groin of Robert or father but I suppose they were there. I washed my sisters and Marshall Howe carried them out." A sob escaped then which she could not hold back. "He had to tie a rope around Father's feet. Though I know from others he has favoured the neck, so I am grateful to him for sparing me that."

"He is a brute Emmy. They say he caught it himself early on but recovered? I suppose he now thinks himself invincible? My kin here say he took plenty for taking out Syth, William and Amy. I hope it brings him no pleasure and no lasting wealth! To pillage from the dead just to see them put into the ground, not even sacred soil!" He could see this upset her. She had turned her face away from him and was staring out across the green hills. He chastised himself for this speech, knowing how much harsh words aimed at others were abrasive to her kind and gentle nature. He desisted from his berating of Marshall Howe and his deplorable conduct as sexton and changed topic.

"How is your mother?" he called. Again, he saw her take a deep breath.

"Like a ghost," she replied. Emmott had hoped her mother would begin to come out of the crippling fog that grief had encased her in, that the near-constant attention from Joseph, her only remaining young child, would cause her maternal heart to fix its direction again. She was adrift, as if her North had gone and now she was like a compass needle spinning round and round without bearings or destination, aimlessly floating on an ocean of loss.

"I'm sorry Emmy," he almost whispered. She could see by the way he fidgeted that he just wanted to cross the void and hold her close. She wanted that too. More than anything. But the image of her father reduced to a swollen and defeated man was enough of a reminder that they each must stay on their respective sides of the Delph. She wanted to touch Rowland so badly but she was convinced that if she had to watch him perish as she had her father, her heart would surely stop beating with the pain of it. As it was, she felt her heart skip beats now and then and flutter with the feathers of the fearful thing that had roosted in her breast. In a melancholy moment, she thought, perhaps, the missed beats were the ones that used to beat for her father and if she were to live without Rowland perhaps her heart would cease to beat at all.

"It's alright. I'm alright," she called out to him, making an effort to appear brighter and raising her hand to a wave.

"I'll come back next week," he promised her. "Be here?"

"I'll be here," she said, nodding her head.

"Make sure you are!" he called. She could hear an undertone of fear to his voice, though he had tried his hardest to conceal it. The notion that to Rowland the idea of living life without her was unthinkable made her feel somehow more contained and even more cherished. And oh, how she wished to be taken care of, for someone to stroke her hair, take her feet into their lap and let her sleep. She missed the days of sleeping normally. Now her nights were often fretful. At times she couldn't go to sleep, though her eyes were gritty and her eyelids full with heavy exhaustion. Other times, she would wake in the early hours, just before dawn, waking even before the birds but with no song in her own heart. This was her life now. This was her family; small and frail, her only living relatives a vacant mother and a little boy. Emmott was their salvation. She knew it and she had rallied to the necessity of it, but she was also crushed by it and nobody could relieve the weight she carried.

'I am the North now,' she told herself. 'I am the breadwinner, the father, the mother, the sister, the keeper of the door and the gate, so that the sinister visitor does not reprise its visit'. A whole month had passed since Alice had died and Emmott was fairly sure their family of three were now firm survivors. Yet still they kept to their house, with Emmott only venturing out for supplies. Most times she was out in the village she would see Catherine Mompesson, basket in her arms, delivering food and concoctions for ailments to families most in need or afflicted by the pestilence. November had been thankfully kinder in the number of families stricken by the plague and Emmott began to hope for a December that would see the village clear of danger.

"He had roses," she suddenly called out, reigniting their conversation.

"What? Who had roses?" Rowland asked, turning back to face her.

"He did. My father. He was the only one. Angry marks flaring on his skin. They spread across his chest, like they were blooming. They reminded me of the ones in the gardens opposite ours. Different shades of pink and red. I wish I could lay roses on his grave now. But I hardly get chance to leave the house now to go looking for flowers. I miss my walks in the Dale. I can't leave Joseph with Mother. I don't even know if she sees him. Sometimes I put him in her lap to see if he brings her out of her fog. He's so affectionate. He puts his chubby little arms around her and touches her face. It makes *my* heart melt but she usually just stares out of the window. I have seen her look down at him briefly a few times. I just hope in time she will thaw and see she still has a child who needs her."

They continued their conversation, turning to the discussions of the village elders, particularly the two rectors, who had miraculously begun working together despite being on either side of the religious divide decided by the Non-Conformist Act of 1662. The people of the village had been sceptical of Mompesson and his wife, appraising William by the same harsh judgements they would have made about Shoreland Adams, had he still been the vicar of Eyam. Adams had shown very little interest in them, preferring his other parish and only visiting Eyam on a Sunday from time to time when the weather was most fine and he could contemplate the journey in the wagon. The fact that William Mompesson had *not* used the excuse of the arrival of the pestilence to desert them had already raised his status in the village considerably and won him the respect of those who had been otherwise sceptical or indifferent.

Rowland recounted a story to Emmott regarding the village of Vernham Dean in the south of the country, that had been troubled with plague earlier in the year. The rector had told his stricken parishioners to wait at Chute Causeway, the road that ran towards Winchester as it passed near Hampshire and Wiltshire, promising that he would meet them there with food and supplies. But he abandoned them. Rowland had heard this from a cousin who wrote a letter relaying the woeful tale and on telling Emmott, he added that the rector had died of plague himself and was now said to haunt the causeway, trying to reach his flock and attain forgiveness for his gross betrayal. Emmott wondered if there would soon be ghosts walking Eyam, those souls who, when it came to the ultimate test for their loved ones, would fail miserably and would take their fatal lack of character to the grave and beyond. Thankfully, Mompesson seemed to be cut from different cloth to the vicar of Vernham Dean and Emmott had already proved herself capable of facing the gravest odds.

The general opinion was that each should keep to his own home as much as possible, straying only into town to obtain provisions. Emmott told Rowland about the reports that a woman from Orchard Bank, on the far side of the village, had ventured to the market at Tideswell and been recognised as being from their village. They had pelted her with old produce and sent her back to Eyam. The fate of the village had clearly spread into the shire. Rowland said the mood in Stoney Middleton was one of simmering fear. With Eyam so close, they were concerned about the almost inevitable transfer of the sickness into their own village. His mother had begged him not to come but his father, seeing how much his son feared for his love, patted him on the back and reminded him to keep his distance when pursuing his heart. This was a plague of proximity and for a close-knit community the pestilence tested their connection with each other as they followed the paradoxical notion that they cared best for each other by staying away.

"Do you hear anything from the families at Riley?" he called. "They seem best placed up there to ride this out unscathed, don't they?"

"I saw Elizabeth Hancock down here just last week," Emmott said. "Andrew Merrill has taken himself up that way. He's living in a hut on the hill with his cockerel!"

Rowland chuckled.

"People do what they think necessary. Stay safe my Emmott."

Assuring him she would, she took her leave with a smile and a wave and made her way back up the hill towards Bagshaw House. On entering the lane, she glimpsed the roses in the cottage gardens and a prayer rose up and out of her, unbidden and swift in its assent, a quiet and heartfelt prayer for the beloved father she had lost.

16

Elizabeth

14th December 1665

Elizabeth was busy stitching at the kitchen table, the afternoon light from the midwinter sun glowing only faintly and not lending much illumination to her task. She moved her chair nearer to the window in order to make best use of the sun's weak winter rays and ensure her handiwork was of the best quality. Her stitches were neat and well-spaced, bringing the different fabric together almost seamlessly. It had taken her the best part of a week to deliberate with herself over whether she should go to the tailor and ask to purchase the scraps of fabric. In some ways it seemed ridiculous, to go to the very nucleus of this entire outbreak, but the other part of her conscience reminded her that the plague had now spread wider into the village and away from its starting point at Alexander Hadfield's home.

In the end, the second argument (and the repeated longings of her daughter) had won out and she had descended into the village yesterday, taking eggs and butter to sell so she could make the most of the visit and perhaps even trade with the tailor to conserve precious funds now the smithy was routinely less busy as nearly all outsiders had begun to shun Eyam for fear of what they might unwittingly catch there. As she followed the usual track down into the village, the earth hard and cold beneath her boots, she did not see another soul until she was almost at the row of cottages where the pestilence had first made its presence known back in September.

It was as if all of Eyam had followed the animals into hibernation, closing up their doors and resisting any impulse to come outside and engage in normal activities. She could see from her viewpoint on the hill that there were times when the streets were traversed by several people but today all was quiet. You would not believe it was December and soon to be Christmastide. With the church closed up and few attending the outdoor services held in the Delph because of the bitterly cold weather that had arrived at the start of the month, there was no indication of festivities in the planning. Life was grey and cold, though nobody could grumble at how the arrival of the chill appeared to slow the march of death which had gathered apace in the warm Autumn month of October. For that she, in keeping with her fellow villagers, was grateful.

When she knocked at the Hadfield door and Alexander came to open it, she could see from his expression of thinly veiled surprise that she was not the only one who had considered the dangers of paying such a visit. Whilst she had decided to come, it seemed likely that others had stayed well away.

"How may I help you Mrs…" he asked, smoothing down his apron with his large, rough hands.

"Hancock. From up at Riley," she said for want of reply.

"Ah yes, Riley. Fortunate to be up there!" he said, and she smiled at him, more out of duty than of want.

"Yes, I suppose I am fortunate," she replied. "I was just here to enquire of any material scraps you might have? I only need a few. Some bright colours would be perfect if you have them, if not I'll take whatever and chance dyeing them." He looked at her quizzically. What could have led her to come calling for fabric scraps under the circumstances? Reading the curiosity in the way his eyebrows were slightly lifted, she divulged the reason for her request.

"I'm making a doll," she explained. "It's for my youngest girl, Elizabeth. She keeps asking for one you see, and…well…I thought I might just make it for her, for giving on Christmas Eve."

Ah, the love of a mother will overcome all obstacles it seemed. Alexander pondered the concept. He had seen the same disregard for risk in Mary when she had nursed her two stricken boys, no care for her own danger if there was the opportunity to show the depth of her love in a practical sense when it was needed the most. He disappeared out the back of the house to where his workshop was, and selected some pieces, adding in some small but exquisite squares of beautiful damask he had used when making a gown for Mrs Furness earlier in the year. He hid them between the layers of more muted, ordinary fabric and hoped that Elizabeth would smile when she discovered them there later. Making anyone smile in this afflicted village was an unparalleled reward at this time and Alexander was happy to be able to offer it.

Returning to the door, he placed the scraps in her hands with a smile and Elizabeth asked him what she owed him. At first, he insisted on nothing but when she offered him some freshly laid eggs, still warm in their wrappings, he could not refuse them and accepted them with thanks. Elizabeth tucked the pieces of fabric into her basket where the eggs had vacated a space and began the walk back towards Riley. She detoured past Humphrey Merrill's place, where he and Anne informed her that they had thankfully been much quieter in the past few weeks and the demand for tinctures and concoctions had returned to a more normal pace.

"Although," Humphrey said. "Every daft beggar with a fever now believes himself stricken with plague!" and he roared with laughter.

"I suppose they do," she said, offering a laugh, her second forced expression of joviality of the visit, confirming to her again that she did not seek out social interactions so much as tolerated them for the necessity of having some she could call friends.

The wind blew strong and seemed to wish to pass through her bones as she climbed the hill towards Riley. Later that evening when she sat down by the light of the fire and pulled over the basket to inspect the scraps of fabric, she found the squares of beautiful damask and Alexander's hope of bringing a smile was indeed fulfilled. She would make Elizabeth a beautiful doll. A smile of double worth, both completely genuine and for the gratification of only herself.

17

Emmott

19th December 1665

After the terrifying spate of deaths in October, November had claimed relatively few lives of the village inhabitants. Marshall Howe reported to a small, daring crowd in the Miner's Arms one night that he had buried only five dead during the month. Some said he had complained because the lucrative gathering of family heirlooms and treasures which he *accepted* in lieu of his death services had dried up. Some say he had the devil in his eye. Some say the plague had drained every ounce of decency from him once his buboes had gone down and his fever had broken. But Emmott believed she knew there was kindness in him yet. She had seen it when he had carried out Sarah and Alice. But Marshall liked to bury it deep, as if any kindness were a weakness and it seemed to Emmott that he likely considered her a feeble and pathetic thing for all her compassion and she did not know why this assumed assessment bothered her so much. Why she should spend a second fretting over what others thought of her she would ever know. Caring often knows no bounds, even to the detriment of the one who cares.

The ale houses had been quiet through October as people had made the decision to stay at home until the deadly stalker of the village hung up its cloak and scythe and left. Then, at the start of December, they had begun to fill again, though only the pluckiest returned and there was always space for more should they find the daring to join them. There was a cautious hope that the Christmas season; the season that best reminds men of a God who chose to reside with man, who was incarnate into humanity's filth and struggle and who *healeth all thy diseases*, would bring with it an end to the harrowing of the village. Men, women and children had been taken to their forever resting places with unhallowed haste and Marshall had put them there. He was at once both revered and reviled for his part in placing their loved ones into the ground. Yet no man would dare refuse a drink with him, especially when he was three tankards in and insisting on a fourth.

Half way through December Emmott found herself assisting with a birth. The village had its midwives but with caution still the order of the day, many households looked only to those closest to them to help them. Emmott had not been close friends with Mary Rowe but she knew of her, being of a similar age. She had heard Mary's husband, William, calling in the road outside Bagshaw House, his harried voice being carried on a frosty November wind.

Emmott had pulled on the winter cloak her father used to wear for the night watch, tying it tight around her neck and borrowing her mother's fur collar to keep out the bitter cold. She emerged from the door of Bagshaw House and stood for a moment staring at him, spinning around wildly in the middle of the road. She brought her hand up to her head to shield her eyes from the low winter sun, so she could better see him.

"What is it?' she called out. He spun around, as if responding to a rifle shot during a hunt. For a moment he stared at her without speaking.

"Emmott Syddall, sir," she said, "Have you need of help?"

"Aye, yes!" he called, collecting himself. "It is my wife, Mary. Our young one is set to appear but she is weak and we are loath to ask the midwife in as she recently was in the house of the Rowbotham's and the plague hath recently visited there." Emmott had heard about the fate of William Rowbotham, the head of the household carried off first and throwing the remaining household into turmoil.

"I will come with you," Emmott said, pulling the door behind her. She had been of a mind to let her mother spend some hours with Joseph in her charge and it appeared the day had come for her to trust that her mother's maternal nature was buried, merely shrouded by grief, and not fully gone. She followed him quickly down the road towards Town End.

On arrival at the Rowe's house she was struck instantly by the sweet smell of sweat mixed with a weak aroma of shit, it having been recently removed but still lingering. Mary Rowe was lying curled up on a pallet bed with her skirts pulled up over her knees, her legs bent and pulled in towards her bulging belly, as if she was desperate to pull every aching part of her inwards, towards her. She clutched at her stomach and her face was squeezed into a painful grimace which Emmott instantly recognised as a contraction. Emmott had seen her younger siblings born. She knew that Mary, who was birthing her first child, was likely exhausted from a prolonged labour and would need encouragement to summon her strength to push the baby out.

"May I?" she asked, turning her attention from Mary to William and back again. Emmott could not stop herself from comparing these two to the Holy Family and their arrival in Bethlehem. Except here there was plenty of room but there was still the reluctance of people to draw near to a family in their time of need. Emmott grasped her own skirts and lifted them slightly so as to be able to crouch before Mary. Parting Mary's legs so she could see more clearly between them and peering through the dark of the cottage, Emmott could just glimpse the head of the baby, a mass of dark hair, ready to crown and be pushed out. Emmott remembered her mother giving birth. She had always used a birthing stool, brought in by one of the village midwives but looking around Emmott could not see one here. When she asked William he simply shook his head.

"We could not risk it," he said, 'having someone come in and bring it". Looking at Mary, Emmott felt the fearful thing shift and flutter; the redness of Mary's cheeks and of her chest, at least the part visible to Emmott in the opening of Mary's gown, were all too familiar and Emmott feared the risk had already been taken, though they may not know how or when. Now was not the time to discuss it and the near-terrified look in William's eyes told her how scared he was, though whether of the dangers of birth or plague or a combination of both, Emmott was unsure.

Emmott did not know how to make the ointment that was often rubbed into the belly of the birthing woman and was said to speed up delivery, but she knew how to make a quick poultice with herbs imbibed within it. She set about making the mixture once William pointed out where she could find the necessary ingredients and she whisked it as quickly as she could, with Mary's moans coming more and more frequently. Once made, she quickly set it on to Mary's stomach and whether it was the cool nature of the poultice or the healing action of the herbs, Mary seemed to relax her tightened position slightly. Emmott scattered the rest of the herbs about the bed, hoping that the scent at least would set Mary at ease. Many women made a will the moment they learned they were pregnant, but looking around the simple cottage, Emmott doubted Mary had much that was truly hers which she could bestow upon anyone else. Mary lay on the bed, her only instinct seemingly being to pull at the covers on either side of her.

Emmott heard Mary's moans gather strength, a crescendo reaching its pitch and falling away separated by only mere moments and she knew it was time. Separating Mary's legs again, she could not see any signs of the umbilical cord. Emmott breathed out slowly with relief at its absence. Her brother Richard's birth had been complicated by this and it had taken two midwives to manoeuvre him and retrieve the looped cord, a risky moment which could have seen him lost and perhaps her mother as well. She felt a small stab of renewed pain to think of him lost now anyway.

"Mary, it is time to push. Can you do that Mary? When you next feel the pain build again, can you push?"

"If she could get out of the bed and crouch..." Emmott said turning to William, and then trailing off in acknowledgement that Mary seemed so spent of energy and was likely unable to sustain such a position on her own. She entreated William to get her up out of the bed so she was instead on her knees leaning over it, with William doing his best to hold her up. Emmott could tell by the way his arms began to tremble with the tension that William was likely taking all of her weight. Emmott saw Mary's face grimace even more as a wave of pain gathered in pace and intensity. William looked at his wife, clearly bewildered by the level of her struggling. It was unusual for a father to be here at a birth. This was usually the domain of women; those of the family, female neighbours and the village midwives, who had learned their craft from their own mothers, aunts and grandmothers. Strangely, they were known as 'gossips', a term that confused Emmott, as there were few things she would want to talk about less.

Emmott's mother would be more use here than she was, though not in her current state, Emmott lamented. Emmott knew women usually liked to deliver standing up or squatting down towards the floor and she had seen her mother do this. It was good that they had managed to get Mary off the bed and Emmott prayed William had the strength to keep his wife from collapsing down onto the rough wood planks on the cottage floor. Emmott knew Mary's knees would be painful, leaning so heavily on the rough wood, so she managed to slide some of the folded linen under each knee between one contraction and the next. Childbirth brought to mind the travailing of Eve and Emmott had often looked upon a birthing woman and wondered if her sex were indeed cursed. Though most lived, many died bringing their children into the world, girls even younger than she. Emmott knew Mary was the same age as she was. It was perhaps this, in part, that had led her to follow William to Mary's aid despite the absolute risk that doing so had brought.

It took a lot of effort on Emmott's part to keep Mary focused on delivering the baby. Her head rolled forward onto her chest with exhaustion and the heat (Emmott was increasingly concerned this was fever) and her hands explored the sweat-soaked sheets fretfully, trying to find William's hand though he was unable to offer it as well as hold her upright. He whispered to her, drawing his head next to hers and telling her she could do it. Mary began an indecipherable babble and Emmott's stomach flipped with the recognition of what could be the response to pain or a sign of a fever increasing its grip. Her heart beat fast with the thought of losing both mother and baby.

Whether Mary had the pestilence or not Emmott did not know for sure, but Mary was hot and red, sweaty and speaking nonsensically and clearly very unwell. Emmott knew birth had left her mother hot, spent and exhausted but she had never seen her quite like this and Emmott had feared that these signs were a bad omen for Mary. Emmott had encouraged Mary to push with the next contraction, though she sometimes appeared to be not quite conscious and missed some of the waves of productive pain as they came. Mary gave one big push, calling out with a weakened voice, and finally the child's head had crowned. Between them, William and Emmott had encouraged Mary to push again and it had thankfully taken only one more push to bring out the shoulders and body, bringing the little one into the world.

When the baby arrived, Emmott had gathered him up into the linens William had thankfully thought to prepare before his walk through the streets searching for mercy from one of Eyam's inhabitants. The baby was a boy, he was quiet and he failed to cry, which Emmott reluctantly and painfully accepted was not the sign of a healthy child. She handed him over wordlessly to William, who took him to his mother and tried putting him to Mary's breast. He suckled a little and then fell asleep and Mary herself lapsed into a shallow sleep. Emmott had used the new water she and William had fetched from the village well on their way towards the Rowes cottage to soak new rags in the boiled water so that William could clean the baby and cool Mary's head. She had instructed him to boil more water on the fire and had poured the water into a new basin and washed her hands. Her father had always instilled in her the benefits of this, speaking of the unseen 'seeds' of illness that could be found in soil and fabric and accumulated on the skin of the sick. How he knew of this she had never asked and now it was too late. She knew his fellow villagers had found his ideas somewhat fanciful but to Emmott it made much sense, especially considering how the pestilence had appeared to spring from the box of cloth from London, as if the very material were tainted with infection.

The placenta arrived, mercifully with little effort from Mary, whose eyes, Emmott noted, were wide with surprise that something else would need to be pushed out after the baby. In the absence of a sharp enough knife, William had bitten through the cord to sever it, almost gagging with the effort, and tied the end with twine wound around a length of bark. The child would now make his solitary effort to live. Emmott had uttered a prayer over him before leaving the Rowe abode.

She had left the little family gathered on the bed, with Mary managing to look down into the face of her new son and a feeble smile on her face. This brief moment of hope finding its own breathing room amongst all the fear and pain had caused a salty smile to form on Emmott's face. She realised her tears had fallen from her eyes involuntarily and had collected at the corners of her mouth. There were beads of sweat gathered on William's brow as he lifted a weary hand to thank her. She instructed him on the making of the caudle, hoping the alcohol would dull any pain Mary still felt from the birth. It struck Emmott that the birth had been relatively straight-forward, which for a firstborn was a gift not afforded to all, and William likely could have delivered his son without her, unaccustomed in the art of childbirth though he was. But something about this time meant people still called out for company and connection in their hour of need, despite the obvious danger.

As she walked back towards her side of town, she gulped the fresh air and took long, deep breaths hoping to calm her body of the nervous excitement of the last few hours. As she walked her heart's beating returned to normal and Emmott hoped this little family would somehow escape what she feared had perhaps already taken up residence with them. She stared at her hands, her lively imagination imagining the 'plague seeds' that could still be on them. She vowed to wash her hands again on arrival back at Bagshaw House. It had gone against Emmott's fears to help the Rowes, yet her sense of duty and her inability to ignore the call of the needy had driven her to the cottage despite her reservations.

Several days later, when she had relayed to Rowland her helping the Rowes, he was incredulous. How could she have done something so reckless when the appearance of infection was so possibly upon Mary, perhaps upon all of them? Emmott tried to give voice to the irresistible pull towards compassion she felt, even in such uncertain days. The news of the Rowes sad demise had reached her. The baby had returned to his place amongst the angels the same day of entering the world, with Mary following soon after him and William four days after that. Since it had been a week and Emmott was still in good health, she was encouraged to believe that her reckless mercy had not resulted in her own demise.

Rowland made her promise no more missions of mercy. She reluctantly made the promise in order to calm his obvious distress and dis-ease at her having put herself in harm's way, though she could not say for certain that a cry for compassion could go unheeded by her ears in days to come. Even in these times of fear and mistrust, Emmott's belief in the necessity of humankind to help each other in times of distress and meet each other with kindness and compassion was resilient. It had been the creed of her father and she saw it daily worked out in the actions of the rector's wife. If now was indeed a time to abandon all hope and leave others to their fate, she was unlikely to yield to it so easily. There was no version of herself that she would want to exist where she could knowingly avoid giving assistance where it was so genuinely needed.

18

Catherine
24th December 1665

As she sat in the parlour she was all of a sudden aware of it being Christmas Eve. The day had passed as they all did these days, with trips to Humphrey Merrill to procure the latest concoctions he had made and taking them to those households who had sick. That afternoon she had been to the Rowes, Rowbothams and the Rowlands and the smells and agonising groans she heard coming from inner rooms had made her delicate shoulders feel unquestionably heavy.

The children had been subdued, finally defeated by weeks of staying indoors and existing in such close proximity to their parents' anguish. Tonight, there would be the traditional midnight mass but neither Catherine nor William expected there to be a sizeable attendance at their church open to the elements. It was probably just as well, a crowd of people herded together in close proximity was not something that would benefit them all at this time of fragility and fear.

She sank down further into the chair by the writing bureau and contemplated the sacred mystery that usually accompanied this night and had always captivated her since childhood. She closed her eyes but it wouldn't come. Then, from the cottage window she thought she heard singing. It took a concerted effort to hoist herself up and out of the chair now she had finally sat down, but Catherine pushed herself up using the arms of the chair and padded over to the casement. The window had been left ajar, likely by Jane for the fresh air that William insisted was so important, and through the gap drifted a melody.

She recognised snatches of a carol; the lines of Luke woven into *While Shepherds Watched*. There was an ensemble of voices she detected, likely made up of the courageous survivors of the cottages that were in the vicinity of the rectory. She could just about make out the sweet singing of a young voice and thought it might be Emmott Syddall, perhaps singing her young brother Joseph to sleep. There was a man's voice too. Not strong, but putting in some effort nonetheless. And behind that she could hear someone harmonising faintly, all the notes mingling in the air before they found their way to her straining ears. That they could form this spontaneous and beautiful choir, precious in its vulnerability, brought her genuine gratitude for being in this village at this moment, despite all that was going on here.

She listened for a while and then pulled the window shut. The evening chill still hung about her but there was something of warmth in her heart this night. Sitting down again, the peace lulled her into a fretless sleep, the first she had had in a long time, her night's repose being frequently interrupted by bad dreams and sudden awakenings. The heifer in the church, the sounds of children crying, they moved themselves together in her dreams and sometimes on the hills she thought she could hear Gabriel's hounds, a sinister pack of spectral dogs, the howls of which were believed to foretell death and misfortune and echoed down towards them.

Yesterday had been difficult. She had got in the habit of helping Humphrey Merrill and had become quite fond of him. At sixty, he was not as quick on his feet as he had once been and traversing the length and breadth of Eyam was very wearing on his old limbs. The demand for remedies and herbal concoctions was often great, particularly in Winter where households battling winter ailments and afflictions turned to him as well as those afflicted by plague. It was for this reason Catherine had rendered her services to the old man, offering to carry his cures to homes and even learning how to make some simple herbal remedies herself. Though the demand had reduced somewhat with a drop in the deaths from plague, he was still entirely grateful of her service.

When she came out of his cottage to begin one such delivery errand, a woman had spoken to Catherine with such barbed conviction that the words still stung even a day later. She had been accused of straying from her job as a rector's wife and of mixing the separate disciplines of sacred sanctity and nature's therapy. '*Choose one, dear, and stick to it. You will only confuse the people further in this time of suffering. They will go to their deaths not knowing whether to beg God for mercy or beg Humphrey Merrill for his herbs!*'

Catherine was troubled by it. She did not want to increase the bewilderment of their parishioners but neither did she want to shy away from anything that would possibly help them. The remedies Humphrey Merrill shared gave the victims and their families some hope, even if only for a moment. She had seen it on the faces of those she handed the bundles to. What harm was it for her to offer scripture or prayer to them also? Surely there was no hierarchy when it came to easing the pain of another? This she believed. The Lord has given many gifts, all to the benefit of his people. Besides, it suited Catherine to be busily employed during this time. She was not fashioned to sit at home in the rectory and do nothing, and if she was honest, there was a small amount of pride that she felt when people thanked her for her service and she didn't want to let go of that. But knowing that some in the village might not look on this favourably gave her some distress.

Catherine had awoken determined to straighten out her thoughts. When William approached her at almost midnight she had resolved within herself to continue the work with Humphrey Merrill. Her husband had not condemned her for it and she determined that neither would the Lord, for she did it for the right reasons. To *save*. Wasn't that what the Christian path was all about? She set off with William for the Delph. The night was cold and cloudless, giving the stars above an extra brilliance. She was confronted by the unchangeable nature of the night sky; the way the stars still stayed there and shone just as brilliantly if the world below were in revelry and merriment or in desperate distress. When the sky was darkest the stars shone all the brighter and she thought there was something of truth for the soul to be mirrored in each of them. It was good to keep the midnight vigil even in such times.

As she listened to William speak the words of the first nativity Catherine couldn't help feel again the wonder of the incarnation, of the Christ baby being born into human suffering and limitation. That He was here even now in amongst their trials and trauma, she did not doubt. Her eyes fell on a couple huddled together not far off, her belly swollen with the promise of a growing child. The babies born in this time would be received into a world of peril and she hoped there was kindness and courage in the hearts of the residents of Eyam to help them even though they were rightly fearful.

She had done much to overcome her own fear since those first days and weeks and the more recent death counts were lower and not as horrifying as the toll in October. Now, as William spoke of the joy of Emmanuel, *God with us,* she slid to her knees in the cold, damp grass and prayed fervently to know the reality of that and for a start to the new year that awaited them, 1666, that saw the threat very greatly reduced.

19

Elizabeth

1st January 1666

It was the first day of the new year and nobody in Eyam could deny the significance this carried. This was the year that would decide their fate. This was the year that would resolve the course of the outbreak one way or another and elect who would live and who would forever have '1666' written next to their name in the parish register as the year they crossed the eternal boundary. For many, the turning of the new year was bittersweet. There was always the sense of hope that the winter would purloin the disease's power once and for all, and there was also the sad recollection of loved ones placed unceremoniously into the earth who were forever left behind in 1665.

Elizabeth and John had ensured their children had enjoyed a quiet but special family Christmas at Riley. She had exchanged eggs and butter for various other provisions so that the Christmas day meal resembled a feast, in variety if not in size. There had been pies and cheese, bread and meat and plum pudding. John had managed to trade some smithing work for a pig's head and it graced the centre of their table, surrounded by fruits and nuts. It made Oner laugh when she saw it on the table with the lemon in its mouth, her beautiful giggle echoing around the farmhouse, but Anne was sensitive and she cried when she saw John unwrap it ready for cooking. Elizabeth had distracted her, enrolling her to help make the mince pies, the two of them spending hours mixing together the flour, eggs and sugar with the strong smelling raisins and currents she had bought in the village. They rarely had means for this kind of food but somehow they had managed it for this Christmas.

John had brought in the yule log on Christmas Eve and she spent close to an hour turning over the farmhouse looking for the brand from last year's log with which to light it in keeping with tradition. Eventually she found it and while John got to work in lighting it, she stepped outside to cool off after her frantic searching. She had stood for a few moments in the quiet, enveloped by the December cold and the growing dark of night falling. Then suddenly there was a song on the breeze, being carried up the hill towards Riley. She recognised it as a carol, people singing in the village. *They have not quite lost all their cheer then* she'd said to herself and as she re-entered the farmhouse she realised she was humming it without planning to.

John took up the song with gusto and William, who would soon be turning sixteen, rolled his eyes in protest. Elizabeth laughed. The yule log was burning well in the grate and the heat had caused the greenery she had gathered that morning with Alice, and hung about the farmhouse rooms, to put out a beautiful festive scent. She closed her eyes and breathed it in and opened them again to take in the happy faces of her family, dappled by the glow from the fire.

When it came to giving their gifts, John had made beautiful soldiers for John, a new hunting knife for William, two delicate metal flowers for Alice and Anne and a very loud metal rattle for Oner. Once he had stopped handing out his gifts, little Elizabeth had looked desolate for just a moment before Elizabeth pulled the doll out from its hiding place in the bedroom she shared with John and Oner and placed it in her hands. It was simply wrapped in a sheet of parchment and Elizabeth had tied the parcel loosely with twine and tucked in a perfect hellebore flower, which is also known as the Christmas Rose. Elizabeth looked at the carefully wrapped parcel and then up into her mother's smiling face and then back to the parcel.

Elizabeth saw how the little girl touched the petals gently before carefully removing it and working her fingers over the twine. The bow came loose easily and she pulled the twine away, turning the package over. The parchment fell open and for the first time little Elizabeth saw the doll her mother had made. The smile that spread across her daughter's sweet face was one of pure joy and Elizabeth clapped her hands together in her own perfect moment of gladness to see her daughter so happy.

"You have been asking for a doll since just after Christmas last year," she said, watching the girl as she ran her fingers over the beautiful pockets of damask in the doll's dress. Elizabeth had skilfully included the scraps from Alexander Hadfield in the skirts of the doll's costume and used the rest to make two small bows for its plaited yarn hair.

"I love it Mama," little Elizabeth said, throwing her arms around her mother's waist and nestling her face into the softness of her belly, rounded by years of childbearing. Elizabeth stroked her daughter's hair and wished it was always so easy to make her children feel happy and safe and loved.

Now today, on this New Year's Day, the first day of 1666, Elizabeth and John sat together and watched their children. The days of Christmas, whilst not as full of food or gifts as Christmas Day itself had been, had so far been lovely despite their continued seclusion from the village except for essential trips. William had put his new knife to good use and was able to prepare some rabbits with it after he and John had set up some traps in the east woods. She had shown him how to cook them, with Alice also helping, so that they enjoyed a good stew, full of flavour from the herbs she had been drying above the hearth.

They had been invited to the Talbot farmhouse on one of the nights and had proceeded with the visit having enquired, with some embarrassment on John's part though none on Elizabeth's, if they were all quite well and free from signs of fever or swelling.

"We have to be able to ask, John," she had told him. "It's not casting suspicion, it's just asking the question on everyone's lips right now." And Catharine had not minded at all, although Richard had teased John a little over it. There was a lot of ale and plenty of singing and when they walked their way back towards their own house the darkness was thick and utterly black, such that they tripped and giggled a little as they found their way. There had been stars that night as many as she had ever seen, as if God himself had set some more in the sky just for them alone to enjoy. This is how she encountered God; in the sky and the earth, on the wind and in the scent of the trees. This was her church; creation in all its glory.

Later in the kitchen, leaning over towards John she laid her head upon his shoulder and welcomed the day's joys into her bosom. He smelled of wood smoke from the fire and something that smelled like the earth. She breathed him in. Tomorrow she would need to go down into the village again to sell whatever she could and trade the rest, but today she wanted to savour the possibilities of a brand new year.

20

Catherine
30ᵗʰ January 1666

The new year had started with more promise, and only four deaths soured the month of January. The Rowbotham family had been devastated by loss and only the widow Anne survived with one of her daughters, Joan. The Rowlands too had been further afflicted, with the plague returning to claim one from their number each and every month, as if driven by some evil clockwork that had the death bell tolling despite the tormenting weeks of seeming-safety that spread out in between each demise. *Would they be able to face a new month without fear?* February waited on the threshold and Catherine hoped for a further decline in the fatal tally.

Her work with Humphrey Merrill had truly inspired her and she had persuaded William to let her section off one part of the vegetable garden in the rectory's grounds so that she could begin to grow her own herbs. Walking out into the dale and beyond to find what she needed was increasingly tiring for her and these walks coupled with those she took to deliver the remedies Humphrey concocted had made her feel very much weaker in these past weeks. The consumption showed itself in terrible fatigue and loss of appetite, which greatly concerned William. The cough that often accompanied it was thankfully no worse, because she often found that coughing and spluttering near to her fellow villagers only sought to make them retract from her in horror, as is she herself might be afflicted by the very thing she was delivering remedies against.

Catherine bent over the earth, kneeling in the cold soil and pressing her hands into it so that it found its way between her fingers. It was cool, being almost February and there was a dampness to it that reached her knees as she worked but the feel of the earth and the smell of the soil kept her working, long after her shoulders became sore and her breathing laboured. She knelt onto her apron in order to save her dress from the worst of the soil and Jane a difficult job of washing. When she brought her handkerchief to her mouth as she coughed there were drops of blood on it as she took it away. She would not tell William. She knew she was working her weak body too hard but after this, once the plants were established and growing and so much nearer to her for collecting, she would be able to rest again. Despite the chill in the air, her brow felt warm and sweaty with the effort of this simple work and these plants Humphrey had given her to transfer were hardy, in a way similar to how she was beginning to regard herself.

Catherine was not one to discard her blessings. She knew all were made in the Lord's image, *imago dei*, and as such she should be wholly thankful for her body, despite the weaknesses it presented her. But something inside her was also growing with frustration. She had found something that she could do, something that would be recognised by others as a legitimate and much-needed service to the village during these turbulent times. It felt good to be praised and needed, to be thanked by desperate villagers and looked upon with eyes that communicated relief and gratitude. She was worried that William would see her deteriorated health and demand she stop, turning to the scriptures that spoke of women as the weaker vessel to ensure her servitude in this matter.

But she didn't feel *weak*. In body, yes. But in soul, in spirit, in the part of her that strained to be alive and vibrant, she felt strong. A new-found purpose enlivened and emboldened her and she had a reason to be here, not just a necessity as the rector's wife. People looked upon her now as one of their own. She was of Eyam! William approached and broke into her thoughts as she sat upright, secreting the bloodied handkerchief away from sight and doing her best to appear healthy.

"You are a busy thing!" he declared as he looked down at the young plants she had deposited into the soil. "Will you walk with me?" Catherine summoned the strength to her knees as she pulled herself upright. She hoped he did not see the way her face involuntarily grimaced a little at the ache in her limbs as they were forced to bear her weight. She enjoyed these walks with William but she noted with some chagrin he always sought to take them when it was most convenient for him and not for her. It would do no good to bring it up now; he clearly had something on his mind.

They walked up behind the house, where the wild flowers grew that most delighted Catherine. She loved the beautiful array of colours to be found there in spring and early summer. Now there were mostly yellow and white flowers; daffodils and snowdrops, each putting out a gentle beautiful scent in the cool, fresh air. She let her hand trail over their delicate blooms.

"I do love how the flowers sweeten the air," she said to William, breathing in deeply. In spring the air seemed imbued with the floral scents, like no other season. The cold winter air seemed to deaden any aroma, in autumn the prevailing scent was the smell of rotten leaves and in summer the heat seemed to deaden any sweetness the flowers offered to her. But spring was full of the fragrance of the blooms all about.

She bent over slowly to examine a plant that she was almost certain was cowslip, though it had not yet flowered. She was sure it had medicinal properties, unexpectedly retrieving a conversation between her uncle and her father from years ago in his study, where she would sit and listen to grown up conversations without interrupting, just storing away the fascinating pieces of wisdom and wonder should there be a future use for it. She selected some stems, pulling the plant carefully from the ground. She would take this to Humphrey. Perhaps he could incorporate it into one of his new remedies if he wasn't using it already? They had both tried several new concoctions of late, hoping that the properties of the newly added plants would do something to relieve the suffering of those who were visited by the pestilence. She carried it in her hand as they walked, revived by the hope it could bring and suddenly impatient to return so she could get on her way to see Merrill, the excitement of a new discovery bringing her a renewed sense of energy.

"I have had word that the Reverend Stanley has conducted some of the rites of Holy Unction," he told her. She could not immediately perceive his feelings on this from his tone or his words, but knowing he was a proud man she supposed that his sense of propriety might have been wounded by the bypassing of him in favour of the services of the old Puritan minister.

"Unacceptable!" she said. "He is no longer the minister here. They should most certainly have come to you for such acts of holy order. The sacraments are not to be doled out at random by anyone they choose." She looked at him for his reaction.

"By the contrary my dear, I have been feeling I should reach out to him. He has the support of a good number in this village and if he has helped me with their suffering I do not begrudge him for it. I only hope neither of us has to do any more of such holy work. I have seen more people die in the last few months than I ever cared to. Each time I write another name in the Parish Register I pray to God it is the last. I only hope it is." William's face conveyed the seriousness of his wishes and she felt his conviction in the way he gave her hand a squeeze.

He went on to tell her about his sadness at saying the prayers for the dead over the Wilson boy. Isaac had died two days prior, not yet seven.

"He had a look of George about him," William said, the last word getting stuck in his throat and she saw him look away for just a moment. Their concern for their children had grown with each new death that William recorded. Whenever it was a child their anxiety found its expression in the way William got a little gruff when his manservant tarried and the way Catherine was so often startled by Jane. They spent long moments just watching George and Elizabeth, even creeping into their bedrooms in the dead of night to watch them sleep, placing tentative hands on resting brows to check for signs of fever. When people feel their children are threatened there is no level of vigilance that seems too much.

If Elizabeth or George were to sicken with plague it would be a most cruel and unfortunate thing, seeing as from the new year the only people they had seen were their parents, Jane their maid and William's manservant, John. William and Catherine had kept them within the rectory vicinity at all times, encouraging them to spend most of their time in the fresh air of the garden, away from any bad air that may have accumulated in the house itself and secreted away from anything that came in and could potentially carry 'plague seeds'. They were forbidden from taking mail from the delivery boys or helping Jane with any goods procured in the village. Eyam and their children must stay separate, with each on either side of an imaginary divide. Catherine felt ashamed of the extremity of their position and her sorrow at having not kept her promise to Robert Thorpe to bring George along on her next visit as a playmate for William particularly distressed her.

Later that afternoon Catherine made a short visit to Alice Rowland, a mother who had lost all but one of her children to the disease and her sole offspring was in his twentieth year. Her husband had followed the children to the grave in February. The sound of children had vanished from her life and in its stead a heavy silence had grown inside her home, swelling and expanding so that every corner seemed full with it. *How could emptiness be so full, so present?* Catherine came away with a heavy heart, having witnessed the utter sorrow that gathered in Alice's eyes. Her daughters, Hannah and Mary had not seen the year turn and her youngest boy, Abel, was lost in January. By the time Thomas died, all but his oldest son had gone on before him.

Catherine wondered at this occurrence that played out time and again in the village, of fathers following their children to whatever awaited them in eternity. John Syddall and Thomas Thorpe had likewise died after losing several of their children. Were these strong men troubled to leave their beloved children to the unknowns of the afterlife without their protection? She imagined the children's joy at having their fathers appear so soon after they had made the one way journey from this life.

Francis Rowland troubled her. He seemed to her to be wholly aware that he was not a child and yet he was now Alice's only surviving offspring. He saw how his mother longed for the children she had held close to her, kissed goodnight and dressed in the morning. He could not be those things for her and yet he was still her child. The child that survives, always caught in the terrible limbo of the grace and gratitude of still being present and the hardship of not being the one who was gone and that everyone missed.

She had smiled at Francis, hoping to convey all that she felt on his behalf, and her kindness had rendered him unable to remain in the room and he excused himself. It appeared that some people were destined to carry painful truth that they can neither deny nor throw off and so must find their own ways to live with, whatever course that meant they must take. As he left the room he laid his hand on his mother's shoulders and left it there for just a few moments and Catherine realised, he was her parent now. At least for a while, but most probably in some measure forever, as she was so broken and reduced by loss, as if returning to the capacity of a child when a beloved toy is taken away or lost.

21

Emmott
20th February 1666

Christmas had been quiet, a low and somewhat sombre affair, though Emmott had done her best to mark the occasion, making small wooden gifts for her mother and Joseph; for her, a wooden heart carved with her father's initials and for Joseph, a rather crude looking knight. Her efforts to fashion a horse had ended in multiple dismal attempts and so she had reluctantly given up on this. Joseph did not seem to mind, he had a good imagination and had immediately run around Bagshaw House with the new figure. Her mother's response to her gift had been less animated but Emmott had been heartened to see her mother draw the heart to her bosom and keep it there.

When they had sat down at table to have the rabbit Emmott had caught using the simple traps her father had shown her, she was acutely and most painfully aware of the absence of her father and siblings during what was usually a happy and raucous family feast. Their empty spaces had only served to make their absence more obvious and so Emmott had removed one entire bench from the table, so that only the three of them dined and in some ways, this was worse, though it struck Emmott there was never going to be an easy way to have this first Christmas together after such harrowing loss. For every blessing they had- and the neighbours had been kind- there was a hardship as they were confronted with what they no longer had. She missed her sisters' voices thrilling with song after dinner and the whooping laughter of her younger siblings as they engaged in games and told stories. Though her heart was heavy, when the melody of a carol had reached her on Christmas Eve she had still pushed open the window and contributed a few bars of her own, her song escaping into the bitter cold night air like puffs of smoke. The village was singing, despite the fear and the weight of loss. Is the human spirit ever so utterly broken that no songs escape at all from the lips of even the most accursed and suppressed when even just a little hope is presented? The wonder of Christmas seemed to have raised the villager's spirits just enough that night to join them together in communal song.

Everywhere Emmott looked conjured up the memory of something lost that could never be recovered. Each corner of their home like a resting place for a lost joy, calling to mind the happy times, the laughter and the tears, the rhythm of daily life in a large family. The embroidery that Ellen had lost her temper over, the stool that had broken under Robert tipping him onto the floor, the window where Sarah had sat to showcase her latest grievance on her grumpy, outward-staring face. All around this cottage were the objects of memory and she danced with their ghosts every day. She was afraid of dying and afraid of not dying. How could this be? *Did she somehow long to be with them, to meet her painful, feverish end, yet also fight against that awful possibility with all her might?* The dichotomy was exhausting.

January had brought mercifully few deaths, with only four cases of death by plague recorded. William Mompesson kept a meticulous record of families affected and the number of those for whom 'dust to dust' had come too soon, following their infection. Emmott had learned from Rowland, who was connected with the Rowbotham's via a second cousin, that the month had claimed all the male members of that household, leaving only Anne and her daughter, Joan, untouched by disease and death. These families, like her own, now existed with huge holes in them where once precious fathers, brothers, mothers and daughters had been. Everything still moving on, village life continuing much as before though with a tangible wariness, but now it was all playing out for the infection-visited families with this giant void, this absence that somehow weighed so much. She kept her father's memory alive by doing the things he had done and honouring him with the labours of her hands. She worked in the garden and made things with wood, she set traps in the woods and helped her fellow neighbours where she could, keeping a distance whenever possible. She had even offered to take her father's place on the watch bill, though the older men of the village were nothing short of scandalised by the proposal. Rowland had laughed when she told him.

"Oh Emmy!" he had chuckled, when they had last met at The Delph. "These men aren't ready for you yet! You will be wanting to be the rector next!". She had pouted in protest but her small annoyance at being teased was immediately dissipated by the appearance of a beautiful bouquet of roses he pulled out from behind his back, a bit comically and awkward, like the jesters she had heard about at the courts of the King.

"I remembered what you said. About John…about your father… and the roses and how you wished you had some. So, these are from the garden of my Aunt and Uncle. They don't actually know this, so maybe it would be best not to tell them after…after all this is over." As he spoke he grinned coyly and looked down at the floor, as if afraid of her reaction. Perhaps he feared she would think it silly, frivolous in such times, or perhaps it would be too painful and he had over-judged the gesture as one she would recognise as love and not a harmful reminder?

Emmott's reaction assured him. She moved forward, as if she would run to him, and then corrected herself, standing still and staring at him with a broad smile spread over her face. He was too far away to see the tears that were running down her face but he heard the little inhale of breath followed by a quiet sob.

"I…I didn't mean to…" he began.

She interrupted him, "No! They are perfect. Thank you. Thank you. Will you leave them when you go?" she enquired.

"Yes, I'll leave them right here Emmy. I thought you might like to put them on his grave?" he said, looking down.

"Yes, I will," Emmy had reassured him, thanking him over and over. The desire to run across the dell and into his arms was almost undeniable. Nobody would know, nobody was here to see. It hadn't strictly been forbidden anyway, just cautioned against by the ministers. They were anxious to protect other villages as much as their own.

Emmott was confronted by an unwelcome image of Rowland back at home in his village, overcome with fever and swellings like her father and sending the pestilence abroad into Stoney Middleton. She had sincere affection for the place and for several people who lived there and were friends and family through her connection with Rowland.

When they were first betrothed she had talked with him hopefully about living in Eyam and his deep-rooted altruism had led him to reassure her they could live wherever she most felt at home. For her, her father was such a signifier of home and love and safety on this earth that even with a husband she could not imagine life lived away from him, even the few miles down the dale to Stoney Middleton. But now, since her father had gone and it was possible she would now always see the village through a veil of worrisome anxiety and distrust, she had loosened her grip on the notion of this as the only place she could live a contented life. It would be good to start again after this was over, in a new place, with him. The thought kept her where she was, rooted into the ground like the ragwort that was defiant in its colonising of Cucklett Delph. Rowland must stay away and Stoney Middleton must stay well if she was to have a future less painful than her present.

She said her goodbyes, watching him for a while as he walked away, and then approached the place where he had stood, stooping down to pick up the roses. They were such a beautiful array of hues of pink and red and instinct drew her hands immediately up to her face, burrowing her nose into the soft blooms so that the petals stroked her face. It was good to feel embraced again, if only by flowers. She whispered 'father' into the delicate carpels of the roses and closed her eyes for a second. She could still see his face smiling at her quite clearly but she worried that this clarity would fade with time. Would she forget what he looked like? The Bradshaws of Bradshaw House, the village's wealthiest habitants, had grand portraits hanging all through their house. Emmott had never seen them but one of the village girls, who was a maid in the grand Tudor house, had told some of the other village girls about the paintings hanging in every room, giant representations of those living and long gone, immortalised in oil and canvas.

The Bradshaws had fled the village now to go to one of their other properties further into the county and perhaps they would not return, though their ancestors would maintain residence in their absence, hanging there in silence even now. Her family home had no paintings capturing the visages of the dead, only the clothes and trinkets they had left behind. Her father's only framing would be in her mind and she hoped her mind's rendering of him was as clear and as lasting as any painter's.

Emmott took the long way back after her rendezvous with Rowland, taking the opportunity to feel the early spring sunlight falling across her face in gentle rays as she walked slowly beneath the trees. She welcomed the chance to look at the first of the Spring flowers, noting white clusters of snowdrops and the odd crocus bravely emerging into the fresh morning air. She likened herself to these courageous young shoots, newly emerging after the utterly burying experience of the winter of her days. It felt time for her to begin to face the sun again, to imagine a future for herself and what remained of her family. The numbers of dead had remained below ten souls now at the end of this month and the word buzzing around the village like early wasps was that perhaps, just maybe, they had beaten their silent enemy, and those holed up in their cottages could come out of their lengthy, fearful hiding behind doors and shuttered windows.

Emmott had heard from Humphrey Merrill's wife, Anne, that Andrew Merrill, their relative by some means, was adamant he would stay up on the hills above Eyam with his cockerel companion and would make no attempt to return to the village just yet. Humphrey himself had been working on new concoctions of herbs he hoped would provide a cure. He had seen some signs of promise with the Wilson girl, Alice. She appeared to rally and he hoped that he had found a way his faithful commitment to the mysterious healing properties of plants would pay a priceless dividend. With a cure they could release the village from captivity, fear itself being the most potent guard. His celebrations were too premature though and Alice Wilson had suddenly declined, becoming the fifth of the Wilson children to go to an early grave. Beginning in December with little Thomas, January had claimed Isaac and February had sealed the utmost grief for their grieving parents by taking John, Deborah and then Alice. Emmott knew hers was not the only family to be utterly stripped by this disease, yet despite this shared pain of communal loss each family bore the burden of it themselves, intensified behind the closed doors of the village.

Emmott missed the market and Sunday services in the church. She missed being close to strangers, with everyone just going about their daily business, mingling next to each other in the rhythms of their days. She even missed the loud ale-soaked musings of those pouring out of the village's ale houses late at night and waking her from her sleep with their noisy journeys home to their cottages. Without the common punctuation of days, marked at start, middle and end by the greetings and salutations of friendly encounters with friends and neighbours on the village's streets, every day seemed to have no bounds and flowed in endless sameness into each other with nothing to distinguish them.

The roads had begun to show signs of their lack of use. As she walked back up the lane towards Bagshaw House there were determined stalks of knot grass starting to appear in the centre of the track, usually kept at bay by constant footfall and the tramping of horses and carts. There was significantly less movement through the village streets during the winter months, as people sought to gather provisions at times when others would not and those from the villages surrounding Eyam stayed away. As Emmott returned to the house she hoped the low death toll for January would mean life in Eyam could begin a return to normal, whatever that rediscovered normal would mean for her and for them. How good it would feel to see a friendly face up close, or to welcome a new face to the village!

On turning towards Bagshaw House, Emmott was surprised to see her mother at the doorway of the cottage, and even more taken aback to hear her laugh. Elizabeth Syddall had begun to come out of her grief fog towards the end of January, seeming to take a renewed interest in little Joseph and joining him in the garden at times. The weather had been mild for the time of year and she had shown him how to plant seeds so that they would have root vegetables for harvesting in early summer. It had prompted a surge of contentment in Emmott's heart. The fearful, nesting thing that in September had taken up residence in her heart like an unwanted cuckoo, was slowly being coaxed out and Emmott hoped it would soon fly the nest completely, leaving her with only her sadness to contemplate.

Drawing closer, Emmott could see who her mother was engaged in conversation with: a man, certainly older than she was, with greying hair and clothes that had seen better days. They were talking together quite animatedly and he was laughing too. The sounds seemed so foreign to Emmott's ears having lived through months of silence and whilst it should have been a joyful sound somehow the sound of her mother laughing with this unknown man dragged up grief, and something else. Shame. It was the same feeling she had had when she began to think forward to the Wakes and the time she now again anticipated, with a renewed and fragile hope, would take place in the summer and make her Rowland's wife. It had felt like a stab of betrayal to be so buoyed by the idea of moving on from this time, the shame of forgetting the tragedy of her father and siblings' deaths too soon. It was shame she felt now too, on her mother's behalf, seeing Elizabeth Syddall so happy to laugh with a strange man with John Syddall only having been dead for four months.

Emmott was concerned it appeared brazen. She looked about her, hoping no neighbours had chosen this moment to abandon all fear and pour out into the street. But the road was quiet, save for the chuckling. Emmott took a deep breath and composed her face as she got nearer to Bagshaw House. As she approached the wall that ran around their house the man took his leave and continued on what Emmott assumed was his original journey, not looking back. Elizabeth watched him, smiling, as Emmott walked up the short path to the house.

"You were laughing," Emmott said, trying to keep her voice even so that none of the jostling emotions she was wrestling with would suddenly betray her by appearing in her tone or pitch and she hoped they would not make themselves present on her face either. Her face so often undid what her voice tried its best to conceal. She forced a smile for her mother, who smiled back at her; one of only a handful of smiles since that day in September when Sarah had died and started the unhappy chain of events that had hollowed out the Syddall family.

"Yes, I suppose I was, wasn't I?" Elizabeth replied, putting her hand to her forehead and then bringing it down to rest beneath her chin, slightly leaning on to it and still smiling.

"Do you know him?" Emmott enquired.

"No. Well now I do, obviously. His name is John too would you believe? John Daniel, I think he said. I went out to look towards the rectory. I had a sudden idea I might catch the attention of Catherine, Mompessons's wife. I'd so like her to come here with William and pray over…over your brother and sisters. I said 'John', because I do that sometimes when I think about your father. Did you know I do that? I thought I had said it in my head but I must have said it out loud because there was an answer! I turned to look and there he was! Says he's a widower with a son. Not plague, his wife died a while ago. We just got into conversation and he was so funny. I didn't mean to laugh but somehow I was." She looked at Emmott, looking her in the eyes and trying to puzzle out her daughter's expression.

"Well, it's good to hear you laughing again, and we should be grateful for this chance encounter you had with…with John." Saying her father's name but meaning the other man seemed to summarise for Emmott everything she was struggling with. It made no sense to feel such dis-ease with using his name; there were at least thirty other men named John in the village. It wasn't a unique name, yet using it now felt like it should be reserved solely for him. Together they went into the house and Elizabeth soon changed the subject but something about the encounter felt duplicitous to Emmott.

22

Elizabeth
14th March 1666

"Which family is it?" John asked her. He was only really half paying attention as he arranged things in the workshop. Since there had been only one death in March so far and January and February combined had not quite made ten, the timid amongst the villagers had grown a little less cautious and he had found some trade had returned to his blacksmith workshop. In fact, there was quite a lot of work to be done due to the surfeit of people putting off everything non-essential or at least those things not considered worth risking infection for. Elizabeth got the impression he found her dialogue a distraction but she continued anyway.

"The Wilsons," she said, watching him move from one bench to another and back again without looking up. "John Wilson, the father, he died at the start of the month and I have since found out that all their children have died, some each month since December, and now it is only her, the wife and mother, left. Oh, how awful John, to be left alone without husband or children!" Of course, there were times when her wildest thoughts of fantasy were to be completely alone for five minutes of peace but to lose one's whole family, it made her shudder to think of it.

John shook his head, finally stopping his activity and standing up tall to look at her. "Tis a monster for sure, this disease. It shows no compassion to those families once it gets in. Only Joan Rowbotham and her girl left, and Robert Thorpe tells me that the Rowes of Orchard Bank have all perished, husband, wife and new-born. There isn't a street in the village that doesn't seem to at least know someone." He shook his head again. He could see in her eyes how moved she was for those who had been so despicably bereaved. He walked over to her and took her face in his hands.

"Didn't I say I'd build you a fortress? And look, I have," he said, spreading his arms out and laughing. He cupped her chin. We are safe up here, and we should say a swift prayer for our blessings." She nodded and he leant forward and planted a tender kiss on her forehead. She liked how he would still talk of prayer, though neither of them knew much of what it meant to pray in the liturgical sense, yet they found a way to express that part of themselves that leaned towards a higher power in their own simple ways.

"I will go down into the village today," she said. "I can take William with me. He's been itching to see Robert Thorpe and see how he is doing on his own with Alice and William. Hard to believe isn't it, that he's the head of the household now at fifteen? I think it fascinates William in a way because he and Robert are the same age. Do you think I should let them speak?" she asked him.

"I think that will be a fine thing to do, Elizabeth," and he squeezed both of her shoulders lightly before turning to continue with his work. She took her cue to leave and went in search of William. Finding him by the hen house, repairing some section of the fencing which had become weakened, she asked him if he would like to accompany her to the village. His first response was to decline the invitation, but when she mentioned perhaps calling on Robert Thorpe before returning to Riley he acquiesced.

They chatted easily as they walked down the hill and into Eyam and it lifted Elizabeth to have this comfortable conversation with her boy. She and John had not been sure how much to tell their children about what was going on in the village. Whilst the two households at Riley remained in good health it seemed better to preserve their ignorance, but William, being the oldest at almost sixteen, had been privy to a few of their conversations and knew more than the others what destruction the plague was wreaking in some households. He had been particularly worried about his friend Robert Thorpe, whose parents had been some of the first to die, along with a younger sister and a brother. Now Robert headed up what was left of their family, taking care of his younger sister and little brother as best he could.

"I don't think I could do it," William was saying. There was concern in his eyes but his tone was light and he followed it up with a chuckle, "I would never get Oner to do anything!" Elizabeth laughed then too. Oner most certainly had a mind of her own. But where she excelled in stubbornness, she also excelled in charm.

"Very true!" she agreed. "But you don't have to," she said, and she felt him put his arm around her. He was now noticeably taller than her, that moment coming when he would stop being a boy, her boy, and become a man. She found that she didn't mind it. Having two men in the house would not be a hardship. She had always found men easier to understand and shied away from female company, finding the small talk and endless gossiping somewhat disappointing. It suited her to live up in Riley out of the thick of it and every time she came down into the village she was always ready to get back there, no more so than in the last six months.

On entering the village, she noted the definite increase in activity since her last visit back in February when people were out of their homes but only in ones or twos. It was almost a different village to the endless closed doors of October, where wood and metal had been tentatively regarded as an essential defence against an invisible threat. Elizabeth observed how people put so much faith in prayers and herbs and wood and words and wondered what it would feel like to truly be dependent on any of these things in a moment of dire need. Today the overgrown roads were being trampled by more people than she had seen in months. Just having the one death so far in March seemed to herald a hiatus to their suffering and people were keen to take advantage and enquire as to the welfare of their neighbours, do a little trade and purchase things they had been waiting patiently to obtain.

Elizabeth effortlessly sold the eggs and butter she had brought down into the village with her and in fact could have sold them twice over. She made a mental note to herself to return to the village sooner than usual and take advantage of this sudden upturn in profits. William had gone to visit Robert, and though she felt a brief pang of worry watching him walk into that part of the village unattended, she knew she had raised a smart boy and that seeing him would also do Robert good.

When they walked back towards Riley, William was quiet. When she asked him how he had found Robert, he was silent for a few moments as if gathering up his thoughts and then he spoke.

"He was strong, Ma. I don't know how else to describe it. It's like it has *made* him, somehow, having to look after Alice and William," he said. She wasn't sure if there was some mild envy in her boy to see his friend's sudden elevation to manhood and responsibility. But what he said next made her realise all he felt was compassion.

"He's like a father and he still needs one himself," William said. When they arrived back at the farmhouse she saw how he stood a little closer to John, eventually placing a hand on his shoulder and asking him if he could help him with anything. She watched them go off to the smithy together and, though she wasn't devout in any sense of the word, she let a grateful prayer bubble up from her heart and up and out of her lips.

23

Catherine
30th March 1666

Only two. Catherine and William could hardly contain the hope they felt as the month closed and the death toll for the whole of March was just two souls. John Wilson followed all his family to the grave on the very first day of the month and since then there had been no other deaths save for Ann Blackwell on the 22nd. Death had first arrived for the Wilson family in December and then with each month more and more of his children were led away to the grave, as if death engaged in a merry procession that went on and on and trailed the Wilson family through weeks and weeks of repeated wailing and weeping. Mary Wilson alone was left, having watched her entire offspring laid into the ground by Marshall Howe.

Catherine could barely imagine Mary's pain. The only thing that seemed at all consoling was that she had not had to lay them into the earth herself, as some poor families had been forced to do in October when deaths had been more regular in their occurrence and Marshall Howe could not keep up with the demand he found placed upon him, he himself recovering from the plague, something others seldom achieved. No others came forth to take his place when he himself was stricken by the illness and in his absence, some decided to make their own burials, on their own land as the churchyard remained closed. When Marshall recovered, an event that had proved to Catherine that the Lord does not just reserve his mercies for the righteous, he found several bodies were waiting for him to be laid out, some only very recently deceased. He set back to work with the strength of an ox and the guile of a snake.

Yet even the empathy she felt for Mrs Wilson, left alone in a cottage once bustling with the noise of a family of seven, could not temper her rising spirits at a month with so few losses. The horrors of October, when a shocking twenty-three people perished by plague, were finally behind them. William looked at his wife. He could see how hope kindled itself in Catherine's cheeks, bringing back a light flush of pink as she spoke with animation about the prospect of a return to something like the ordinary. Her eyes were bright, not moist with ever-threatening tears as they had so often been of late, but with renewed optimism. Faith did not achieve its goal in the absence of doubt. It was only in the prospect of the thing you most hoped for and most desired being perhaps unobtainable that faith found its true grit. It had cost them both to continually offer reassurance and to hand out the scriptures like treats to children desperate for some form of sweetness.

Now, as he looked at Catherine's optimism, it embodied her movements and gestures so that everything appeared to take on a new lightness and grace, and he hoped their faith would be further rewarded as March gave way to April, like keys unlocking an unknown door. What would this new month unlock? Further confirmation their hope was fulfilled or a sudden return to the dread of October? He feared the warmer weather, knowing from what few reports came from London via letters from kin there, that when the sun shone its hottest the plague was more virulent than any fire. It spread in the capital as swiftly as flames would on dry wood and William's prayers were the deep intercessions of petitioning heaven for a lack of kindling that would start a raging blaze of infection in their own village.

That evening they asked Jane to put the children to bed and William took Catherine up into the woods while there was still plenty of light. He was mindful of her fragility. Her walking was unhurried and deliberate and any attempt to pick up the pace resulted in an audible increase in the sound of her breathing. He walked beside her and listened to the muffled softness of her breath, the inhale and exhale shallow but even. She had been the perfect choice of wife, at least for him. Not just her beauty, which he truly regarded as God's greatest blessing; living with Catherine was like spending your days beneath the gaze of a sumptuous painting, but for her dogged resilience despite the limitations her health had brought upon her.

He liked how the gentle exercise brought a flush to her complexion and the chattering about her new-found love of plants and herbs. She stooped now and again to examine flora he hadn't cared to notice before and when she came to get herself upright again he liked how she reached out her hand for his so she could push herself up against his readied palm. They had faced a monster. There were nights he would come back late from a death bed or a will-writing and she would just hold him. He found her ability to understand without the need for words to be like balm for his wearied soul. The things he had seen and heard, the smells and the bitter taste of death that he imagined clinging to him, so that he stripped off his outer coat and hung it outside in some pathetic attempt to be rid of the fell atmosphere of houses that had been visited.

"You know, in London, they write 'Lord have mercy' upon the door posts," he said quite suddenly to Catherine. She was kneeling, examining some wild garlic, contemplating her likely success of uprooting the plant and transferring it in its entirety to her little apothecary herb garden adjacent to their vegetable patch in the rectory garden.

"They do?" she said as she stood with the aid of the tree branch next to her and turned to look at him, sweeping the back of her hands across her forehead and disturbing the brown curls that had fallen across her eyes. "Would you have advised that here?" she asked him. "If we had been overcome by it I mean." They had taken to making tentative assumptions that the besieging of the village was, in fact, now past, never quite saying it out loud but both of them thinking it nonetheless.

"I might have," he said. "Repentance and pardon have their place as cures for the soul do they not? There are worse things than casting ourselves on God's mercy," he said. Catherine had wondered at her newfound craft of weaving flora together in a bowl to find relief and how this trust in the medicine of plants found its footing alongside her faith. The people of Eyam had tried many things as a barrier between them and sickness and pain. Some had written what seemed to her to be akin to spells in their windows; an upside-down triangle of *abracadabra*, dropping a letter each time until it was just '*a*' at the bottom. *A*-what? She felt more inclined to depend on the '*I am*' than the '*a*' but she knew within their village that desperation had led those afflicted to reach for anything that might halt the inevitable. She could understand that couldn't she?

"Yes, but they also need something they can place their hands on, something they can draw to their breasts and fix upon with their eyes. I'm not sure a whole sea of red-daubed doors, drawing to mind the visitation of the Angel of Death on the Israelites, would have worked for us here William. The people reach out for solace, for a cure, for an end to it. We can't always provide it, but there is something in using what nature offers, alongside our blessed scriptures, that brought hope, even if it was a hope unfulfilled. It gave the gift of moments of possibility and in those moments, people were momentarily themselves again, not just powerless victims."

William had never heard her talk this way. She had always been so resolute, pious even, when it came to the Word of God, never adding anything to it or placing anything alongside it. Perhaps he had been unwise to allow her the freedom of working with Humphrey Merrill?

"I still believe it!" she declared, as if sensing his thoughts. "The scriptures, I mean. With all my heart! Lord have mercy indeed. And He has, hasn't he William? He's had mercy upon us?" He gathered her to him.

"Yes, He has," he whispered into her hair. The light was beginning to fade from their path beneath the trees and he was keen to return to his study and work on his sermon for the coming Sunday. Perhaps there would be opportunity to open the church again. It pained him to see it stand there so unused during a time where spiritual comfort was at its highest need.

As they returned home, each quiet and walking with their thoughts, Catherine realised her sorrow at leaving behind the work she had done with Humphrey Merrill. The demand now would be less. He wouldn't need her. How perverse to lament the passing of dire need. Did she wish there was still a threat? She chastised herself for feeling the ache of disappointment. The wild garlic was in her hands and she suddenly felt foolish to have uprooted it. No, she would plant it anyway. It was known commonly as 'bear garlic', stemming from the belief that in ancient times bears had eaten of the plant to fortify their strength. It was good for stomach complaints, as well as being a key ingredient for poultices for infected wounds. As a girl her grandmother had given her a wild garlic tea infusion whenever she got sick. People would always be ill in Eyam; the usual everyday complaints would require remedy. Perhaps there was a place for her still?

24

Emmott

29th March 1666

With March came a renewed hope for normality for Emmott. She thought about Mary Wilson, a little older than Emmott's own mother, left all alone in her cottage, destined to live now with the ghosts of her family. Emmott wondered how her own mother would have fared in such circumstances. Her mood had brightened since her chance meeting with John Daniel but she still had large periods of time where she appeared vacant, only eating and washing because Emmott put food in front of her and filled up a bowl with fresh water.

The month had also claimed Ann Blackwell, another friend of her sister Sarah's, having taken young Anthony at the end of December. It was a sobering reminder to Emmott that families could be visited twice by this evil guest and she was at great pains to keep her mother and Joseph safe. Though her thoughts at times had taken her to dark places during the winter months, these past weeks, buoyed by the downturn in deaths, Emmott had found that her thoughts about the future were gradually becoming brighter, finding their way between fear and doubt like resilient and determined rays of sunshine breaking through the tree canopy in the dense woods that surrounded the village. She considered how the village's compact society would need to be rebuilt, not the physical constructions of stone and mortar, but through trust and assurance that a close knit community could again function together in proximity and the warmth of physical contact. How quickly daily life as they knew it had vanished and now she had begun to harness her imagination in a joyous coming together again after such an isolated winter.

With only two deaths, the prospect of The Wakes seemed suddenly more of a living hope and her thoughts of becoming Rowland's wife took up residence in her heart again, pushing out the cuckoo of fear that had made its nest so confidently in her bosom since September had delivered the first agonising blow to their family. As Emmott went about her usual jobs in Bagshaw House's kitchen, she more frequently found herself smiling. One morning she had even noticed herself humming, harmonising with the song of their beautiful linnets in their cage by the window.

Emmott had considered releasing the linnets. She had sat one day during the darkness of December contemplating the cage and seeing herself in the little birds surrounded by encasing bars. Winter had swelled the sense of feeling trapped; not just by fear of going out into the village where nobody knew where the infection waited, but by the responsibility she felt to bring Elizabeth and Joseph safely through the months of chill and dread and into Spring. Her trips to buy meat and purchase flour had become nerve-racking missions for their sustenance, always keeping her distance from those she encountered. She had been encased in a heavy sorrow, the kind of sadness that does not bring tears but instead makes you heavy with extra layers of yourself; cold, rigid layers that make it that bit harder to move, to think, to breathe. Winter was hard enough ordinarily, with the manual tasks made more challenging by frozen water and chilled, stiff fingers. But the emotional cost of being so secluded from others had taken its toll.

During those months of frost and snow, Emmott had fallen into bed every night with aching all over her body. She had noticed her body slowly changing with the increased labour. Her arms now had small, well-defined muscles and her shoulders had grown strong with all the lifting and carrying. She hoped Rowland would not mind this change, that he would not find his lady too firm and sturdy through her necessity now to live as if she were the man of the family. She imagined herself kissing him. Some kisses you just want with your very essence, and Emmott wanted nothing more than to wrap her newly strong arms around his neck and kiss him with all that she was. The compulsion was so strong after so many months of being apart that she worried the next time she saw him at the Delph she would be overcome by the longing and tear across the grass towards him. Only she knew she wouldn't. Because real love, love where you want only what will make the other stronger, more utterly themselves, is stronger than any beguiling kiss and if her lips were to deliver death and diminishment, how could she claim to love at all?

By the end of the month Elizabeth Syddall was quite transformed. Her days of living each day as if wrapped up in a fog were apparently now behind her. She became interested again in Joseph's welfare and took on some of the household chores once more, significantly lightening Emmott's load and giving her the much-welcomed time to herself she so wanted and needed. Emmott was sincerely glad to be gifted hours to take her walks in the dale again and to be able to sit down and write long letters to Rowland instead of the rushed notes that had had to suffice for the past few months.

She marvelled at his dedication to her over all this time, their love affair reduced to what could be said across wide open space or summarised in the limits of written language. There were times when she was plagued with doubt over his ability to keep waiting for her without their close physical contact and she had banished several overly-vivid thoughts about him beginning a new love affair with some easily accessible girl in Stoney Middleton. But Rowland's intensity and fervour when they met across the expanse at the Delph always managed to convince her that her torturous fancies were ill-conceived and unlikely. That he loved her, she had no doubt. That she loved him, and would gladly wait another six months to see them safely reunited and joined in matrimony was confirmed to her. She took out memories of their times together from the vault of her mind, considering each one with heart full, as if polishing a jewel and then returning it carefully to its hidden place of safety. They may not be as rich as the Bradshaws but Rowland had already given her a precious tiara of recollections that beautified her head when dark thoughts threatened to enter. The difficulty of living through such harrowing times is that you can never entirely know that such times will not come again. Those who suffer often have the unfair misfortune of meeting with sorrow again.

It was painful for Emmott to admit, but the friendship her mother had struck up with John Daniel seemed to have been a catalyst for the change she had wanted to see come over her mother, albeit not at all the means or method she would have chosen. Following the initial chance encounter between the two of them, when he had walked past Bagshaw

House last month, he now purposefully and frequently turned up outside, always staying close to the external wall, with her mother speaking to him coyly from the threshold, as if she was a young girl and new to the prospect of courting. Emmott often heard her laughing coquettishly and his full throated laughter returned enthusiastically. She was at a loss as to what they could possibly find so amusing, so often, to account for the persistent level of doorstep revelry.

Whilst on the one hand she welcomed this new light-hearted incarnation of her mother, which had lessened her work load and dramatically lifted the atmosphere in the cottage, Emmott still found herself overcome with sadness in defence of her father. Her cheeks burned red at the imagined judgements being made by the neighbours, though, to their credit, those living in the cottages thereabout never once uttered a word to her about it. Yet still she imagined the whisperings: *That Elizabeth Syddall, taking on a new lover before even a year is out.* Her father deserved better. He deserved not to be replaced so soon. He deserved for his memory to be more enduringly prized.

Emmott tried to manage her anger towards her mother. Their interactions within Bagshaw House were calm and civil, but Emmott knew her resentment simmered below the surface of their everyday exchanges and she wondered if her mother knew it too. One morning it became obvious to Emmott that she did. John Daniel had just said his goodbyes and Elizabeth had entered the house positively beaming from her dalliance with him on the doorstep.

"He sends you his regards," Elizabeth said to Emmott with a smile. Emmott was cutting bread and she lay the knife to one side of the board and gripped the sides of the wooden table, bowing her head as she spoke.

"They are sentiments I neither wish nor encourage. I do not want to pursue a friendship with this man who comes so often and I wish you would not either."

Lifting her head, she looked directly into her mother's eyes. The resistance she saw there made Emmott feel defiant. She felt her resolve to not have this conversation with her mother -for fear of returning her into her spectre-like state- slide away, like ice when it melted on their roof and slid off into the wooden gutters.

"I cannot bring myself to even try to understand how you could do this? How could you forget Father so soon? Not even a year! Does his memory mean nothing to you? Did you sever your promises to him the minute Marshall Howe laid him in the ground? I cannot watch you with this man, this new 'John', laughing like two children in the street. Why do you encourage his coming? Why, mother?"

Elizabeth's smile fell from her face as she regarded the earnestness of her only surviving daughter's questions. Emmott's usually pale face was flushed and her eyes were glassy with ready-to-fall tears. She took a step towards her daughter and then stopped, leaving space between them. The answer was hanging there between them before she spoke.

"Because when I laugh, when he makes me laugh, I feel joy again and I thought that never would be. When we talk, and he makes me smile, it's like I feel that good feeling all the stronger because I know now with absolute certainty that this, all this, can come to an end. Just like that. When we lost…them…I could have become a ghost with them. I almost wished it. I felt so far from myself. I saw you and Joseph but I couldn't make myself reach you. I wanted to, Emmott. I wanted to, but you reminded me of all that no longer is. But then John, he managed it. And I wasn't expecting it or trying to make it happen, but that first day when he made me laugh, it was like something broke through to the broken part of me and I discovered there was still something light in there. I'm sorry Emmott. I know…"

"You don't know!" Emmott replied. You haven't seen me. You haven't asked me. You kept me out while you just weren't here and then when you opened up again you didn't let me in, you let in a complete stranger! You choose a man you have known for a month to bring you back to life all the while I have been holding onto the fragile threads of this family. For you! And for father. Because…because…he would never do this. Never abandon you in your grave if some laughing woman were to walk down the street. So no, I don't want regards from 'John'."

Emmott turned quickly on her heels and left the room, leaving her stunned mother alone to digest her words. She went out into the street and walked without purpose, ending up out towards Town End, her hands balled in fists at her sides. As she approached the village square she became aware of how hard she had been biting her lip and how close she was to letting her tears burst out hot and flowing like the water rushing over the river rocks when it is at full bore. She feared if she began with her weeping she would not be able to stop, that the people who lived in the houses in this part of Eyam would empty out of their homes to see who was pouring out their grief like a fountain in the village square. She closed her eyes and stood for a moment, trying to compose herself.

Emmott reflected that life in the village looked set to return to its usual rhythm and vitality. The threat appeared to be behind them and it was a time for counting blessings and embracing hopes that have been temporarily buried. She resented her mother for sullying the waters of her hope with this unwanted and inappropriate intrusion of a stranger into their family remnant.

On passing the Lydgate, Emmott saw Mary Darby walking with her father. She knew Mary just enough for a polite greeting and brief exchange of words where they stood on opposite sides of the street. Kind and warm in nature, Mary confirmed she was in good health and Emmott noticed how she squeezed her father's arm just a little as she informed her that her father was well also. It pained Emmott to look upon Mary with her father, though she could not allow herself to give voice or expression to this in front of them. Mary was a beautiful young woman, about the same age as Emmott and with such kind eyes that Emmott couldn't help but smile at Mary with genuine warmth. Her father was older than Emmott's father had been but he carried his age well, with a straightness of back and silvering hair that gave him a look of distinguished wisdom. What Emmott would give for one last walk around the village on the arm of her father.

The thought reminded her of her pending wedding and how, now, when she married Rowland this summer at The Wakes, John Syddall would not be there to give her away. She had neither brother nor grandfather who would be present either and Emmott had the absurd thought of asking George Darby if he would attend her wedding, though she really did not know him at all. The Darbys said their goodbyes and Emmott watched them walk together up the Lydgate and disappear from view.

The encounter with Mary and George had succeeded in breaking through Emmott's anger and as she returned to the Syddall cottage she was glad to feel it ebbing away, leaving her. She stretched out her fingers and let her shoulders fall down from where they had crept up around her ears in tension. She resolved to talk to her mother, to find out her intentions with this John Daniel. The idea of a new beginning was not lost on Emmott and she could allow her mother this much; that after a tragedy hollows you out, there is room for new things to grow, like seeds planted in dark, heavy soil. There is a magic to the breaking that eventually prompts a new, green shoot to make its way from darkness into the sunlight and Emmott herself had been entertaining imaginings of a new version of herself.

The experience of helping Mary Rowe, though tainted with its tragic end, had shown Emmott that she had uses outside of the tasks she performed routinely in Bagshaw House. She had kept herself calm, overruled her fear and used what little knowledge she did have to bring comfort and support to William and Mary at a time they needed it the most. She wanted to do more of that. Perhaps Eyam could use another midwife? There were plenty of older women who could show Emmott how to help women in their labour and birthing and she could be of use, if not here, then in Stoney Middleton.

Her thoughts drifted again towards Rowland and their future house. The villagers of either village would come together to build it and their first marital home, though likely to be humble and small, would bring her more joy than the echoing empty rooms of her childhood home now did.

As she approached Bagshaw House again she saw John Daniel outside and her mother at the threshold in animated chatter. Incredulous that he was back so soon, it crept up again, the burning resentment, like bile from her stomach, but she pushed it down and resolved not to bring the quarrel back into the house now she had taken it for a walk and burnt it out. She gave John Daniel a small smile as she entered the cottage and she knew both he and her mother understood it as a small gesture with much larger possibilities if they could win Emmott over. Emmott wasn't sure she wanted to be won over though and she wondered where all this would lead.

25

Emmott

18th April 1666

The morning had begun sadly for Emmott. On entering the kitchen at first light she could see almost immediately that something was wrong in the cage hanging by the window in the corner of the dimly lit room. What little of the dawn light found its way into the room was cast into the cage, sending gentle lines of light and dark onto the cage floor as it found its way between the bars. She could see one of the linnets, its red mottled breast glowing in the sunlight. But its head hung low as it stood over its mate, prostrate and lifeless on the floor of the cage. Emmott could see by the way its little feet stretched out rigid and straight that life had left its little body and the male bird, looking down at its lost companion, looked so sad and helpless in its solitary state.

She had taken the dead female, perfect in death, with its red chest cold and as still as the heart no longer beating beneath it, and buried it tenderly in the garden, leaving the lone linnet staring out of the cage and moving restlessly from foot to foot, as if in confusion of how to be now it was alone in its confinement. The loss of the bird had brought a surprising amount of pain to Emmott, which puzzled her when compared with the magnitude of what had already been taken away from her. But when something so immense, so significant, is taken away, even the smallest grain of additional loss is too much to bear.

It had been a disconcerting few weeks. With only two deaths in March, the villagers had been convinced they had seen the back of the malevolent guest from London. Fifty-three people had died up until then and they had all pinned their hopes on the notion that Death would now be satisfied and the village would be left to pick itself up and find a way forward. William Mompesson was considering calling the congregation back from the open air meetings of the Delph into the church building of St Lawrence once more. Also, traffic to Humphrey Merrill's shop had slowed right down, according to his wife Anne, which she welcomed as she said her husband was getting on in years and the incessant demand for tinctures and potions had near exhausted him.

But then another Blackwell was taken ill. Joan, not much younger than Emmott, had followed her parents to be laid to rest in the field behind the Miner's Arms, leaving only Francis and Margaret left of that family. Catherine Mompesson, the vicar's wife, had visited them and Francis, being twenty-seven years of age, had assured her he would take care of his remaining sister, who had only recently turned fourteen. Catherine was guaranteed of his devotion in taking care of Margaret and when she saw Emmott on the street outside the rectory she had commented on how fatherly the young man was in his commitment towards his sister.

The Blackwells had been tormented by the deadly disease, with it leaving and returning over and over, so that they lost family members in December, February and March, spreading their agony and suffering out across the months. Emmott tried to imagine what it would have been like for her sisters, Alice or Sarah, to have been left without either parent so young. Alice Thorpe, Sarah's best companion, had died on April 15th, the week after Joan Blackwell, leaving only Robert Thorpe and little William alive of the once bustling household of seven. It was unthinkable.

In the case of the Rowlands and the Rowbothams, who had both lost family members between November and February, a child had been left solely with their mother. Emmott had wondered what would have become of her own mother if Emmott herself had been taken too, and only Joseph was left. It was surely God's providence that she had been saved for the good of her little brother. But did she really believe that? Did she believe God was selecting and choosing people to fall or be spared? Where *was* God in all this?

There were times when she was at the Delph waiting for Rowland or sitting quietly after he had gone, when she would feel a tangible peace come over her body. Her mind would reach, without prompting for higher thoughts and she would often, in these solitary moments, find herself moved with compassion for her fellow villagers- those who had suffered and were still suffering- pouring her soul out in fervent prayer on their behalf. Was this God moving her? Was she inspired by the Spirit to lean towards her fellow villagers and not away from them, as the insistence of the fearful thing in her breast sometimes still seemed to urge when it felt the need to stretch? She wasn't sure how these experiences tessellated with what William Mompesson preached from the rock pulpit on Sundays but when he quoted the Psalmists she felt a flicker of recognition with their lines of praise within the torment, of that sense of reaching and hoping. She wondered how Andrew Merrill could so easily remove himself from all of the suffering and remain alone up on the hill where he could not see it unfold? Yet each must choose their own trail when adversity arrives and sets up home.

Emmott was with Joseph in the kitchen, showing the little boy the seeds she had collected from last year's sunflowers and talking with him about growing new ones. Now it was April and the sun had begun to grace them more frequently with its warming presence, she was beginning to think of sowing and planting, the way her father had taught her. This year she would sow alone, unless she could tear her mother away from her doorstop dialogues with John Daniel, or engage Joseph's infant concentration long enough for him to give her a helping hand.

Mary Cooper was calling from outside the cottage, her voice carrying faintly inside, so Emmott gathered the seeds into a small pot and left Joseph sitting on the dusty floor with his wooden soldiers for company. He was a good boy and rarely wandered off to engage in mischief. Not at all like Robert, she remembered with a pang. Emmott thought that Mary's face seemed to have aged since she had lost her two boys in October, among the earliest victims following George Viccar's demise. Yet today she seemed to have some reason for hope and it touched her eyes in a way that was a welcome change for Emmott.

'What is it Mary?' Emmott said, stepping outside the door and pulling it to behind her. She half wondered where her mother was if she wasn't here on the threshold talking to John Daniel, but Mary looked ready to regale her with some tale so she put the thought to one side in order to proffer her some attention.

'It's Margaret Blackwell!' she replied. Emmott's heart sank in the way in which she was sadly now accustomed. These rising hopes too often gave way to precipices of adversity. She knew Margaret was ill but had hoped it would not turn out to be plague and that she would not leave her brother Francis all alone as the sole survivor of the disease's onslaught on his family.

"No!" said Mary, seeing Emmott's pale face and aghast expression, "She has recovered!"

Emmott's hands found themselves, clasped together in front of her heart, as she uttered the words 'Thank God!'

"Yes, indeed, all praise. I heard from Francis that he was most concerned to leave her as she was in the throes of the sickness and he was almost certain he would return to find her dead, but they had to have more coal and so he had gone to fetch some. When he came back she was a lot brighter and when he enquired as to how she had come to be better, Margaret described a severe thirst that had driven her to consume the contents of the pitcher she had found in the kitchen. It was not water as she had supposed but bacon fat! She said she had vomited violently but on emptying the contents of her stomach and laying down again, her fever had broken and she began to feel much better. 'Tis a miracle!"

"Aye, it is!" replied Emmott, marvelling at Mary's ability to be delighted about the well-being of a young, near stranger when she herself had lost her own precious sons. Emmott had seen how she had been comforted by Alexander, her husband of only one year having previously been widowed, and had not disappeared beneath a heavy fog of grief like her mother had. Yes, she had shed tears for those boys, ceaseless and hard in the first few days, but she had performed some kind of heart alchemy that turned the power of her pain outward and Emmott was inspired by her helping of other villagers. Perhaps she was reassured by her own avoidance of infection despite her proximity to its outward symptoms, similar to how Emmott herself had been when she had undertaken to help the Rowes and found herself untouched? Emmott wondered how many people remained of the homes that had been marred by disaster and whether for all of them there was some mystery resistance that coursed their veins. Whether it was from God she could not say.

"How wonderful for Francis to have kept his sister. Is he well?" Emmott asked.

"Yes, no signs of the pestilence on him at all, more's to be praised."

Emmott felt her heart thrill at the idea that death could sometimes be thwarted even when its grip was poised so stern and sure.

"Marshall Howe has been truly scandalous this week, mind," Mary went on.

"Marshall? How so?". Emmott knew many were scandalised by Marshall Howe's recent behaviour, the way he was so pitiless with the corpses he retrieved, much to the chagrin of the loved ones looking on, and his insistence in receiving 'payment' in excess, taking into his possession many a family's heirlooms, as well as more basic goods like clothing, blankets and food. His apparent recovery from the pestilence appeared to have made him bold and had hardened him even more than the coolness of his manner prior to the outbreak. Emmott wondered how Joan, who seemed so delicate and unassuming, could have found love with such a brute of a man. Though Emmott had glimpsed a softer side to him when he had carried out Sarah, she guessed Joan would be even better at mining Marshall's good points than she was.

"He only went and carried out Unwin, over on t'other side of the village, before he was even dead! The poor man awoke from his unconscious delirium to find himself being carried out on Howe's back! Imagine it! He was planning to bury him before he was even dead! He's near making a fortune out of this. Possibly the only person praying for it to not end whilst the rest of us have been begging for mercy! Poor Unwin asked him for a posset!"

"Oh my!" exclaimed Emmott. She was always inclined to see the good in people, wanting to believe people were just doing their best in the circumstances they found themselves in, but now and again the behaviour of some would stretch her willingness to give people the benefit of the doubt just too far.

"Poor Unwin! What has happened to him, do you know?"

"I have not been able to find out," Mary admitted.

It was at that moment that Emmott saw her mother approaching up the lane. Not alone, but arm in arm with John Daniel! Emmott had reluctantly realised that their relationship would not long be confined to conversations on doorsteps but it seemed that they had now deemed it appropriate for them to take walks together. The ways her mother leaned into him and his arm encircled her waist made Emmott's cheeks pink up and she was acutely embarrassed that Mary Cooper was also witnessing the revealing of this new development in their relationship.

"Oh!" whispered Mary, somewhat involuntarily Emmott surmised. "Oh, I'll...er...be going now. Must get back to Alexander. I have to help him a lot now...now George is gone, and I have no other distractions..." her voice trailed off as she turned back towards her cottage across the street. She gave a quick wave and called out 'Elizabeth', nodding at John Daniel, before bustling over the road and in through the black door to the tailor's without looking back.

Emmott took a deep breath, holding it slightly before exhaling. She did not want to discover the source of the jubilant look on their faces though she was sure they were about to try to tell her. They walked purposefully towards her together, and when they were within a few feet Elizabeth began to speak.

"Emmott, my love, we have some news."

Emmott could barely believe what she was hearing. She could already predict what this news would be and it made her feel sick to her stomach. She stood staring at them both, her mouth slightly opened and her forehead furrowed in anger.

"Don't say it," she said. "Don't! I do not wish to hear your news. I have tolerated this friendship because of you Mother, because you have been your old self again! And for so long I wondered if you ever would be again. But this! This is too much. Do not tell me you are to be married! I cannot bear it!"

"But we love each other!" Elizabeth retorted, dropping John's arm and advancing towards her daughter. She went to take up Emmott's hand but Emmott pulled it away.

"How can you love him?" Emmott cried, "When not even half a year ago you loved my father! And for 25 years too! How does one love so long and then leave it all behind so soon? I could never…"

"I pray you never will have to find out how a person has to drag themselves up from the pain of losing your life's companion, let alone almost all your children. John has given me reason to smile, to want to live, to want to make new plans. Surely you can understand that?" Elizabeth appealed to Emmott, all the while John Daniel stood back and stared at the ground. Emmott could not deny he was a reasonable man and his manner seemed gentle and accommodating enough but she could not shake off the betrayal this all seemed to her father's memory.

"I can't," Emmott said, "And I will not stand by and watch you marry another man so soon. The infection may not yet be over. How will you even convince William Mompesson to marry you?"

"We haven't asked him yet. Perhaps we will ask Reverend Stanley instead," Elizbeth responded, trying again to take her daughter's hand.

"Well, whoever it is, I cannot be there! I'm sorry, but I simply cannot."

And with that Emmott left Elizbeth turning back to look at her betrothed on the street outside Bagshaw House. She went straight up to her mother's room, lying face down on the bed where her father had breathed his last breath and sobbed into the bedclothes in memorial of the last scraps of the life she had once known giving way to a future she didn't recognise. With horror she realised John Daniel would soon lie here on this bed and that he would soon sit at their table and she would be sharing this house with him. She did not want this change. Life was hard enough to live following such unspeakable sorrow without adding negotiating daily life with a stranger into the day's demands. It was with a heavy heart and forceful sobs that she exhausted herself into sleep, waking much later to find her mother asleep beside her, her arm laid gently across her.

26

Catherine

20th April 1666

April did not arrive in the way in which both Catherine and William had hoped. Almost two weeks after Ann Blackwell had perished on 22nd March, news of the death of Thomas Allen reached the rectory. The Allens lived in the Town Head part of the village and Catherine knew through Mary Cooper that Mrs Allen had only very recently given birth to a son. Catherine was concerned about the young mother being alone. Her early days with Elizabeth and George had been made all the easier by the presence of their then maid, Bridget. Catherine had been significantly weakened by both births, but especially George's, and having Bridget there to take the baby, if only for a short while, so she could sleep, was a God-sent blessing. She would search for a solution for the Allen woman. It was her maternal conviction that she should offer the young mother succour if she could.

In the meantime, there was some small hope that presented itself beside the now sullied prospect that the infection had ceased in March. Margaret Blackwell had caught the terrible disease and survived! Catherine relayed the story to Jane in the parlour of the rectory. She sat to conserve her energy, which was somewhat depleted from the renewed demand for remedies and their delivery. Yet even Jane could see what this small hope did to her mistress's eyes and she gave a small smile to the fireplace as she dusted and cleaned the ashes from the fire pit.

"Bacon fat! Can you believe it Jane? I rush about handing over the combinations of herbs and prayers for recovery but in the end a soul is saved by warm bacon fat! The Lord's ways are indeed unfathomable aren't they Jane?"

"Yes mi 'lady," Jane answered, by duty more than sincerity. She had long come to doubt this Lord and His mysterious ways, despite living in the rectory and being perpetually surrounded by its assertions. How could the same Lord who intervened for this Blackwell girl have let all the Thorpes die one by one? Dear, sweet Alice had been the latest of that tragic family to suffer a cruel and agonising death. She had often come to the rectory garden to speak with Jane, handing her the Mompesson washing as she hung it up to dry on the line, or helping her fetch fruit or pull up vegetables.

At fourteen years, she was a greater help to Jane than trying to insist the Mompesson children assist her with these tasks. Alice liked to talk and Jane supposed that in a family so large, though there was always much work to be done, one person's absence might not be so well noted. She would miss the girl and hoped she had not suffered too much at the end, for she had heard some most dreadful stories of burst swellings and hideous red sores. A girl so innocent and kind-hearted as Alice had been should not suffer so. It made Jane angry with this God, though she had not the bravery to voice it with any fervour to her mistress, preferring only to state the sad fact of her young friend's demise.

"Not so for Alice," Jane almost whispered. Catherine was silent then. She had been greatly saddened to hear that Alice had sickened and had sought to help Robert as he tried to help his sister, through the bringing of Humphrey Merrill's remedies and fresh linen for rags for him to use with water to cool her fever. With no parent to tend to her, it fell to local women to assist the boy; brave and compassionate women like Mary Cooper. They took turns to nurse her, each spending an hour in the house before swapping with someone else. It was a new suggestion made by the Reverend Stanley to try to minimise the risk of plague seeds being transferred through the least amount of time spent within the house of the victim. Catherine thought it a good one, though William had questioned whether the greater amount of human traffic in and out might undo the benefits of the lessened time of exposure.

She had expressed her own wish to take a turn but William had most vehemently opposed this notion. It had taken a long time for him to give his blessing to her assisting the apothecary and making deliveries to plague-visited homes, though she had continued to do it anyway in the face of his disapproval. Never in their marriage had she pursued something without his consent, let alone in direct contention of his expressed will, such was her dislike of conflict. She would much rather acquiesce to his wishes and retain a comfortable peace than risk his displeasure and days of discomfort. But the times in which they found themselves living had greatly heightened the absolute necessity she felt to do something of consequence. She could not leave it to others and preserve her safety within the walls of the rectory. It was hard enough to accept that this was what she was already doing for her children in keeping them so secluded at home. She was prepared to navigate the risk in order to feel some sort of sense of purpose during times that made people feel so helpless.

Yet William had been resolute. He would not see her die and leave their children without a mother! And so, it was *he* who took an hour's watch, assisting Robert in caring for Alice. It had humbled him to see the way the gracious child accepted the fate the pestilence presented to her. It weakened her so that she could barely swallow and her neck was especially swollen by the characteristic swellings, now being given the term 'buboes', named so by the physicians in the capital who were beginning to write down theories for how the disease was unfolding and how it might best be treated. However, none of this would likely reach the village of Eyam quick enough or in any sense that would ultimately help them.

Alice had died relatively quickly, not lingering for days as some had done. In the end he had been glad of it, and ashamed to tell Catherine so, for nobody should be glad of the death of a child. But in her suffering, he could not bear to prolong the inevitable. He did not pray for such, for it would have been contrary to his calling as minister, but in his heart, he had recognised he had wanted it. When he conveyed this to Catherine she could see how much the experience had unsettled him.

His usual calls to visited households were quick visits to administer Holy Unction or to say the prayers of the dead over a recent corpse and, most recently, to assist in the writing of wills. William was not well-experienced in this but having an uncle who found his living in the realms of law and order he was managing this latest requirement of his flock moderately well. It was because of his devotion to Catherine and his inability to conceive of a life without her, and *only* because of her, he had condescended to join the women in caring for the girl and she had loved him for it.

'No, not Alice, sadly not Alice," Catherine answered Jane with a sigh.

They were interrupted in saying more by a knock at the rectory door. Visitors of late had been fewer as less souls were added to the list of the dead in February and March and even then, the only visits they received were for William's services. Fifty-eight of the village inhabitants had died, from sixteen households of Eyam's families. He had been called out to them many times. Catherine presumed it to be another call for aid against the malevolent threat the plague presented to them all. When she opened the door, she was surprised to see Elizabeth Syddall standing there, and even more so by the huge smile that was on her face.

Catherine knew from Emmott's confiding in Mary Cooper that Elizabeth had been slowly brought out of her debilitating grief by the visits of a man named John Daniel. Neither William nor Catherine were familiar with him, but both were gladdened to hear that Elizabeth had begun to engage with life again, renewing her maternal affections for both little Joseph and Emmott and taking up speech again as if she had never given it up. Catherine smiled at her neighbour and waited for the mistress of Bagshaw House to divulge the reason for her call.

"I shan't ask to be admitted," she said, "We Syddalls, as a family most severely visited, have somewhat of a name around the village now I expect." Catherine opened her mouth to contradict her and ensure her she had not heard such aspersions cast upon their family, but Elizabeth was already talking again.

'It is no matter!" she continued. "I have not come to lament upon village gossip. I have come to ask… to request of your husband…" She was struggling for the words and Catherine was slightly bemused by the grown woman's bashfulness, though she hoped she was not showing it on her face. Catherine was fairly sure she was not requesting aid for a sick Emmott or Joseph and she was glad of it. She waited patiently for the woman to articulate her request.

"For his services in performing a marriage ceremony," Elizabeth finally found the words she was looking for.

"A marriage ceremony?" Catherine said, "Do Emmott and Rowland wish to bring their wedding forward?".

"No," Elizabeth replied. "The wedding ceremony will be for me," she added, her eyes remaining firmly fixed upon the ground at her feet.

Doing her best to disguise the surprise in her voice, Catherine repeated the words.

"A marriage ceremony?", the incredulity creeping out against her will. John Syddall had been dead six months. While it was true some bereaved wives did re-marry quickly, usually it was customary to see out the first year as a widow before embarking on new matrimony. To say that Catherine was shocked at the request was something she was now sure showed in the surprise on her face. She saw colour flood to Elizabeth's cheeks as she waited for the response of the parson's wife.

Catherine had always thought John and Elizabeth Syddall well-matched. They worked together to bring up their large family and she had always noted continued affection on Elizabeth's part, even seven children later and with her oldest daughters in their early twenties. It seemed unlikely that she would be ready to pledge her affections to another so soon, and yet here she was requesting that very thing.

"I will inform Reverend Mompesson of your request," Catherine assured her, wrinkling her eyebrows together and smiling in a way that pulled in her lips towards her teeth and that likely betrayed her confusion.

"Thank you, Mrs Mompesson," Elizabeth responded. "We would like to do it soon, perhaps even next week! In the Delph if he pleases, as we know gathering in the church may not be wise in these times even with a small group."

"Will Emmott be joining you for the ceremony?" Catherine asked. She had an affection for the young woman, in whom she saw a generous heart but which was sure to be bruised by this new relationship. Catherine fancied that Emmott would cling to the memory of her father in such a way as this would appear to be a betrayal. Her love for her father, and his love for her, had been clear to those who lived in the homes that neighboured Bagshaw House. Parents should not have favourites but sometimes the bonds of affection were seen most sincerely and deeply between a parent and one child than they were with others, though the professing of love be the same towards all.

Catherine saw Elizabeth drop her gaze. It was a few moments before she spoke.

"I'm not entirely sure she will," Elizabeth said, and in that confession was contained the confirmation of Catherine's surmised thoughts on the matter.

"Perhaps she still will," said Catherine kindly, for though she believed the swiftness and timing of this new marriage was questionable, she could see a mother's pain in Elizabeth's response and Catherine would not seek to injure her with lazily scattered judgements.

"Perhaps," Elizabeth said, offering a sad smile. "Thank you for your service in relaying my request to your husband. If he is too desperately over-worked with…with offering succour to those caught up in sickness, I will make my approach to Reverend Stanley if…"

Catherine cut in on her. "That won't be necessary! He will do it!" she said quickly. Although her husband had been generous towards Thomas Stanley for administering sacraments to the sick and deceased, Catherine was still of the opinion it was her husband's job and duty, as the rightful and proper vicar of Eyam, to perform the sacraments for the village, and most certainly a wedding!

Elizabeth, a little startled by Catherine's definitive answer on behalf of her husband, nodded and thanked her. As Catherine watched her walk away she felt discomfited that she had been so forceful and bold in asserting her conviction in what must ultimately be a decision for her husband to make. She would tell him of the request and if he agreed there would be no need to tell him she had already given his assent to the plan. If he were to resist, well, she was not yet sure what she would do. She went straight to his study to find out how he would react.

When she knocked he barely looked up. To her eye it looked as if he were puzzling over some sort of legal documentation, perhaps a will he had been asked to help write and witness. Instead of waiting she took a step into the dimly lit study and approached his desk. Sensing her presence, he looked up and slid the spectacles from his nose. Catherine rarely interrupted him when he was at work in his study and besides, he did not mind to pause and look at his wife's beautiful face instead of the sombre contents of his current work. Who orphaned children were to be left with was not a subject that he wished to spend any more time than necessary pondering. She really was a fine-looking woman and he could see some mischief dancing in her eyes which made her all the prettier.

"What have you to tell me?" he asked, inclining his head to one side and fixing her with a quizzical look.

"Well," she said, bringing her hands together and bobbing up onto her tiptoes momentarily. "It's a wedding!"

"A wedding?!" William exclaimed, clearly incredulous at this news. "Who can possibly be getting married during this precarious time we find ourselves living through?"

"Well, it is a Syddall wedding. Before you jump to conclusions, it is not the joining of Emmott Syddall with Rowland Torre. That wedding is still scheduled for The Wakes, God bless them. It is *Elizabeth* Syddall who seeks your blessing for a ceremony."

"Elizabeth Syddall?" he queried. "John's widow?" He knew it could only be the more senior Elizabeth Syddall, for he was all too aware that the younger Elizabeth had perished soon after her father and sister and he had written her name into the parish register. Yet the surprising request had him asking incredulously anyway. "Well, for goodness sake, who is she marrying?"

"His name is John Daniel. Are you acquainted with him?" Catherine asked him.

"I can't say I am," he replied. "Well this is some turn around isn't it? I never would have suspected. To go from near-spectre to blushing bride so rapidly," he shook his head involuntarily at the unexpectedness of it all. Human beings never ceased to amaze him.

"I think Emmott especially feels the sense of impropriety. I fear others may also. Elizabeth was unsure whether Emmott would attend the wedding. She would like it to be in The Delph rather than the church, which I'm sure you will agree is wise. Much better to have the air about and the ability to stand at a distance, although you know how much I love the giving of a ring at a ceremony before the altar."

"I do my dear," he said, and brought his hands together, resting them on his lap. Catherine sensed he was contemplating this strange request. She had one more thing to add.

"She says she can approach the Reverend Stanley if you are too busily employed with the needs of the suffering."

His mind was made up. "No need my love. I shall indeed conduct this marriage service, though I find the timing and haste of its coming about rather unexpected… She is not still of childbearing age, is she?" he asked suddenly.

This made Catherine smile. She had heard from Mary Cooper that Elizabeth's womb had declared itself closed and her bleeding ceased soon after Joseph was born. As to how these conversations ever arose, Catherine had no understanding. She could imagine Elizabeth Frith just boldly asking under what working order a woman found her reproductive parts and laughing it off as one of those 'ordinary things' that is never talked about and yet happens to everyone and so really should be. Anyway, regardless of *how* this conversation came to be, Mary was adamant there would be no more Syddalls and since Joseph was now three and no others had followed, Catherine suspected the judgement must be right.

"I do not believe it is a marriage made to hide a growing child," Catherine said. "Mary has told me she has seen him outside Bagshaw House on several occasions and the two of them laughing like merry infants. I suspect he was the cause of her laying down her paralysing grief and re-negotiating a place within the world again. I will let her know you will do it, husband."

She left him at his desk, sliding the spectacles back up onto the bridge of his nose and stroking his chin in a manner that seemed to indicate he was still somewhat perplexed. Eyam was not a village to be circumscribed by the ordinary, even if the unprecedented things that occurred of late were pertaining to the scale and severity of death. Hardly a thing to be known for! Yes, it would be good to have a wedding. Catherine smiled to herself as she set off across the road towards Bagshaw House to deliver the news.

27

Catherine

23rd April 1666

April had not kept the promise she had so desperately wanted it to make and as the days ticked by, three more Eyam souls had perished since Joan Blackwell on April 6th. It was with great distress that Robert Thorpe had knocked on the rectory door late last week to inform William that his sister Alice had died. Catherine, who was already in bed as it was past the hour of eleven and the kitchen and parlour candles had already been extinguished, heard William's steps coming up the stairs with a definite heaviness and she felt her body grow tense beneath the covers. Suddenly they had felt altogether too heavy, smothering and she had thrown them off and sat up as he entered the bedroom.

"What is it?" she said. The moon shining through the window fell across his face and she could see his sad expression, beautiful but mournful, as if etched in silver. She had known the news would not be good.

"I have just come from visiting Robert Thorpe," he said.

"How did he seem?" Catherine asked, the lump in her throat growing and slightly choking her words as she thought about Robert. What was this evil that called upon orphaned children to take care of each other, even escorting each other to the grave?

"He looked tired, poor lad. But he was strangely resigned to Alice's passing. In losing so much perhaps one is more accepting of more being taken away? There must come a time when the heart cannot break any more than it has already, perhaps?" Catherine doubted this. She was certain the capacity in the human heart to feel pain was as endless as it was to feel joy. But it was not the time for her to debate with William.

"And what of William?" she asked.

"He had left him sleeping soundly and says he doesn't yet know of the passing of his sister." Catherine had stated her intention to visit with Robert and William first thing in the morning and William had left soon after, fulfilling a promise he had made to Robert to hail Marshall Howe. Catherine had found that by the morning when she knocked on the door to the Thorpe cottage, Alice was already in the ground alongside the others.

The sexton was quick and thorough, she could not argue with that and she hoped he had been tender towards Alice for the sake of her brothers. Robert seemed to indicate such when she enquired of the sexton's actions. He had given Marshall an expensive locket, an heirloom of his mother's family, as payment. Catherine wondered if he had chosen it with the knowledge there were now no girls left of her line who could wear it. Catherine imagined Marshall Howe's treasure trove was growing to match that of any pirate's she had read about as a girl. Was any collection worth the suffering the givers had endured? She wondered how he dared take it and keep it.

In the days that followed, another two people died and both Catherine and William wondered what momentum might be building, still hoping that there would be a slump again, as there had been during the hopeful month of March. She had grown to dread knocks at the rectory door, terrified that each one heralded a new infection or the announcement of the most recent corpse. If each rap on the door were a portent of disaster, the numbers would have reached unthinkable heights. Three or four deaths a day! She could not conceive of it. But thankfully villagers still knocked at the door for more benign things; seeking William's letters for delivery or requesting that they might have a half hour alone in the church for silent prayer.

William was busy preparing for the Syddall wedding, due to take place in four days' time. He was inclined to say a few words at hand-fasting ceremonies and given the somewhat interesting circumstances of the matrimony of Elizabeth Syddall with John Daniel, William was disinclined to use one of his usual sermons for such occasions. He would need to think of something more fitting, something that better reflected the current circumstances. Had ever a parson written a sermon for a wedding between a recent widow and a near stranger during a plague outbreak he wondered? He doubted it, and if it did exist he had never set eyes on such a sermon, despite his study being stocked with a well-blessed library.

Catherine had decided she would speak with Emmott at the Syddall wedding, if she was indeed there, about Mrs Allen. The girl knew a good many of the young women in the village and perhaps she could recommend someone in need of work. Whilst they had not escaped the plague, and the fact it continued after a brief lull did not bode well, it was true that there were some in the village who deeply needed assistance and companionship. The enduring fear of entering each other's homes had left some desperately lonely and in dire need of help. If she could secure Mrs Allen just a bit of assistance and respite, and it be safe to do so, she would.

Catherine had begun to harvest the herbs and plants that were reaching their maturity within her dedicated area of the garden, building up a fine collection of supplies any apothecary would look upon with a jealous eye. She repurposed jars found in the kitchen larder, spending hours cleaning and labelling them, insisting she do it herself and not Jane. Relieved of duties, Jane had taken herself to the garden and whiled away an indolent hour or so in the Spring sunshine.

For Catherine, taking ownership of her contribution to combat this ongoing catastrophe was essential. She could not think of anyone else doing one single step of it for her. The cleaning of the jars had been exhausting. Her shoulders ached and more than once when she coughed she saw tiny speckles of blood on her handkerchief. The pattern reminded her of the willow warbler's eggs she had discovered in a nest in the woods during her walk last week. She had noticed the nest because of its distinctive dome shape and, finding the adults absent and no juveniles yet making their presence known, she had peered inside and seen the clutch of four or five eggs within.

It was the first time she had ever seen the eggs of this beautiful bird and the fragility of the exquisite white shells with their reddish-brown speckled markings had immediately invoked some sort of sense of kinship with the eggs and their inhabitants waiting to be hatched. Delicate like her, they were waiting to find their place in the world and so was she. Willow warblers, delicate and slim birds, shed their feathers twice during the year, making them quite distinct amongst their feathered peers. Catherine herself was ready to shed the sole occupation of simply being 'the rector's wife'. Mrs Mompesson was preparing to throw herself into a new manifestation of herself as apothecary's apprentice, should her gathering fears find expression in a deadlier spread of the infection as the weather warmed up.

Having cleaned and labelled the jars, she sat down at the kitchen table with swathes of herbs, flowers, seeds and fruits, all gathered in large baskets. Some would need drying but some were ready to be ground and mixed immediately. She took out her pestle and mortar and set to grinding up the herbs most commonly called for by Humphrey Merrill. She had piled up her onion harvest in a large crate in the corner of the pantry, in readiness of a new cure that had been reported in London as coming from the College of Physicians.

One took an onion, filled it with figs, rue and Venice treacle, and then wrapped it in sodden paper before laying it in the hot embers to soften and congeal. These onion poultices were applied to the swellings in the neck, armpit and groin whilst hot, and in quick succession. Catherine imagined the discomfort this cure itself might bring, perhaps worse than the pain of the swelling itself. But she had gathered them anyway, determined to offer any means to treat the disease if she possibly could.

She had heard through village gossip that some were discussing the merits of placing a live chicken on the sites of the red sores that were common on the bodies of victims. The basic premise being that the infection would be drawn up into the chicken, thus killing it. As a means of extracting the poison of the pestilence Catherine thought it sounded most barbaric, for the chicken and for the sick person who had to endure a bird sitting on them whilst feverish and in agony. She would not be rearing chickens.

When the herbs that needed drying were all hung up in neat little bundles and anything that could be ground with the pestle and mortar had been suitable pounded and shredded, she found she had the satisfaction of eight full jars and the capacity for six more, once drying was completed. Her shoulders and arms ached and she sat down in the parlour chair by the fireplace only intending to rest. Sleep found Catherine easily and she dreamed, of the heifer in the sanctuary again, lowing before the altar with a chicken beside it and an onion slung about its neck. When she awoke it was with a deep sense of foreboding, as if something unexpected, something they thought had been prevented, would suddenly catch them

28

Emmott

24th April 1666

Emmott had railed and resisted, quite unlike her usual calm and accommodating nature, and insisted she would not be present at the wedding of her mother to John Daniel. Her mother had pleaded and implored her to reconsider but on seeing that her daughter was resolute she eventually stopped trying. Elizabeth was not incapable of understanding her daughter's feelings and the reasons behind them, she had just hoped her own happiness would be enough to overcome Emmott's resistance and she struggled to not feel hurt by her continued opposition.

On the day of the wedding Emmott awoke early. Last night she had helped her mother choose a dress and had laid it out ready for the morning. On her walks in the dale during the week she had gathered flowers, wanting to weave a beautiful headdress for her mother to wear; a sort of peace offering to make up for her planned absence at the ceremony itself. She had done her best to select the most beautiful of flowers available, choosing blooms of blue, yellow and pink. She had assembled sprays of Jacob's Ladder, considering as she did so her own wrestling with God over how all this could be and how it was at all possible for her to be as sad over a marriage as she was over a death. She wove the blue flowers in amongst sprigs of winter heath with just a hint of the pink to come, and studded every few inches of the floral crown with columbine. Her mother would look beautiful wearing it.

After a while Emmott could hear movement in the rooms downstairs and she came down the stairs to find her mother bustling between tasks, neither dressed nor ready for her pending nuptials. Joseph was sat at the table, shovelling squares of bread into his mouth with his chubby fingers. He would need a face wash before he would be ready to go and she began pouring some warmed water from the hearth into an earthen bowl. Joseph hated having his face washed so she fully anticipated getting somewhat wet in the attempt and tied her apron around her waist in readiness.

"How are you feeling?" she asked her mother, who had moved between at least five different tasks in the last three minutes, orbiting the kitchen table several times. She couldn't stick with anything and her nervousness was evident.

"Like a child!" cried Elizabeth, throwing her hands in the air. "I can't think straight!"

Emmott laughed and took the bread knife from her mother's hands.

"Let me get you some breakfast, Mother. You can eat this and then go and put your dress on. I left you something on the bed. I'll sort out Joseph. You will take him with you?"

"Yes, yes," she said, lowering herself into the chair and staring into the linnet's cage.

"What happened to the other one?" she asked. Emmott shook her head.

"It died. Last week."

"Oh!" replied her mother. She quietened then, as if a thought had entered and captured her and subdued her body into the quiet rhythm of simply eating and breathing.

Emmott successfully wiped Joseph's face and hands, though the little boy resisted with all the strength his little body could muster. It cheered Emmott to feel him so alive and strong and resistant. She hoped he would always stay this way. When her other younger siblings had died she had worried about how Joseph would fare with only adult company in the house, but if anything, he seemed to have thrived somehow, responding to the increased adult contact and letting himself become immersed in his imagination.

He had a mind like hers, she could tell from the way he muttered little phases as he played and used household things as props and staging for his games. He was out in the garden as often as he could be and enjoyed feeling the sunlight on his face. She sometimes saw him standing still with his eyes closed enjoying the sun's caresses, just as she often did herself in the warm space of the Delph. April was often cool and wet but this year they had enjoyed such bright and luminous days, which greatly assisted them in bearing the heaviness of what had been lost. Yes, she was happy to have him and reminded herself to be more thankful in her daily devotions.

When her mother came down the stairs and into the cottage's small reception room she looked radiant. The flower diadem encircling her head looked every bit as lovely as Emmott had hoped and the smile on her mother's face confirmed to her that this gift had communicated what she wanted to: that she did wish for happiness for Elizabeth but her devotion to her father was too strong to be overcome so soon.

"Thank you," whispered Elizabeth, taking both of Emmott's hands in hers and giving them a gentle squeeze. Emmott smiled.

"I…"

"I know," Elizabeth interrupted her. For a moment the two women stood just looking at each other.

"I really must go!" she said with a smile. Emmott nodded and went to bring Joseph from the kitchen, passing his little hand from hers into that of her mother. She watched them go out through the door and onto the road, her mother looking back just once and smiling at Emmott. Emmott smiled back and waved. There was the unsettling sense of her heart dropping down into her stomach and she watched them go in the direction of the Delph. William Mompesson had overcome his own reservations, Emmott thought largely due to the supplications of his wife, and agreed to marry Elizabeth Syddall and John Daniel in what had become his outdoor church.

Emmott climbed the stairs and lay down. She hadn't slept much the night before, kept hostage by frantic, disquieting dreams of John Daniel and her mother interspersed with images of her father. At one point he had leaned right forward as if to whisper to her and said only one word, *Why?* She had been awake and asleep so many times before dawn that in the end she had got out of bed before the first light of morning and written a letter to Rowland by the light of the candles in the kitchen. She hoped she could send it first thing via the messenger boy and that he would come to meet her later.

Now she was tired but sleep would not come because she couldn't shake the shame of letting her mother go and get married without her. Rowland often told her she cared about what others felt and thought to her own detriment but Emmott would rather live with the discomfort of having put herself out than she would the burden of having been the cause of someone else's upset or pain. Never had it been more unclear what she should choose. If she stayed here she honoured her father. If she went to the wedding ceremony she brought pleasure to her mother. And it was in looking at it this way that she realised what her father would have her do. He would never deny her mother the chance of joy and Emmott realised with a rush of certainty that propelled her up off the bed and out of the bedroom door, that she absolutely should be there to see her mother marry.

As she raced out of the house, her skirts flapped around her legs and she lifted her skirts scandalously high to allow her knees to pump freely, one hand on her cap to prevent it from flying off her head, her hair escaping wildly from beneath it. She flew past Mary Cooper who looked physically shocked to see Emmott rushing by in such haste. Emmott was too out of breath and focused on reaching her destination to acknowledge Mary beyond a fleeting wave as she flashed by. She just caught Mary shaking her head as she found the path down to the Delph. Now she had decided to go she was anxious to arrive before the ceremony had begun, or at least right at the very start of the opening prayers.

When she could see the figures standing there, her mother and John Daniel standing side by side, with William Mompesson in front of them and Joseph standing to the side with Catherine, she gave a wave towards the rector and folded forward, out of breath, her hands on her knees. William stopped what he was saying and the bridal party all turned round to see Emmott bent over, her head down yet waving frantically at them. Her mother ran straight up to her, overjoyed to see her, and holding Emmott upright as they walked, she leaned her head against her daughter's and whispered an earnest 'thank you'. Emmott smiled and squeezed her mother's shoulder, her breathing still heavy after her exertion.

"We had better not keep the rector waiting," she chuckled and Elizabeth laughed in return. When Elizabeth returned to John Daniel's side, Emmott saw him turn and look over towards her, giving her his own smile, which Emmott returned with newfound grace. If she was going to have to share a house with him, even if it was only for a few months until the Wakes when she would gain her own, it would do neither of them any good to start off on a frosty footing.

The ceremony did not take too long. Elizabeth and John said their vows to each other and William conducted them in the giving of the ring that joined them together as man and wife. If her father disapproved, Emmott felt no sense of it, though she said her own silent prayers, telling God, and her father, that she would always honour his memory and keep it alive in word and action, following the things he showed her to do and talking of him whenever she got the chance. She hoped John Daniel was of an accommodating disposition and could share his house with the ghost of his predecessor.

As they walked back up the hill towards the cottages, with Joseph racing ahead and Elizabeth and John strolling arm in arm, Catherine caught up with Emmott. Emmott, knowing how Catherine, as the rector's wife, would be well placed with knowledge of how it faired with the families of the village, asked her how things really were in Eyam.

"Praise the Lord, it is fairly quiet. The Blackwells and the Wilsons have been most badly affected in the last few months and such a tragedy that the house of Thorpe is depleted further with the death of Alice. My heart cannot bear it to lose the children. And then there's the Allens. Poor wife left alone with their new-born son."

"The Allens?" enquired Emmott. She didn't recollect anything being mentioned about the Allens, especially not by Mary who was usually the source of Emmott's knowledge about what was going on in the village. Emmott didn't know if it was because she had survived nursing George, Edward and Jonathan through the pestilence and not got sick herself, but Mary seemed more confident than most to be close to other villagers, even entering some homes when families had need. Emmott was inspired by Mary's ability to be quietly supportive of families in their time of need despite her own pain and loss.

"Yes, so sad. The husband, Thomas, died of plague at the start of the month and the wife has recently given birth to a boy, only in the last few days I think. She is struggling with the baby, I hear. You would know how hard it can be, having had all those siblings," Catherine said. Emmott liked the way she had talked about her brothers and sisters without hesitation or fear. People generally tried to avoid any mention of them or her father, as if Emmott had forgotten they had died and saying their names would remind her. She had not forgotten. She thought about them so often in the hours of the day that it was almost like breathing. Though the majority of her thoughts about them now were to recall the bittersweet good memories and happy times, there would sometimes be the unsuspected pang of pain, like the sharp stitch-like sting of an inhalation following a bout of heavy running.

"I could call in on her," Emmott told Catherine, the words escaping before she had made the conscious decision to utter them. Catherine looked surprised but an appreciative smile spread across her face and she caught up Emmott's hand and gave it a squeeze. She went on to remind her where in the village the Allens lived and confirmed to Emmott that the wife had shown no signs of illness, though she could not speak for certain of the health of the baby boy. Catherine's brow furrowed as she relayed this to Emmott, wanting her to understand that such a mercy mission could not be regarded as free of jeopardy.

"I will go." Emmott assured Catherine. Catherine put her arm around Emmott as they walked back up the hill.

"Thank you," she said. "You are as brave as you are kind. Please do your best to keep yourself from danger." Catherine said. "We do not understand how plague seeds find their way to some and not others."

"I will do my best. I haven't been troubled by it so far and there have been quite a few times, now, that I have been with those afflicted." Catherine smiled at her, acknowledging the unspoken reference to Emmott's nursing of her siblings and father in their final hours. When she looked at the young woman it was with sincere appreciation of her resilience through a time that had claimed so much from her. Catherine did not know what Emmott's faith was like, though she was a routine attendee at Sunday liturgy, but Catherine recognised a quiet assurance that she herself felt and always credited to her belief in a kind and omnipresent God, even when times were dreadful and took their cruellest toll.

"I know. But one never truly knows," Catherine said, "One can only trust in what one believes to be so." They said goodbye in the small lane to the side of Bagshaw House and Catherine made her way over to the rectory. William had already gone inside. The outbreak had kept him busy; more people wanting Last Rights and to write wills. Emmott supposed he was off to write another letter or compose another sermon. She was glad people did not look to her for such spoken wisdom in such times. Her response was in action not in eloquence.

Later that same day she left her mother and John Daniel chatting animatedly in the cottage kitchen. He seemed instantly at ease, having taken his small bundle of possessions up to the room Elizabeth had shared with father.

She couldn't fault his manner. He had been kind and courteous towards Emmott, and his merriment- she noted he did seem to laugh very often- lifted some of the sadness that had settled like dust around the rooms of the house.

At times she believed she could hear her father's heavy footsteps on the step and if she strained her ears perhaps the wooden eaves would yield the memory of her sisters' singing voices and soft chuckles trapped there over the years. How near their voices sounded at times and yet now so eternally far. With a haste that was both shocking and inevitable, they had been reduced from nine to three, and now they had increased by one. Life was all a series of additions and subtractions Emmott reflected. It was with this thought of increase that she made her way to the Delph that afternoon, thinking about her own upcoming wedding when two would become one and her family would increase again.

Since her mother's return to something close to normal, Emmott had given herself over to the habitual gazing on beautiful things; flowers bursting with colours on the moors during her afternoon walks, the mottled beauty of the rock beneath the rushing water at the swallow, and the stars in the night sky, twinkling like tiny jewels on the velvet gown of some well-to-do woman she had never the fortune to meet. She knew her father's eyes would never see the stars again and the realisation of it made her shiver and pull the shawl closer around her narrow shoulders during her walks at dusk when they first began to appear in the evening sky. She took her time walking to the Delph, enjoying the joys of Spring; the buzzing of the early honey bees, the mating calls of the robin and blackbird and the blossom full on the apple trees in the orchards behind the grander houses of the village, now quiet and abandoned, their opulent families having taken themselves to safer localities.

As she walked, her mind was cast back. At the Wakes, just eight months ago but now seeming like another life, she had danced with Rowland without a care in the world. All eyes had been on them and she hadn't minded. Usually she was content to stay in the shadows of daily life, content to watch and applaud the vivacity of others, but he had whirled her round on the village green and she had laughed as her eyes caught the happy glances of her sisters and the quiet nod of her approving father. The past few days the memory and the anticipation of their future happiness had taken up residence in her thoughts again more and more, and now, as her eyes found Rowland silhouetted in the archway of the rock as he waited, she picked up again the delicate dreams she had had about houses and children and the joyous possibilities of being a wife.

She took a moment to stand and look at him before he realised she was there. Just to see him, even from afar, gave her such happiness. She had decided not to tell him about visiting Mrs Allen. After the Rowes he had made her promise she would not put herself at risk again. She felt vaguely confident she would be able to do it without danger, having now been exposed to nine others with the infection and lived to tell the tale, but she knew Rowland would consider any risk too high. Yet how could she deny her nature? From the moment she heard about poor Mrs Allen left alone with her baby she had felt moved to help. If everyone resisted the pull to help another in a time of need the village would perish at a quicker pace than the pestilence itself would achieve. The spirit of Eyam was one of kindness and comradery; she had been raised on it, breathed it like air. She would help them.

She stopped, the agreed distance away, and breathed a breathy greeting that rose and fell on the air of the darkening early evening. He turned towards her and the weight of his gentle gaze caused a throaty laugh to tumble out of her. It was good to feel such joy again. She was making space for it, purposefully creating space for laughter and hope, because the space inside her that was carved out by grief needed to be filled with something and she had reached a new-found resolve that it should be with good things and not more pain.

"Hello," she whispered again. "It's so good to see you."

Rowland stretched his arms out wide.

"I wish I could hold you. It's been so long." His face looked a mixture of pained expression and absolute longing. She recognised it as her own dichotomy of feeling.

"I know," she said. "Six months! It feels like The Wakes was another life. But things seem to be improving. Catherine Mompesson said only five people died this month and two in March. Everyone is hoping that is the end of it. It been so hard staying away from each other. I know the village isn't tiny but we were so used to popping into each other's cottages, minding children, doing jobs. It's been sad having everyone so retreated into their own houses. You should see the main street! The grass has started growing up down the centre because of the lack of horse and carts and people walking."

"I can't imagine it. I hope I can come into the village again soon. Do you think I can come soon?"

"I hope so Rowland. I want you to, of course. But I want to be sure, to be safe. I cannot watch you die like I watched them die. I won't ask you to risk your life."

"I know. I know you wouldn't. It's just hard not seeing you, not being with you. I think about you being my wife, all the time."

"I do too. It's another four months until we get married. You'll be able to come into Eyam before then and then we can start our preparations."

He smiled at her.

"Emmott, my love. I will marry you. When the village gates are opened again I will be the first one through them I swear and I defy anyone to see a more deliriously happy groom." She smiled and it tasted salty as the tears that had travelled down her cheeks so freely found their way onto her lips.

He told her all about the goings on in Stoney Middleton. It was both exhilarating and strange to hear about normal life in a village not afflicted by the sudden arrival of the pestilence. She was exceedingly glad to know nobody was sick. The Torres were in good health and one of Rowland's sisters had just had another baby, bringing another niece into the world and adding to the ready-made quota of nieces and nephews she would acquire on saying their vows. She would welcome these new little ones into her life with open arms. How she missed the energy and the boisterous clamour her younger siblings had brought to the house. Even with John Daniel's penchant for laughter it was still so much quieter than it had been when they were a family of nine.

"How are you getting on with John?" Rowland asked tentatively. He knew how difficult Emmott had found her mother's decision to remarry so soon after her father's death. She had poured it all out in her letters; the shame, the anger, the sorrow and the nagging sense of betrayal that had led her to resist the idea of him for so long.

"It hasn't been so bad," Emmott replied. "He is a jolly sort, always seems inexplicably buoyant. Remarkable really. But then he hasn't lost anybody. He seems to make mother happy. She is more herself and much more attentive to Joseph. I find it very odd to see them disappear together into the bedroom she shared with father but he is a practical sort and has helped me with the garden and they have sown a patch for growing more vegetables. He chops the wood now so my shoulders have been given a rest. I think he will even take up father's place on the watch roster.

"That's good. I was worried. You were so averse to it." Rowland said.

"Yes, I was. And I still feel she should have waited longer, to honour my father. But it does not seem as bad as I feared. And Joseph seems to like him. He climbs up into his lap and everything. I had better get back," Emmott told him. "I said I would prepare the meal tonight."

"Soon we will eat together my Emmy, eat and kiss and love and all the things young married people do," Rowland said with a mischievous look upon his face. Emmott blushed though he was too far away to see it.

"Yes, I cannot wait to be your wife Roly. This space between us cannot last forever. Give me two weeks and I am near certain you will be able to enter the village. Soon we will be in one space, on one patch of earth. You and I for the rest of our days. I love you," Emmott said. They had become used to these public declarations of affection, though nobody was in the Delph to hear them. This is where their love hung around, in the open air of the dell, imbibed in the green of the grass and the blue of the sky. She would forever associate this beautiful natural space with Rowland and where their love was put to the test by separation but won out despite the trial. She easily picturing them visiting this space hand in hand as newly-weds, running around with their little ones and leaning on each other in their older age. Some places just spoke of meaning in your life in ways others never would and Cucklett Delph was now forever a geographical waymark for their love affair.

When they said goodbye, she watched him until he disappeared. As he faded from view the light was suddenly diminished and for a moment the warmth of the sun ceased as it was hidden behind cloud like the game she played with Joseph, covering up his toys with a cloth and seeing what he could remember was there. A creeping doubt shadowed the joy of her happy planning with Rowland and for a moment Emmott felt afraid again, like a reunion with a long gone acquaintance who you would much rather have parted ways with for good. She shook off the feeling and stepped into the sunshine as it once again put forth its rays across the glade of the Delph. She breathed in deeply and took in the scent of the flowers and reminded herself that doom was behind her and ahead lay only new beginnings.

29

Emmott
25th April 1666

Emmott woke to glorious sunshine and the smell of bacon drifting up from downstairs. Having John Daniel around had actually vastly improved Emmott's daily life; reducing her chores and lifting her spirits, though she had fiercely resisted it at first. Laying down an idea you have spent some time honing and growing is not easy and she had been determined to keep John Daniel at arm's length. She lay in bed considering how her initial feelings of clinging to how things were when her father was alive had given way to a more generous acceptance of things changing. Sometimes the vision you have in your head of how things should be, keeps you from embracing what you have in front of you and then you miss out on something good you hadn't had the capacity to imagine. *Who could miss out on bacon first thing in the morning?!* Emmott smiled to herself.

It was actually nice to have a room to herself, she thought as she looked around the room filling up with the morning sunshine, though she missed her sisters so deeply. She could almost conjure them in her mind, doing ordinary little things in the room around her. Just ordinary, everyday things that she never appreciated she would miss when they were suddenly gone and no longer around to potter about. She stretched her legs down towards the end of the bed. She had been doing it since she was a child. When she was small, her grandmother, now long gone, had given her the advice to walk her feet down the bed every morning and every night so that she would will her body to be tall. Emmott *was* tall, willowy and slim, but as to whether it was from stretching her legs twice a day she wasn't sure. What she liked was how it stretched her spine, making her back feel lithe and agile and ready for whatever the day would bring.

She slid her legs out of the bed, her nightdress gathered around her ankles and her feet touched the cool of the wooden floorboards. She pressed her feet down onto the wood and stood up, taking a deep breath. Today she would go to the Allens. She had already decided but made the resolution not to mention it to her mother, just as she had omitted to tell Rowland. They would only worry and she was perfectly safe, wasn't she? The idea that she couldn't get the plague had planted itself in her mind. She couldn't have just been 'lucky' nine times, could she?

When she reached the kitchen, her mother was already seated and John Daniel was at the kitchen hearth, removing crispy layers of bacon from the skillet above the fire.

"It smells good," she told him, offering a smile. Her mother cut up hunks of bread and offered some to Emmott as she sat down. They were the picture of domestic bliss. *How is this possible?* Emmott wondered. Since committing to marrying Rowland she had become deeply invested in the notion of true love and Rowland being her 'one and only', that they would only ever be married to each other. She knew her mother had loved her father and didn't doubt it. But she had found a way to be ready for a new love far sooner than Emmott's heart could explain to her own satisfaction. Perhaps it was not love but companionship? When Emmott left, Elizabeth would have been quite alone, with just Joseph for company. Perhaps Elizabeth already knew that would be too lonely for her and so reached for a companion when one arrived on her doorstep?

They ate breakfast together, with Emmott feeding Joseph strips of bread and bacon. He was growing chubby, his face rounding and his adorable dimples showing when he smiled. She wondered if he had any concept of what he had lost in the loss of his siblings. Surely, he had noticed they were not around? But when she recollected what she could remember from being three years old it was very vague, just a fleeting imprint of a certain person in a certain place or often just a feeling that couldn't quite be wrapped in words. It pained her to think that he wouldn't remember them vividly like she did. His memory would be of the *idea* that he had five other brothers and sisters. She would be his only sibling in any sense he could experience. She glanced between John Daniel and her mother and for a moment wondered if that would always be true. Her mother was forty-six and since Joseph her menses had become altogether less frequent and often disappearing entirely, but while she bled at all it was still possible, wasn't it? Emmott pushed the thought from her mind. Making room for a substitute for her father had been hard enough. She wasn't at all ready for baby brothers and sisters, especially as they wouldn't be 'Syddalls'.

At the end of breakfast, she wiped her mouth with the linens her mother had laid out and stood up. She offered her gratitude to John for the meal and shared her intention of going out. Her mother enquired as to where she would go.

"You know you must still be careful Emmott," Elizabeth said suddenly. "The pestilence still insists upon staying in the village. It just hides away. Let us hope it is now gone, but until we can be sure you should suspect it hiding in every house and behind every closed door!" She was not hysterical but her voice was a little shrill as she spoke.

It surprised Emmott to hear her mother speak so plainly about the disease. It had rendered her speechless and depleted as it ravaged her family. She had said as many words this morning alone as she had in the four months that passed between when they had died and John Daniel had shown up. This was the first time she had acknowledged it at all, staying eerily mute when it had made its presence known.

"I will be careful," Emmott said as she pulled her cap down over her head and gathered her shawl from the back of the chair and pulled it round herself. The days of late had been blessed with sunshine but the mornings still proffered a chill in the air and it was a bit of a walk to the Allens on the Town Head side of town. Thankfully, her mother did not quiz her as to where she was going, knowing that Emmott enjoyed her walks and likely assuming she would wander through the dale and gather flowers as she was often known to do.

"Go with you!" Joseph said as she stepped away from the table.

"Not today little brother," she said, ruffling his hair and stooping down to plant a kiss on the top of his soft, wavy hair. "Tomorrow we can take a long walk to the woods if you like?" Joseph smiled his approval of that plan and Emmott realised how much she would like to see the woods herself. Wandering beneath the tree canopy and weaving in and out of the dappled light, her hands brushing the ferns and breathing in the earthy smell beneath her feet was a great tonic for Emmott. She felt somehow connected to the woods and what memories of childhood she did have were nearly always played out here with her father. For a moment she considered abandoning her plan to find Mrs Allen and to head to the woods instead, but dropped the alternative just as quickly as she had taken it up.

Eyam was quiet this time in the morning and she walked the streets towards Town Head without encountering many people at all. A man she did not recognise carrying a bundle of firewood tipped his hat at her and a woman who she had seen several times with Mary Cooper enquired how Mary was doing having 'lost her brood, poor love'. As she neared Hawkshill and the turn off up the hill towards Humphrey Merrill's place, Emmott encountered a familiar figure. Marshall Howe stood before her, his large frame blocking out the light so that she stood in shadow. Seeing him there brought a pang. She could not look at him without remembering his rough hands winding a rope around her father's shrouded legs and pulling him down the stairs, or the way he lay Sarah's limp body across his arms as if she weighed nothing at all.

"Good morrow," Emmott swallowed her ache at seeing him so unexpectedly. "How are you this day, Marshall? And your wife and son? I hope all of you are well."

He nodded in response. "'Tis well with us," he said. "We don't usually see you over in these parts. Taking a walk or are you up here to visit Humphrey Merrill?" She could see despite his gruff expression there registered in his eyes something of concern, that another of her family members might be in peril.

"No, no, no need for me to see Humphrey Merrill today. I usually take my walks in the Delph. I'm a great lover of the space there and like to pick the flowers. They bring some cheer to a home, don't they?" She could see from his expression she had wandered into territory he had no experience or opinion of. "I'm actually heading up to the Allen property. Do you know it?" she asked.

"Aye, I do. 'Tis that way," he said, pointing further up the main road towards Town Head. Emmott guessed Marshall probably knew where everyone lived, such was his job. "I took Thomas Allen out of there near the start of the month. He had all the signs of having had the pestilence. Are you sure that's where you want to go?"

"Yes, I believe his wife had a baby? I thought perhaps she could use a hand? Perhaps just another face to look upon?" Emmott replied.

Maybe Marshall didn't understand such things, because he looked at her as if she had attempted to convey her thoughts in a foreign language.

"Anyway," Emmott said. 'I should get on. Good morning to you Marshall."

"Aye," he replied, not knowing quite where to look or what to say next, taking their conversation into the realms of awkward for a third time. Emmott gave him a smile and small wave before pressing on towards the direction he had indicated for the Allen's house. As she walked she reflected on him. He was stern, you could not argue with that. And with some ales inside him she had no doubt he was intimidating. She had heard tales from her father and Thomas Thorpe about his antics in the Miner's Arms and the King's Head.

Yet there was something about Marshall that Emmott thought was deeply buried but somehow just detectable, at least by anyone who believed there was good to be found in everyone and anyone. She wondered what it was like to live

with him. His house was just nearby. Did Joan see more of
the parts he chose to hide away from the rest of the villagers?
What was he like with his boy? Did he catch him up into his
arms? Play? It was hard even for Emmott to imagine with her
propensity towards fantasy, but she felt there must be more
to this brusque sexton. He had, after all, become a godsend to
the families who had been afflicted by the plague, even if his
manner was so often offensive. Having to bury one's own
dead added a layer of grief that was tough and hard to
overcome as the days passed into weeks and months. Laying
a once warm, living, breathing loved one cold into the earth
and letting the dirt fall upon them, closing them in, was a
deeply troubling experience.

Her musings about Marshall Howe occupied her
thoughts so much that Emmott walked past the Allen house
and had to be directed back down the road by an old woman
who was tending to her garden. She had the most beautiful
peonies. Straight away Emmott thought to tell Ellen and then
was met with the remembrance that she could neither show
nor tell Ellen anything. She wondered if she would always be
so unexpectedly seized by these lapses into times past that
brought the agony of reality crashing into the present without
a moment's warning? In the past month she had done her
best to nurture the quiet but growing pull towards hope and
tried her hardest to open up her heart to it and to healing, and

to imagine a time beyond these painful days where joy could characterise her days more than sorrow. She felt the balance tipping towards that again and she was at pains to hold onto the memory of her lost family whilst looking forwards to brighter days and perhaps soon a family of her own, if the summer were to hold fast to its promise of a wedding.

When she reached the Allen house she entered through the gate and approached the modest house through a garden not much tended and certainly more mud than flora. She paused for a moment before knocking on the door. Was this something she wanted to do? If the fearful thing still firmly nestled in her breast she knew it would stretch and make itself known at this moment. But in the past days and weeks she had ejected that cuckoo and instead nurtured prayers and watered them with her many tears so that faith and hope could feather her heart instead of fear. She knocked.

Mrs Allen opened the door wearily. The baby was in her arms. She seemed surprised to see Emmott standing there. They had never met before and to all intents and purposes Emmott was a stranger standing on her threshold with unknown intentions.

"Sorry, to intrude upon you. I'm Emmott Syddall. I live down in the village opposite the rectory and Catherine

Mompesson had mentioned that your…that Thomas… had died from plague and…well…I lost nearly all my family and I'm good with children. I have a little brother who is three. Sorry, I'm talking too much... I just thought you might need some company or some help? How is he? Your son I mean?" Emmott gestured towards the baby sleeping in her arms.

"You can come in," the young woman said. "I haven't seen anyone since Tom…since he died. I can't stop thinking about it. It was so awful. He was in such pain. Did you see your…your family…when they passed I mean?"

'Yes," Emmott replied, doing her best to stop the harrowing sequence of all their deaths passing through her head as it often did just before she drifted into sleep. "I nursed them all. I know how bad it is…at the end."

Mrs Allen smiled wearily at Emmott and pointed to a stool in the furthest corner of the room, gesturing that she should sit.

"My milk is not good," she said, jadedly. "I have to feed him so often, I don't think I have slept more than a couple of hours since he was born". Emmott looked at the young woman. She looked exhausted. Her skin had a grey tone to it and under her eyes were dark shadows.

"Why don't you let me hold him and you can take some rest?" Emmott said.

She needed some convincing, and Emmott could understand it- a complete stranger turning up and offering to hold your baby while you slept was unusual and new mothers should always be cautious.

"He hasn't nursed as much today," she said after transferring him into Emmott's arms and moving towards the stairs. "Not quite himself, poor love".

Emmott sat on the stool and held the baby close. His sleep was light. She could see his eyeballs moving under his near translucent eyelids. He snuffled slightly and she could feel his heat warming her own body. As she sat holding the little boy, Emmott contemplated her own future as a mother. Would she have a son? What about a daughter? If she had a girl she would name her after her sisters: Ellen Sarah Alice Elizabeth Torre. A bit of a mouthful but full of meaning and memory. A son would be John Robert, of course. She tried to picture her belly swelling, her womb full with the substantive proof of her love for Rowland. Yes, she so wanted to be a mother. They should not wait. By this time next year this could be her sitting in her own home nursing an infant. The thought warmed her in a way that few thoughts had this past year.

Mrs Allen slept for little more than an hour and then returned down the stairs looking like she would have benefitted from a few more hours of sleep but Emmott could understand her reluctance to not prevail too much on the kindness of a stranger. The baby had begun to get fractious, Emmott assumed because he wanted to feed. His cheeks looked flushed with the effort of looking for his mother's nipple and Emmott had pacified him by moving him up to her shoulder. His warm cheek brushed hers and she could hear his faint snuffling next to her ear. It was with some reluctance she handed him back to his mother. Holding a baby during times of crisis brought an immeasurable sense of peace and a hope that things could be different, could be better.

"Thank you," Mrs Allen said to Emmott. "It was unquestionably kind of you to do this for me. I have been so tired since he was born. I don't know if it is the loss of Thomas or if new motherhood is always so exhausting." She gave a little laugh as she spoke, trying to appear light-hearted, but Emmott could see in her eyes that she was truly brought low by the experience of the past few weeks.

"Perhaps I could come again?" Emmott enquired.

"You are an angel. That would be really, really wonderful. I really do appreciate this. The scriptures say we sometimes entertain angels unaware don't they? I don't know them well but I remember that bit. It always sounded so exciting as a child to imagine you might meet angels and not know it. Are you sure you aren't an angel?" she laughed again.

Emmott blushed. "Oh no, most certainly not an angel. I am just grateful to be able to do something that is a blessing to others. It's been a difficult few months. I am sorry about Thomas." She added. She was half inclined to tell the other woman about her own sorrow in losing so many members of her family but her story was as precious as it was painful and she did not feel quite ready to share it with this new acquaintance. Perhaps on the next visit? She wondered if Mrs Allen had had to tend to Thomas all by herself, heavily pregnant and fearful. Mary Cooper, who appeared to somehow know everything about the comings and goings and the deeds of the various inhabitants of Eyam, had told her that when the time came she had birthed with the help of the local midwife, and Emmott urged herself to remember to contact this wise woman so that she could further pursue her inclination to learn the craft of midwifery from her.

On her walk back towards Bagshaw House Emmott looked about the village. Smoke still issued from chimneys, she could hear the chopping of wood in backyards and the braying of animals in their pens. People just did the things they knew how to do, that is how they survived. The 'living through' was in the everyday details of families; of women making meals and keeping homes, of children helping fathers and mothers and trying to get out of chores to play, of men making their livelihoods down the mines or selling their wares and worrying about putting food on the table. When life presented a crisis, people responded by doing more of what they knew how to do.

The most challenging aspect of this particular calamity was that usually people would naturally want to help each other. Eyam was a close knit village and people genuinely supported each other where they could. But with the virulence of the disease and the horrifying end results for those who were unfortunate enough to be felled by it, people were forced to stay more apart. People like Mrs Allen living by herself with her new-born were those most in need of human touch and the feeling that someone else in the world had a care for their existence. It made Emmott feel good to know she had taken a brave step in showing up at the Allen's door. Being seemingly out of the disease's reach had its rewards.

As she walked she gazed up on the hills overlooking Eyam, towards Riley Farm where the Hancocks and the Talbots lived. People living on the outskirts of the village must have felt safer these past months tucked away up there on the hills. She wondered if Andrew Merrill would now come home. According to Mary he was still up there in his hut with only a cockerel for companionship. There were times Emmott had thought about taking her mother and Joseph to one of the dilapidated huts on the edge of the woods. Old poaching huts, she was sure they could make modestly hospitable and trade less rudimentary living for safety. Rowland had even suggested it in one of his letters, even coming up with a plan to bring provisions from Stoney Middleton and leaving them at a designated spot at the edge of the woods. Yet in the end they had not needed it. Surely this month would see the end of it?

30

Emmott

29th April 1666

Emmott was sick. It had begun yesterday with a slight headache and a feeling of light-headedness which she had shrugged off, believing it to be the natural consequence of a day spent in busyness. She had bathed Joseph, fetched eggs, and flour for bread from the village and taken a moderate walk up towards the woods on the eastern borders of Eyam. The weather had been so lovely she took some of the bread and a tiny morsel of cheese and stayed out for most of the day, taking lunch on the edge of the trees from an elevation that allowed her to look down over the rooftops and down towards the centre of Eyam.

She spent some time turning over the idea of destiny, like pebbles tumbled by the river when it ran full and fast. Her mind had been awash with questions and ideas. She surely had been spared for a reason. Was her survival tied to some as yet unknown fate? She had been brave and careful and not shrunk away from doing what was necessary when death had turned up within the walls of her own home. There was a satisfaction within Emmott to know she had been tested and was not found to be in want of either character or fortitude. Her father would have been proud. She knew that. When the headache began to make itself known she began the long walk back to the village, believing she had overdone both the sunshine, which was unusually warm for April, and the exercise.

She stopped to look at a beautiful crop of delicate common orchids but hurried the pace when she was overcome with a wave of nausea and on entering Bagshaw House she told her mother she felt a little out of sorts and was going to lie down. Such was the belief that she, Emmott and Joseph were the happy survivors of the plague's assault on their family, it did not even enter Elizabeth's head that Emmott could be gravely afflicted. She simply smiled at her daughter and wished her a happy rest, promising to bring her up some pottage when it was cooked.

Emmott found the ascent up the stairs difficult yet managed it. Her legs felt heavy and aching yet she had not walked all that far to account for the painful heaviness in her limbs. She removed her outer skirts, taking care to lay them neatly on the chair that sat in the corner, so they would not be too creased for tomorrow, and lay down in her shift on top of the bed. The thought of having the covers over her was unwelcome and her head on the pillow felt leaden. She tried to close her eyes but sleep would not come and she lay there willing the thought to not enter her head, holding it at bay as the village watch would ward off an objectionable visitor with the halberd in the dead of night. *This could not possibly be it could it? She could not possibly be infected with plague, could she?* She had encountered it nine times and not once had it proved to her a deadly foe. For it to tease her thus and then return in force on the tenth encounter seemed to Emmott beyond cruel. She had allowed herself to believe in a future, her future, and to dream. She managed a light sleep, for how long she could not tell. The sounds below came to her as if muffled by water, distant but ordinary. There was no sense of urgency in the house. Nothing to suggest they would soon be shifted backward into danger.

Emmott was not sure what rose first- her fever or her fear. She felt the heat gathering in her cheeks and on her forehead and when her fingers reached up and ran along her hairline the tiny beads of sweat gathered on the tips of her slender fingers. Her hands felt clammy and her throat felt thick. It was as if the few moments of sleep she had fallen into had caused some unseen army to advance disastrously, so that they appeared without warning at barricades most unready for battle. The despair took hold of her and it was utterly smothering.

Her thoughts snapped to Rowland, who could not come here now even if she wanted him to. Her mind wandered to Margaret Blackwell and her miraculous recovery. Perhaps if she had been in such close proximity to the disease so many times it would be unable to grip her quite so hard now it appeared to have finally come to wrestle for her soul? Perhaps she could ask John to boil up some bacon fat so she could drink it like Margaret? Perhaps she could live through the arrival of death and that was her destiny? In amongst the turmoil of it all she realised she should call down to her mother.

It took her several minutes to summon the strength to haul herself up off the bed and over to the staircase. Recalling how quickly her father was overcome by it she was fearful she would slip into delirium upstairs alone without being able to warn anyone of her affliction. She called out. Her voice was weak and feeble and she seemed unable to muster the strength she would need to make it any louder. Frequency must prevail over volume. She called again and again until finally she saw the small shadow of Joseph draw near to the bottom of the staircase.

"Joseph," she said, losing breath in a sharp exhale as she spoke. She leaned against the wood of the beams that ran around the top of the stairs and felt her body slide down the wall a few inches. "Joseph, get mama. Please." Her voice was drowsy.

She saw him toddle off, unimaginably glad in that moment that he was smart and quick and not rascally like Richard. He might have thought it a game and teased her. No. She admonished herself for the thought, remembering how much she had loved Richard's mischievous side and the recollection brought a weak smile. Her lips were salty from the sweat. She ran her tongue over them, desperate for some moisture as her mouth and throat felt so dry. She remembered her father always said the best cure for a disease was to try to avoid catching it in the first place. He had not managed to follow his own remedy and now it seemed neither would she, despite the cruellest indicators of the contrary.

As she waited she contemplated her exposure. How had plague seeds come to reside in her body and found their way towards this untimely germination? With gentle recognition she retrieved the painful truth of her exposure in this past week, as if snagging her finger on the thorn when reaching for a rose. The Allen baby boy. She would need to have her mother find out whether he had sickened.

Her mother came quickly up the stairs, finding Emmott sat at the top leaning against the wall, unable to stand for herself.

"My dear, dear girl," Elizabeth whispered and a moment past between them as their eyes met and each acknowledged the reality of the situation they were in. Emmott let out a little sob as Elizabeth helped her to the bed, calling for her husband over her shoulder. Calling for John. How Emmott wished it was her father who would climb the stairs and answer the call and tend to her. When she looked at her mother there was a tiny pang of what Emmott realised was jealousy at the thought that her mother was twice a bride whilst now she herself might never be. The thought of the loss made her sick to her stomach, causing her throat to spasm and she leaned over and vomited onto the wooden boards.

"I'm sorry," she whispered, her hands beginning to tremble. Her mother shook her head with such a look of loving concern that Emmott began to weep.

"Do not trouble yourself with thoughts of this," Elizabeth said, settling Emmott into the bed. She noticed how cold her daughter's hands and feet were. *Was this normal? Why did she not know?* She cursed herself for not having watched the others pass from this life, for having become a ghost even before they did. Now she could not tell if Emmott's symptoms were following a similar path, if they were better or worse than John and her children. The pestilence had visited them at Bagshaw House many times but this was the first time Elizabeth was looking it full in the face. She had no idea what to do.

Emmott's voice was hoarse when she whispered her thanks. She lay for a length of time she could not judge whilst her mother disappeared and John Daniel appeared at her bedside. He had brought up a steaming bowl of the pottage, now cooked, but the smell made her nauseous and she could not think of eating any food and, besides, her belly felt hard. Her hands felt the roundness and it brought forth another sob as she thought of the hopes she had her womb would be swelled by children in good time. Her pulse was bounding and there was no position in which she could sit or lie where she did not feel faint and pained. The headache had grown into an intense throbbing that made her eyes hurt and her neck felt so weakened she could only lean it forward or to the side, having not the strength to keep it upright.

Emmott thought about how well she had felt at lunch time, enjoying her simple meal of bread and cheese under the sun, cooled by the gentle breeze that had kissed the treeline. Now she was too sick for dinner and she had the ever-growing sense that perhaps tonight she would supper with the dead, if the heavenly banquet she had heard about at church services was to be believed. There was an unexpected sense of resignation despite the uncertainty and the thought of seeing her father and her brothers and sisters again on the far side of eternity was a hope she wanted to reach for. Yet, her will to live was indomitable.

John Daniel placed the bowl of pottage out of the room so as not to cause Emmott any further discomfort. He had meant it with the kindest intentions but could see now he had misjudged how afflicted Emmott was. The speed with which the illness advanced had shocked him. He heard tales of it in town, how it turned up in the morning and sent victims to their graves by dusk, but had never seen with his own eyes the way the disease could diminish someone so quickly.

He had grown fond of Emmott. Though she had been resistant towards him at first, he understood her reservation and recognised her rectitude. She had wanted to hang on to the memory of her father and he could not blame her for that. He had loved his father deeply also and lost him early and understood the ache of losing a man who had meant so much.

"No," Emmott croaked. "Don't sit so close." Even in her own suffering her thoughts turned to others.

"It is alright lass," he said. "I will sit. Your mother has gone to speak with Mary Cooper. She will ask about the fate of the Allen boy. She'll be back soon."

Emmott managed a frail smile but she could barely keep her eyelids from closing. Her breathing was rapid and had become shallower as the hours had passed. She seemed to reach beneath the bedclothes, feeling some serious discomfort but as her mother was not yet back John decided it best not to look for the cause and to preserve the young woman's modesty instead.

"She'll be back soon," he repeated, trying to reassure her. "She will look to your… pain," and he nodded at her. John applied cold water on wet rags to her forehead and was surprised by the heat he found there. After a while she quietened and though her head still turned often from side to side, she slept and he was grateful. He decided to take the opportunity to replenish the water and find new rags, and to talk to his wife as soon as she returned from her visit with Mary Cooper. He did not want to admit it but he was afraid. As a man who liked to laugh at life he felt moved to tears by the effects of the disease upon Emmott and terrified by the possibility of her death arriving soon.

"You're back," he said, stating the obvious as Elizabeth came through the door, closing it behind her. He had been to check on Emmott twice more, applying fresh cold rags and trying to break her fever, unsuccessfully.

"What did...?" he enquired.

Elizabeth cut him off. "Tis plague!" she cried, sinking onto the chair by the kitchen's hearth. "The Allen baby died yesterday and he had all the signs of having had the pestilence, poor mite. The mother shows no sign of the sickness, which is probably what made Emmott so confident to go in there and pursue her mercy mission. Oh Emmott, why did you go there? I can't lose another child!" she sobbed, grabbing hold of his hand and pulling it close to her face so that he felt her hot tears fall down over his fingers. He held her a short while before telling her gently that Emmott had grown worse even in the short time Elizabeth had been away from the house.

At these words Elizabeth rushed up the stairs to her daughter. Emmott had felt the delirium creep up on her, like a hot madness that promised to relieve her of her fear as it also relieved her of her grasp on reality. She felt nothing and everything, alternating like the faces of her fellow villagers spinning past her as Rowland had spun her round at The Wakes. Now her head was a blur, like walking through the fog that would sometimes envelope Eyam in winter, and her room would not stay still and her eyes would not stay open. She could not focus but she recognised the shape of her mother as she felt the fever take her under again, blackness in exchange for light.

Elizabeth sobbed to see her daughter so taken and yet still somehow hanging on. She pulled back the covers and it was as she had feared when John mentioned Emmott's discomfort. There were painful swellings at the top of her legs, beginning to darken, and her beautiful, graceful neck had also thickened on each side, though her armpits were mercifully clear of engorgement. She could not bear the pain of watching this unfold but she knew she must not fail at this test a second time. Emmott had nursed everyone else, and now she must nurse Emmott. The pain of losing another child must not change that.

John came up the stairs to show Elizabeth something that had been left on the cottage's outside border wall. It was a muslin bag tied loosely with twine and bore a scribbled note on a scrap of parchment that seemed only to read "Yours, MH".

"Did you see anyone?" Elizabeth asked.

"No, I just found them out there. Do you suppose it is from Mary? You did tell her about Emmott's condition?"

"Yes, I told her. But she would not shy away to leave it on the wall. What is it? It is not the time for trifles!"

John opened the bag and found inside a mixture of herbs and dried flowers. "Looks to me like one of Humphrey Merrill's remedies," he said. "From someone who knows she is sick." The thought made him think of Rowland. Emmott talked about him so often. He knew she would want to see him if she was...he couldn't bring himself to say the word. "Rowland, should we tell him? He would..."

"He would..." Elizabeth said, her voice thick with emotion. "Oh, he would. And she would too. But he can't. He can't come here into this house. It would risk sickening all of Stoney Middleton should he take back the seeds of plague. We cannot. May they both forgive us!" she sobbed, and crossed herself. When John went up again he heard Emmott muttering in her sleep. Just one word. *Rowland.*

Emmott lingered in a shadowy twilight between living and being gone. As she came to the edge of herself, she felt the lines beginning to blur and the join with her body became free and loose. Things flashed before her eyes as the fever ran up and down her frame, causing wakefulness and sleep alternately like blinking. She felt detached, like a taut rope being let out slowly. She wasn't sure if this was her life unravelling or her being gathered up into a new mode of existing. It felt like loss and gain all at the same time.

She saw herself at The Wakes in August, dressed in white and floral-crowned and Rowland standing in front of her, smiling, always smiling. She tried to smile back and Elizabeth and John saw the faint twitching of the corner of her lips. Then suddenly she was a girl again, sitting on her father's knee. He was giving her the doll she had given to Sarah and he stroked her hair as she nestled into his strong chest in gratitude. Now her sisters were there again, Ellen and Elizabeth, and they were all walking arm in arm down the main village road, towards the square and the lydgate. Then Marshall Howe was there, his big hands were reaching for her. He wanted to carry her out but she was still here, wasn't she? Now he was whispering, 'sorry'. They were all saying sorry, the faces of her family in earnest waiting and watching and their arms spread wide.

Emmott felt the ground leave her feet, which was strange as she was in bed, wasn't she? But now she came to think on it, she did not feel like she was lying down at all but instead upright and moving, walking, as if to the dale, to the Delph, as if to meet Rowland. She waved to him. He waved back. Why did he look so sad? And then it was dark, only for a second, but in that moment, she stopped feeling pain and fear and the light found her and wrapped itself around her, all of her, somehow both inside and out, and she stopped reaching for the ground and let herself drift, like the seeds of the dandelion clock spreading far and wide when all you want is to know what time it is.

31

Catherine
30ᵗʰ April 1666

Catherine sat still as the river when it froze in the dead of winter. She did not appear to move and as William watched her he was acutely aware of the presence of pain in his wife's face. The hope of March had turned out to be a fool's hope and he could not argue with the Book of Proverbs' pronouncement that 'hope deferred makes the heart sick'. When he looked on his wife, he could see her heart ailed with the events of the past week.

The dreadful illness had swept through the Allen house for a second time and taken with it the baby of Mrs Allen, the lone mother Catherine had been so concerned about. It was out of that concern she had mentioned the plight of Mrs Allen, alone with her new baby once her husband was claimed by the pestilence, to Emmott Syddall. Now as he looked at Catherine and the way her eyes stared across at her herb garden yet seemed somehow not to really gaze upon it, he knew she would be taking the suffering of blame and bringing it in close to her heart, where it made itself known as pain and drained her eyes of their usual brightness.

He missed that playful look she had gotten when she found herself some real purpose in assisting Humphrey Merrill. To begin with, William had not wanted her to do this work, preferring her to stay less prominent and less open to public exposure as the rector's wife. But when he saw what animation and vibrancy it brought to her beautiful face, he had become increasingly glad of it. She had busied herself, managed her own energy levels well, and still made herself available to him as a wife. He marvelled at her ability to juggle so many things and stretch to do them with integrity and dedication, even though her health was not the greatest and he could see her tiredness, yet it was a happy exhaustion and he was glad she had discovered it.

Catherine could not stop thinking about Emmott. It was impossible to believe she was gone, and had joined her sisters and brothers and her father in the earth. Catherine had spoken to Marshall Howe herself. She found the stern sexton intimidating and could not deny a feeling of revulsion, having heard of the harsh way he treated corpses and the burden he placed on the remnants of bereft families to part with their family heirlooms to pay his grave-digging fees. With so many Syddalls laid in the ground already, Catherine was unsure what Elizabeth Syddall had left to pay the man. Yet Catherine could not let her intimidation prevent her from asking Marshall to do the very best he could with regards to

Emmott; to be slow and tender in his removal of her and to honour her with a sound and respectful burial.

When she spoke with the sexton she thought, beyond her expectations, that there was a softness in his eye as he listened to her request. He had removed his hat and brought it to his chest and answered her request with a slow nod of his head and a 'Yes, Mrs Mompesson' and despite his dreadful reputation, she found herself trusting him.

Later when she approached Bagshaw House, John Daniel answered the door. He informed her that Elizabeth was lying down, quite exhausted by this new grief. Joseph played quietly by the hearth and Catherine found herself wondering how such a young child could possibly understand how, in the space of half a year, he had lost all his siblings and was now alone with a new step-father and a mother again felled by grief. His play was almost silent and he moved very little, as if he dared not take up any more space in this house that, whilst full of room, was crammed full with the memories of the dead.

It was then that she had discovered Emmott was not buried behind Bagshaw House with the other Syddalls, but had instead been buried in the Cussy Dell. Her heart went out to Marshall then, that he had somehow known that Emmott would be most happy in her eternal home in the surrounds of the lush green which she most loved. It was something the two women had in common, a love of walking through nature and appreciating the wild flowers and the trees, though they had not known each other well nor ever taken a walk together.

As she sat in the garden, the sounds of birds filling the air around her and the aroma of the herbs filling her nostrils, she could not help but let her eyes grow cloudy with tears. It was she who had mentioned the Allen woman to Emmott. Even though she recalled talking with her about the dangers and the inability to predict complete safety, she knew she had shared Emmott's belief that she seemed to somehow be protected from the awful disease and had not pushed her cautions very hard. There were certain people in the village who seemed to have flirted with death repeatedly and never succumbed to its charms. One such was Mary Cooper and another, she had believed, was Emmott. There were likely more in the village who had lived with households taken one by one and were yet untouched. Of the players in the Allen situation, it appeared it was Mrs Allen, who remained unaffected despite losing her husband and child, who had true resistance to the plague, and not the guileless, compassionate woman who had entered their home full of intent to do good.

If only she could go back to the day of the wedding and insist Emmott not visit the Allens. If only she had not mentioned that family to her at all. The wedding had been a rare oasis of joy and celebration in the nightmare that had befallen the Syddall family. She recalled the words of her husband during the hand-fasting service in the Delph, speaking about not despising 'the day of small things' and how from this small ceremony great joy would grow, not to undo the pain of the past but to bring hope to the future. Emmott had smiled, no doubt she was thinking of Rowland in that moment.

Rowland. How it would hurt him to hear of this. He no longer came into the village to visit Bagshaw House and Catherine knew that the lovers often met at Cucklett Delph, having seen them there a few times, conversing from a distance. She had heard them once or twice and felt as if she had stumbled upon a scene from the classics, like nymphs meeting with mortal men in the secret spaces of nature. She always tried to tiptoe away, not wanting to disturb them or embarrass them through revealing they had been discovered.

How would anyone tell Rowland? He would come and wait for her in their usual place but she would not be there. Nor would she write to him either. Catherine knew he would want to find out the fate of his love but she hoped he would not come into the village despite the pain of his not-knowing. To take the plague back into Stoney Middleton would be most calamitous and place all of Derbyshire at risk.

Yet how could he bear to stay away and not know what had befallen her? It made Catherine want to weep with the sorrow of it all.

How sad it would be to face The Wakes again and not have the wedding she and William had hoped would bring the village together and bring with it a return to a more pious devotion for Eyam's inhabitants. Catherine supposed they had achieved their goal another way, morbidly aided by the horrors of the silent foe that brought even the most hardened sinner and anti-church men and women to their knees. People had approached the rectory who had never once set foot in the church the whole time the Mompessons had been in the village. There were requests made for blessings and prayers that came from the most unexpected of places and William was always so quick to grant them, never thinking to put up any barriers or give any lectures on prior disengagement. For him it was like the one sheep being found every time. He glorified in the ninety-nine and threw up his hands in praise for this new one. This flock was penned in and oppressed by fear and he was glad to welcome new sheep and do his best to alleviate the suffering of his flock where he could.

"You couldn't have known," William broke into her thoughts. She turned her attention towards him, feeling the tears displace with the shift of her eyeballs. She covered her face with her hands and he came over and gently prised them away from her face.

"You couldn't have known," he repeated, cradling her head with his hands and drawing her towards himself. She felt her tears soak into his shirt and the beat of his heart against her ear was strangely soothing. She imagined it was the sound children could hear in the womb, the rhythmic insistence of life, reassuring in its regularity. It comforted her to be close to him, to be held. She felt like a child. Like an inexperienced and naïve girl who had made a wrong decision and invited all kind of calamity in because of it.

"We should take a walk. It does you no good to sit here this way and dwell on what might or might not have been. The past is unobtainable Catherine. All we can do is look at it with grace and cast ourselves on God's mercy, knowing that he sees the heart." In that moment Catherine did feel like a walk. She had one place in mind. "Shall we walk?" he said again, and this time she made a reply.

"Yes. I would like to go to the Cussy Dell," she said, standing up and brushing off the bits of leaves and seeds that had fallen from the trees around her and gathered in her skirts while she sat. They walked slowly, her limbs seeming to match with the lacklustre of her thoughts. When they arrived, she saw the thing she had come here for. The earth was mounded up, fresh and dark. It was impossible to imagine Emmott lying beneath it, her slim figure made still from its constant business, her pretty face marred by death and her chestnut hair lying limp around her head.

The stark contrast of the dark earth against the green of the dell gave her heart a pang of sorrow, but what she saw atop the death knoll caused a smile to find her lips despite the sadness of the scene. Laying on the grave was a crude wreath of wild flowers, simple in its weaving yet somehow beautiful in its simplicity. She imagined the sexton's large fingers working the stems together, unskilled in the art of floristry. That he had bothered to do it softened Catherine's heart a great deal towards the man, and seeing Emmott so honoured released just a little of the sorrow she felt over the loss of this young woman. A valve had opened and out of it would trickle all the sorrow and guilt in time.

"We can walk back now," she whispered, taking William's arm. They took their time returning to the rectory and he felt perhaps she leaned on him just a little lighter and her head seemed just a little more tilted up towards the sun.

32

Elizabeth

3rd May 1666

It had been a long time since she had held him in her arms, but as he lay there quiet and still she stroked his blonde, wavy hair and it reminded her of when he was a little one, her second child, when she was still learning how to be a mother. She had approached it with such methodology, seeing it as a series of tasks to be completed that were necessary for the growing of a family. She had been ill-prepared for the giant wave of love that had swept over her at that moment she had first held Joseph, her eldest son, in her arms. She had expected it to feel somehow less when she became a mother for the second time but the rush of adoration she felt when she first held William was of the same intensity as with her firstborn, proving love would only multiply with addition.

When she had looked down after the pains of birth had subsided and saw him lying there helpless, fast asleep, with flakes of her own blood on his perfect cheek and streaked in his hair, she was immediately besotted. She was not an emotional woman but the strength of affection for each child as he or she arrived into her world prompted a passionate feeling of absolute devotion. Today she had discovered it doesn't go away even as they near adulthood themselves.

Now she saw the way his adolescent jaw was set and his beautiful brown eyes stared off somewhere beyond her, beyond them both. The cruel news about Robert and little William had reached them at Riley that morning. John had received the update from a man who had ventured up from Eyam to have a saddle's stirrups replaced and when John lumbered into the farmhouse towards midday Elizabeth knew immediately something was wrong. He had this habit of avoiding her eyes when he had something difficult to say. She sat down at the table so she was below him and his gaze more easily fell on her.

"It is news from below," he had said. "Some is good and some is not. The numbers have stayed low. Only seven who perished in April."

"That is indeed good news," Elizbeth had replied, recalling the horrifying reports of deaths in October. "And the bad?" she asked.

"There were two died yesterday… They were Robert and William Thorpe," he said, his eyes returning to the floor. Elizabeth placed both hands on the table and breathed out slowly. John told her the other particulars of the Thorpe boys' passing but she grasped only a few details because her thoughts had gone immediately to William. She knew their son would be devastated to hear what had happened to his friend, especially as he had only seen him so recently. *How recent was it?* Her brain started to scramble back through the past few weeks.

It could only have been a fortnight ago as she had made one more trip to Eyam since then and the visit for this week was scheduled for tomorrow. *Was Robert sick then?* William had not mentioned anything about him looking unwell. *Had William gone inside?* She had told him not to and trusted him to follow her wishes. *He wouldn't have gone inside, would he?* Her mind was saturated with questions, but the thought of her devastated boy cut through them all, swift like an arrow, and she rose slowly from the table.

"I will tell him,' she said, passing John, who reached out and held her hand, holding onto it until she had walked out of his reach and it slipped from his hand and he watched as she headed for the door that led to the yard at the back of the farmhouse. She found William feeding the hens and she made some small talk with him about their egg-laying tricks before she asked him to come and sit with her on the edge of the well. She knew he could tell something was wrong and so she moved to tell him as quickly as she could.

"Son, Robert is gone. The plague has taken him, just as it did the rest of his family, and little William too. They went together, curled up on his bed your father says. I'm so very sorry," she told him. She could see her son battle with himself, as if he stood on a knife edge between manhood and boyhood and this was his defining moment. She saw his eyes start to glisten and the way he clenched his near-manly jaw in response to the threatening of tears.

"But, I only saw him that day we made the visit together. He was alright then," he said, and Elizabeth felt relief flood her. "He was even laughing though I knew he wasn't quite his real self. How can he be gone?" he asked her, and he leaned his head against her shoulder. She stroked his cheek and asked him if he would like to go inside. Now here they were both lying on the bed she shared with John and William was staring as if he could see Robert on the otherwise of eternity. She stroked his head for a bit longer and then asked him if he would like to eat. He did not speak but she was pleased to see him nod. *Not much comes before a growing boy and his food* she smiled to herself, glad to know he was not so overcome with grief as she had feared he might be.

He rested upon her and she slipped out from behind him and lay his head gently onto her pillow, as she had done so often when he was a boy and had needed a nap in the afternoons. She could almost see that toddler version of him still left inside the almost man she saw stretched out now. *Motherhood was nothing but changes, always changes and how you coped with them*, she thought to herself as she went into the kitchen to find bread and cheese and perhaps some meat if they had any. The kitchen was quiet and she worked in near silence, alone with her thoughts about a family completely wiped out and her hopes that May would be kinder than this grave start it had made.

33

Catherine
30th May 1666

It was incredible really, how the hope had crept back in after they had such certainty all was lost. The month of May had, unexpectedly, claimed only two lives. But the lives it had claimed had filled Catherine's heart with sorrow. Both Robert and William Thorpe, the only survivors in the Thorpe house, had passed away together on the 2nd of May. When some women from the village knocked their door and received no answer, they had pushed their way in and found the brothers dead, curled up together on the same pallet bed, little William's arm cold and resting over his older brother's still chest.

When Catherine heard this, she cried. All the remaining sadness over Emmott and all the wretchedness of the Thorpe boys suddenly came flooding out. Jane held her mistress while she sobbed, her delicate shoulders heaving up and down and her breath coming out all raspy with the effort. *How could a whole household of people just be gone?* It wouldn't find a way to make sense in Catherine's thoughts. She kept returning to it, again and again. A whole family, a living, breathing lineage of seven simply gone. In years to come, would anyone even know this family had existed? She knew William was most meticulous in keeping the parish register up to date. Every single soul who had been lost had been entered, sometimes late at night when his eyes were tired from writing wills. She had often found him, taking great care to write their names clearly and boldly, so that what was no longer present on earth had its place, solid and stark, on the pale parchment.

She had waited with nervous anticipation when a week passed, and then two, and no more deaths followed. Nobody sickened, demand for Humphrey Merrill's herbal concoctions died right down to his normal level of custom once again, so that he didn't need Catherine's assistance at all in the latter half of May. She missed the work, and the interaction with the old man himself. She had grown quite fond of the old apothecary. Spending her days in the presence of such simple, earthy wisdom had had a profound effect on her and she was overjoyed to have found a new skill she could nurture and nourish as her own. Her herb garden was flourishing and she was more naturally able to combine plants and flowers now, knowing their medicinal properties and using them to treat little ailments in her own family.

The lull in the horrifying outbreak had given her additional time to spend with her children. They were increasingly fractious from having been kept within the rectory grounds for weeks and had essentially been neglected by both their parents, both too occupied with meeting the needs of the village than to spend time with them. Thankfully they had Jane, and Catherine had even seen William's man servant engaging Elizabeth and George with a ball game on several occasions. They were so very fortunate. To have two adults at their disposal, whilst other children nursed their sick parents, was luxury many families who had suffered did not have.

It had been twenty-eight days. The longest the village had gone without a plague death. A whole four weeks of pausing, holding back suspicion and taking out hope from all the little, secret places in the homes in Eyam it had been hidden away. They were behind closed doors, dusting off the hope they still had and tentatively enshrining it again, placing it on mantlepieces and hanging it up in windows. For Catherine that meant releasing the children from the effective prison she had kept them in. Taking them each by the hand, she led them out onto the street and they took a walk to the church yard.

"Where are we going mother?" Elizabeth asked. "I thought we did not go out from the garden? We might see people!" Catherine could hear the anxiety in her little girl's voice, the slightest indication of worry that only a mother would detect. She had shut her children away to protect them, but it wasn't without cost. Sometimes when we protect our children from something vast, we give them a series of small things instead, which can be just as difficult to navigate.

"It is alright, Elizabeth," she said, kneeling down to place her hands on either side of Elizabeth's waist and looking her directly in the eye, George taking the opportunity to lean on her back as she spoke to his sister. "We needed to be safe. I know it was hard. But it is better now. We can take a little walk."

"What if we see someone? What if they have it? What if they have plague?" Elizabeth asked, concern in her eyes. They had taken care to not talk about it openly in front of their children, keeping to low voices in William's study or out in the garden away from the house. But children being children, they secrete themselves away, hang about at doorways and incline their ears towards conversations not meant for them. Clearly, they had taken up the notion of the infection having arrived and how serious it was.

"If we see someone, we will speak to them, polite like always," she said, pinching Elizabeth's cheek softly and putting her arm around George, who was in danger of toppling her over into the street, his leaning having grown into a sprawl. She stood up slowly; coming up to full height from a low position was always such an effort. Taking both their hands again, they proceeded towards the churchyard. She could see Bagshaw House just beyond, smoke creeping up into the sky in a thin, steady stream. It reminded her of incense. The Syddalls had provided such a sacrifice. She squeezed the hands of her children, causing them to look up at her. Smiling down into their trusting faces, she felt afresh the great responsibility of bringing children into the world and leading them body and soul through times you never once expected to live through. Looking at the church, looming ahead of them, she was glad to have the guidance of the Bible and the Book of Common Prayer to help her in guiding their course.

On entering the churchyard, they were almost immediately met by Elizabeth Frith. Catherine smiled at her friend. It had been weeks since she had last seen her and Elizabeth had a way of making Catherine feel lighter.

"Good morrow, look what the wind has blown in!" Elizabeth declared, looking down at the two children and offering a wink. Suddenly overcome with unusual shyness in the presence of Elizabeth's larger-than-life personality, they shuffled so they were ever so slightly behind Catherine and for a moment she thought she might have to remind them about the importance of politeness. But they recovered themselves before she could speak.

"Good morning Mrs Frith," little Elizabeth said, followed by an equally polite and respectful greeting from George, albeit from behind Catherine's skirts.

'My, we are polite little children, aren't we!" Elizabeth chuckled. "Run along now, I want to talk with your mother!" Were it anyone else, Catherine might have baulked at someone being so directive with her own children, but there was something so good-natured in Elizabeth's forthright manner than she merely chuckled instead. She hoped the children would be sensible. She had not given them any guidance for what they should do should any other children appear in the churchyard and she felt too foolish to issue such directives now in front of Elizabeth. If she thought them unnecessary, she would likely say so, and Catherine doubted she would take that so easily as the run-along directive.

"How do you fare, Elizabeth?" Catherine asked, mustering her bravery and looping her arm through the arm of the other woman.

"Me?" she cried. "How are *you*? You must be relieved this misfortune has passed. So many people looking to William for direction! He was more popular than muck to a fly!"

Despite the crudeness of the analogy, Catherine couldn't help but smile.

"Well yes, we are rather," she muttered, her attention taken by the graveyard. There was room here for all who had perished. She wondered if she should ask William to have all those buried on non-sacred ground reinterred here. But when she mentioned it to Elizabeth, she was most upset to think about the disturbing of so many children from their eternal sleeps, having been laid down to rest already. When Catherine also thought of Emmott she could not imagine bringing her out of her beautiful place of final repose. She admitted the error of her thinking to Elizabeth.

"Do not be daft, woman," Elizabeth said. "You only suggested it because of how much you care for these lost souls. But we have to believe God's got them, don't we? And Francis says William has been round darn near all of these resting places," she said, gesturing towards the village, "and said all the prayers that can be said to move their souls on towards paradise. There is nought else can be done, nor should be done, except care for those left."

"Yes,' Catherine nodded. "You are right Elizabeth, always so right." She thought she saw the other woman blush slightly with the compliment, an endearing feature for a woman who seemed so sure of herself. Catherine knew that people often presented a façade, she often presented one herself, as if she was playing a role: Catherine Mompesson, rector's wife. She supposed some of how Elizabeth came across could be pretence too, but in the case of the older woman she sincerely hoped not, and that Elizabeth was equal parts both self-assured and soft-hearted.

They spoke for a while about the Thorpes, about the certainty that this was over that another week would bring, and about Catherine's herb garden and all she had cultivated there since the early Spring. Catherine shared some simple remedies with Elizabeth and the older woman promised to call by the rectory some time so Catherine could demonstrate some of the skills she had learned from Humphrey Merrill. As the light fell across the Saxon cross and found the sundial on the church wall, Catherine realised the time and called for the children to come back as noontime was fast approaching and Jane was sure to have some vittles ready for them to eat. They gave their goodbyes to Elizabeth and walked the short journey with a sense of normality, the wind in their hair and the sun warming their faces.

"That was nice," her daughter whispered.

"It was," agreed Catherine. And George gave his agreement by running off up the street and in through the gate to the rectory.

34

Elizabeth
14th June 1666

May had been kind, as if the month itself had gathered up her hopes and taken it upon itself to ensure they would be preserved. The only two souls to perish from the pestilence were Robert and William that whole month. She had been worried about her own son William and his unexpressed grief for his friend, as if to show his tears so close to his sixteenth birthday would somehow interrupt his transition into manhood. Then one day she heard him in the forge when John had finished his work for the day, making low, muffled sobs, and despite his anguish she was glad. When he emerged, she pretended not to notice, busying herself with the linen, and simply told him supper would shortly be ready. He had been hiding his tears, but as he strode towards the farmhouse it was hard to hide the fact that he was indeed almost a man, her boy.

June was only half way done but already it was an ill-favoured, piteous cousin to the more sympathetic May. Down in the village the Thornleys were picked off one by one by the deadly infection and it began to visit new houses, sweeping in and announcing itself with fever and sickness and swelling. She could not imagine the horror those first signs must bring to all those within the household; both stricken and well alike.

Her trips into the village were left longer and longer, as much as she could avoid it, but in the end, necessity would present itself and down she would go, growing more and more cautious as the weeks ticked by. She saw the vicar's wife working alongside Humphrey Merrill in his little shop adjacent to the house and was strangely enamoured by the sight of her there, grinding up herbs in the pestle and mortar at Merrill's side. *With disaster comes surprises* her mother had always said, meaning that there would always be the opportunity for those who had lingered in the background to suddenly find themselves in the midst of calamity and do their part to lead others through the maelstrom.

John found that his work decreased again as the disease added to its number, but the work he had had in the early Spring had certainly helped to keep her from the village more often than was absolutely necessary. From the customers he did have they gleaned some idea of how life was in the village. There were tales told of a woman of Eyam from Orchard Bank who had ventured to the market at Tideswell. When asked where she was from she had given her place of abode as Orchard Bank and not Eyam, but this embellishing of the truth had been found out when she was recognised as being a resident of their doomed village.

"They threw all of yesterday's vegetables at her and some muck from the road for good measure!" John told the family when they sat down to eat. There were roars of laughter from the children but all Elizabeth could do was imagine the woman's desperate need to escape the village, even if it was just for one normal afternoon of buying provisions. She could not bring herself to laugh at the woman.

"There is talk of the two parsons working together," John said, changing the subject. "As it worsens down there they will need to make a plan. The heat is what gives it chance to thrive, if it is the same pestilence as they fight in London, and all the signs are there that this will be as hot a summer as any. Some expect they will call a meeting," he said.

"At the church?" she asked.

"No, not the church. They have not been using it for services they say. At the Delph most likely, where they hold their Sunday Liturgy. We shall see. Nothing has been announced as yet but it is all worried eyes and faces in the village and they are the only two who can take the lead with the grand houses all now empty," he added, shaking his head. The Bradshaws and Sheldons and Furnesses were long gone, safely ensconced in safer dwellings.

"We shall see," Elizabeth said in reply. "Time shall deliver up its secrets when it is good and ready."

35

Catherine
20th June 1666

The month of June had been incredibly difficult. When Catherine thought back to her hopefulness at the end of May she realised they had simply been in the hollow of a wave, appearing to be embraced by calm and space when actually they were moments away from having their fears crash back in on them. She had seen the waves of the ocean as a child, on the Northumberland coast when she had lived in Durham growing up, and she had been in awe of how the waves just kept coming onto the shore. She remembered sitting on the sand and daring them to stop coming, but they never did. Now, it appeared this infection was not going away, merely teasing them in May with the eye of a storm, which now appeared to want to re-commence its raging.

On the very first day of May this particular wave began to break in the Thornley household, first taking Isaac Thornley, the thirteen-year-old stepson of Elizabeth Thornley, the widow of Francis, who had passed away the September before any of this began. Ever since, Elizabeth had been raising his three children, as well as her own two and the new baby, also named Francis, who Francis senior had died too soon to meet. Catherine could see how much

Elizabeth had suffered already, losing her husband and raising a whole household of children she had barely had time to get to know.

When Catherine spoke with Elizabeth soon after Isaac had died, she found the widow most preoccupied with the guilt of losing one of Francis' sons. He had gone and left her with them, entrusting his children to her care and she had promised him on his death bed that she would love them as her own and see no harm come to them. She had wailed then, quite overcome with the weight of having failed in her vow. Catherine was dismayed by the expression of her grief, so unbridled and dramatic. How grief finds its path is a mystery. Sometimes forced through resistance and finding its way to expressionless blankness, and sometimes flooding and wrenching through and out with loud screams and bodily convulsions. Each soul manifests its own grief and each grief is as different as the soul it devours.

Catherine had done her best to soothe Elizabeth's pain, though she did not know the woman at all well and she had been asked by Elizabeth Frith if she would call, when her neighbours reported how unending her grief appeared to be. She pointed out to the distraught widow that, far from being angry with her, her late husband was likely to be comforted by the arrival of his son in the afterlife, being a father who could welcome his child into what waited beyond death and not have to send him on ahead alone as so many other parents had had to do with their children during this visitation. Mrs Thornley did appear to take some comfort from that idea and Catherine took the opportunity to lead her in prayer, using some supplications from the Book of Common Prayer.

Not knowing in early June that the month was ramping up to bring a barrage of infections and emboldened by the low death toll in May, Catherine had entered the home and sat with Mrs Thornley and her other children. Within a week four more of them were dead, including her infant son Francis. The knowledge that she had sat so long and comfortably with impending death troubled Catherine to her soul and seemed to crumble her resolve to serve the village during this time. *Why had she not seen it? Why hadn't God given her some foresight?*

Her conversations with William were emotion-laden and frantic. She had allowed in the tiny grain of a thought, the awful contemplation of losing her own children and it had grown, putting down terrifying roots and wrapping its tendrils around her heart and squeezing it so that even to look at her children was to bring about a sense of dread so visceral she was overcome with faintness on several occasions, much to the upset of George and Elizabeth who could not understand why simply looking at them caused such distress in their mother.

"We must leave William!" she implored him. "All of us, we cannot stay. It is imperative that we survive this. Then we can come back! We can come back and rebuild. It will be a kindness to the village to have someone who hasn't suffered great loss to lead those left behind who have. They will need someone strong enough to do that."

"What are you saying Catherine?" William said, doing his best to hide the disappointment and surprise his wife's words had prompted in him. "A shepherd does not abandon the flock when trouble arrives! You would have me cast as the vicar of Vernham Dean and desert my parishioners! I cannot leave these people to die alone Catherine! It is hard enough to see them struggling with their corpses to bury them on their land or behind the ale house, when I know they are truly desperate to have their loved ones buried here in the churchyard. I cannot fail them further." His voice had become bolder and stronger as he spoke, but he did not wish to upset his wife. He could see she was frightened and had let her fear conquer her faith, though he hoped it was only a temporary defeat.

Taking a step towards her, he enveloped her in his arms and held her head against his chest, stroking her hair.

"I know your fear is for Elizabeth and George. It is only natural you would have this maternal urge to protect them and spirit us all away from this place, especially having seen families yielding their babies to the earth. I do not blame you, my love, for wanting to leave Eyam, but I do impress upon you that you must do so without me. I make no claims to hold you here as my wife, as rector or as husband."

Catherine felt the battle of maternal and pastoral duty rise up in her, the two responsibilities tussling against a backdrop of shame for having voiced her fears and not her faith. The effect was fury, not at William or at his words, but at the agonising decision that lay before her and she did not wish to make. The weight of it crushed her. Her hands were drawn into fists and she brought them up in front of her chest, taking a deep inhalation before letting out what sounded like a violent sigh. She left the room, unable to speak her quandary, and William watched her leave, sinking into his chair behind the desk of his study. He called for his manservant, requesting a glass of wine, much to the man's surprise, it being mid-afternoon on a week day. It would take more than wine for William to find the strength to carry out what he believed he had to do, and he sent his man out to request Thomas Stanley pay the rectory a visit, while he drained his glass.

Catherine paced the garden, her thoughts a furious whirlwind resisting taming. After a while she felt her anger ebb away, replaced by a feeling of resigned disquiet. She could not simply resist the decision. To do nothing was to make a decision. To do nothing was to stay. She gazed at the herb garden, with its neat rows, and mentally compiled her lists of merits for staying and merits for leaving. They were equally stacked and she felt sandwiched between them, struggling to let a solution emerge, like a seed she had once seen jammed in between two rocks yet determined to germinate. She remembered showing Elizabeth and George how the seed coat was rupturing and beneath its dark layers there was the promise of something green, something new, yet none of them could fathom where its new shoot would grow.

A weed grew between the impeccable rows of her herb garden. She frowned at first, priding herself on keeping this little green space thriving and pristine. Yet this weed was beautiful- indeed she struggled to see why such pretty flowers were oft regarded as weeds and unwanted- and from it bloomed two small but simple flowers. Between the thoughts of staying and leaving, a new idea found space to present itself. She herself would remain here in Eyam, but the children would leave. They could send them to Yorkshire, to William's Uncle, John Beilby. They would be safe there. She would stay here and support William as he led the village through the valley of the shadow of death, and offer her services to Humphrey Merrill again as he was sure to be busy with new demands made for apothecary cures in a hopeless bid to defeat plague when it struck.

As she turned to face the house, Catherine saw William's man arriving back, accompanied by another fellow. Even from a distance she could see it was Thomas Stanley, Puritan and prior rector of Eyam. Though old, the man walked tall and erect. She saw him glance in her direction and he bowed ever so slightly. Catherine issued a wave and set off across the lawn to catch the men up, eager to know what new plan William had set in motion that would require the support of Reverend Stanley, her fury now forgotten.

An hour later, the plans were finalised and they sat in the rectory parlour looking at each other. In the absence of Jane, who they had asked to remain in the kitchen, fearing their plans would escape the rectory and gallop into the village too soon, Catherine stoked the coals of the fire and turned to face the two men, sitting silent with their own thoughts.

"If we do this, you will need to convince them. I fear not even your respective allegiances will be enough for you to secure the will of all the people. They need due reason.

You must find scripture to back up your request." Catherine said.

William knew she was right and Stanley nodded along, pursing his lips in symmetry with his furrowed brow. Both men knew the gravity of what they proposed. By closing the village to preserve the rest of the county, indeed perhaps the country, they asked the villagers to face certain peril and to run the risk of this disease passing through them like fire, taking with it much of what was cherished. The reality was that many would die and yet they must ask them. The weight of the decision was vast, and Catherine could see it in the lines of her husband's face and the dark circles that cast his eyes into shadow. It was also there in Reverend Stanley's slumped shoulders and the way his hands found and unfound each other repeatedly in his lap.

"It is perhaps that we should turn our attentions to John, chapter fifteen," William said. "Verse thirteen…" Thomas cut in on him then, before Catherine's mind had chance to retrieve the verse.

"Greater love hath no man than this, that he lay down his life for his friends," his voice spoke, hushed, as if this verse from the Bible were a great and terrible secret. Indeed, there was power in it. With these words, barely a line, would the weight these men carried be shared amongst the villagers, laying its heavy rest on hearts and minds alike. Catherine stood behind the two men, laying a hand on each shoulder.

"It is as you say," she whispered, the gravity of it keeping them all quiet in their locution. She patted them each gently on the shoulder and then left the men to work out the details of their dire but necessary suggestion. She knew for some it would be too much and they would leave almost immediately. She too sought to send her children on the next coach to Yorkshire and awaited the availability of her husband for discourse on the matter she had now settled in her own heart. She would stay and help him shepherd his bewildered flock, but their lambs would be safe away from this village with its resident malevolence.

William made plans to hold an open air gathering the next day, so that he and Thomas could present their scheme to the citizens of the village. Those who were churchgoers had grown used to his sermonising on the rock in the Delph. But tomorrow he would urge all to come, those of conformist and non-conformist persuasion, the puritan and the more liberal, those with belief and those who professed to have none. All must come, for the disease was not selective. It would just as soon invade palace as priory, the rectory and the humble abode, the home of the poor and the wealthy. As such, it was a great leveller for those who still remained. The Bradshaws had left Bradshaw House at the very start; the terrified widow and her daughter, no doubt overcome with the terror of reports out of London, which they would have been better placed to receive, had abandoned Eyam in October when it had appeared George Viccars would not be the only victim. So too had the Sheldon family, retreating to their property in Hazleford, and the Furnesses, who were fortunate to own a farmhouse outside of Eyam and could wait out the curse of the pestilence there. For most though, they could not escape, pinned here by their commitment to farming or mining, and it was imperative he assemble as close to everyone as he could.

With a view to spreading word, he sent out Jane, Stanley and his manservant to deliver the particulars of the gathering at Cucklett Delph and he himself went from door to door. By the time he returned home hours later, Catherine opened the door to a truly exhausted incarnation of her husband. She guessed from his drawn expression that the villagers had tried to pull from him the particulars of his designs for their village and the constant rebuttal had taken its toll. Yet, she must still speak with him about the children, and it was with a pang of guilt she asked him to sit with her in the parlour. Taking his hand, she addressed him.

"I have given it some thought, and I am sorry for the way I let my sentiments take me somewhere far from the faith and hope I know you wish for me." He opened his mouth to protest but she continued. "It is not within me to abandon you as either husband or rector, and so I have determined to stay. Yet I must ask you that you write to your uncle this night and send on the letter ahead, for it is my determined wish to send the children on to him tomorrow and I will not be deterred from that. They must be safe William and, though it pains me to say it, we cannot guarantee that for them whilst they stay here at our side."

He took her hands in his, gazing into her eyes. He found the emotion he expected to see there, an agonising concoction of grief, fear, love and hope.

"Are you sure?" he asked her. Her answer came as a sob, through which she managed to croak the word 'yes'. He held her and let her cry. Being parted from her children was her deepest dread and yet she had found the strength to choose it. All disappointment he felt in the words she had previously expressed about leaving Eyam vanished in the presence of this brave and determined woman he held in his arms.

36

Catherine

21st June 1666

They had awoken early, Catherine pulling the children from their beds before the sun had even crept under the eaves of the rectory and into their windows. Both children were drowsy with sleep, remaining floppy of limb even after several attempts to raise them to standing. She had instructed Jane to make an obscenely early breakfast and Catherine had finally succeeded in dressing both George and Elizabeth by the time it was ready. They ate quietly, with Catherine suspecting they were suspicious that something out of the ordinary was unfolding. Glimpsing the trunks by the door, Elizabeth was the first to voice her enquiry.

"Why are the trunks packed mama? Must we make a journey?" she asked, her eyes imploring.

"I love travels!" declared George, jumping up and down on the spot, until his sister tugged on his arm so that they both stood still in front of her.

"You are to travel, yes," she told them, kneeling down in front of them. "Though your papa and I must stay here. The village is greatly threatened by the spread of plague. Father has great work to do as rector and he cannot do it by himself. We both want you to be safe, more than anything in the world, and so you must travel to your father's Uncle John in Yorkshire. You will not be gone for too long we hope, but father and I will be greatly encouraged in our work here if we know you are safe and waiting to return when all this has gone away."

Elizabeth collapsed into her, wrapping her arms around her neck. She did not cry but Catherine felt her breath coming rapidly, as if she fought to hold back a sob. George, knowing not what to do, joined them, and for a moment they stayed, a knot of human affection in the hall of the rectory. It was when Catherine heard the sound of the hooves of horses approaching on the road outside that she raised them from their affectionate embrace on the cold flag stones and opened the door. She called up to William, who descended quickly from his study, where he was re-working his notes for this morning's address. She was not convinced he had slept, his black coat crumpled and his short collar at an angle.

Together they took the children out towards the road. It was not yet full light and the road was still. No fires yet burned in the surrounding cottages and the chimneys were void of smoke. There was nobody thereabout to witness this heart-rending separation of Catherine from her children. William loaded the trunks into the coach, giving instructions to the driver. Unable to spare either Jane or William's manservant to make the journey with them for fear of the monumental tasks that lay before them if their fears for the village were correct, they must entrust their dearest children to the coachman.

William had sent his letter on ahead, passing it to one of the most trusted mail boys before dusk last night. He hoped it would have found passage on the night coach and arrive at his uncle's home in Yorkshire before the children did. Having instructed the coachman, Catherine saw him pat the man on the back, and his expression gave her reason to believe he found the man to be trustworthy and of honest regard.

She could not bear a long farewell, so in saying goodbye she drew them to her side, bent down to smell their hair and plant a simple kiss atop each crown and brought them close to her with one final squeeze. Their little arms circled her waist and she willed herself to remember this moment, the feel of their limbs tight about her and the warmth of their bodies so close to her heart. She helped them up into the coach as William held open the door. His goodbye was a simple kiss to the cheek of each child, to intreat them that they be good for their great uncle and to echo Catherine's words that they would not be gone long and would be back with them in Eyam soon.

Elizabeth did her best to be brave but Catherine could see her daughter's bottom lip begin to tremble. It was all she could do to stop herself from reaching out, opening the coach door and pulling her out again. George hid has apprehension with silly faces designed to make her laugh and she did not resist, offering him a faint, feigned chuckle. As the coachman raised the reins and brought them down swiftly on the horses' backs and the hooves began their clip-clopping, Catherine looked at her children as the coach pulled away. Something painful whispered to her that she would not see them again. It was as a barb to the soft-flesh of her tender heart and she longed to tear it out, keeping the smile on her face until the coach rounded the corner and she could no longer see them. Only then did she collapse into William's arms and he led her back into the house. The people would be assembled in less than an hour and they had little time to pull themselves together and get to the Delph.

William looked out at the swarm of people that gathered in the Delph below him. Though this was by far the safer option than the church, he was still unsettled by the gathering of families so close together, imagining plague seeds crossing between them malevolently. They did their best to stay apart from their neighbours as they had been instructed, and he recognised in their faces and the way their eyes darted about that they felt the same trepidation he did. Since the start of the month, they had kept out of each other's homes. The movement on the street was near non-existent, with those from surrounding villages making circuitous routes, taking them miles out of their way, to avoid Eyam and the risk of infection altogether. Those who lived on the outskirts of the village, up at Riley and out at Shepherd's Flatts, had made the journey to join with the village they recognised as home despite the distance. He could see them there; Mortens and Kemps, Talbots and Hancocks.

As he stood waiting for stragglers to arrive, he was reminded of the Lord's sermon on the mount. How Jesus had looked out at those who gathered, and moved by their bewilderment as lost and scattered sheep, he had instructed them on the blessings that were theirs, despite the many challenges they faced. Blessed were the poor in spirit, the meek, they that mourn, they that hunger and thirst for righteousness, the merciful and the pure in spirit, the peacemakers and the persecuted. As he looked out, he could see them all gathered here and it seemed fitting that he should use the words of Christ, the One who had proven Himself to be the True Shepherd, to convince them that their duty, as Christians, as men and women, as citizens of not only the village but the nation, was to commit themselves to sacrifice for the good of others.

As he looked at them, picking out faces he knew would nod along immediately and faces he knew would scowl and shake their heads or perhaps even cry out in opposition, he felt a hand on his shoulder and turned from the crowd to see Thomas Stanley standing next to him. All sense of rivalry was gone from between them and he had come to greatly revere and appreciate this older, wiser man, without whose support he could barely hope to succeed in what he had planned.

"Thomas," he said. Returning the gesture, with a hand on the other man's shoulder. They stood for a few moments, simply looking at the masses, a visual representation of the enormity of their task and the living, breathing reality of their request. Yet no matter how many there were before them, the earth around Eyam was testament to the many who were already gone and the earth made itself ready for those the great many they both feared would follow. In London, one sixth of the capital's population were believed to have fallen fowl of plague. Already they had lost a comparative amount and the pestilence showed no signs of abating, now it had found a sure foothold during the course of this month.

By some mystery, the crowd began to hush as William and Stanley prepared to speak. A wind rushed through the crowd and he felt it find its way round his body, in a way reminiscent of the Holy Spirit showing up with great insistence in the upper room. Before him, his disciples cowered and looked up at him, no emboldening flames of fire on their heads, just the frightened yet desperate expressions of those who know they must face their own doom. He took a deep breath, catching Catherine's eye where she was waiting just beneath him at the foot of the rock he had come to embrace in these last few months as a pulpit.

Gazing up at her husband, Catherine felt the force of the crowd behind her, yet nobody touched her. She felt the hair on the back of her neck begin to rise, encouraged by the cool breeze that ran past her. *If the people would not listen, what then?* If they left in great swathes, taking the plague out into Derbyshire, trading it with their wares at the market in Bakewell or passing it with affectionate embraces with their relatives in Stoney Middleton, what then? Would the county survive such widespread devastation. As she heard her husband begin speaking she held her breath.

"Thank you, my fellow villagers, for assembling here this morning," William called out into the green amphitheatre, the crowd silent in the face of his opening words. They looked up at him almost quizzical in their expressions, like anxious children trying to figure out what their punishment might be. He remembered the times in the Gospel where Jesus looked out at the crowds and was moved with compassion for them. As William gazed down over his flock, he felt the magnitude of what he was about to impress upon them and the weight of it moved him. Was he about to manipulate scripture to get this flock to remain in the sheep pen? The gratitude he felt for Stanley as his fellow shepherd, standing to the side and slightly behind him, was immense.

"As you know, our hopes at having escaped the pestilence have been crushed. The few deaths we saw in spring gave us false hope and now as summer arrives and the days increase in warmth, we must face the hard reality that our village has not been released from the grip of this evil foe. I stand here this morning to tell you that since the month opened, sixteen souls have been taken, more than March, April and May all combined." He saw their faces absorb the shock, finding its way into worried brows and open mouths. There was the faint whisper of a collective gasp and it hung on the wind for a moment before being carried away. He continued.

"We must assume this is the beginning of a wave of plague that will only grow as summer reaches its peak, and it is for this reason that Reverend Stanley and I," he said, gesturing to the man to the side of him, who took a small step forwards, "believe we must take measures to prevent the spread of the pestilence into the surrounding villages and out into Derbyshire and potentially wider into the country. Our local neighbours avoid our village, travelling longer routes to bypass Eyam. It is unlikely we will receive visitation from outside that will spread the disease. So, I call upon you all to ensure their safety by remaining within the confines of the village. Many have already left, including the family of the manor house who would ordinarily take a civic lead during such times. In the absence of the Bradshaws, Reverend Stanley and I are assuming leadership and it is after a great deal of consideration that we are instating a Cordon Sanitaire."

The villagers began to look at each other then, the reality of his statement falling upon them. He saw wives shuffle closer to husbands, instinctively pulling children closer to themselves. Those who had already lost children and spouses, looked at bewildered families with a sense of sorrow. Andrew Merrill, standing so far towards the back that he was almost out of the Delph completely, stooped down to pick up the chicken that had accompanied him from his hut on the hill. Catherine had told him that she had been told by Anne, Humphrey's wife, that Andrew was considering returning to his house in the village when May claimed only two souls, but his decision to tarry had kept him safely closeted away on the hill and not seen him return as the death toll once again increased. This was the closest he had been to the other villagers in months; his caution keeping him separated from others.

"The quarantine line will reach to the edge of the village. You will not be permitted to pass the well in the north or the boundary stone beyond the Lydgate. Keep to the village limits at Townhead and do not venture beyond the Delph."

"What about food?" somebody called out. "Provisions? We will die by starvation sooner than the pestilence!" The contributor's words were met with ayes and affirmations from those who were not too stunned to speak.

"I have written to the Earl of Devonshire. He has agreed to ensure we have provisions in exchange for our vow to stay within the confines of the village. You will be able to request specific provisions and payment must be left within holes in the boundary stone filled with vinegar, which Humphrey Merrill insists will kill any plague seeds, or within the rushing water of the well on the outskirts of the northern wood, where plague seeds will be cleansed by water. The stone troughs of The Cliffe, between here and Stoney Middleton, can also be used for the delivering and removing of goods. The Earl of Devonshire has promised to keep us well-supplied with bread and other essentials."

'We will die!" someone called out, a feeble voice that wavered with emotion and yet was fortified with the agreement of so many. He looked at their ashen faces. Were they soldiers, such an undertaking would be a feat of discipline. Yet these were frightened men and women, many of whom had already lost so much and not troops obligated by duty. He glimpsed Elizabeth Syddall in the crowd, clinging onto John Daniel, with Joseph sat unnervingly still at her feet. So many had turned up for the church service that preceded this meeting, their troubled souls searching for solace in the scriptures. He must use it now to insist on their adherence to his plan. He went to speak but faltered. In the seconds where his voice failed him, Reverend Stanley found his.

"Yes," he called out to them. "There is a chance many more will die. We are asking a great deal of courage and commitment from you. William and I are agreed in the necessity of this or never would we impose such a thing upon you all, the very people we have committed to lead and protect. Yet the love of Christ compels us to think beyond ourselves. We have searched the scriptures on your behalf and we believe this is what we must do." He reached out and lay a gentle hand on William's shoulder and the younger man felt his nerve again in the company of this brother made for adversity.

"Greater love hath no man than this," he declared, "than to lay down his life for his friends." He let the words find their target, watching each person take a breath as they struggled with the enormity of the task laid before them. "It is for us to save Stoney Middleton, for us to save Tideswell, and Bakewell, and every other village that lies between us and the next county. It is for us to save Derbyshire, and we do it by choosing the path that puts us in greater peril but keeps multitudes safe. Without our…" he paused slightly, not wishing to use the word 'sacrifice', "…offering of ourselves in this way, this disease would carry tens of thousands to the grave as it has in London. We were set on this path the day George Viccars received the tainted cloth from the capital and we have walked it as best we could, and now we must put up our barriers and brave what future may come to us. Yes, many of us may die, and we may watch those we love die. I see before me the eyes of those who have already seen their loved ones depart this life. It is a task of faith and immense courage I lay upon you, and I urge you to carry it with the grace and mercy that comes only from our Lord."

He expected another voice to call out, but there was silence as the many inhabitants of Eyam pondered their fate and the implications of following the plan William and Thomas had laid out for them. Catherine felt the silent prayers being said by those all around her. She sensed the imploring and pleading of hearts to her right and to her left. She joined them, entreating God earnestly to give them the strength they would need to follow her husband's plan.

As he began to speak again of the new duties of the watch to ensure nobody would leave or enter and the particulars for requesting specific items to be left at the village boundaries, her thoughts went to her children, already safely half way to Yorkshire, and she felt the pang of shame that many parents here would carry the brunt of the cordon sanitaire more than she would, being faced with having their children locked inside a village of death for however long God deemed for them to wrestle with this foe. She dreaded the fury of the villagers when they discovered Elizabeth and George were gone. They would be rightly angry and she could say nothing in her defence. She had acted with the unapologetic selfish impulses of a mother and must accept the criticism of her actions when they came.

When William and Thomas concluded the meeting with prayers for fortitude and courage, the people of the village began to shuffle away. Despite the import of what they had just heard their assent had been given in silence. No further contentions were heard and William and Reverend Stanley praised their gathered congregation for their bravery. There were gathered there those who very rarely ventured to church and William had expected a challenge that never came. The conviction to spare life existed across the bounds of conformist, non-conformist and those who claimed neither affiliation. They were united in their desire to save and the mood, whilst sombre, was one of a united village, stoic and moving back towards their separate homes to assess what the cordon sanitaire meant for each family.

William climbed down from his position on the rock pulpit and took Catherine's hand and she gripped it tightly as they walked back towards the rectory. Jane had gone ahead of them to ensure there would be some food for William, who was exhausted and weakened by the gravity of his announcement. Catherine herself was slow and steady, tired out by the early start and the continued weakening the consumption placed upon her. The silence on entering the rectory was deafening. No noise of children making mischief, or bickering or whooping or constantly asking for something. Though often their constant chatter gave her a headache and wore her out, there was nothing in the world she would have rather heard as she entered the house. She sent love out over the hills to her children, hoping it would carry beyond the cordon sanitaire, out over the protected villages that surrounded Eyam and up onto the moors of Yorkshire where they would soon arrive into perfect safety.

37

Elizabeth

21st June 1666

The walk back from Cucklett Delph had been conducted in near silence. Of the children, only William had been permitted to attend along with Elizabeth and John to hear what the reverends Mompesson and Stanley would have to say to the villagers gathered beneath the rocky pulpit. Elizabeth had listened wide-eyed to the plan to impose a cordon sanitaire, to keep the village shut off from the rest of the county and the villagers themselves contained within. She couldn't help but feel like a prisoner, though she had no trouble understanding the logic or reasons behind such a plan, being a very reasonable and logical sort of woman.

"So, we can't leave and nobody can come in?" William asked John as they climbed the incline up towards Riley. Elizabeth detected some concern in her son's eyes and the slightest wobble in his voice, which had grown otherwise deep and manly in the past few years.

"That's about the size of it. Sounds like the Lord of Chatsworth is willing to be very generous in order to keep the plague from reaching his own doorstep," John replied.

'We'll be just fine up here on the hillside," Elizabeth said, seeking to reassure William and realising she was also hoping to soothe herself. Making the problem so utterly the responsibility of the village and its inhabitants to contain had made it somehow seem more dangerous. Sixteen people had died so far this month and there was every indication that as the summer heated up that number would grow into something monstrous. The vicars were right to be proactive and what they proposed made sense but she felt trapped, suddenly hemmed in by the choices of two men.

"Of course, we will be fine," John concurred, placing his arm around his son's shoulders. "It might be best if we keep to ourselves mind, not so many visits with the Talbots. I'll talk to Richard," he said, turning his attention to Elizabeth. She nodded her assent.

Later when all the children were safely tucked up in bed, she lay on the mattress next to John, her elbow bent so her face rested on her palm and speaking in a whisper so as not to wake Oner, Elizabeth shared some of her concern with her husband.

"They expect an onslaught, don't they?" she murmured. Even from down in the Delph she had seen the grave concern in the eyes of the two men orating above her. June was already laying claim to more lives than the first half of the year combined if the numbers that filtered up to Riley were to be believed.

"Yes," John said. "I think they do. The Mompessons will be much freer to deal with it now they only have themselves to worry about."

"What do you mean?" Elizabeth asked, pushing herself up so that she was sitting on the bed facing John.

"Well, it seems they sent their children away. That's what John Torre told me at the assembly this morning anyway. Gone to Yorkshire I think, to his uncle," he added.

Elizabeth was incredulous. She stood up. Her hands found their way to her hips and she stared at John in disbelief.

"They sent their children to safety but here we are now locked into a village with our children unable to leave or for us to send them away to safety?" she cried, forgetting to keep her voice low enough to prevent disturbing Oner. She whimpered in her sleep and Elizabeth saw her daughter turn over but thankfully she did not wake. She lowered her voice back to a whisper.

"This is outrageous!" She could hear the anger in her own voice even though it was hushed. She was angry at them, at William and Catherine, but she was cross with herself too for having not even considered it. She thought of their oldest son Joseph in Sheffield where he was an apprentice. Perhaps she could have sent the children there? At least Oner and John and perhaps Elizabeth too. But now it was too late. The fate of her children now rested on her and John to keep their family safe in what was now a sealed plague village.

John got up and made his way towards her. He wrapped his arms around her and she let herself be swallowed up in the strength of his embrace. Being surrounded by John's muscular hold felt safe compared with the suffocating containment of the cordon sanitaire. She let him stroke her hair and undo her apron. His fingers worked easily to take off her clothes, each layer barely an obstacle to him. She wanted him to touch her, to hold her.

The sense of any control over what happened in the village was lost and she mirrored it in her own abandon as he took her beneath him and she found herself opening to him quite desperately. The rush of it swept her frantic thoughts away and she let herself be swallowed up by the love of this man, the heat of him and the insistent way in which his body wanted hers. They found each other in low moans and resolute touch and for a moment she forgot about Oner sleeping, forgot about the sanctuary of Sheffield lost to her and forgot about the village beneath them going to sleep in fretful apprehension tonight.

38

Catherine

5th July 1666

Catherine was still shaken from an incident in the village, even days later. She chastised herself for letting it get to her, for she had expected it and should have been prepared. Whilst leaving Humphrey Merrill's shop she had encountered one of the women from Riley, Elizabeth Hancock. The families up at Riley barely ventured into the main village these days, keeping their distance up on the hill, and no one could blame them. Some necessity must have driven Elizabeth into the village that day and when she saw Catherine she did not return Catherine's warm smile but instead her eyes narrowed and she said as she passed, *making sure your own children are safe, you should be ashamed to think only of them and not of any other young ones here.* She had gone on her way without turning and Catherine had stood for a good many moments in the street as if rooted to the spot after watching her leave the shop. She knew Elizabeth Hancock was not a hard woman. She was just a mother, scared for her children.

Catherine knew the Hancocks had six children up at Riley Farm, three times the number of young souls she had been concerned about. As a mother it was only natural

Elizabeth envy her some way of keeping them safe. But what troubled her was not the anger in Elizabeth's face but the genuine fear in her eyes, that something would befall her babies and that no escape from this village had presented itself to her. It was the look of a trapped animal. Catherine could not shake that look. She recognised it for she had seen it in the looking glass, her own eyes staring back at her. She beseeched God to forgive her the one sin of selfishness she had taken in order to keep Elizabeth and George safe. She had exercised her privilege as rector's wife and it caused pain for those who could not do the same, and she could not undo what she had chosen, though she knew in her heart she would choose it again just the same.

When she looked in the eyes of the men and women all around her, she tried to ignore the changes she saw in their faces, or the way their actions unwittingly displayed their apprehension. Despite their terror they somehow continued, each one doing the daily chores and tasks they needed to, attending to the necessities of life going on, not knowing for how long life would linger for them or those they loved. The threat of the pestilence turning up behind their doors was ever-present and their inability to see it or trace it created a general wariness and dis-ease despite the appearance of business as usual. They waited to see how this race through the summer would end. What would await them at the start of Autumn? Another chance of hope or more distress?

Catherine could see that the people doing what the people knew how to do stopped the panic from being overwhelming. When people could still see men in yards chopping wood and women airing linen they were heartened. Though the air was frequently filled with the groans of those who suffered, leaking out from the cracks in closed doors meant to confine their misery, there was the feeble hope that life would, at least the possibility that it *could*, return to what was ordinary one day. They were not cowards and neither were they heroes, they were just people doing what they knew how to do and clinging on like those caught in a current holding fast to the riverbank. How many of them would be swept away still remained to be seen.

Amongst the scenes of habitual village life there were the scenes that chilled Catherine's heart. Behind the Miners Ale House graves had begun to appear. Yesterday morning she had climbed through the woods to the well on the moor, taking payment to leave in the water and a list of provisions, a system set up by William with the Earl at Chatsworth, which had so far been working efficiently for both basic provisions of bread, cheese and meat and also to obtain some specific items. She had appealed for certain herbs at Merrill's request. As she returned passing the public house she saw

Marshall Howe digging a grave, with Mary Darby weeping at his side. The young woman's beautiful face was contorted in the agony of losing her father. They were so frequently seen walking together in this part of town, traversing The Square arm in arm. Now he had gone somewhere she could not accompany him. Catherine had hurried past, reluctant to add her own sadness to the young woman's grief.

Days in the rectory were long and quiet without the children present to engage her. Her rounds delivering Merrill's remedies took most of the afternoon, and she had taken to holding up a nosegay to her nose, knocking the door and leaving the muslin bundles on the doorstep whilst she stepped back. She would enquire as to who was well and who sickened and be sure to tell William, for he and Thomas Stanley were doing their best to stay abreast of how the plague was gripping their village. They could see the way it clustered, as if it were passed by some silent pest through the very walls from cottage to cottage. She did not see William for most of the days and he often returned exhausted after dark, having performed sacramental rites on the dead and dying and witnessing wills for those who knew their time on earth was up. He did not speak of the horrors of what he saw and heard and she did not ask.

Catherine was sat at the kitchen table with her pestle and mortar and some of the herbs from her garden when

William returned to the rectory. She could see in his eyes there was more doom to be shared.

"What is it?" she asked him, taking off his coat and slipping it down his arms before seating him in the chair by the fire. He ran his hands through his hair and exhaled slowly before telling her.

"Two things," he said in reply. "It has arrived at Riley..."

"Not the Hancocks?" she cut across him, Elizabeth's eyes coming into her mind.

"No, not the Hancocks. The Talbots, their neighbours" he said. The Talbots were in the farmhouse adjacent to the Hancock Farm at Riley. "They have lost their oldest daughter, Bridget, and a younger daughter, Mary, and it is confirmed as plague. I had thought they would be safe up there on the hill, barely coming into the village except for needed supplies. But it thwarts our attempts to resist it at every turn. There is an invisible map traced on Eyam by this pestilence and none of us can see it. Only the disease itself knows its routes and where it will strike next. I see the people grow ever fearful with the unknowing.

"So, the two things are Bridget and Mary?" Catherine said, making the sign of the cross as she whispered a prayer for the souls of the two young women.

"Sadly no," William continued. "I have just learned of the death of John Daniel." He wiped his brow with his handkerchief as he spoke.

"Elizabeth Syddall's new husband?" Catherine asked. "But he can't be dead! She only just married him. How can she be made a widow again so soon? Oh William, I really must go to her. The poor woman!" she said as she stood up.

"You cannot," he said, taking her hands in his. "She has taken Joseph and fled to the huts in the Delph to be with relatives there. I have instruction from her on what should happen if…if anything happens to her and the boy is left."

"What will we do if there are babies left William? Young children without parents?" she questioned him. The thought of little ones left all alone caused a lump to swell in her throat. If their parents died without anyone knowing what would a young child do?

"You must not let this idea trouble you. Thomas and I are in contact with as many households as our days permit and we have expressed our request that each household is mindful of the situation for their neighbours, so if whole families sicken, we will be aware of potential orphans and can act accordingly. It does you no good my dear wife to imagine always the worst. We must hold onto what hope we have, dig around for optimism and always remember our faith is not in flesh and blood but in He who created us." He said.

The question that kept a silent vigil in Catherine's head rattled once more inside her. *Where was God now?* She still believed in Him with all of her heart but never had she felt more connection with the cry of her saviour on Calvary: *My God, my God, why have you forsaken me?* She told William everything, but this she would not utter.

39

Elizabeth
7th July 1666

Elizabeth had clung to the idea that they could be safe up at Riley and perhaps if they were the only farmhouse up here they would have been. But a few days back she was dismayed to find Catharine Talbot rapping on their door in the early hours of the morning in hysterics over their eldest daughter, Bridget.

"What is it?" Elizabeth asked, though the sudden dropping feeling in her stomach told her she already knew what the matter would be. She pulled John's old coat around her nightgown in the cool morning air. Light was beginning to creep in at the edges of the darkness of the sky like a sable cloak, hemmed with gold and dawn was not far off.

"It's Bridget!" Catharine cried into the near darkness. "She's feverish and delirious with it, I think I can see the swellings. They are in her neck and armpits. I think she has it!" She sobbed and Elizabeth reached out a hand and placed it on her shoulder before withdrawing it just as hastily as she had placed it there.

"How would she have got it?" Elizabeth enquired. "Was she recently in the village?"

"Yes," Catharine sobbed. "She paid a visit to Elizabeth Heald. Their daughter Emmott died and Bridget took them some eggs. Elizabeth sickened herself and died on the first day of July and now Bridget is sick."

"Where have you got her?" Elizabeth asked. "You should try to keep her separate to everyone else. What about the barn? You could nurse her there easily but away from the others." Elizabeth suggested. Catharine nodded and Elizabeth pulled the door to behind her.

"I will help you set up a bed. Then you and Richard can bring Bridget out," Elizabeth said. Catharine's breathing stopped coming in big gasps as she stopped crying, emboldened and focused by her friend's ability to offer solutions and not simply match her panic.

"Thank you, Elizabeth," she whispered. It had taken them twenty minutes to set up a bed for Bridget, using a straw filled mattress on top of a wooden pallet. Elizabeth made sure there was water in a bowl and plenty of rags for soaking to cool Bridget's fever. All the courage Elizabeth felt in taking charge of the situation drained away as she saw them bringing Bridget out.

The young woman was draped across their shoulders, barely able to walk. Her skin was red and glistening with the sheen of sweat. Even from a distance Elizabeth could see the way Bridget's neck looked swollen and beginning to darken.

It was a horrifying sight and Elizabeth had soon offered them her condolences and promised to go down into the village at first light to procure them remedies from Humphrey Merrill, before she made a hasty retreat.

She woke John up at once, though there were still several hours left for sleeping until morning. He was sleepy and a little gruff at being woken so early.

"What is it?" he asked.

"They have it. They have it John. The Talbots," she said. He didn't respond for a moment, rubbing his eyes whilst the meaning of her words found traction in his newly-wakened brain.

"The plague? They have the plague?" he said, sitting up. "Who? Who has it?"

"Bridget," she replied. "She visited the Healds. They are all dead now except for Robert Heald," Elizabeth said. Robert was the sole survivor of his family. They were all gone except for him. Elizabeth thought of him sitting all alone in that house that was once another home alive with the vibrancy of life. No longer father. No longer husband. *How could he endure it? How could anyone bear being the only one left?*

"Is anyone else sick?" John had asked. She could tell he was concerned but did not want to worry her further by giving full vent to it.

"No, not yet. Just Bridget. I got them to move her to the barn. But she looks after the little ones John," Elizabeth said.

"Do not make such great leaps just yet. You gave them good counsel advising they move her into the barn," he said, praising his wife and placing his hand over hers.

"I have promised to go into the village at first light to get remedies from Merrill. I will not go for long. Just to the apothecary and back. Oh John! I had hoped we would escape up here," she said, sitting down next to him, her head hanging low with the weight of seeming defeat.

"We still may," John replied, trying to bring some optimism to his voice. "We still may. We can stay away," he said, and Elizabeth wanted to believe him.

When dawn found its way into the windows of the Hancock's farmhouse, Elizabeth set off on foot towards the village. She noted how everything looked the same even though it now felt all their lives were built upon fragile shifting sands and not the rocky limestone ledge the village rested upon. She had heard tales of what lay beneath them from the lead miners; huge caverns full of water. She imagined herself falling into one, falling, falling, drowning. Was it much different, what was happening now? The devil had come to Riley. She tried not to imagine what change even these few hours had wrought upon Bridget. Her conversations with fellow villagers had educated her in the progress of the disease and it was neither tardy nor pleasant.

It was here outside Merrill's shop she had seen Catherine Mompesson on the street. Elizabeth was not given to fury but the sight of the vicar's wife, knowing her children were safely shielded away in Yorkshire, had incensed her. She couldn't help but voice her anger. The younger woman had looked confounded and gave no utterance in return due to her shock, and afterwards Elizabeth had felt a pang of remorse, though not enough to approach the rectory and offer an apology.

Now Elizabeth entered the room Humphrey Merrill used to mix and sell his herbal concoctions and tinctures. The air was rich with the smell of herbs and spices and Elizabeth breathed it in deeply. Humphrey was occupied and barely looked up from his work. Beside him, his wife Anne poured liquid from the mixtures pooled in mortars, funnelling them into glass vials. When Elizabeth asked about their welfare they told her they were busier than ever but with Catherine Mompesson helping with delivery they could just about cope. Perhaps Elizabeth had been too hard on the woman? The thought was dissipated by the memory of her children up the hill, now so uncomfortably close to the contagion.

Anne talked more than Humphrey and while he made the remedies Elizabeth had come to secure for the Talbots, she told Elizabeth of the carnage the disease was wreaking in the village.

"Just this morning we had news that John Daniel has died," Anne said.

"John Daniel?" Elizabeth enquired, unsure as to the man this name belonged to.

"Aye, John that married Elizabeth Syddall after she was widowed last October. They have only been married since April and now she is twice a widow in less than a year!" she added. Elizabeth could not imagine being once a widow, let alone twice. She knew of the Syddalls and their fate from a conversation she had had in the spring with Mary Cooper who lived opposite Bagshaw House, the Syddall's residence.

"What of the boy?" Elizabeth asked. She was aware they had a little boy of a similar age to Oner and that until April only he and their daughter Emmott had survived of their seven children. When Emmott died, the little boy was left alone with his mother and her new husband, who it now appeared was also gone.

"Joseph? He is well," Anne said. "She has taken the boy and fled to the huts at the Cussy Dell. Perhaps to be closer to where Marshall Howe laid Emmott, God rest her soul. I believe Elizabeth has family staying in the huts so she is not alone and I hope the boy will be well cared for."

Elizabeth nodded. "And what of Riley?" Anne asked, concern crossing her face. "I fear you are not down here requesting all this on a trifle errand."

Elizabeth shook her head. "The pestilence has found its way to Riley. Bridget Talbot sickens. She is feverish and has the tell-tale swellings. I had her moved to the barn to try to keep the infection away from the others but I do not know how successful that will be. John and I are worried. We are but a few yards from the Talbot farmhouse," Elizabeth said. Anne smiled a crooked smile and there was pity in her eyes.

When Elizabeth returned with the remedies, John met her as she came up the hill.

"It is too late for Bridget," he said. The words registered in Elizabeth's brain with a jolt. *Too late?* But it had been mere hours since she had seen Bridget stagger out towards the barn between her father and step-mother.

"But these may help Mary," he said.

"Mary is sick too?" Elizabeth replied.

"Yes," John replied, "and based on how quickly Bridget was taken, Richard does not expect her to see tomorrow. They did not know it but Bridget took Mary with her when she went to the Heald's." Elizabeth struggled with the notion that by nightfall the Talbots would likely be down two daughters. Suddenly, the urge to get back to her own children was irresistible. She looked in earnest apprehension towards the farmhouse.

"I will take these," John said, lifting the basket from Elizabeth's arm. "The children were worried when they awoke to find you not in the kitchen. Go and settle them and I will deliver these and return."

Now, it had been two days since Bridget and Mary had died and they had seen Richard digging two graves beside the house and Catharine weeping over them. Nobody else sickened in the Talbot household and Elizabeth sat at the table in her kitchen taking stock of the decisions that lay ahead. The visits she made to the village were not as frequent since May and they had survived on what little income they got from the smithy, but now with provisions running low and traffic to the blacksmith's workshop slowing down again with each new day that passed with a climbing death toll, she would almost certainly need to sell eggs and butter or trade them for the goods they needed. She would do it. No need for anyone else in the family to go from the limits of the farmhouse grounds. They would stay here. She would create a fortress. Only she would leave it. They would stay and they would be safe.

Her thoughts were interrupted by a knock at the door. It was Catharine. Little Anne was sick.

40

Elizabeth

31st July 1666

Once plague had found its way into the Talbot farmhouse it appeared there was no way of stopping it. During the month Elizabeth and John had done their best to support their ailing neighbours as one by one they were taken into the arms of death by the disease. Anne died very quickly, held in the arms of her mother as she sobbed over her little girl. Then there came a cruel ten day gap in which Richard and Catharine bravely counted their losses, assembling crude crosses and laying hand-fashioned wreaths of wildflowers on the mounds of earth that covered the bodies of Bridget, Mary and Anne; three roses of Riley buried in the dirt. They had buried them themselves, preferring not to bring the services of Marshall Howe up onto the hill.

Then, nine days after Anne died, Jane fell sick with fever. The red marks bloomed across her chest by evening and when Catharine woke from the exhausted sleep she had fallen into without intention, she found her daughter cold and staring, no longer struggling with fever or wrestling death for her meagre seven years on the earth. Not only did Catharine wake to shock, she also woke to fever herself, and though

Richard cared for her tenderly, she fast became his second wife to leave him a widow.

A week later Robert died and then Richard himself, followed by Joan and Ruth together the next day, so that as July grew to a close there was only Jonathan left at the Talbot farmstead. John and Elizabeth helped the young man as best they could and it was on a clear morning towards the end of the month a tearful Jonathan approached the Hancock farmhouse with a bundle of what Elizabeth believed were rags in his arms. It was not rags. Jonathan carried a baby girl of three or four months old. Elizabeth looked at him standing there with this mewling bundle, incredulous as to where the baby had come from and through his tears, Jonathan explained how she was the daughter of his older brother Robert and his wife Ruth who lived in the village and had both been taken by the disease within days of each other. He had been driven by loneliness to seek them at the farmhouse, hoping to find a welcome with his own kin, but instead he had found them both dead and the little girl whimpering in hunger. Just a teenage boy left alone, he did not know how to look after her by himself and his only surviving brother, George, was not in the village, having found work elsewhere, and could not return now to help him even if he had the mind to come back.

Elizabeth felt her heart pound with a mixture of fear and pity. Her hand went up to her forehead and back as the decisions flew within her mind like birds scattered by the sudden introduction of a boisterous hound. A babe from a plague house was not a wise addition to their household but she could not ignore the cries of the child nor the tears of the overwhelmed fifteen year old boy who stood in front of her. In a moment of clarity, it came to her; she would take the infant to Richard's mother, Bridget, who was living in the village. She was an older woman, past her sixtieth year, but still capable of caring for a single child. Elizabeth had taken the baby from Jonathan's arms and given her some milk sucked from sodden rags. The child quietened into a peaceful sleep and while she slumbered Elizabeth made John aware of what had happened and what she planned to do about it. He could see how the baby moved her and the conflict it gave her when faced with keeping her own children safe.

"I think your decision is a wise one Elizabeth. If Bridget cannot take care of the child, she can seek the help of the Mompessons," he said, and held her tenderly, looking into her eyes as he spoke.

"There is still the question of what to do about Jonathan," she whispered, for it was early and none of their children were yet making a sound from the rooms in which they slept.

"Yes, I do feel for that boy alone in the farmhouse. It must feel so oppressively silent after all his years of growing up in that house," he replied, shaking his head and sitting down at the kitchen table. "I will give that some thought myself."

Elizabeth set off for the village, as ready as she could be to burden the girl's great grandmother with the news of the fate of her family and the care of the infant. As she walked, the baby snoozing soundly on her shoulder, Elizabeth contemplated keeping her. But the idea would not take root. Instead it presented her with all the responsibility she already had in keeping her own six children safely away from the peril that now strayed so close to them. If the elderly Bridget would not take the baby, named Catharine after her grandmother, Elizabeth would take the baby to the rectory and impress upon the vicar's wife the need to find suitable care for her. Catherine Mompesson had already found a home for the orphaned daughter of the Banes family in the village.

When it came to it though, Bridget had welcomed Elizabeth into her modest cottage and she had taken in the child, weary and worried but only too happy to know she had a surviving family member. After the old woman had stopped her tears over the loss of her son and all but one of his family up on the hill, she took little Catharine into her arms and pressed her little face to her own, still wet from her grief. Elizabeth watched the scene in silence, feeling her soul reach towards God in hope of the survival of this little duo of Talbot women.

Fate was cruel and it had declared most painfully that it was not the end of the Talbot reaping though. Yesterday, Elizabeth sat with Jonathan as he took his last breaths. He had taken ill just days after bringing her from the home of his dead brother and sister-in-law. She could still see the terror in his eyes as he faced his own death without his family, wild with having been left 'til last and facing the unknown without them. It terrified Elizabeth to sit with him while he moaned and writhed in pain. To sit so close to death, to touch it, to almost *invite* it with proximity. She was terrified for her own family but what could she do? How could she leave a young boy, just fifteen and so like William, to die alone? Could a maternal heart be so easily stopped just because it was not your own flesh and blood in agony before you? When it came to it, pity had triumphed over terror and compassion reached out and did what fear had tried not to.

"I'm scared," he had said, his words being forced out with difficulty through the thickening at his neck and the parching of his tongue through fever. She had wanted to hold him close then, but even in the pang of her pity she knew doing so would put her own family in even more danger if she carried plague seeds back to them. Instead, she sat at the distance she could best maintain to wipe his brow and reassure him he was not alone.

"Do not be," she said, summoning a sureness to her voice which she did not feel. "You go to your family, and if the rector be right, a much better and kinder place than here," she whispered, and touched his arm ever so quickly and gently. His skin burned beneath her fingers. He did not linger many more hours after that and she was grateful. When he passed she leant over and tenderly closed his eyelids so that the eyeballs no longer stared.

John had buried him the next day. He wrapped his body in an old sheet and laid him in the ground. She had told him about Marshall Howe's method of tying a rope around the neck or feet but she could see in his face that he could not do it. He had the heart of a father and he could not drag out Richard's son at the end of a rope any more than he could drag out his own. Afterwards, they stood around all the Talbot graves to pay their respects. If the people in the village across the dale could look out at that moment they would see all the Hancocks assembled, heads bowed in silent farewell to their neighbours at Riley.

41

Elizabeth

2nd August 1666

The loss of the Talbots created a silence up at Riley that Elizabeth had not known during all her time living up here on the hill overlooking the village of Eyam. Always there had been a hum from the two farmhouses but now theirs was silent and her own was engaged in a hushed vigil as they went about their daily chores with all the noise of monks in a monastery. When they looked at each other she could see they were afraid. They stopped looking each other fully in the eye, as if to glimpse the full nature of the fear in the eyes of the other would make it too horribly real.

The latest news from the village was that Alexander Hadfield, the tailor, was sick. Elizabeth could barely believe that Mary Cooper would face another loss and there was likely to be a strange symmetry with Bagshaw House that stood across the street and was home to the twice-widowed Elizabeth Syddall before her grief at the loss of her second husband led her to flee to her family in the huts in the Dell. Elizabeth liked the tailor. He had been kind with the giving of his scraps of damask. In some small way the gift of the sumptuous fabric undid a microscopic proportion of the damage done when the plague seeds had arrived from London in the folds of damp material.

"It will take literally anybody won't it?" she said to John. "It has even stolen up to Shepherd's Flatts. Robert Kemp has died and the Mortens are all overcome with the terror of it. Matthew Morten's wife is ready to give birth. Oh, I cannot imagine it John!" and she ran her hands over her flat stomach, never being more grateful for it being empty of child.

Their conversation was interrupted by the sound of sobbing. She had told him she would be right back. She had followed the sounds of the sobs into the room that the younger children shared and found Elizabeth and John lying together on the pallet bed, her doll between them. As soon as she looked at them she knew. Just this morning they were out on the grass laughing and rolling around in between the chores she had set them. Now they both looked hot and sweaty, their bodies still and energy-less, except for the whimpering sobs coming from both their mouths.

"We don't feel well Mama," John said. "Lizzie is all hot," he added and touched his sister's red face. Elizabeth tried to move away from his touch. She strained her head to one side and Elizabeth could see the beginnings of a thickening. She rushed to them, reaching out her hand to touch both their foreheads at once, both feverish under her cool palms. She lifted up John's shirt and there was no red blooming but the gesture repeated on little Elizabeth showed a posy of red wheels and rings and a large swelling already in her armpit. Turning away from her children for a second, Elizabeth screwed her eyes up tight and prayed a most desperate prayer. She felt her eyes become hot and wet with the tears of unfathomable dread.

"Mama," John said, and she turned back to him. She sat down and took both their hands, telling them it would be alright, that she would look after them and she would just need to get a few things but she would be coming right back. *How could she tell John?* She went to move the doll and as she did so John spoke.

"Can't we keep it here mother? Jonathan liked it when he was sick. I think it made him feel better, like his sisters," he said.

"What?" she said. "When did Jonathan see your doll?" she turned to Elizabeth. "When did he see it?" Elizabeth turned her head slowly to look at her mother, the weight of sadness and sickness in her young eyes.

"We took her to see him. We knew he was sick and she always makes me feel better mama. It was only for a minute. We just wanted him to feel better," she said, beginning to cry again as her mother closed her eyes and brought her hands up to her lips together as if in prayer.

"You took the doll to Jonathan? When he was sick?" she asked them again, hoping she had misunderstood, praying she had.

"Yes," Elizabeth whispered. "He really liked it. I told him to give her a little kiss and she would make him feel better," the little girl whispered, her voice hoarse and rasping from the fever. Elizabeth could cry with the kindness of her daughter and the absolute heartache of all it would bring. There wasn't space in her heart nor strength in her body for what she would have to do next but she would have to do it nonetheless.

She tucked the doll in next to Elizabeth and said she would be back very quickly. In the time it took to tell the rest of the frightened family what was happening, their eyes wide and then full of tears, Alice had fetched water and linen and placed them on the kitchen table. When it came to it, she hadn't even needed to tell John. She just stood in front of him and looked him square in the face, the whole weight of it there between them, the weight of what was unsaid and the weight of all that this would mean. It was the heaviest moment to ever pass between them in the long years of their marriage, surpassing even the moment when she had delivered their first child barely formed and already eternally asleep those many years ago.

John had pulled her into him and they stood there in the pain of that embrace for only a few moments, time being a luxury that they could not afford. She wanted to collapse, to just go to the floor and stay there and not have to do this. Not nurse her babies into death, not see them in pain and watch them leave her. But she could not collapse, she could not do anything else but do and be what this moment asked from her. John would not let her do it alone. He came with her to the children's room and they gave the others strict instructions to stay outside.

They sat with them, through the afternoon and into the evening. At some point the day passed to night, the light giving way to the dark but they did not notice. Alice knocked on the door softly. When Elizabeth opened it, she saw the red rims around her oldest daughter's eyes, the aftermath of hours of tears. She had cooked for them. Elizabeth felt her heart make room for some pride amongst all the desolation and sorrow. William took care of Oner, despite him saying he wouldn't be able to get her to do anything. She remembered, in the conversation they had had after he had seen Robert. He dressed her and fed her and put her down to sleep. He did those things and Oner let him.

They took shifts to eat, though doing it for the physical strength it afforded and not for appetite, and they returned to the bed where their little ones lay. They watched them as they lapsed into delirium due to fever, as they clutched at their necks and arms, their restless heads turning back and forth on the straw-filled pillows as they tried in vain to find comfort. Elizabeth tried to give them Merrill's tinctures. John prayed, made up prayers right there on the spot and she gave them the deepest amens of the four decades of her life. But they could see the life slipping away from them. She could see death in her house, as if it was standing in the corner shrouded and waiting and it was all just a matter of time. She had not been able to protect them. John had wanted to build her a fortress but they had no portcullis, no moat, no weaponry at all to stop an invisible foe.

They died within an hour of each other, Elizabeth first and then John. They looked so small on the bed but she was relieved to see them now still and not in pain. From John a howl broke out from deep in his chest. It frightened her and yet she understood it. She wanted to howl too but it would not come. No sound would come from her mouth. She could not stop him from falling onto them, pulling them in towards his chest and rocking them both as he had done when they were smaller, one on each knee to tell ghost stories when there was a full moon. He would not let them go. She placed her hand on his shoulder gently and kept it there and in his own time he released them and lay them down again.

They looked like they could be sleeping. He had closed their eyes and then lay down at the foot of the bed looking at them, and sleep took hold of him fast. She took herself to the kitchen. It was just approaching dawn and light had begun to find its way into the farmhouse. The house was still, those who slept making as much noise as those who now slept eternally. She slipped out of the door and into the yard, picking up one of John's shovels as she walked. She began to dig. There was a place just out a little way from the house, a good spot that looked over the dale with Stoney Middleton nestled away on the other side.

She dug for hours, until the sun came up and she could feel the first rays on her already sweaty back. She dug a place for each of them, side by side. She stared down into the two pits, knowing this is where she must lay them but completely unable to comprehend what that really meant. When she went back into the farmhouse, all was still quiet. John stirred as she lifted their son from the mattress and carried him out. A moment later he appeared behind her with Elizabeth. She lay limp in his arms, just like the doll she had taken to comfort Jonathan. The tears swam into Elizabeth's eyes then.

She lay out the two sheets she had brought outside and they lay the children in each one. They cried then, she and John, as they bound them. The two of them letting their tears fall onto the linen. John lay them in their graves, dug by their mother. She helped him cover them with earth. There was the sound of the door opening and William appeared with a sleepy Oner in his arms.

"What's this?" the little girl asked, pointing.

"This is my heart," Elizabeth said, pointing at the earth and then at Oner and at William and at John. "It's all in separate pieces now," she cried. "A little piece for all of you."

42

Elizabeth

7th August 1666

This day looked set to bring her more pain than she could possibly bear. It had begun two days ago. They were sat at the table, neither of them talking much, their minds and hearts elsewhere, beneath the dirt of the two mounds of earth they knew they would see, if they ventured to the window. She began to avoid it. It seemed so preposterous that two of her own, two of her babies would be outside in the dirt when the rest of them were in here and life just continued regardless.

"I cannot bear them to be out there without me," she said and she looked over at John for he did not make a reply. He had spent the morning in the smithy but the exhaustion which she saw on him could not be accounted for by a mere morning's work. He could work all day and into the night and not look this overcome. The August sun was warm and so there was no need for a fire to be lit in the grate but when she looked at him she saw the way his face glistened as if he were sitting too close to a raging blaze. She had expected the horror of this moment to affront her quickly, like a knife taken to her heart, but when the realisation found her it was like creeping ice, slowly climbing like a chill up her spine and escaping in a ragged breath from her open mouth.

"John!" she cried, their eyes meeting in a mutual gaze they had been avoiding for days. He gave her the saddest of smiles and lay his head down onto his hands gathered into two fists on the table.

She thought this moment would make her heart stop, but now it was here she pushed herself into action. She began pulling out bowls and filling them with water from the pump. She took old linens and ripped them into strips. She fetched the remedies she had bought from Humphrey Merrill all the time hoping she would never need them. He would not be able to help her this time.

She helped John to their room. He could walk but she felt some of his weight transferred onto her and felt the question rise of how she would lift him after...*No!* she screamed inwardly at herself. She would not let him die. She would find a way even if all those other widows and widowers in the village had not. She would do it. She could not face her tragedy alone. He looked at her, the sweat gathered across his forehead and beginning to run down his temples like little rivulets. "John," she said again, and they both cried then.

The moment was broken by the appearance of William holding Oner close to his chest. She saw how the little girl was limp and her head drooped onto him. She saw the wild look in the eyes of her oldest son, now her only son here with her. It was not possible that they could all be sick, was it?

"She's hot," he said. "And I think I am too. I feel weak and a little dizzy." She took Oner from his arms and as the little girl nestled into her she could feel the heat from her, like a hot coal, the awful confirmation of her fears. She guided William into her room, where John was already laid out on the bed. William turned to look back at her, shocked by what he saw of his father, and she nodded.

"Yes," she said, and William cried then. He lay down next to his father, who opened his eyes and began protesting that they leave the room.

"You are all taken with fever," Elizabeth said. She lay Oner between William and John and the little girl looked so feeble between her father and her brother. "I will care for you all in here. I must go and talk with Alice and Anne and then I will return. Keep the door closed." None of them responded. The air around them was still and stale and she was suddenly overcome with the heat and the lack of air. She pulled the door shut behind her and went to the window, breathing in huge gulps of fresh air and willing herself to be strong.

The girls were in the other room together alone. When she opened the door, they looked at her and she went over to where they sat and squatted down on her haunches in front of them. She cupped their faces as she spoke, their cheeks reassuringly cool. She could barely keep eye contact with them, their terror so evident in their eyes and she so unable to provide any real relief from their dread. When John and Elizabeth had died she had allowed them to say their goodbyes, but now the risk of it seemed reckless and she could not repeat it.

"Your father, William and Oner are all sick," she said, and the two girls immediately commenced crying as if they were of one entity. "I know you want to cry and I know you are scared but I must take care of them. I need you to stay in here and not come out unless you need to get food or water. Do not come into the room where they are sick for anything," she told them.

"Should we go to the village?" Alice asked. "To get help." Elizabeth smiled at her oldest daughter, already trying to do what she could to assist her. She had wanted to foster independence in Alice, to prepare her for life as a wife and mother that was not far off, but now when she looked at her, all she wanted was for her to stay a girl and to stay safe.

"No, my girl. I have all I have need of here. There is nothing anyone from the village can do to help me," she replied. But her thoughts drifted to Marshall Howe unbidden and the terrible thought of how she would move John if he died, especially now William was also sick. But she knew as she had always known, she would do whatever it took. Alice and Anne held onto each other and promised they would do as she had asked. She left them and made her way back to the room where her remaining family were, growing sicker as the minutes passed. She pressed her forehead to the wood and tried to suppress the nausea that now gripped her stomach and to still the tremble that shook her hands. The tears were ready to spring from her eyes and the lump in her throat made it hard for her to swallow but she opened the door regardless.

The hours that followed were as if from hell itself. She had watched them fade despite all she administered and all the efforts she made to break their fever. The disease performed its awful dance, overcoming their bodies so they contorted with pain, muttering with delirium and then falling still as they fell back into the feeble consciousness of fever. She wanted to cry and never stop, she wanted to scream and never hear the end of her lament. One day ran into the next and they faded with the daylight into the dark of night.

Oner barely saw the first hour of the new day. She cradled her, smelling her daughter's hair, tracing her fingers over the roses that bloomed across her perfect little body.

Sometime after midnight she felt the grip of her daughter's fingers around hers begin to loosen. She dabbed at her head with the soaked cloths of linen but the fever raged. William and John murmured in their feverish sleep and could not help her. She watched to see Oner's chest rise and fall again but it did not, as still as the hill on which their house stood. She lay her down, soothing out her sweat-drenched hair so that her curls lay about her face. She closed her eyes and remembered that sweet moment after her difficult birth when she had gazed on her much like this. She could just be sleeping. Only sleeping.

John and William lingered longer. She kissed them on their foreheads and held their hands. The girls did what they were asked and stayed in their room. Alice made a simple broth to feed her sister and left some outside the door for Elizabeth but she could not eat. Her stomach was knotted in unspeakable grief and bone-deep exhaustion and though she was tired and weak she could not think of eating. When they were still she watched them and inspected their bodies for the incipient signs. The swellings came and with them came pain. She prayed they did not burst as they had for some. She busied herself with making poultices to lay upon them and hoped they brought some relief.

When the afternoon began to draw on John tried to speak. She drew her chair close to him so that her ear was near to his mouth. His breath was sour and came with a rattle. With some effort he managed three words and before she had the chance to reply he was gone, his eyes staring past her and no amount of her looking into them changed the emptiness she saw. The light had gone from him. Where always she had looked into those eyes and seen the warmth of his soul she now saw only the reflected image of herself. Was there a feeling lonelier than that felt in that moment when you see your reflection in your dead husband's eyes? She lay her head to his chest willing it to move but there was only stillness and, in that moment, she wanted to die right here with him.

The movement of William on the bed made her sit up. She could barely look at her son, his mouth dry and his lips cracked. She offered him a drink of water but he could not drink it, spluttering and coughing on the few small drops. He lifted his hand as if to touch something but he merely swiped at the empty air. She took his hand and held him, her heart broken over the husband and father he would never be. When he took his last breaths she held him close, as she had done when he was first born. She felt his agony as her own, in every part of her. She whispered to him how proud he had made her.

It took all of her strength to lift John. It would have been made easier with the help of Alice and Anne but she would not ask them and though they cried out wanting to know what she was doing, she insisted they stay in their room. It took an hour to drag him slowly, so that she would not harm him and she had to stop to rest several times. She lay him across her back and looped her arms through his, her footsteps all staggers. When she got him outside she lay him on the earth beside the mounds where John and Elizabeth were already waiting. John had been her heart's home and now she would bury him and her home would become the earth.

She carried Oner out next, cradling her and almost succeeding in convincing herself the little girl was only sleeping, and she lay her by her father before going back for William. Her son was tall and lean and she lay his cold arm across her shoulders and pulled and dragged him out of the farmhouse. When they were all laid out she began digging. It took hours and hours. The light faded and the dusk was waiting, ready to rush in and swallow them all up in blackness. She wanted it to. But when she looked at the cottage she saw the candles were lit and the faces of Alice and Anne at the window looking out at her.

She imagined the people of the village on the other side of the hill looking out of their windows at her too. Could the people of Stoney Middleton see her now? Could they see this real, visceral scene of her digging in the dirt to bury her kin? Could they see the way the dirt mingled with her tears and made dirty track marks down her face? Could they see the agony she felt dragging her husband into that hole and throwing the dirt in over him? Or the moment when she clung to her little one unable to perform the unnatural act of letting her go, ashes to ashes, dust to dust. Did they watch her as she lay William down next to his father, so close that their hands could touch? Did heaven watch her in her excruciating toil? Did anyone see? *'Look at me!'* her soul cried. *Look at me!*

43

Elizabeth

10th August 1666

The few days that passed following the deaths of John, William and Oner were lived as if she were inside a dream. The reality that more of her family were in the ground than were in the farmhouse with her sent her into a numbness that Alice and Anne seemed to share. The three of them sat around the kitchen table in silence. At first, they had wailed with grief. When she entered the farmhouse after she had finished the burials, she had told them in the gentlest voice she could muster that their father, brother and sister were all gone. She could barely believe the words she was saying and she expected them to argue with her over how it could possibly be, but they just crumpled into grief. She had gathered them to herself and their sorrow became a corporate lament in each other's arms.

Now none of them could cry. They sat and barely ate. Elizabeth was sure she would not have eaten at all if it were not for Alice pushing herself up from the table and putting together a simple meal of bread, cheese and potatoes for Elizabeth and her sister. She pulled the young girl close, breathed in her hair and kissed her hands, inhaling the scent of earth where she had pulled the potatoes from the ground.

None of them had tended the hens. It was always William's job and now it was nobody's.

"We will need to check for eggs," she said to her girls. "There will be a few now and we can sell them." She suddenly felt the weight of needing to support her family, even though it was now much smaller than it had been. The anvil was silent at Riley. No more would she hear the sharp clanging of John pounding metal and emerging from his workshop sweating and satisfied after a long day's work. She could not conjure the image of him and it bothered her. The thought of day after day after day without him was smothering and she could hardly breathe.

The girls nodded and when she stood up, they got up from the table too and followed her out to the yard behind the house where the hen coup was. For a moment her mind tricked her with the expectation of seeing William there and the split second it took for her to remember brought with it the shock of losing him all over again, like a barb to her heart. She could not stop thinking about them all, how they had lived inside her and were still part of her, like some living part of herself was buried in the ground and yet she was still here, expected to function like a normal breathing person. It almost made her laugh with the absurdity of it.

In the time they had been paralysed by the shock of their loss, the hens had been busy and there were eggs all over the coup, filling up their usual favourite laying places and then just scattered haphazardly. Alice and Anne gathered up their skirts to collect them in and then brought them to their mother and Elizabeth laid them carefully into her basket. They would need to be taken into the village. She would do it. The girls could stay here. Would anyone buy her eggs if they knew they had been visited by the disease? Any yet she could not pretend that they were not dead. The world simply failed to be the same, as surely anyone would see it on her face the moment they laid eyes on her?

Yesterday she had shared her intention to go down into the village. The girls insisted they would come with her but the risk was too great. Together they would be a trio of potential hazard and though she should also probably stay away, they needed money. The journey alone down into the village was one she made slowly, as if her feet were made of lead. She saw barely anyone and those she did see looked upon her with the same heavy sense of sorrow she herself felt. Their exchanged glances were fleeting and painful and she looked away as soon as she could.

She decided to try to sell her eggs to houses over towards the Lydgate where she was not at all well known. Some houses remained shut up no matter how much she knocked and some doors opened but the people behind them peered out cautiously and shook their heads at her, not unkind but definite in their refusal. Eventually she came to a house where the door was opened by a young woman with kind eyes. Elizabeth had passed a mound of earth in the front garden, where the grass was beginning to grow up in young tender shoots and a crudely-made grave post of slate with hastily scratched letters showing G.D. stood erect from the ground.

"Just leave the eggs in the basket by the wall," the young woman indicated, "and I will put my coins into the vinegar in the pail here," she added, pointing to the bucket by the door. Elizabeth thanked her.

"I am sorry for your loss," she said, turning to look at the mound of earth.

"My father," the young woman said. "Sometimes I wish I had gone with him." Elizabeth could see the young woman's eyes moisten. She was pretty and the sadness in her expression only seemed to add to her beauty. Elizabeth did not feel the same could be said for her. She felt hollow and haggard, as if all that was ever good about her, all that was ever beautiful, had been taken away when John and her children took their last breaths. She knew what the young woman meant. Since the moment she had thrown the last lot of earth on top of them she had wanted to lie down and die there with them. It had been hard to keep living after John and Elizabeth but even harder now that William, Oner and her beloved husband had joined them.

All Elizabeth could do in response to the young woman's expression of her grief was to nod. She stepped towards the basket and laid the eggs in carefully, and then made her way to the bucket where the coins had been tossed into the vinegar. Over the months the villagers had developed all kinds of ways to try to avoid the spreading of plague seeds. Those who used the well and the boundary stone to obtain provisions arranged for the village by the Lord at Chatsworth, also made use of vinegar and the rushing water of the well as a way to cleanse the potential threat. Elizabeth wiped the coins onto her apron, feeling the sting of the vinegar's pungent aroma reach her nostrils.

"Thank you," she said, and the woman replied with another of her sad smiles before closing the door. Elizabeth looked again at the grave. Perhaps she should try to fashion some kind of markings for each of the graves she had dug? For a moment she thought to ask William and then the truth crushed her once again. William could not make the grave markings. William could not do anything again. Her thoughts went to Alice and Anne alone back at Riley and she began to walk back towards the village. There was one place she must pay a visit on her way home.

Elizabeth stood at the door to the rectory and for a moment she did not move. How many people had come to knock on this door with this news she wondered? She was not unique nor special, but somehow the breadth of her loss felt uniquely terrible, at least to her. She knew there were whole families wiped out; the Thorpes and the Thornleys all gone and of course the Talbots too, her neighbours on the hill no more. There were households empty save for single mothers or fathers left alone with just the memories of their spouses and children as their only company. She was lucky to still have two daughters. She knocked and took a step back away from the door.

She had expected Catherine to answer, or perhaps a maid or manservant, but it was William himself who opened the door and greeted her with a surprised but warm greeting. For a second, she was embarrassed at her lack of church attendance but the absurdity of it given the magnitude of what the village faced caused the moment to pass quickly.

"How can I help you Mrs..." he said and she gave him her family name, not expecting any recognition.

"Hancock?" he said. "You are John's wife?" She remembered that he had requested John's witnessing of the will of William Thorpe and would have made his acquaintance then. "I hope all is well up at Riley?" he said and she knew the next question he would ask when she did not reply and she could not bear to say out loud the answer she would need to give. She looked down at the threshold and took a deep breath before speaking without looking up.

"I have come to inform you that I have buried my husband and four of my children. I have two daughters left with me at Riley. When I left this morning all three of us were well, but as you know, that means nothing," she said. There was a rustle of skirts behind him and she saw Catherine appear beside her husband. There was such a look of compassion on her face she could not maintain any anger towards the woman with regards to her having sent her children away.

"We are so sorry for your loss, Elizabeth. May God have mercy on you," Catherine said.

"Thank you," Elizabeth replied, the pain of it reaching her afresh in agonising waves. "I thought you should know. I know you keep the parish register up to date. I should also inform you that all of the Talbots are dead," she said.

"*All* of them?" William asked, incredulous.

"Yes, all of them. Jonathan was the last and it was from him that the pestilence passed to us via my children," Elizabeth said. The mentioning of the children made Catherine look away, her memory of that day outside Humphrey Merrill's house clearly still lingered.

"If there is anything we can do for you, please ask," Catherine added.

"Many thanks mistress," Elizabeth replied and for what felt like the millionth time in her life offered a smile she did not feel. She turned and began to walk away but was recalled by a question.

"Did you say you have buried them?" William asked. "Yourself?"

"Yes," she replied. "I have buried them myself." She left them standing together on the doorstep, bewildered by the feat she had accomplished alone.

When she had returned to Riley she was arrested by the silent stillness. There was no noise from the Talbot farm. She had driven their animals down into the village. No clamour from the forge. No movement from her own farmhouse, just the fluttering of leaves in the trees amongst the cluster of graves that housed her loved ones and the broken fragments of her heart. The girls were not at the window as she had thought they might be, watching and waiting for her return. She tried not to panic at the eerie stillness and what it could mean and stopped herself from running towards the farmhouse to find out. What awaited her would still be there, would still happen, no matter how quickly or slowly she approached it. Fate had gripped her and squeezed her and could squeeze her still more.

When she entered the house the silence of outside was matched within, neither Anne nor Alice to be seen. She walked towards the door to the room they now shared alone and pushed it gently. The smell hit her before the scene before her could; sweat and vomit mixed together in a pungent herald of sickness. Alice lay on the bed with Anne sitting next to her, a look of absolute distress across her face.

"How long?" Elizabeth asked.

"Almost immediately after you had gone," Anne said. "We were sitting mending and she suddenly said she felt unwell. I wondered whether I should chase you down into the village but Alice begged me not to leave her. She got a fever out of nowhere mama, I tried to stop it but she was too hot and weak," Anne said and she started to cry.

"You did nothing wrong and everything right," she told her daughter, taking her by the chin and looking into her frightened eyes, wide and searching for salvation from this horror. Elizabeth knew with certainty she could not give the girl the thing she wanted and it felt as if unseen giant hands were pummelling her and would not be satisfied until she was ground into dust. She lay her hand across Alice's forehead and straight away felt the fever that Anne had tried to keep at bay. The horror of going through this again was too horrible to be suffered. She felt a numbness build in her and began the motions again of nursing and tending with the knowledge that it could achieve nothing. She could do nothing. She would watch them sicken and die and then she would be alone.

Anne's fever also began to burn within hours of Elizabeth's return and she willed the numbness that enveloped her to stay with her until the end, lest she be overcome with the desperation of watching the last of her children perish beneath her hands and be unable to do what she needed to. Their armpits and necks swelled and she watched the beautiful faces of her girls take on the red lesions that were the mark of the sickness. They writhed when the fever burned within them and lay inert and still in the moments it gave them respite. She stroked their hair and held their hands, dripped water onto their hot faces and soothed their pain with the last of Humphrey Merrill's tinctures.

Anne cried and held her head, complaining of the pain and Alice was sick. Elizabeth's fingers felt for their pulses and found them to be weak and erratic as if their precious little hearts could not decide between life and death. She knew the disease would choose for them and that soon she would be the only living person still at Riley. The thought was utterly confounding. Only a month earlier, seventeen souls lived out their days up here at Riley, laughing, loving, living. She wrestled with the punishing jolt of all that could be lost within the days of a month.

Alice died before the night had covered the hill with its blackest mantle. She kissed her daughter's cooling hands and whispered to her how much she loved her. It would soon be too dark for her to think about burial and it would need to wait until morning. Her back still ached with the memory of the graves she had dug a week ago and the pain of it, though bringing discomfort, was a lingering connection with them and she held on to it. Tomorrow she would feel it again, the physical aching of laying her heart's desires into the earth which matched the sense of torturous loss that waited on the other side of her current numbness.

Anne stayed with her until this morning but as the sun crept along the ridge towards the farmhouse she muttered some words Elizabeth could not make out, the senseless loquaciousness of delirium. Her little chest rose and fell in an unsettling rhythm until she gasped and her little mouth fell open and never closed again. Elizabeth felt a tear roll from her eye, a single stream of saltwater that had broken ranks from those she had been holding back. She felt something gather in her chest, deep down from a primal place and a loud wailing rolled up her chest and out of her mouth. She had never made this noise before and were she not already so overcome with weariness and grief she may have been scared by the expression of pain her soul let out.

Elizabeth wailed and howled and rolled herself into a ball on the bed. She wrapped her arms around herself in a feeble effort to hold herself together but the agony would not stop pouring out of her. Great sobs wracked her body so that she heaved and shook and the depth of her loss felt like the great stone chasms beneath her, pain roaring through her emptiness. Never had she felt so untethered and so alone. The pain of her loss was absolute.

Burying Alice and Anne took the painful toiling of an hour or two. She wrapped them both in blankets and carried them out, laying them across her arms and nestling her face against their shrouded faces before placing them tenderly into the pits she had dug. Her tears fell on their swathed forms as she pushed the earth over them with her bare hands, feeling the soil press between her fingers. She lay down in the dirt, pressing her cheek into the soil and feeling the tears run down her nose and become soaked into the earth beneath her face. If there was a thought that could bring death she would think it, but no such powerful incantation would come. Her lungs emptied and filled in spite of her no longer wishing them to. She did not know how long she lay there in the dirt, her arms spread out across her family, as if to gather them all to herself. The ground cradled them, the earth kissed them, the disease had claimed its prize and it had gone. She closed her eyes and let sleep come.

44

Elizabeth
13th August 1666

Elizabeth waited for death. She did not eat for there seemed no necessity for it. She only breathed because her body continued to do so. She sat alone in the farmhouse kitchen hemmed in by a deafening silence. From time to time she thought she could hear them: John calling her name from his workshop, Oner's giggle, William's whisper, the happy chatter of John and Alice and Anne and Elizabeth. But in reality, the silence was stubborn and kept all the mysteries of the those once living secreted away, inaccessible now because of the finality of death.

She walked around their property. Walked to the Talbot farmhouse and stood outside, feeling it an intrusion to go in even though she knew it was utterly empty. The door stood a little ajar, as if they had all just slipped out and would be back soon. She pulled it firmly shut and wondered what would happen to this house now. Would a new family move in and replace the family that now could only lay claim to the land in which they were buried and no longer the stone walls and slate roof that had contained the fullness of their life?

She walked back towards her own house, stopping at the hen houses to collect any eggs they may have laid. They had continued to lay despite her having been remiss in giving them the corn to feed them. It enraged her that the world just kept on going despite all that she loved being under the earth. Did these stupid hens not know that the world had ended? She collected the eggs anyway, annoyed with her own perverse drive to go through the motions herself. What now? Would she go down into the village to sell them? Why? Who was she trying to sustain?

She stood for a while looking down at the houses and cottages that crept their way down towards the centre of the village. How many of those houses now cocooned a broken-hearted survivor? Inside how many of those walls did people cling to life without hope? How many were taking their last breath and how many were watching in agony as they did? From up here all looked as it always had, but all had changed. She knew she needed to tell William Mompesson she had buried her last two children. Were the people of Stoney Middleton able to enter Eyam they could have told her sad tale for her from their vantage point on the hill opposite.

The next morning, she made her way into Eyam, passing in silence as she heard the moans and cries that emitted from cottages that she passed. Behind each door a family was living out their own personal agony and she knew too well the lasting pain of it. She had thought to check on

Bridget Talbot and to hear about the welfare of the baby Jonathan had brought to her, but as she approached the old woman's cottage a neighbour rushed out and told her that Bridget's house was visited by the disease.

"What of the baby? Does she sicken?" Elizabeth asked.

"No, not yet at least. The vicar's wife has taken her to another family. I know not who. But Bridget is stricken."

"I am sad to hear of it," Elizabeth replied, though in all honesty she had no room left within her heart to feel the pain of others, so overcome with her own loss and grief. The neighbour shuffled back into their cottage without further comment, closing the door, and Elizabeth looked at Bridget's window, a scrap of paper with the ABRACADABORA spell written out upon it in crude letters. All of a sudden, she wanted to laugh, not with mirth but with the sheer desperation of it all, where people put their faith in parchment enchantments and the throwing together of plants and herbs.

When she called at the vicarage the maid opened the door and informed her that her master and mistress were out in the village, administering to the sick in whatever ways they could be of assistance. Elizabeth bade her to tell the rector that she had buried her last two children and was now alone at Riley. She could see the way the news registered as pity in the eyes of the young maid.

As she climbed the road back to Riley she considered the danger in which the Mompessons placed themselves. She had been angry with them for sending away their children but they had placed themselves within the reach of the disease repeatedly where she had tried her best to hide away from it from their advantage up on the hill, which in the end had proved no advantage at all. Once peril arrives it matters not how small or large your circle is, it will do what it will within it.

45

Catherine
15th August 1666

The deaths in July came thick and fast, sometimes five or six in one day. Nobody in the village worked harder than William Mompesson and Thomas Stanley, Humphrey Merrill and Marshall Howe. The former set about their task of supporting the village with stoic resolve, their days beginning before dawn and lasting well beyond dusk as they comforted the dying and the bereaved with prayer and supplication. More wills were written, so many that a request for parchment had to be made and subsequently arrived at the boundary stone, sent by the Earl of Devonshire. William was forced to pick up even more work around the church, with the death of Francis Frith, the husband of Catherine's dear friend Elizabeth, on the 10th of the month. Death crept ever closer to the rectory.

Humphrey Merrill, despite the length of his years also worked long days in his workshop, mixing new remedies and dispensing them in haste to afflicted households: Thornleys, Naylors, Chapmans. Catherine learned with great sorrow that Elizabeth Thornley had succumbed to the disease herself, having lost her own children, Edward and Elizabeth, Francis's remaining children, Jonathan and Jane, and finally her new born son named after her late husband. With her household empty, Elizabeth had gone to the grave alone and Catherine enquired of Marshall Howe the manner of her burial, having been moved by the woman's desire to protect her step-children.

"Did you bury Elizabeth Thornley?" she enquired of the sexton as he called at Merrill's house while she was there to collect the day's orders from the apothecary. The sexton reached into his pocket for a crude book, bound with leather and parchment pages roughly sewn together. Catherine fancied Joan had made it for him. She suspected Marshall could not read or write so she peered down at the pages with interest. Instead of letters she found drawings; the streets of Eyam sketched out with recognisable landmarks and homes marked by an X with numbers. He thumbed through it, finding the street he knew the Thornleys resided and gave his reply.

"Aye, I did. Her and all her young ones. They are buried in the Miner's field. You want to pay your respects, do you?" he asked her.

"Yes, I think I do," she replied. She turned to walk away and then turned back to the sexton.

"How do you do it?" she asked him. "I mean, how do you bury so many children, whole families, as if it is the most normal thing in the world?" She did not mean it to sound accusatory but there was a thought inside her that found its way into the question; how could a man benefit so seemingly contentedly from the misfortune of those around him?

"Well I had it didn't I? So, I don't worry about it now. I just go in and get them. No ceremony, I ain't no rector. I just gets them and puts them in the ground." Catherine had heard of his crude methods of burial; how he used ropes around the neck, or the feet if he was feeling merciful, to drag the bodies from the house and out to the allotted burial space, digging the graves in advance so they lay waiting, like hungry mouths ready to devour the next prey. There had been rumours that one man in the village had been so determined to not be dragged out so undignifiedly by Howe, that when he had sensed the end was coming he'd taken himself outside to lay in the grave that awaited him, dying there and removing the necessity for Marshall Howe's ropes and hauling.

"You may not be a man of God, Mr Howe, but you are accountable to Him nonetheless for your services here. I should think your wife and son would not wish to be so unceremoniously bundled into the soil." She had gone further than she had intended with her words. The mention of his family caused him to bristle with painful realisation. She could see she had affected him and should feel remorseful but in truth she hoped he might be less brutal in his manner of removal and burial on account of her observation. "I'll say my goodbyes now Mr Howe," she said, crossing the pathway and into Humphrey Merrill's house. "Have a good day."

"You been upsetting the sexton ma'am?" Humphrey Merrill said with a chuckle.

"You heard that?" Catherine said, her cheeks beginning to flush at the knowledge of her boldness being witnessed.

"I did," he said, moving towards the jars on his shelves and taking down a selection, placing them on the large wood table. "It isn't a bad thing to remind a fellow to be a little more compassionate," Humphrey said.

"I've seen him do it, when he carried out Edward Cooper. He was gentle then. Surviving the disease seems to have made him conceited somehow. He takes payment beyond what is necessary and furthers the pain of the bereaved with his pitiless manner. The only person I have seen him genuinely moved by was Emmott Syddall. He left a posy on her grave don't you know?" she asked Humphrey.

"Did he now?" the old man replied, beginning to grind herbs, so that the smell found its way to Catherine's nostrils, pungent and strong.

"He did. A pretty little wreath of wild flowers, crudely woven by him I believe. It is a wonder she managed to affect him such. But she was wondrous kind that soul. May she rest in peace," she added.

They worked in near silence after that. Catherine completing some of the remedies for him and transferring the mixtures into muslin bundles and small glass vials. She would take these on her visits this afternoon. She had begun accompanying William and Thomas on their calls around the village. What they provided with sacred words and wise legal counsel, she bolstered with remedies and what she hoped were sympathetic words. Where children were left with ailing parents, Catherine did her best to make arrangements for them to be taken into the homes of neighbours, though there was a growing sense of mistrust and fear that this was causing the plague to spread. Many children simply remained in homes alone, with neighbours leaving provisions for them as best they were able.

Catherine was doing her best to keep track of these adult-less abodes, and took provisions herself as often as she could. What kind of suffering was this, where children could be so bereft, unable to be comforted or cared for because of the terror that compassion would be repaid with sickness and grief? Already that narrative had been played out again and again like an evil tale repeated. She thought of Emmott often. The girls' kindness had cost her so dearly. By now Rowland must have guessed the fate of his love. Yet still he stayed away, facing his probable agony from a distance and honouring the cordon sanitaire established by the two rectors.

Catherine loaded the bundles and bottles into a large basket that she slung over one arm. The basket was heavy and the weight of it tired her. Since the morning she had been troubled by a cough, and as she walked she coughed at regular intervals, tiny blood spatters on her white handkerchief at times. People she passed on the road moved away from her, fearing her cough was a sign of impending illness, despite her assurances she was not afflicted by plague. By the time she returned to the rectory she was ready to lie down, but on entering the house she found William and Thomas ready to make a visit and they requested she accompany them. Catherine assented, though she leaned heavily on William's arm the entire way to the Bocking house.

Alice Bocking had died during the morning. Together she and Francis had nursed all six of their children on their successive death beds, three of them, including their infant daughter Mary, dying on the same day. Catherine had heard about each tragedy in detail, for Alice was Francis' second wife and Mary Cooper's sister. Catherine knew this latest loss would hit Mary hard. She had been deprived of her two sons and now a beloved older sister. The two were inseparable, just a year in age difference and with Alice matching Mary's compassion for others but not quite her verve for life as being a more quiet and reserved soul. Catherine wondered if something more of Mary's soul would slip away with the last breath of Alice. It was troubling to watch such a large, warm soul lose some of it light in the face of continuous tragedy and hardship.

Francis Bocking opened the door to the trio, pulling the door close to himself to let them in, as if he wished to press the life from himself and disappear. Catherine stood slightly behind the men, using her slightly hidden viewpoint to look at the man's face. She had become captivated by the changes she witnessed in the faces of her fellow villagers; the way grief weaved lines and shadows, caused the skin to look grey and wan. She saw the way fear narrowed the eyes and the way people conducted themselves with mouths slightly open, as if dismay might escape from their lips at any time. Francis looked like an old man. He was already a decade older than Alice had been but what she saw before her was a man exhausted by life, shuffling as if in senility. This pestilence robbed men and women of life even when they survived its deadly onslaught.

They would not go in. From the house there came the smell of the destruction death wrought on a body overcome by disease. She could almost imagine it on him, clinging to his person, there on his hands, in his every breath. It was enough to make her recoil a step but she forced herself to step forward as she heard her husband speak. William enquired where the children were buried, and what his plans were for Alice. Francis's voice was gravelly with emotion as he relayed that his children were in the field adjacent to the Miner's Arms and that the sexton would return this evening to take Alice to them. Thomas led with several prayers for the dead and he enquired as to Francis' will and whether he would like to consider another family that might benefit from his meagre wealth should he himself succumb to sickness. When he closed the door, Catherine felt the weight of his sorrow. That night as she slept she dreamed of closing doors, hundreds of them all closing at once, all around the village.

46

Catherine
23rd August 1666

Elizabeth Frith had come to the rectory distraught. It was unsettling for Catherine to see her usually aloof and confident friend so undone with fear and worry. Having lost her husband, spending days nursing him herself, recognising every sign and symptom as it appeared to mark and disfigure the body of the man she had loved her whole life, her attention was now turned towards her children and her fears for them. She pressed Catherine on advice with regards to which herbal concoctions would best treat the pestilence and her requests were punctuated with tears as Elizabeth grappled in her own wrestle with death as it turned up to threaten her family as the next victims on an ever-growing list. Her thought always on her family and not upon herself, Catherine recognised the un-ending concern of a mother in Elizabeth's words and tears.

As Catherine closed the door on her departing friend, with promises to bring a selection of remedies to the Frith house forthwith, Catherine found herself wracked with guilt at the suffering she had spared herself in sending away her children whilst the opportunity for others to do the same had been taken away by her husband's plan, including her friend's chances to save her sons and daughters. The thought of Elizabeth resenting her, or even worse- blaming her- was an immense burden on her which found its way into her fingers as she ground the herbs with the pestle, imagining all her fragile friendships crumbling in the presence of such a deadly threat.

Each household was finding their own way of living through these times. Some households had left the gathering at the Delph, closed their doors and done all within their power to not need to open them again since. When they did open them, she glimpsed frightened faces peering out as if to check the world still *looked* the same beyond their little patch of earth, even if it *felt* so unimaginably different. She saw some families gathering provisions- chopping logs and piling them behind their cottages, catching hares and rabbits in the woods in simple snares to smoke and dry the meat. Even the most cautious of families could not avoid venturing out for water and the troughs not being used as vinegar-filled sanitation sites for leaving money to pay for provisions, still hosted a gathering of animals. However, the wells and springs around Eyam were accessed by villagers standing cautiously away from each other and hurrying to complete their task of getting water. With a threat unseen and a transfer so secret and impossible to trace, the villagers had come to believe there could be plague seeds anywhere, on any of them and that the only way to continue to live was in a state of ongoing caution which suspected everybody of being the next victim.

There were some households who refused to be drawn into a life of fear and doubt, though these dismissive reactions to the obvious presence of danger were relatively few. Of the few she saw continuing to live in proximity to normal, in what she could only assume was defiance of death, the sexton, Marshall Howe was the most pronounced in his belief he was invincible to the pestilence, having survived its attack once. He swaggered in and out of afflicted homes, dragging corpses out with bare hands and caring not which houses he entered during the course of a day. Even homes with several ailing, or perhaps even several dead, did not deter him from providing his services and leaving with goods and money in payment. When a family member took ill, the likelihood of it spreading to others in the same family was very high and Marshall quickly became aware of these new family invasions of disease, as if the first afflicted person themselves were a plague seed which would plant itself and grow an entire crop of corpses. For a grave-digger, another house visited by death was not so much a tragedy as a steady income stream, and as the months passed the disdain for the sexton grew and took hold and Catherine could not blame her fellow villagers for their growing aversion. Howe appeared haughty and she was sure from the words of scripture that the proud would ultimately be brought low, though not perhaps before wounding innocents with their unfeeling actions.

Elizabeth had asked Catherine to bring the remedies that afternoon, clearly hoping to do the only thing she could to be prepared should death be hovering since the death of her husband.   Catherine had ruminated over her friend's request. Was her friend expecting her to go in to the cottage? Could she leave the remedies at the threshold and feign some other errand that required her urgent attention and called her away? In her mind there was an ongoing pull of ideas that criss-crossed the values she had always held dear, and the mental battle caused her heart to ache and her stomach to churn with anguish. Never had she refused a friend in need. She wondered if Elizabeth's own anguish would soften her ability to feel cross with a friend who faltered when courage was required?

Catherine had taken her time mixing the remedies. Humphrey Merrill had taught her the merits of allowing some of the herbs some time to release their aromas before throwing them into the mix of a concoction. The smells in her kitchen seemed to clear a place inside her awareness that was clouded by her own worries. She took deep breaths, inhaling the scents the earth had provided to offer a hope of health and wellness, or at least a moment of relief from pain and suffering. Was it so very far from biblical doctrine to glimpse the creator even in this? She thought about the myrrh-bearing women arriving at the tomb of Christ with their spices, to use their knowledge of the properties of plants to express their love and tender care for their beloved who had suffered. They arrived with a balm to sweeten death, just as she did. If only she could also encounter resurrection as they had.

When Catherine had arrived at the door to the Frith household she hesitated only a minute before reaching out her hand to knock on the heavy wooden door. The door was answered not by Elizabeth but by one of her grown sons. The young man was handsome, his arms strong beneath his shirt and his stature tall and straight as an arrow. Catherine gazed up at him and saw him smile.

She was aware that she was older than he was but close enough in age for her beauty to still inspire a response in him, no matter how much he tried to hide it and she did not want to cause it. Usually this resulted in her looking away and introducing herself as 'the rector's wife', though in this case there was no need as Thomas Frith already knew this information and it didn't stop him from appreciating a beautiful woman at the threshold. Catherine felt herself blush. Despite the dangers of the times they were in, men still looked upon women with attraction and those with the propensity to wear their embarrassment on their faces still felt their cheeks grow warm under scrutiny.

"Our mother is inside," he said, pushing the door back and away from him, whilst gesturing with his arm for her to enter if she chose. There was something in the way he did it that had appeared as a question to her, and she hesitated only a second in giving her answer, moving forwards and feeling her soft skirts brush upon his legs just a little as she entered the Frith cottage. Any smell or sign of death had been brushed, scrubbed and aired out of the cottage, it being over a week since Francis's passing. Afterwards, she could still imagine Elizabeth sitting there, quiet in her rocking chair, saying only a few words as Catherine talked of her work in the village, and only really stirring from her seat to gift Catherine with a beautiful lace handkerchief she had made for her. She passed the beautifully crafted square to Catherine and her fingers brushed Catherine's hands in the affectionate exchange.

Elizabeth had smiled at her friend with genuine warmth, allaying Catherine's fears over her friend's potential anger. Though her words had been few, and seeing her animated friend so reduced in expression and energy by grief and anguish had unsettled Catherine, she was glad to have made the visit. For just three days later, Elizabeth was dead.

William had woken Catherine early this very morning to tell her he had had a visit from Elizabeth's son Henry late last night after Catherine had already retired to her bed for the night, informing him his mother was gravely ill.

William himself, feeling indebted to the family in respect to the late Francis' services as churchwarden, had gone to administer the last rites to Elizabeth, finding the woman indeed on the cusp of immortality and with no available time left to rouse his wife from her sleep. Thomas Frith had knocked the rectory door at first light, raising a disgruntled Jane from her bed and delivering the sad news that his mother had joined their father in the afterlife soon after William had departed. It appeared the boys had shunned the services of Marshall Howe and wrapped their mother in the sheet on which she died, carrying her out to the land behind their house and laying her to rest in the earth with every affection held between a dedicated mother and her sons.

Catherine received the news with a mixture of shock and dread. That her friend could be so quickly taken to the earth was an idea too bewildering for her mind to allow the news to settle. Instead it flew around inside her head like a caged bird, brushing against every doubt and fear and worry she had ever had during these past few months. She went back over the image of her friend in her mind. How did she miss the signs she was already sick? Elizabeth was wearing her bonnet so she could not clearly see her forehead where typically the signs of a fever would make themselves known in beads of sweat like a malevolent string of pearls. Her hands had seemed warm but she had put it down to the heat of the fire. But was there a fire, in August? She could no longer remember.

After William left the room Catherine lay in bed, staring up at the ceiling. Her thoughts came upon her fast like arrows fleeting through a darkened sky. She anticipated them only moments before they landed. *What of the handkerchief?* She knew William and Thomas had been emphatically insisting that each house visited with plague should destroy all goods that had been associated with the deceased during sickness and death through the means of fire. The only person who seemed to not put his mortal existence at risk in accumulating such items was Marshall Howe, who boasted an apparent resistance to the plague seeds feared by so many having already succumbed to the disease once and mercifully recovered, a feat achieved by very few, with Margaret Blackwell being the only other survivor Catherine was aware of.

Catherine encountered the usual early morning weakness she typically felt when she roused herself from the bed, but she propelled herself towards the chest by the bedroom window and wrenched the top drawer open. The handkerchief lay there pristine and beautiful, all signs of any corruption as invisible. She used the coal tongues from the fireplace to retrieve it from the chest, blackening it with coal soot as she did so and lay it on top of the logs and kindling Jane had arranged in the grate should her mistress require a fire during an unseasonably cold August evening.

Catherine called for the maid, her voice ringing out through the empty rooms and passageways of the rectory, and Jane soon appeared in the doorway, regarding her mistress knelt in front of the fireplace as if in devotions at the holy altar with some alarm.

"Can I assist you Mrs Mompesson?" she enquired, stepping forward to stand parallel with Catherine and wondering if her mistress had perhaps fallen or had lost something.

"Yes Jane, please, I require a fire," she said, with an urgency that communicated some amount of distress to the confused maid.

"But you appear to have dropped..." said Jane, kneeling and reaching her hand out as if to retrieve the handkerchief from its resting place atop the logs.

"No, leave it!" Catherine said in a whisper of urgency, and Jane removed her hand, attempting to conceal her shock and began preparing the fire for lighting, just as

Reverend Mompesson entered the room. He did not look upon the grate and Catherine stood as quickly as she could, impeding his view of the fireplace with the skirts of her nightdress as she faced him.

"You are cold?" he asked, bending a little to the side in an effort to see past her to what the maid was doing.

"Yes, just a little. 'Tis a trifle chilly for me this morning," she said, ushering him out of the bedroom and towards his study, where she quickly sat in his chair in an effort to hide from him the sudden feeling of faintness that threatened to overtake her. The thoughts of the handkerchief swam in her head like an evil swarm, causing her great difficulty to focus her eyes on her husband and her ears to attend to what he was saying.

"How can you possibly feel a chill this morning Catherine? Look at the sun already shining so warmly," and he chuckled softly at his wife's propensity to be contrary when she put her mind to it. Though when he looked at her she did seem wan and he saw how she sought to stifle a cough. She always tried to hide her weaknesses from him, as if they were a shame too awful to share with a loving spouse, and yet it was the way she carried on, unhindered by her physical limitations, in her quest to serve his flock, that he found so very endearing and inspiring in his wife. She was relentless in her commitment to support his cause and her help during this most challenging of times had proved to him what a perfect help meet God had afforded him in making her his wife. Indeed, he could not imagine how he would have fared thus far without her gentle and steadfast encouragement.

"We should take a walk," he said. "It need only be about the garden," he added when he saw what he believed to be a look of tiredness in his wife's delicate face. The death of Elizabeth Frith had shaken her and it had pained him greatly to share it with her that morning. No matter how many times this dreadful act of demise and death played out on the stage that their little village had now become, there was always a reaction to be had from them, the audience and their recoil and sorrow never diminished no matter how high the number of victims rose. The deadly repeated performance had reached the outlying farmsteads of Riley and now Shepherd's Flatts, and bad news reached him from every far-flung corner of the parish.

He glanced down at the parish register where he spent each evening painstakingly updating the pages with the day's deaths. To date, a terrifyingly high total of two hundred and six souls had perished in Eyam. Two hundred and six from the flock he had been greeted by only two years ago, albeit with some suspicion and a sense of him needing to earn his place. Now he was rector of a much smaller band of troubled people, many of whom felt utterly forsaken by the God he was here to lead them towards, and yet they followed his direction anyway, living each painful day to show they had taken his words to heart; that 'greater love hath no man than to lay down his life for his friends'. August had provided him with an understanding of his saviour's parting words in a way no study at the seminary had made possible. *Father, into your hands I commend my spirit.*

Catherine agreed to the walk around the garden with a slight nod of her head and a weak smile. They usually took their walks in the evening during the summer, when the night breezes rushing over the hills cooled them and the sun dropping behind the slopes shone gently and without the dazzling the glare of the afternoon. Catherine loved to stop to look at the common orchids that grew along the sides of the worn paths towards the woods and she pointed out butterflies to their children when they had taken walks as a family.

The thought of the children brought a spur to his heart, and he clutched his arms about his chest remembering how he had lifted and embraced Elizabeth and George in turn before placing them into the coach. It had been now two months since their departure on the morning of his solemn meeting in the Delph to share the plan he had concocted with Reverend Stanley to stop the plague reaching Tideswell and Bakewell and the horrifying notion of the pestilence's arrival in the towns of Derby or Sheffield where two hundred and six could so easily become a devastating toll of tens of thousands.

Catherine descended the stairs in front of him, taking each step slowly and with great precision. Her body felt weaker than she had felt in many months but she was reluctant to show weakness to William when he still had so much to face in leading the village. She would take this walk and then perhaps she would find somewhere to quietly rest. The burden of grief for her friend and the weight of her anxious thoughts seemed to be as leaden shackles around her ankles and she felt herself perspiring almost immediately on stepping out into the warm rays of the sun casting its bright gleams onto the panes of the rectory's mullioned windows as she passed in front of them.

As they walked William talked and she did her best to lean lightly upon his arm. She heard his voice pass in and out of her conscious thought as her quiet deliberations went to her two sweet, absent children and to Elizabeth Frith, to Emmott now gone three months and the harsh words of Elizabeth Hancock after the meeting that announced the cordon sanitaire in June. Then all of a sudden, the strangest and most beautiful of scents cut across her thoughts, stopping the swirl of them in their tracks. It was unlike any other scent she recognised in her garden, and she looked about to see if a new flower had found its way in carriage by some feathered merchant. She turned to William.

"Oh! Mompesson! The air! How sweet it smells!" she said with a smile that she hoped would delight him, but all she saw in the eyes of her husband was the look of utter dismay. Though Catherine could not know it, William had read of this, the sudden smelling of sweetness, as a sign of infection in plagues past. What she accepted with elated gratitude, he heard as the beginning of the doleful peals of the death bell.

47

Elizabeth
25th August 1666

August had ushered in utter devastation within the village. As of yesterday, sixty eight had died since the first day of the month. A man from Orchard Bank had arrived at the smithy yesterday, having not heard the news of John's demise and in need of a new hoe to till his earth. At first, she had assumed she had imagined his voice, so prone had she become to easing her sheer loneliness with the imagined voices of her lost family. But she had not imagined it, and when it became more insistent in its calling she rounded the back of the farmhouse to the forge and found a man standing there peering in through the shuttered windows.

She had informed him that her husband was dead and he had been so very sorry that she had fallen to her knees in sobs and he looked most bewildered, though she bade him not to approach her. When she had recovered enough for speech she asked him what news he had of the village for it had been weeks since she had been down the hill. He rattled off the names of families who were afflicted, some she recognised and some she didn't. In a hauntingly similar tale to what had happened here at Riley, it appeared the Kemps of Shepherd's Flatts had given the plague to the Mortens and

Matthew Morten had lost his wife and children and their new-born infant, unable to secure a midwife to help him as his sick wife laboured. All over the village there were people like her, alone.

He also delivered the news that Catherine Mompesson herself was taken ill with what was presumed to be the pestilence and her husband was distraught. Elizabeth was moved by this news, more than she could account for. William had chosen for the village. Chosen with the best of intentions. He had hemmed them in, chosen what had amounted to death over life for so many of them and he had carried the weight of it. Now he would feel the weight of loss on his own shoulders and she knew the heaviness of it and did not wish it upon him.

After the man had left she felt her aloneness pressing in on her. Everywhere she looked she saw the remnants of them. She could not look across the hill without seeing their graves all gathered there, as if *they* were still a family but she was over here, no longer part of it. Without them, this place meant nothing to her. She realised she did not care if the farmhouse grew derelict around her, fell in on her even, the roof opening itself up to the sky. She willed it to do so, to entomb her in stone like she was sure William would his wife, no doubt affording her a space in the churchyard where he could bring his children back to say their goodbyes when all this was finally over and done with.

The thought had been growing in magnitude in her mind but this day it seemed to dwarf her. She would leave. She knew she shouldn't. She knew hundreds had not left and they had died for their staying. But she had waited to get sick. She had counted the days, notching each one on the wooden beam above the hearth. It had been four days from Jonathan to John and Elizabeth. Four days more until John and William and Oner, and another three that saw both Anne and Alice taken to the grave. But it had been over two weeks since then and she had not become ill.

Each night she lay alone in her bed, listening to the wind, waiting for the fever, but it had not come. In the morning she explored her body, looking for swellings, searching for the ominous marks of infection, but they never came. For whatever reason, and she could not bring herself to call it God 's blessing because if he did exist she was angry with Him; she had been spared and providence had selected her for life. At first, she had raged against it, wanting to die, wanting to be quickly taken into the arms of death and reunited with her family. She had even made a plan that she would dig her own grave at the first signs of it and lay down in it when her sickness was far enough advanced. She had heard about a man in the village who had done the same rather than invite Marshall Howe to earn another penny. The man from Orchard Bank had also told her how Joan Howe was sick and Elizabeth wondered how the grasping gravedigger would survive this likely deadly consequence of his greed if it meant losing a wife and a son.

But her plan had not been needed and the realisation she would not sicken had given rise to a new idea: abandoning the village. She tried to dismiss it but the desire to see her surviving son, Joseph, grew and grew until it was stronger than her reluctance to leave her dead behind. She would go tonight, when the cover of darkness could hide her sin and ensure she would not be stopped. The village watch did not reach up along the Manchester to Sheffield road and she could follow it using only the moon tonight as it was full and would cast sufficient light for her planned flight.

There was not much that she cared to take with her, just some small trinkets that John had made for her or her children had given her. She wrapped up bread and cheese within a fabric bundle and poured water into a flask that had been John's father's. As she went to leave the farmhouse she glimpsed the doll she had made for Elizabeth. She had meant to bury it with her but it had fallen under the bed, out of sight and out of mind.

She could not bring it for fear of plague seeds within it still and she probably should have burned it, and perhaps the farmhouse too, as she knew this was the new advice of Mompesson and Stanley, having seen conflagrations from time to time in the houses of the village below. But she could not bring herself to do it, so she tucked the doll into bed where her daughters had once slept their peaceful, beauteous sleeps. She remembered how they looked like cherubs as she kissed their still faces goodnight each night. She left the farmhouse, closing the door behind her.

Elizabeth paused on the craggy hilltop, her feet squared and sure on the dirt road, her hair blowing unbridled in the wind for she had removed her cap. She reached up a thin hand and swept her hair from her forehead and cheeks. Her fingers brushed the lines about her face and she wondered if they told this part of her story and if anyone would ever want to hear it. She took one last look at the place where her family were buried. She could feel again the weight of them on her back and in her arms. This is the place where they would become dust, where her heart, which would never again be whole, would rest in seven pieces beneath the earth.

She looked down at the village below in its unseen agony and gave it her apologies. She wished for hope for William Mompesson as he faced his own loss and she hoped he would not think so badly of her when he realised she was gone, for a part of her would always remain here at Riley forever.

48

Catherine

25th August 1666

The room felt smaller than usual and almost tomblike, the four walls encasing her as she struggled for each new breath and the pain in her neck and armpits throbbed with each weak beat from her heart. Yet she was still here, still the dutiful wife accompanying her husband as he battled a deadly foe. Each beat confirmed she was still alive. But she could see in his eyes the fear his words would not betray, and after two days of accepting small mouthfuls of thin pottage and watered down ale and her only sickening further, Catherine had begun to feel the apprehension in her own heart. Piety however, resisted making room for panic, and though she felt herself drifting towards absolute uncertainty, she clung to the hope of scripture coupled with Humphrey Merrill's skill as an apothecary.

It was very early morning and William had gone to the home of Humphrey and Anne as soon as first light had broken through the rectory windows. He had been tending to Catherine in her bed since that moment three days ago in the garden when she had smelled that sweet air and been overwhelmed by a sudden tiredness. William had looked at her with a terror in his eyes she would never forget, and had helped her into her bed and she had not since removed herself from it. Now as she lay here, battling with delirium, the sheets stuck to her where her sweat had dried and the fever toyed with her like a cat with a mouse, as if it did not mean the encounter to end fatally but at every sign of escape a taloned-paw returned as a reminder of the nature of your captivity. There were moments she fancied she was rallying; a slight appetite forming or the clearing of the headache that rattled her skull and dulled her thinking, even if just for a moment.

But somehow Catherine felt a knowledge growing, that this day would bring a clarity to this narrative, and try though she had, through feeble attempts at prayer, she was unable to grasp hold of any surety that she had for this life any longer. As she lay on the bed, her face turned up towards the ceiling, she made her attempt to turn her soul towards God in the sincerest manner she was able.

The fever made her feel separate from her body somehow, as if she could look down upon herself and see herself lying there, battling the foe she had tried to help so many others overcome in vain. William would soon return and spoon another remedy into her mouth, but Catherine knew he knew as well as she did, that it would likely also be in vain. So few of them who sickened had recovered. As an enemy the pestilence had proved to be deadly in every sense of the word. It was wondrous how long they had evaded its snare when she, William and Thomas had daily entered the homes of those who had been overcome by the disease. There was a sense of inevitability that wrapped itself around her as real as the damp sheets that clung to her slight frame. Why shouldn't she be here in this bed? Why shouldn't she be next to taste immortality? It struck her that she should perhaps be more afraid, but though the doubt of her survival grew, the fear did not.

To begin with, the scripture had helped her to summon her bodily strength. William read her favourite psalms and she lifted her arm enough to cross herself, her voice feeble but sure in its Amen. Then he had opened the Book of Common Prayer, deliberately reading every prayer for the sick to be found therein, but avoiding those said over the souls so evidently set to leave this earthly life and taste eternity within the hour. She had called for him in the night, requesting he go through the catechism with her again, so she could affirm all the questions of faith it raised and make her preparations for eternity in heaven if that indeed was where she was so headed.

Catherine tried to picture it, this notion of foreverness. But her head seemed always to swim with other thoughts, with the scraps of things people had said to her, the little tokens of gratitude they left for her, and the images of her children as clear as if they had been just this moment painted and hung on the walls of her chamber.

You should be ashamed; she recalled with some still-lingering shame the words of the Hancock woman that day on the road outside Merrill's house. Catherine knew the plague had claimed all that Elizabeth held dear. She had heard from William that Elizabeth had buried her entire family with her own two hands, with no help from anyone from the village. The tender sorrow she felt on that woman's behalf had been amongst the deepest pangs of sympathy Catherine had ever felt in her life. She could not imagine, and she didn't have to because she had sent her children to Yorkshire instead of to the grave.

Catherine knew she should be ashamed, that no mother should have to bury her children in the earth with her two bare hands the way Elizabeth Hancock had, but when the faces of her dear hearts, Elizabeth and George, swam before her in the gaps the fever left free, she could feel nothing but pure joy that her two angels were safe and healthy, no doubt laughing at the terrible jokes William's uncle liked to tell and enjoying the many treats his aunt always bestowed upon them.

A moment of piercing clarity shocked her through the increasing fog of the disease's grip as she pondered whether her precious children would remember their ever-loving mother if she faded into eternity this day as she now fully expected to. *Would they? Would they be able to recall her face as clearly as she now saw theirs?* She had no doubt William would do his best to tell them about her, to regale them with stories of her character and her life, but they being so young, she could not be comforted that this would be enough.

This painful doubt expressed itself as a sob, but her body was too exhausted to cry; her eyes painfully dry where tears should have been. The air of her room felt cloyed with the aromas of sweat and sick and a smell she unwillingly recognised as belonging to death. She turned her face into the pillow and waited for William to return, her whole body aching and her pulse racing through her wrists and climbing up into her neck. If she slept, she could not tell, her mind lapsing and returning as if time had given up its natural rhythm and instead span round in circles, backwards and forwards, carrying her with it. If he were gone five minutes or the best part of a day she could not tell.

Believing William to have finally returned, Catherine heard the door handle turn and with great effort she turned her head towards the bedroom door. But it was Jane who stood there, and on seeing her mistress lying so stricken in her bed, she pulled her cap from her head and clutched it to her breast, muttering 'Oh mistress, mistress,' as she did so.

Catherine felt the bizarre urge to laugh, believing herself to obviously be a most ghastly sight to the poor maid, but her body was unwilling to expend the energy a peal of laughter would have required. Instead, Catherine hoped Jane could see the smile she tried to arc her lips into, though even to attempt it seemed to hurt her face.

"Don't..." Catherine whispered, and Jane came closer to catch her mistress's words, though Catherine could see she was afraid to come too close. William's man servant had managed to catch the plague and yet, by some miracle, be one of the very few who had rallied after being treated with some of Merrill's concoctions, and Catherine believed this was behind her husband's determination to pursue the apothecary so doggedly for every possible tincture he could provide. But Jane had not sickened and was doing her very best to show reverence to her employer whilst exercising as much caution as she could. Catherine could see the compassion on the young woman's face as she asked her to repeat her words again if she felt she could.

Catherine swallowed, and with great difficulty she tried again to speak.

"Don't...worry...about me, Jane. I go to...a place of...serenity. All will be well," she said, hoping the maid would listen to her words. She knew how Jane resisted their piety, having heard her tell the manservant she had 'no time for them holy ways' once in the kitchen when Jane believed her master and mistress were still out on their walk. "I am...sorry," she continued, but Jane cut in, asking her what she could possibly be sorry for before she could get the words out. "For any...cross...word...I ever said...to you," Catherine concluded. She could not have said more in that moment if she had tried, but when she looked at the maid she could see the way Jane's eyes glistened with tears and the way she clung to her cap as though wringing it out.

"There is no need mistress Catherine!" she cried. "No need at all. You have always been most heavenly to me," Jane said, her last words carried on a sob, the sincerity of which touched Catherine deeply. She had never felt so tired, so completely ready for rest, though shutting her eyes brought no relief from the pain that built at the top of her legs and pulsed under her arms.

"Oh Mompesson!" she said, her body contorting between the sheets and Jane seeking to comfort her with the conviction William would very soon return home and was sure to have with him a remedy that would relieve her suffering and usher her back towards good health. Catherine wanted to believe her but the longer she lay in the bed, the deeper she swam in the sea of her own doubts.

As the hours passed, the fever gripped her in a deep wave of alternating delirium and nothingness, yet somehow the noise of the front door being opened found its way into her consciousness and in her next lucid moment she was aware of William being once again at her side. She could hear the chink of a spoon against earthenware and guessed he was sat at her bedside with yet another concoction of herbs and flowers, but her eyelids seemed not her own and she could not raise them. She felt the spoon against her lips and the combined sweetness and tartness of the remedy briefly filled her mouth, though she found she could not swallow it and instead felt the liquid run down her chin and down into the creases of her neck. He dabbed at it and she could hear the way he took two small breaths, the kind that follow a fit of crying.

"Prayer," she said, her voice so faint he struggled to hear it even sitting right next to her.

"Prayer, my darling?" he whispered. "Of course. Oh Catherine, you have been as a martyr to my interests here. I will pray you to the end and out the other side!" William said, and she felt him clutching her hand.

"One drop of…my…saviour's blood…to save my soul," she whispered, and appeared to fade for a moment, though he could see her chest was still rising and falling. He left the room briefly, returning with a small glass of wine, tipping it so that it moistened her lips. She was barely aware of the wine, just a sensation of warmth, almost pleasant on her dry lips. There seemed to be an uncoupling, like the stitches of a well-loved garment being gently undone in order to let down a hem. Catherine felt a sensation of being loosened. All about her there seemed a light not possible for the time of day. It being still early, the sun could not yet burn as at midday and yet she felt caught up in it, as if standing in the full glare of the sun's hottest rays between the trees in the woods where they most loved to take their walks together.

She let herself be released into the light. Her husband's voice found her on the edge of her journey. His fingers flicked through the pages of a book. She heard the utterances in Latin echoing as if he had called them down into a well. They drifted up to her as if she was above them and could catch them with her hands as they passed by.

"My dear, dost thou mind?" he asked, a quiet desperation in his voice.

"Yes,' she answered him, in a voice that silence would use if it could speak. "Yes." He saw her chest rise and fall and not rise again. Her mouth was parted where her last words had escaped them. Her last utterance on earth he realised, with such pain he flung himself forward so his head rested on her bosom, his ear straining for that beat that had been the rhythm of his days. He waited for his head to rise with her breath, but it remained heavy and unmoving and the only movement that came was from the wracking sobs that shook his shoulders as he called out her name, dropping tears on her still face as if like another baptism, bringing Jane and his man running into the room in response to his weeping. Gently, he felt their hands about his shoulders, pulling him back, and he tried in vain to block out the words as they said them: *She's gone.* It just could not be. His wife, the two hundredth person whose name he would be forced to ink into the parish record. A momentous death in every sense it could ever be. Had God ever provided a wife more serving of a husband as she had been to him in this peril? He believed not. He had stood between the dead and the living, as Moses had in the desert, lifting up the snake before the Israelites, and she had stood next to him, resolute despite her fragility and determined to make her sweet mark in this senseless age. And she had.

49

Rowland

15th November 1666

Word had found its way to him, rumours of her death. But despite this being conveyed to him time and time again, by many who meant well and felt he should know the truth, he could not bear to believe it until he saw with his own eyes that she was no longer in the village, nor working in Bagshaw House or walking in the dale as she loved to do. He had to see her absence, feel her loss, know she was missing and would not ever return to him. She would never be his wife, they would never make children or live in the house the villagers would have built for them. For sixth months he had lived a half-life, always torn between grief and hopeful longing. Death was so cruel. It took the person you loved most in all the world but, not satisfied with that, it also pillaged your future, your dreams. He could not think of what lay before him without pain.

Mompesson and Stanley had only just deemed it safe to re-open the village, having kept it shielded and barricaded to keep the plague in and limit the chance of transmission to other villages. They had chosen for everybody and everybody had gone along with their choice. They had chosen for *him*, their suggestions of necessary distance keeping her there when perhaps he could have brought her out after her father and siblings died. Perhaps he could have saved her, taken her far away to live in a hut on the land, so that April had never happened? That was the problem with death. Even long after it had moved on it raised questions and they were always built around an 'if'.

He pushed the village gate wide. It squealed on its hinges, unused to being forced into movement this past year. It had been so long since he had been in this village. To start with, he had met her here at this gate secretly, but as the victims had begun to increase they had moved their rendezvous point to the open space of the Delph. What words they sought to say to each other were then called over the distance or stashed away into letters brought from here to Stoney Middleton by boys of the village, until that too had to stop. He had heard it told by one such boy, sometime in May or June, that his precious Emmy was buried in the Cussy Dell and this dreadful confirmation of what her prolonged absence had come to hint at had caused him such pain he had never felt before. That her name had been added to the list of the dead crushed him.

The roads of Eyam were in bad condition, with grass and weeds having claimed the central run. They would need to be cut back and pulled up he noted, and then chided himself for having thought about something so ordinary when the reason he was here was so much more important. He made his way towards Bagshaw House. He knew that Elizabeth had married again, a John Daniel, but heard from others that her new husband had died in July and she had followed only weeks ago. He would have liked to have spoken to her, to have found out what Emmott had said at the end and how his precious love had left this life.

It had taken him a while to find out what had become of Joseph, Emmott's loveable little brother who had, by some feat, become the only surviving member of the Syddall family he had once loved and spent so many happy times with. He had entertained the notion for a brief moment that he might raise him, bring him up to know his sister. But word had reached him that Elizabeth had left instruction that her surviving son should reside with a Robert and Margaret Thorpe, who had lost all their children during July and August and that the bringing together of Joseph with such parents would restore a sense of family. Rowland would not seek to disrupt that plan.

As he drew near to Bagshaw House, he could almost imagine Emmott standing there waiting for him, as she had so many times before. That she wasn't there hit him deep in his gut like a violent shot, though he knew the likelihood of her being there, of the rumours he had heard told being untrue, was so low he had hardly dared to imagine it and further torture himself with the truth. No smoke issued from Bagshaw House and all around him there blew a breeze as though composed of a thousand sighs. Nobody came out to meet him and as he reached the boundary wall he bowed his head and gripped the stone, so overcome with loss. He was so inclined to go and knock on the heavy cottage door with its gnarled wood but he knew within his heart that all who once lived there were dead and the only possible resemblance of those he had grown to love would exist purely as spectres behind those doors and it did his heart no good at all to think of them so.

He stood for a moment feeling the pain in his heart and letting it sit there, letting himself recall a string of memories, of him and Emmott laughing with her sisters, of the way she looked at him the first time he suggested marriage, of her father laying an approving hand on his shoulder afterward and the way he knew he had kept his hands on her waist just a few moments too long at The Wakes but he just couldn't help himself. He had wanted to make love to her, and perhaps if the plague hadn't put an end to their meeting, they would have before the ceremony in August. He ached for her and she had known it and he believed she had wanted it too, though she was always such a modest thing and had never said so out loud. He could tell though, by the way she had looked at his lips and inclined her hips towards him ever so slightly when they held each other. He would never know what it would be like to truly love her.

Someone calling his name brought him from his melancholy brooding and he turned to see a man approaching him. If he wasn't mistaken it was the village sexton, the infamous Marshall Howe. He had heard terrible tales of Howe's treatment of the dead and his tendency towards over-compensating himself with goods from the household before leaving. Yet Emmott had seen a different side to the gruff man who stood before him now. News had reached the people of Stoney Middleton, who chronicled the desperate happenings of Eyam in their daily tidings with one another like gathering them into the pages of a book, that the sexton was much changed having lost his wife and child to the pestilence. It was likely his own avaricious actions that led to the bringing of plague seeds into the family home. When he was close enough, Rowland could see in his eyes that sorrow had indeed claimed its place in Marshall Howe's soul.

"It's this way," he said, gesturing with his hand to the path that ran behind Bagshaw House and down towards

Cucklett Delph. Rowland should have known that Marshall Howe would be the one to bury her, her father having already been placed into the earth himself. He hoped beyond hope that he had treated her tenderly but could not bring himself to ask, fearing the sexton would recount his methods and break his heart further. Instead he followed him silently, as if in a liturgical procession, to the spot that had been their meeting place and the vividness of her standing before him there became so clear in his mind he could barely stand it. He put his hands up to his eyes intuitively to shield them from the blinding brilliance of this memory, yet this November morning boasted no sun and very little warmth.

When they stopped, Marshall stood aside and before Rowland was a shallow mound of earth and atop it were some flowers, wild flowers likely picked from the meadow about. None lived of family to remember her so tenderly and it was when Rowland saw the sexton bow his head and remove his cap, bringing it to his chest, that he realised who had placed them there.

"She was a good sort, your Emmott," he said. And then strode off without further utterance, away from the Delph and back towards the village. Rowland was alone with his thoughts. He tried to imagine her lying there beneath that veil of soil, beautiful and full of youth. It seemed so beyond belief that she could be laid in the ground, taken to her grave even before her marriage bed. Kneeling before the mounded earth, he wept and his tears fell onto the flowers, their essence escaping them and reaching his senses. To have known such sweetness in this life, if only for a short time, had given him memories to recall for a lifetime in exchange for the love of this sweet woman.

50

William
21st November 1666

He had buried her in the churchyard, though he had long since barred the opportunity for anyone else. When it came to it, he could not do it. He could not bury his wife in the garden when the hallowed ground of the church of St Lawrence stood on the other side of the rectory boundary wall. He hoped the villagers would meet his decision with grace, perhaps recognising that he had given his most cherished possession in defence of the safety of all the villages that surrounded them.

He had summoned Marshall Howe that same day and entreated him to dig a grave where he instructed. When he had finished, and had carried her shrouded body and lain her in the bottom of the deep pit, William had said farewell to all his happy days and watered the ground afresh with the tears he feared might never cease. Indeed, they were his faithful companions throughout September and October, so much that Jane called upon the wisdom of Reverend Stanley, who being wise, advised her to let him be.

He had chosen a burial space near to the Saxon cross, imagining her standing there beneath it with that sweet smile on her face framed by her beautiful brown hair, leaning on it like the wayside preachers passing through had done for centuries past as they professed their devout words to those who gathered. She had begun an eternal journey without him and though three months had passed since she slipped from him, he had grown no more used to her being gone than he had in those very first moments when he had cast himself upon her lifeless body, utterly bereft. Time had brought few comforts, but these past two weeks in November appeared to usher in the long-awaited moment they had both hoped for. He was reminded of Simeon and Anna at the presentation of the Lord in the temple. Yet his Anna had not seen what she had hoped for and he was not afforded the sweetness of death that was given to Simeon on having his hope realised.

There had been no deaths since the first day of the month when Abraham Morten had passed away. They had been here before. He cast his mind back to March and May, when he and Catherine had taken to their knees before the altar and prayed in earnest that it be the last of their testing. He could almost feel her hand gripping his at the altar, such had been the fervour of her prayers. But there was something new now that he felt, which had been missing then. There was a confirmation, a deep feeling of an ending, that he had not known before. He wished she was there to feel it with him. He wished he could race back to the rectory and find her in the parlour reading or at the kitchen table experimenting with her herbs, the way that always brought a pleasure to her face that shone in her eyes even when she was weak.

The only thing to spark his joy now was the thought of the return of his children. Now their Golgotha was once again just a quiet village nestled in a Derbyshire hillside. He had written to them about their mother; the hardest letter he had ever had to write. '*Dear Hearts, I am not only deprived of a kind and loving comfort, but you also are bereaved of the most indulgent mother that ever dear children had.*' He told them of her most devout life, and how he was convinced she now wore a crown of righteousness.

Before signing off the letter, he recounted her words of love for them that she spoke as she lay dying and how desirous she had been to see them one last time. In her delirium she had reached out to touch their faces, mumbling about how much she loved her two masterpieces. It had made his heart ache to hear it and yet he hoped it would bring comfort to their two disoriented little souls.

Now, as he wandered back towards the churchyard, the smell of burning wafted through the village as the surviving villagers burnt all that had come into contact with anyone who sickened, purging any plague seeds that sought to remain. He picked some flowers from the rectory garden. They were roses, red and vibrant. Though the thorns pricked him, he carried them with a smile towards the grave of his dear wife and lay them gently upon it. "Long may you be remembered, dear one," he whispered, kneeling with his head bent so near the ground that his forehead almost touched the cold, hard earth that had claimed so many this past year.

51

Joseph

30th November 1666

He had asked her to come with him but she would not, could not. Word had reached Elizabeth and her oldest son in Sheffield that the plague in Eyam was finally ended. Seventy six families were visited by the disease and if William Mompesson's parish register was correct, two hundred and fifty nine souls were taken by it, including Joseph's father and all his siblings. His mother had arrived one morning in August, cold and windswept but in good health, having walked all through the night and into the next day. Joseph had heard some of what had been happening in Eyam but with the village shut, closed off to visitors and those who would seek to leave alike, there had seemed little he could do. It was a surprise, therefore, to see Elizabeth standing on his doorstep but he had instantly seen in her face that she had been broken by despair and he could not bring himself to question her as to why she had broken the cordon sanitaire put in place by the village's two clergymen.

She relayed to him the deaths of his father and brothers and sisters as they sat by the fire of the small rooms he lived in funded by the meagre pay of his apprenticeship. Joseph could hardly bear to hear the details of his family's demise nor the harrowing particulars of how Elizabeth had buried each one of them by herself. He knew she wished she had sent them to him in Sheffield, and though it would have been near impossible for him to have done his work whilst having them in his care, he wished she had sent them too. So many of the children sent away from Eyam now returned to the village to find their home changed beyond their understanding, some without a parent or siblings they did not know they were saying goodbye to forever when they were sent away. Some bereaved of everyone and never to return.

A desire grew in Joseph to see the place where she had buried them, to witness the dirt that her hands had dug in and the final resting place of his tragic family. But when he pressed her to come back with him, to return to Riley, Elizabeth shook her head and said she could not. So, he had come without her. The roads of Eyam were grown tall with grass and even though the carts and wagons were beginning to roll along the highways again, and there was footfall unmatched during the past year, there was a sense of a village held in time, as if it still held its breath here amongst the hills to see if and how it would now survive. Those who remembered him waved at Joseph and he waved back but was conscious of an atmosphere of sadness that lingered despite these displays of joviality.

Joseph passed the churchyard which was now open again and witnessed the clean new stone of the tomb the rector had erected for his deceased wife. Atop it there was a bunch of red roses, like those growing in the gardens of the cottages where he was told the plague first made itself known last year. The village was one sprawling graveyard and as he passed by the cottages and public houses. He saw all about him the mounds of earth that marked the final destinations of each life and soul doomed to live and die here in the past year. They were everywhere.

As he climbed the hill he saw his old home looming above him, and the Talbot farmhouse beside the Hancock farmhouse. Nobody had yet dared to attempt to claim either as their new abode and as he approached his old house he was arrested by the stillness and the silence. He tried to imagine his mother here all by herself after they had perished and he understood her reluctance to come back. She was a living ghost, his mother. Sometimes when he looked at her, he would catch a glimpse of the pain she hid there, behind her eyes.

He did not enter the farmhouse but followed the direction she had given him to where the graves of his family lay, their bodies becoming bones beneath the ground. He saw the way the earth rose up in mounds a little way off and made his way towards the spot. They were gathered here, his father, his brother William, the closest to him in age, his sisters Alice and Anne and Elizabeth and little Oner who he had barely met, and his little brother John, named after his father. They were all here and now so was he. He could not imagine the strength it must have taken Elizabeth, of body and of mind, to bury each one in the earth. The respect he had for his mother in that moment would never be matched.

He saw the way the wild wanted to reclaim this spot, the way the grass had begun to creep over the mounds and the shoots of wild flowers sprang up from the earth. Another year and they would be covered. He imagined people stumbling upon them in the future and being perplexed as to what this mossy uneven mass of earth might be. He wished he could build great tombs for them as the rector had done, down in the village for his wife. So that they would never be forgotten, so what she did would never be overlooked or erased from memory.

When he again retook the Manchester to Sheffield road he looked back one last time and imagined her standing there, her hair blowing in the wind, her back straight and her face lifted towards the sky. Elizabeth may no longer be in this village and she may never return, but some of her heart would remain here always and her spirit would forever be carried on the wind.

Epilogue

This book is dedicated to the memory of Emmott and Catherine and Elizabeth, three very different, but real, women of Eyam who faced the trials of 1665-1666 each in their own way, with courage, compassion and integrity. They lived out their brave stories in the dale, on the hill and in the village during two of the hardest years in the parish records. Much of this book is fictionalised; the flesh of imagination built around the bare bones of sparse historical facts. The personality and character exhibited by these three women in the actions that we do know of, speak of vibrant women who lived, laughed and loved during the visitation of the plague, and whom I have tried to bring to life. You may wish their stories had ended differently, and at times so did I, but even within their tales of tragedy there is much to celebrate in the lives, and deaths, of these three women and their stories. Thank you for walking their paths with me.

About the Author

Jennifer Jenkins lives in a village outside of Rugby in Warwickshire, with her husband, two sons and her dog. Formerly a primary school teacher and assistant head teacher, her interest in the story of Eyam in Derbyshire was first kindled over a decade ago when first teaching her class of seven year olds about the plague as part of history lessons. Having visited Eyam many times, and reading every available piece of literature about the plague-stricken village, she was inspired to write a novel about the brave women she had encountered in her research and to attempt to bring them to life.

Jennifer currently works for Coventry Diocesan Board of Education, supporting local schools with Religious Education and spiritual development. She would like to write more novels.

Printed in Great Britain
by Amazon